Paycheck

Also by Philip K. Dick

Philip K. Dick
Paycheck

GOLLANCZ

LONDON

First published in Great Britain in 2003 by
Gollancz
An imprint of the Orion Publishing Group
Orion House, 5 Upper St Martin's Lane,
London WC2H 9EA

A CIP catalogue record for this book
is available from the British Library

ISBN 0 575 07001 3

Typeset at The Spartan Press Ltd,
Lymington, Hants

Printed in Great Britain by
Clays Ltd, St Ives plc

Contents

Paycheck

All at once he was in motion. Around him smooth jets hummed. He was on a small private rocket cruiser, moving leisurely across the afternoon sky, between cities.

'Ugh!' he said, sitting up in his seat and rubbing his head. Beside him Earl Rethrick was staring keenly at him, his eyes bright.

'Coming around?'

'Where are we?' Jennings shook his head, trying to clear the dull ache. 'Or maybe I should ask that a different way.' Already, he could see that it was not late fall. It was spring. Below the cruiser the fields were green. The last thing he remembered was stepping into an elevator with Rethrick. And it was late fall. And in New York.

'Yes,' Rethrick said. 'It's almost two years later. You'll find a lot of things have changed. The Government fell a few months ago. The new Government is even stronger. The SP, Security Police, have almost unlimited power. They're teaching the schoolchildren to inform, now. But we all saw that coming. Let's see, what else? New York is larger. I understand they've finished filling in San Francisco Bay.'

'What I want to know is what the hell I've been doing the last two years!' Jennings lit a cigarette nervously, pressing the strike end. 'Will you tell me that?'

'No. Of course I won't tell you that.'

'Where are we going?'

'Back to the New York Office. Where you first met me. Remember? You probably remember it better than I. After all, it was just a day or so ago for you.'

Jennings nodded. Two years! Two years out of his life, gone forever. It didn't seem possible. He had still been considering, debating, when he stepped into the elevator. Should he change his mind? Even if he were getting that much money – and it was a lot, even for him – it didn't really seem worth it. He would always wonder what work he had been doing. Was it legal? Was it— But that was past speculation, now. Even while he was trying to make up his mind the curtain had fallen. He looked ruefully out the window at the afternoon sky. Below, the earth was moist and alive. Spring, spring two years later. And what did he have to show for the two years?

'Have I been paid?' he asked. He slipped his wallet out and glanced into it. 'Apparently not.'

'No. You'll be paid at the Office. Kelly will pay you.'

'The whole works at once?'

'Fifty thousand credits.'

Jennings smiled. He felt a little better, now that the sum had been spoken aloud. Maybe it wasn't so bad, after all. Almost like being paid to sleep. But he was two years older; he had just that much less to live. It was like selling part of himself, part of his life. And life was worth plenty, these days. He shrugged. Anyhow, it was in the past.

'We're almost there,' the older man said. The robot pilot dropped the cruiser down, sinking toward the ground. The edge of New York City became visible below them. 'Well, Jennings, I may never see you again.' He held out his hand. 'It's been a pleasure working with you. We did work together, you know. Side by side. You're one of the best mechanics I've ever seen. We were right in hiring you, even at that salary. You paid us back many times – although you don't realize it.'

'I'm glad you got your money's worth.'

'You sound angry.'

'No. I'm just trying to get used to the idea of being two years older.'

Rethrick laughed. 'You're still a very young man. And you'll feel better when she gives you your pay.'

They stepped out onto the tiny rooftop field of the New York office building. Rethrick led him over to an elevator. As the doors slid shut Jennings got a mental shock. This was the last thing he remembered, this elevator. After that he had blacked out.

'Kelly will be glad to see you,' Rethrick said, as they came out into a lighted hall. 'She asks about you, once in a while.'

'Why?'

'She says you're good-looking.' Rethrick pushed a code key against a door. The door responded, swinging wide. They entered the luxurious office of Rethrick Construction. Behind a long mahogany desk a young woman was sitting, studying a report.

'Kelly,' Rethrick said, 'look whose time finally expired.'

The girl looked up, smiling. 'Hello, Mr Jennings. How does it feel to be back in the world?'

'Fine.' Jennings walked over to her. 'Rethrick says you're the paymaster.'

Rethrick clapped Jennings on the back. 'So long, my friend. I'll go back to the plant. If you ever need a lot of money in a hurry come around and we'll work out another contract with you.'

Jennings nodded. As Rethrick went back out he sat down beside the desk, crossing his legs. Kelly slid a drawer open, moving her chair back. 'All right. Your time is up, so Rethrick Construction is ready to pay. Do you have your copy of the contract?'

Jennings took an envelope from his pocket and tossed it on the desk. 'There it is.'

Kelly removed a small cloth sack and some sheets of handwritten paper from the desk drawer. For a time she read over the sheets, her small face intent.

'What is it?'

'I think you're going to be surprised.' Kelly handed him his contract back. 'Read that over again.'

'Why?' Jennings unfastened the envelope.

'There's an alternate clause. "If the party of the second

part so desires, at any time during his time of contract to the aforesaid Rethrick Construction Company—" '

' "If he so desires, instead of the monetary sum specified, he may choose instead, according to his own wish, articles or products which, in his own opinion, are of sufficient value to stand in lieu of the sum—" '

Jennings snatched up the cloth sack, pulling it open. He poured the contents into his palm. Kelly watched.

'Where's Rethrick?' Jennings stood up. 'If he has an idea that this—'

'Rethrick has nothing to do with it. It was your own request. Here, look at this.' Kelly passed him the sheets of paper. 'In your own hand. Read them. It was your idea, not ours. Honest.' She smiled up at him. 'This happens every once in a while with people we take on contract. During their time they decide to take something else instead of money. Why, I don't know. But they come out with their minds clean, having agreed—'

Jennings scanned the pages. It was his own writing. There was no doubt of it. His hands shook. 'I can't believe it. Even if it is my own writing.' He folded up the paper, his jaw set. 'Something was done to me while I was back there. I never would have agreed to this.'

'You must have had a reason. I admit it doesn't make sense. But you don't know what factors might have persuaded you, before your mind was cleaned. You aren't the first. There have been several others before you.'

Jennings stared down at what he held in his palm. From the cloth sack he had spilled a little assortment of items. A code key. A ticket stub. A parcel receipt. A length of fine wire. Half a poker chip, broken across. A green strip of cloth. A bus token.

'This, instead of fifty thousand credits,' he murmured. 'Two years . . .'

He went out of the building, onto the busy afternoon street. He was still dazed, dazed and confused. Had he been swindled? He felt in his pocket for the little trinkets, the wire, the ticket stub, all the rest. *That*, for two years of work! But he had seen his own handwriting, the statement of waiver, the request for the substitution. Like Jack and the Beanstalk. Why? What for? What had made him do it?

He turned, starting down the sidewalk. At the corner he stopped for a surface cruiser that was turning.

'All right, Jennings. Get in.'

His head jerked up. The door of the cruiser was open. A man was kneeling, pointing a heat-rifle straight at his face. A man in blue-green. The Security Police.

Jennings got in. The door closed, magnetic locks slipping into place behind him. Like a vault. The cruiser glided off down the street. Jennings sank back against the seat. Beside him the SP man lowered his gun. On the other side a second officer ran his hands expertly over him, searching for weapons. He brought out Jennings' wallet and the handful of trinkets. The envelope and contract.

'What does he have?' the driver said.

'Wallet, money. Contract with Rethrick Construction. No weapons.' He gave Jennings back his things.

'What's this all about?' Jennings said.

'We want to ask you a few questions. That's all. You've been working for Rethrick?'

'Yes.'

'Two years?'

'Almost two years.'

'At the Plant?'

Jennings nodded. 'I suppose so.'

The officer leaned toward him. 'Where is that Plant, Mr Jennings. Where is it located?'

'I don't know.'

The two officers looked at each other. The first one moistened his lips, his face sharp and alert. 'You don't know? The next question. The last. In those two years, what kind of work did you do? What was your job?'

'Mechanic. I repaired electronic machinery.'

'What *kind* of electronic machinery?'

'I don't know.' Jennings looked up at him. He could not help smiling, his lips twisting ironically. 'I'm sorry, but I don't know. It's the truth.'

There was silence.

'What do you mean, you don't know? You mean you worked on machinery for two years without knowing what it was? Without even knowing where you were?'

Jennings roused himself. 'What is all this? What did you pick me up for? I haven't done anything. I've been—'

'We know. We're not arresting you. We only want to get information for our records. About Rethrick Construction. You've been working for them, in their Plant. In an important capacity. You're an electronic mechanic?'

'Yes.'

'You repair high-quality computers and allied equipment?' The officer consulted his notebook. 'You're considered one of the best in the country, according to this.'

Jennings said nothing.

'Tell us the two things we want to know, and you'll be released at once. Where is Rethrick's Plant? What kind of work are they doing? You serviced their machines for them, didn't you? Isn't that right? For two years.'

'I don't know. I suppose so. I don't have any idea what I did during the two years. You can believe me or not.' Jennings stared wearily down at the floor.

'What'll we do?' the driver said finally. 'We have no instructions past this.'

'Take him to the station. We can't do any more questioning here.' Beyond the cruiser, men and women hurried along the sidewalk. The streets were choked with cruisers, workers going to their homes in the country.

'Jennings, why don't you answer us? What's the matter with you? There's no reason why you can't tell us a couple of simple things like that. Don't you want to cooperate with your Government? Why should you conceal information from us?'

'I'd tell you if I knew.'

The officer grunted. No one spoke. Presently the cruiser drew up before a great stone building. The driver turned the motor off, removing the control cap and putting it in his pocket. He touched the door with a code key, releasing the magnetic lock.

'What shall we do, take him in? Actually, we don't— '

'Wait.' The driver stepped out. The other two went with him, closing and locking the doors behind them. They stood on the pavement before the Security Station, talking.

Jennings sat silently, staring down at the floor. The SP wanted to know about Rethrick Construction. Well, there was nothing he could tell them. They had come to the wrong person, but how could he prove that? The whole thing was impossible. Two years wiped clean from his mind. Who would believe him? It seemed unbelievable to him, too.

His mind wandered, back to when he had first read the ad. It had hit home, hit him direct. *Mechanic wanted*, and a general outline of the work, vague, indirect, but enough to tell him that it was right up his line. And the pay! Interviews at the Office. Tests, forms. And then the gradual realization that Rethrick Construction was finding out all about him while he knew nothing about them. What kind of work did they do? Construction, but what kind? What sort of machines did they have? Fifty thousand credits for two years . . .

And he had come out with his mind washed clean. Two years, and he remembered nothing. It took him a long time to agree to that part of the contract. But he *had* agreed.

Jennings looked out the window. The three officers were still talking on the sidewalk, trying to decide what to do with him. He was in a tough spot. They wanted information he couldn't give, information he didn't know. But how could he prove it? How could he prove that he had worked two years and come out knowing no more than when he had gone in! The SP would work him over. It would be a long time before they'd believe him, and by that time—

He glanced quickly around. Was there any escape? In a second they would be back. He touched the door. Locked, the triple-ring magnetic locks. He had worked on magnetic locks many times. He had even designed part of a trigger core. There was no way to open the doors without the right code key. No way, unless by some chance he could short out the lock. But with what?

He felt in his pockets. What could he use? If he could short the locks, blow them out, there was a faint chance. Outside, men and women were swarming by, on their way home from work. It was past five; the great office buildings were shutting down, the streets were alive with traffic. If he once got out they wouldn't dare fire. – If he could get out.

The three officers separated. One went up the steps into the Station building. In a second the others would reenter the cruiser. Jennings dug into his pocket, bringing out the code key, the ticket stub, the wire. The wire! Thin wire, thin as human hair. Was it insulated? He unwound it quickly. No.

He knelt down, running his fingers expertly across the surface of the door. At the edge of the lock was a thin line, a groove between the lock and the door. He brought the end of the wire up to it, delicately maneuvering the wire into the almost invisible space. The wire disappeared an inch or so. Sweat rolled down Jennings' forehead. He moved the wire a fraction of an inch, twisting it. He held his breath. The relay should be—

A flash.

Half blinded, he threw his weight against the door. The door fell open, the lock fused and smoking. Jennings tumbled into the street and leaped to his feet. Cruisers were all around him, honking and sweeping past. He ducked behind a lumbering truck, entering the middle lane of traffic. On the sidewalk he caught a momentary glimpse of the SP men starting after him.

A bus came along, swaying from side to side, loaded with shoppers and workers. Jennings caught hold of the back rail, pulling himself up onto the platform. Astonished faces loomed up, pale moons thrust suddenly at him. The robot conductor was coming toward him, whirring angrily.

'Sir—' the conductor began. The bus was slowing down. 'Sir, it is not allowed—'

'It's all right,' Jennings said. He was filled, all at once, with a strange elation. A moment ago he had been trapped, with no way to escape. Two years of his life had been lost for nothing. The Security Police had arrested him, demanding information he couldn't give. A hopeless situation! But now things were beginning to click in his mind.

He reached into his pocket and brought out the bus token. He put it calmly into the conductor's coin slot.

'Okay?' he said. Under his feet the bus wavered, the driver hesitating. Then the bus resumed pace, going on. The conductor turned away, its whirrs subsiding. Everything was all right. Jennings smiled. He eased past the standing people, looking for a seat, some place to sit down. Where he could think.

He had plenty to think about. His mind was racing.

The bus moved on, flowing with the restless stream of urban traffic. Jennings only half saw the people sitting around him. There was no doubt of it: he had not been swindled. It was on the level. The decision had actually been his. Amazingly, after two years of work he had preferred a handful of trinkets instead of fifty thousand credits. But more amazingly, the handful of trinkets were turning out to be worth more than the money.

With a piece of wire and a bus token he had escaped from the Security Police. That was worth plenty. Money would have been useless to him once he disappeared inside the great stone Station. Even fifty thousand credits wouldn't have helped him. And there were five trinkets left. He felt around in his pocket. Five more things. He had used two. The others – what were they for? Something as important?

But the big puzzle: how had *he* – his earlier self – known that a piece of wire and a bus token would save his life? *He* had known, all right. Known in advance. But how? And the other five. Probably they were just as precious, or would be.

The *he* of those two years had known things that he did not know now, things that had been washed away when the company cleaned his mind. Like an adding machine which had been cleared. Everything was slate-clean. What *he* had known was gone, now. Gone, except for seven trinkets, five of which were still in his pocket.

But the real problem right now was not a problem of speculation. It was very concrete. The Security Police were looking for him. They had his name and description. There was no use thinking of going to his apartment – if he even still had an apartment. But where, then? Hotels? The SP combed them daily. Friends? That would mean putting them in jeopardy, along with him. It was only a question of time before the SP found him, walking along the street, eating in a restaurant, in a show, sleeping in some rooming house. The SP were everywhere.

Everywhere? Not quite. When an individual person was defenseless, a business was not. The big economic forces had managed to remain free, although virtually everything else had been absorbed by the Government. Laws that had been eased away from the private person still protected property and industry. The SP could pick up any given person, but they could not enter and seize a company, a business. That had been clearly established in the middle of the twentieth century.

Business, industry, corporations, were safe from the Security Police. Due process was required. Rethrick Construction was a target of SP interest, but they could do nothing until some statute was violated. If he could get back to the Company, get inside its doors, he would be safe. Jennings smiled grimly. The modern church, sanctuary. It was the Government against the corporation, rather than the State against the Church. The new Notre Dame of the world. Where the law could not follow.

Would Rethrick take him back? Yes, on the old basis. He

had already said so. Another two years sliced from him, and then back onto the streets. Would that help him? He felt suddenly in his pocket. And there were the remaining trinkets. Surely *he* had intended them to be used! No, he could not go back to Rethrick and work another contract time. Something else was indicated. Something more permanent. Jennings pondered. Rethrick Construction. What did it construct? What had *he* known, found out, during those two years? And why were the SP so interested?

He brought out the five objects and studied them. The green strip of cloth. The code key. The ticket stub. The parcel receipt. The half poker chip. Strange, that little things like that could be important.

And Rethrick Construction was involved.

There was no doubt. The answer, all the answers, lay at Rethrick. But where *was* Rethrick? He had no idea where the Plant was, no idea at all. He knew where the Office was, the big, luxurious room with the young woman and her desk. But that was not Rethrick Construction. Did anyone know, beside Rethrick? Kelly didn't know. Did the SP know?

It was out of town. That was certain. He had gone there by rocket. It was probably in the United States, maybe in the farmlands, the country, between cities. What a hell of a situation! Any moment the SP might pick him up. The next time he might not get away. His only chance, his own real chance for safety, lay in reaching Rethrick. And his only chance to find out the things he had to know. The Plant – a place where he had been, but which he could not recall. He looked down at the five trinkets. Would any of them help?

A burst of despair swept through him. Maybe it was just coincidence, the wire and the token. Maybe—

He examined the parcel receipt, turning it over and holding it up to the light. Suddenly his stomach muscles knotted. His pulse changed. He had been right. No, it was not a coincidence, the wire and the token. The parcel receipt was dated two days hence. The parcel, whatever it might be, had not even been deposited yet. Not for forty-eight more hours.

He looked at the other things. The ticket stub. What good was a ticket stub? It was creased and bent, folded over, again and again. He couldn't go anyplace with that. A stub didn't take you anywhere. It only told you where you had been.

Where you had been!

He bent down, peering at it, smoothing the creases. The printing had been torn through the middle. Only part of each word could be made out.

PORTOLA T
STUARTSVI
IOW

He smiled. That was it. Where he had been. He could fill in the missing letters. It was enough. There was no doubt: *he* had foreseen this, too. Three of the seven trinkets used. Four left. Stuartsville, Iowa. Was there such a place? He looked out the window of the bus. The Intercity rocket station was only a block or so away. He could be there in a second. A quick sprint from the bus, hoping the Police wouldn't be there to stop him—

But somehow he knew they wouldn't. Not with the other four things in his pocket. And once he was on the rocket he would be safe. Intercity was big, big enough to keep free of the SP. Jennings put the remaining trinkets back into his pocket and stood up, pulling the bellcord.

A moment later he stepped gingerly out onto the sidewalk.

The rocket let him off at the edge of town, at a tiny brown field. A few disinterested porters moved about, stacking luggage, resting from the heat of the sun.

Jennings crossed the field to the waiting room, studying the people around him. Ordinary people, workmen, businessmen, housewives. Stuartsville was a small Middle Western town. Truck drivers. High school kids.

He went through the waiting room, out onto the street. So this was where Rethrick's Plant was located – perhaps. If he had used the stub correctly. Anyhow, *something* was here, or *he* wouldn't have included the stub with the other trinkets.

Stuartsville, Iowa. A faint plan was beginning to form in the back of his mind, still vague and nebulous. He began to walk, his hands in his pockets, looking around him. A newspaper office, lunch counters, hotels, poolrooms, a barber shop, a television repair shop. A rocket sales store with huge showrooms of gleaming rockets. Family size. And at the end of the block the Portola Theater.

The town thinned out. Farms, fields. Miles of green country. In the sky above a few transport rockets lumbered, carrying farm supplies and equipment back and forth. A small, unimportant town. Just right for Rethrick Construction. The Plant would be lost here, away from the city, away from the SP.

Jennings walked back. He entered a lunchroom, BOB'S PLACE. A young man with glasses came over as he sat down at the counter, wiping his hands on his white apron.

'Coffee,' Jennings said.

'Coffee.' The man brought the cup. There were only a few people in the lunchroom. A couple of flies buzzed, against the window.

Outside in the street shoppers and farmers moved leisurely by.

'Say,' Jennings said, stirring his coffee. 'Where can a man get work around here? Do you know?'

'What kind of work?' The young man came back, leaning against the counter.

'Electrical wiring. I'm an electrician. Television, rockets, computers. That sort of stuff.'

'Why don't you try the big industrial areas? Detroit. Chicago. New York.'

Jennings shook his head. 'Can't stand the big cities. I never liked cities.'

The young man laughed. 'A lot of people here would be glad to work in Detroit. You're an electrician?'

'Are there any plants around here? Any repair shops or plants?'

'None that I know of.' The young man went off to wait on some men that had come in. Jennings sipped his coffee. Had he made a mistake? Maybe he should go back and forget about Stuartsville, Iowa. Maybe he had made the wrong inference from the ticket stub. But the ticket meant something, unless he was completely wrong about everything. It was a little late to decide that, though.

The young man came back. 'Is there *any* kind of work I can get here?' Jennings said. 'Just to tide me over.'

'There's always farm work.'

'How about the retail repair shops? Garages. TV.'

'There's a TV repair shop down the street. Maybe you might get something there. You could try. Farm work pays good. They can't get many men, anymore. Most men in the military. You want to pitch hay?'

Jennings laughed. He paid for his coffee. 'Not very much. Thanks.'

'Once in a while some of the men go up the road and work. There's some sort of Government station.'

Jennings nodded. He pushed the screen door open, stepping outside onto the hot sidewalk. He walked aimlessly for a time, deep in thought, turning his nebulous plan over and over. It was a good plan; it would solve everything, all his problems at once. But right now it hinged on one thing: finding Rethrick Construction. And he had only one clue, if it really was a clue. The ticket stub, folded and creased, in his pocket. And a faith that *he* had known what he was doing.

A Government station. Jennings paused, looking around him. Across the street was a taxi stand, a couple of cabbies sitting in their cabs, smoking and reading the newspaper. It was worth a try, at least. There wasn't much else to do.

Rethrick would be something else, on the surface. If it posed as a Government project no one would ask any questions. They were all too accustomed to Government projects working without explanation, in secrecy.

He went over to the first cab. 'Mister,' he said, 'can you tell me something?'

The cabbie looked up. 'What do you want?'

'They tell me there's work to be had, out at the Government station. Is that right?'

The cabbie studied him. He nodded.

'What kind of work is it?'

'I don't know.'

'Where do they do the hiring?'

'I don't know.' The cabbie lifted his paper.

'Thanks.' Jennings turned away.

'They don't do any hiring. Maybe once in a long while. They don't take many on. You better go someplace else if you're looking for work.'

'All right.'

The other cabbie leaned out of his cab. 'They use only a few day laborers, buddy. That's all. And they're very choosy. They don't hardly let anybody in. Some kind of war work.'

Jennings pricked up his ears. 'Secret?'

'They come into town and pick up a load of construction workers. Maybe a truck full. That's all. They're real careful who they pick.'

Jennings walked back toward the cabbie. 'That right?'

'It's a big place. Steel wall. Charged. Guards. Work going on day and night. But nobody gets in. Set up on top of a hill, out the old Henderson Road. About two miles and a half.' The cabbie poked at his shoulder. 'You can't get in unless you're identified. They identify their laborers, after they pick them out. You know.'

Jennings stared at him. The cabbie was tracing a line on his shoulder. Suddenly Jennings understood. A flood of relief rushed over him.

'Sure,' he said. 'I understand what you mean. At least, I think so.' He reached into his pocket, bringing out the four trinkets. Carefully, he unfolded the strip of green cloth, holding it up. 'Like this?'

The cabbies stared at the cloth. 'That's right,' one of them said slowly, staring at the cloth. 'Where did you get it?'

Jennings laughed. 'A friend.' He put the cloth back in his pocket. 'A friend gave it to me.'

He went off, toward the Intercity field. He had plenty to do, now that the first step was over. Rethrick was here, all right. And apparently the trinkets were going to see him through. One for every crisis. A pocketful of miracles, from someone who knew the future!

But the next step couldn't be done alone. He needed help. Somebody else was needed for this part. But who? He pondered, entering the Intercity waiting room. There was only one person he could possibly go to. It was a long chance, but he had to take it. He couldn't work alone, here on out. If the Rethrick plant was here then Kelly would be too . . .

The street was dark. At the corner a lamppost cast a fitful beam. A few cruisers moved by.

From the apartment building entrance a slim shape came, a young woman in a coat, a purse in her hand. Jennings watched as she passed under the streetlamp. Kelly McVane was going someplace, probably to a party. Smartly dressed, high heels tap-tapping on the pavement, a little coat and hat.

He stepped out behind her. 'Kelly.'

She turned quickly, her mouth open. 'Oh!'

Jennings took her arm. 'Don't worry. It's just me. Where are you going, all dressed up?'

'No place.' She blinked. 'My golly, you scared me. What is it? What's going on?'

'Nothing. Can you spare a few minutes? I want to talk to you.'

Kelly nodded. 'I guess so.' She looked around. 'Where'll we go?'

'Where's a place we can talk? I don't want anyone to overhear us.'

'Can't we just walk along?'

'No. The Police.'

'The Police?'

'They're looking for me.'

'For you? But why?'

'Let's not stand here,' Jennings said grimly. 'Where can we go?'

Kelly hesitated. 'We can go up to my apartment. No one's there.'

They went up to the elevator. Kelly unlocked the door, pressing the code key against it. The door swung open and they went inside, the heater and lights coming on automatically at her step. She closed the door and took off her coat.

'I won't stay long,' Jennings said.

'That's all right. I'll fix you a drink.' She went into the kitchen. Jennings sat down on the couch, looking around at the neat little apartment. Presently the girl came back. She sat down beside him and Jennings took his drink. Scotch and water, cold.

'Thanks.'

Kelly smiled. 'Not at all.' The two of them sat silently for a time. 'Well?' she said at last. 'What's this all about? Why are the Police looking for you?'

'They want to find out about Rethrick Construction. I'm only a pawn in this. They think I know something because I worked two years at Rethrick's Plant.'

'But you don't!'

'I can't prove that.'

Kelly reached out, touching Jennings' head, just above the ear. 'Feel there. That spot.'

Jennings reached up. Above his ear, under the hair, was a tiny hard spot. 'What is it?'

'They burned through the skull there. Cut a tiny wedge from the brain. All your memories of the two years. They located them and burned them out. The SP couldn't possibly make you remember. It's gone. You don't have it.'

'By the time they realize that there won't be much left of me.'

Kelly said nothing.

'You can see the spot I'm in. It would be better for me if I did remember. Then I could tell them and they'd—'

'And destroy Rethrick!'

Jennings shrugged. 'Why not? Rethrick means nothing to me. I don't even know what they're doing. And why are the Police so interested? From the very start, all the secrecy, cleaning my mind—'

'There's reason. Good reason.'

'Do you know why?'

'No.' Kelly shook her head. 'But I'm sure there's a reason. If the SP are interested, there's a reason.' She set down her drink, turning toward him. 'I hate the Police. We all do, every one of us. They're after us all the time. I don't know anything about Rethrick. If I did my life wouldn't be safe. There's not much standing between Rethrick and them. A few laws, a handful of laws. Nothing more.'

'I have the feeling Rethrick is a great deal more than just another construction company the SP wants to control.'

'I suppose it is. I really don't know. I'm just a receptionist. I've never been to the Plant. I don't even know where it is.'

'But you wouldn't want anything to happen to it.'

'Of course not! They're fighting the Police. Anyone that's fighting the Police is on our side.'

'Really? I've heard that kind of logic before. Anyone fighting communism was automatically good, a few decades ago. Well, time will tell. As far as I'm concerned I'm an individual caught between two ruthless forces. Government and business. The Government has men and wealth. Rethrick Construction has its technocracy. What they've done with it, I don't know. I did, a few weeks ago. All I have now is a faint glimmer, a few references. A theory.'

Kelly glanced at him. 'A theory?'

'And my pocketful of trinkets. Seven. Three or four now. I've used some. They're the basis of my theory. If Rethrick is doing what I think it's doing, I can understand the SP's interest. As a matter of fact, I'm beginning to share their interest.'

'What is Rethrick doing?'

'It's developed a time scoop.'

'What?'

'A time scoop. It's been theoretically possible for several years. But it's illegal to experiment with time scoops and mirrors. It's a felony, and if you're caught, all your equipment and data becomes the property of the Government.' Jennings smiled crookedly. 'No wonder the Government's interested. If they can catch Rethrick with the goods—'

'A time scoop. It's hard to believe.'

'Don't you think I'm right?'

'I don't know. Perhaps. Your trinkets. You're not the first to come out with a little cloth sack of odds and ends. You've used some? How?'

'First, the wire and the bus token. Getting away from the Police. It seems funny, but if I hadn't had them, I'd be there yet. A piece of wire and a ten-cent token. But I don't usually carry such things. That's the point.'

'Time travel.'

'No. Not time travel. Berkowsky demonstrated that time travel is impossible. This is a time scoop, a mirror to see and a scoop to pick up things. These trinkets. At least one of them is from the future. Scooped up. Brought back.'

'How do you know?'

'It's dated. The others, perhaps not. Things like tokens and wire belong to classes of things. Any one token is as good as another. There, *he* must have used a mirror.'

'*He?*'

'When I was working with Rethrick. I must have used the

mirror. I looked into my own future. If I was repairing their equipment I could hardly keep from it! I must have looked ahead, seen what was coming. The SP picking me up. I must have seen that, and seen what a piece of thin wire and a bus token would do – if I had them with me at the exact moment.'

Kelly considered. 'Well? What do you want me for?'

'I'm not sure, now. Do you really look on Rethrick as a benevolent institution, waging war against the Police? A sort of Roland at Roncesvalles—'

'What does it matter how I feel about the Company?'

'It matters a lot.' Jennings finished his drink, pushing the glass aside. 'It matters a lot, because I want you to help me. I'm going to blackmail Rethrick Construction.'

Kelly stared at him.

'It's my one chance to stay alive, I've got to get a hold over Rethrick, a big hold. Enough of a hold so they'll let me in, on my own terms. There's no other place I can go. Sooner or later the Police are going to pick me up. If I'm not inside the Plant, and soon—'

'Help you blackmail the Company? Destroy Rethrick?'

'No. Not destroy. I don't want to destroy it – my life depends on the Company. My life depends on Rethrick being strong enough to defy the SP. But if I'm on the *outside* it doesn't much matter how strong Rethrick is. Do you see? I want to get in. I want to get inside before it's too late. And I want in on my own terms, not as a two-year worker who gets pushed out again afterward.'

'For the Police to pick up.'

Jennings nodded. 'Exactly.'

'How are you going to blackmail the Company?'

'I'm going to enter the Plant and carry out enough material to prove Rethrick is operating a time scoop.'

Kelly laughed. 'Enter the Plant? Let's see you *find* the Plant. The SP have been looking for it for years.'

'I've already found it.' Jennings leaned back, lighting a cigarette. 'I've located it with my trinkets. And I have four left, enough to get me inside, I think. And to get me what I want. I'll be able to carry out enough papers and photographs to hang Rethrick. But I don't want to hang Rethrick. I only want to bargain. That's where you come in.'

'I?'

'You can be trusted not to go to the Police. I need someone I can turn the material over to. I don't dare keep it myself. As soon as I have it I must turn it over to someone else, someone who'll hide it where I won't be able to find it.'

'Why?'

'Because,' Jennings said calmly, 'any minute the SP may pick me up. I have no love for Rethrick, but I don't want to scuttle it. That's why you've got to help me. I'm going to turn the information over to you, to hold, while I bargain with Rethrick. Otherwise I'll have to hold it myself. And if I have it on me—'

He glanced at her. Kelly was staring at the floor, her face tense. Set.

'Well? What do you say? Will you help me, or shall I take the chance the SP won't pick me up with the material? Data enough to destroy Rethrick. Well? Which will it be? Do you want to see Rethrick destroyed? What's your answer?'

The two of them crouched, looking across the fields at the hill beyond. The hill rose up, naked and brown, burned clean of vegetation. Nothing grew on its sides. Halfway up a long steel fence twisted, topped with charged barbed wire. On the other side a guard walked slowly, a tiny figure patrolling with a rifle and helmet.

At the top of the hill lay an enormous concrete block, a towering structure without windows or doors. Mounted guns caught the early morning sunlight, glinting in a row along the roof of the building.

'So that's the Plant,' Kelly said softly.

'That's it. It would take an army to get up there, up that hill and over the fence. Unless they were allowed in.'

Jennings got to his feet, helping Kelly up. They walked back along the path, through the trees, to where Kelly had parked the cruiser.

'Do you really think your green cloth band will get you in?' Kelly said, sliding behind the wheel.

'According to the people in the town, a truckload of laborers will be brought in to the Plant sometime this morning. The truck is unloaded at the entrance and the men examined. If everything's in order they're let inside the grounds, past the fence. For construction work, manual labor. At the end of the day they're let out again and driven back to town.'

'Will that get you close enough?'

'I'll be on the other side of the fence, at least.'

'How will you get to the time scoop? That must be inside the building, some place.'

Jennings brought out a small code key. 'This will get me in. I hope. I assume it will.'

Kelly took the key, examining it. 'So that's one of your trinkets. We should have taken a better look inside your little cloth bag.'

'We?'

'The Company. I saw several little bags of trinkets pass out, through my hands. Rethrick never said anything.'

'Probably the Company assumed no one would ever want to get back inside again.' Jennings took the code key from her. 'Now, do you know what you're supposed to do?'

'I'm supposed to stay here with the cruiser until you get back. You're to give me the material. Then I'm to carry it back to New York and wait for you to contact me.'

'That's right.' Jennings studied the distant road, leading through the trees to the Plant gate. 'I better get down there. The truck may be along any time.'

'What if they decide to count the number of workers?'

'I'll have to take the chance. But I'm not worried. I'm sure *he* foresaw everything.'

Kelly smiled. 'You and your friend, your helpful friend. I

hope *he* left you enough things to get you out again, after you have the photographs.'

'Do you?'

'Why not?' Kelly said easily. 'I always liked you. You know that. You knew when you came to me.'

Jennings stepped out of the cruiser. He had on overalls and workshoes, and a gray sweatshirt. 'I'll see you later. If everything goes all right. I think it will.' He patted his pocket. 'With my charms here, my good-luck charms.'

He went off through the trees, walking swiftly.

The trees led to the very edge of the road. He stayed with them, not coming out into the open. The Plant guards were certainly scanning the hillside. They had burned it clean, so that anyone trying to creep up to the fence would be spotted at once. And he had seen infrared searchlights.

Jennings crouched low, resting against his heels, watching the road. A few yards up the road was a roadblock, just ahead of the gate. He examined his watch. Ten thirty. He might have a wait, a long wait. He tried to relax.

It was after eleven when the great truck came down the road, rumbling and wheezing.

Jennings came to life. He took out the strip of green cloth and fastened it around his arm. The truck came closer. He could see its load now. The back was full of workmen, men in jeans and workshirts, bounced and jolted as the truck moved along. Sure enough, each had an arm band like his own, a swathe of green around his upper arm. So far so good.

The truck came slowly to a halt, stopping at the road-block. The men got down slowly onto the road, sending up a cloud of dust into the hot midday sun. They slapped the dust from their jeans, some of them lighting cigarettes. Two guards came leisurely from behind the roadblock. Jennings tensed. In a moment it would be time. The guards moved among the men, examining them, their arm bands, their faces, looking at the identification tabs of a few.

The roadblock slid back. The gate opened. The guards returned to their positions.

Jennings slid forward, slithering through the brush, toward the road. The men were stamping out their cigarettes, climbing back up into the truck. The truck was gunning its motor, the driver releasing the brakes. Jennings dropped onto the road, behind the truck. A rattle of leaves and dirt showered after him. Where he had landed, the view of the guards was cut off by the truck. Jennings held his breath. He ran toward the back of the truck.

The men stared at him curiously as he pulled himself up among them, his chest rising and falling. Their faces were weathered, gray and lined. Men of the soil. Jennings took his place between two burly farmers as the truck started up. They did not seem to notice him. He had rubbed dirt into his skin, and let his beard grow for a day. At a quick glance he didn't look much different from the others. But if anyone made a count—

The truck passed through the gate, into the grounds. The gate slid shut behind. Now they were going up, up the steep side of the hill, the truck rattling and swaying from side to side. The vast concrete structure loomed nearer. Were they going to enter it? Jennings watched, fascinated. A thin high door was sliding back, revealing a dark interior. A row of artificial lights gleamed.

The truck stopped. The workmen began to get down again. Some mechanics came around them.

'What's this crew for?' one of them asked.

'Digging. Inside.' Another jerked a thumb. 'They're digging again. Send them inside.'

Jennings's heart thudded. He was going inside! He felt at his neck. There, inside the gray sweater, a flatplate camera hung like a bib around his neck. He could scarcely feel it, even knowing it was there. Maybe this would be less difficult than he had thought.

The workmen pushed through the door on foot, Jennings with them. They were in an immense workroom, long benches with half-completed machinery, booms and cranes, and the constant roar of work. The door closed after them, cutting them off from outside. He was in the Plant. But where was the time scoop, and the mirror?

'This way,' a foreman said. The workmen plodded over to the right. A freight lift rose to meet them from the bowels of the building. 'You're going down below. How many of you have experience with drills?'

A few hands went up.

'You can show the others. We are moving earth with drills and eaters. Any of you work eaters?'

No hands. Jennings glanced at the worktables. Had he worked here, not so long ago? A sudden chill went through him. Suppose he were recognized? Maybe he had worked with these very mechanics.

'Come on,' the foreman said impatiently. 'Hurry up.'

Jennings got into the freight lift with the others. A moment later they began to descend, down the black tube. Down, down, into the lower levels of the Plant. Rethrick Construction was *big*, a lot bigger than it looked above ground. A lot bigger than he had imagined. Floors, underground levels, flashing past one after the other.

The elevator stopped. The doors opened. He was looking down a long corridor. The floor was thick with stone dust. The air was moist. Around him, the workmen began to crowd out. Suddenly Jennings stiffened, pulling back.

At the end of the corridor, before a steel door, was Earl Rethrick. Talking to a group of technicians.

'All out,' the foreman said. 'Let's go.'

Jennings left the elevator, keeping behind the others. Rethrick! His heart beat dully. If Rethrick saw him he was finished. He felt in his pockets. He had a miniature Boris gun, but it wouldn't be much use if he was discovered. Once Rethrick saw him it would be all over.

'Down this way.' The foreman led them toward what seemed to be an underground railway, to one side of the corridor. The men were getting into metal cars along a track. Jennings watched Rethrick. He saw him gesture angrily, his voice coming faintly down the hall. Suddenly Rethrick turned. He held up his hand and the great steel door behind him opened.

Jennings's heart almost stopped beating.

There, beyond the steel door, was the time scoop. He recognized it at once. The mirror. The long metal rods, ending in claws. Like Berkowsky's theoretical model – only this was real.

Rethrick went into the room, the technicians following behind him. Men were working at the scoop, standing all around it. Part of the shield was off. They were digging into the works. Jennings stared, hanging back.

'Say you—' the foreman said, coming toward him. The steel door shut. The view was cut off. Rethrick, the scoop, the technicians, were gone.

'Sorry,' Jennings murmured.

'You know you're not supposed to be curious around here.' The foreman was studying him intently. 'I don't remember you. Let me see your tab.'

'My tab?'

'Your identification tab.' The foreman turned away. 'Bill, bring me the board.' He looked Jennings up and down. 'I'm going to check you from the board, mister. I've never seen you in the crew before. Stay here.' A man was coming from a side door with a check board in his hands.

It was now or never.

Jennings sprinted, down the corridor, toward the great steel door. Behind there was a startled shout, the foreman and his helper. Jennings whipped out the code key, praying fervently as he ran. He came up to the door, holding out the key. With the other hand he brought out the Boris gun. Beyond the door was the time scoop. A few photographs, some schematics snatched up, and then, if he could get out—

The door did not move. Sweat leaped out on his face. He knocked the key against the door. Why didn't it open?

Surely— He began to shake, panic rising up in him. Down the corridor people were coming, racing after him. Open— But the door did not open. The key he held in his hand was the wrong key.

He was defeated. The door and the key did not match. Either *he* had been wrong, or the key was to be used someplace else. But where? Jennings looked frantically around. Where? Where could he go?

To one side a door was half open, a regular bolt-lock door. He crossed the corridor, pushing it open. He was in a storeroom of some sort. He slammed the door, throwing the bolt. He could hear them outside, confused, calling for guards. Soon armed guards would be along. Jennings held the Boris gun tightly, gazing around. Was he trapped? Was there a second way out?

He ran through the room, pushing among bales and boxes, towering stacks of silent cartons, end on end. At the rear was an emergency hatch. He opened it immediately. An impulse came to throw the code key away. What good had it been? But surely *he* had known what he was doing. *He* had already seen all this. Like God, it had already happened for *him*. Predetermined. *He* could not err. Or could he?

A chill went through him. Maybe the future was variable. Maybe this had been the right key, once. But not any more!

There were sounds behind him. They were melting the storeroom door. Jennings scrambled through the emergency hatch, into a low concrete passage, damp and ill lit. He ran quickly along it, turning corners. It was like a sewer. Other passages ran into it, from all sides.

He stopped. Which way? Where could he hide? The mouth of a major vent pipe gaped above his head. He caught hold and pulled himself up. Grimly, he eased his body onto it. They'd ignore a pipe, go on past. He crawled cautiously down the pipe. Warm air blew into his face. Why such a big vent? It implied an unusual chamber at the other end. He came to a metal grill and stopped.

And gasped.

He was looking into the great room, the room he had glimpsed beyond the steel door. Only now he was at the other end. There was the time scoop. And far down, beyond the scoop, was Rethrick, conferring at an active vidscreen. An alarm was sounding, whining shrilly, echoing everywhere. Technicians were running in all directions. Guards in uniform poured in and out of doors.

The scoop. Jennings examined the grill. It was slotted in place. He moved it laterally and it fell into his hands. No one was watching. He slid cautiously out, into the room, the Boris gun ready. He was fairly hidden behind the scoop, and the technicians and guards were all the way down at the other end of the room, where he had first seen them.

And there it was, all around him, the schematics, the mirror, papers, data, blueprints. He flicked his camera on. Against his chest the camera vibrated, film moving through it. He snatched up a handful of schematics. Perhaps *he* had used these very diagrams, a few weeks before!

He stuffed his pockets with papers. The film came to an end. But he was finished. He squeezed back into the vent, pushing through the mouth and down the tube. The sewer-like corridor was still empty, but there was an insistent drumming sound, the noise of voices and footsteps. So many passages – They were looking for him in a maze of escape corridors.

Jennings ran swiftly. He ran on and on, without regard to direction, trying to keep along the main corridor. On all sides passages flocked off, one after another, countless passages. He was dropping down, lower and lower. Running downhill.

Suddenly he stopped, gasping. The sound behind him had died away for a moment. But there was a new sound, ahead. He went along slowly. The corridor twisted, turning to the right. He advanced slowly, the Boris gun ready.

Two guards were standing a little way ahead, lounging and talking together. Beyond them was a heavy code door. And behind him the sound of voices was coming again, growing louder. They had found the same passage he had taken. They were on the way.

Jennings stepped out, the Boris gun raised. 'Put up your hands. Let go of your guns.'

The guards gawked at him. Kids, boys with cropped blond hair and shiny uniforms. They moved back, pale and scared.

'The guns. Let them fall.'

The two rifles clattered down. Jennings smiled. Boys. Probably this was their first encounter with trouble. Their leather boots shone, brightly polished.

'Open the door,' Jennings said. 'I want through.'

They stared at him. Behind, the noise grew.

'Open it.' He became impatient. 'Come on.' He waved the pistol. 'Open it, damn it! Do you want me to—'

'We – we can't.'

'What?'

'We can't. It's a code door. We don't have the key. Honest, mister. They don't let us have the key.' They were frightened. Jennings felt fear himself now. Behind him the drumming was louder. He was trapped, caught.

Or was he?

Suddenly he laughed. He walked quickly up to the door. 'Faith,' he murmured, raising his hand. 'That's something you should never lose.'

'What – what's that?'

'Faith in yourself. Self-confidence.'

The door slid back as he held the code key against it. Blinding sunlight streamed in, making him blink. He held the gun steady. He was outside, at the gate. Three guards gaped in amazement at the gun. He was at the gate – and beyond lay the woods.

'Get out of the way.' Jennings fired at the metal bars of the gate. The metal burst into flame, melting, a cloud of fire rising.

'Stop him!' From behind, men came pouring, guards, out of the corridor.

Jennings leaped through the smoking gate. The metal tore at him, searing him. He ran through the smoke, rolling and falling. He got to his feet and scurried on, into the trees.

He was outside. *He* had not let him down. The key had worked, all right. He had tried it first on the wrong door.

On and on he ran, sobbing for breath, pushing through the trees. Behind him the Plant and the voices fell away. He had the papers. And he was free.

He found Kelly and gave her the film and everything he had managed to stuff into his pockets. Then he changed back to his regular clothes. Kelly drove him to the edge of Stuartsville and left him off: Jennings watched the cruiser rise up into the air, heading toward New York. Then he went into town and boarded the Intercity rocket.

On the flight he slept, surrounded by dozing businessmen. When he awoke the rocket was settling down, landing at the huge New York spaceport.

Jennings got off, mixing with the flow of people. Now that he was back there was the danger of being picked up by the SP again. Two security officers in their green uniforms watched him impassively as he took a taxi at the field station. The taxi swept him into downtown traffic. Jennings wiped his brow. That was close. Now, to find Kelly.

He ate dinner at a small restaurant, sitting in the back away from the windows. When he emerged the sun was beginning to set. He walked slowly along the sidewalk, deep in thought.

So far so good. He had got the papers and film, and he had got away. The trinkets had worked every step along the way. Without them he would have been helpless. He felt in his pocket. Two left. The serrated half poker chip, and the parcel receipt. He took the receipt out, examining it in the fading evening light.

Suddenly he noticed something. The date on it was today's date. He had caught up with the slip.

He put it away, going on. What did it mean? What was it for? He shrugged. He would know, in time. And the half poker chip. What the hell was it for? No way to tell. In any case, he was certain to get through. *He* had got him by, up to now. Surely there wasn't much left.

He came to Kelly's apartment house and stopped, looking up. Her light was on. She was back; her fast little cruiser had beaten the Intercity rocket. He entered the elevator and rose to her floor.

'Hello,' he said, when she opened the door.

'You're all right?'

'Sure. Can I come in?'

He went inside. Kelly closed the door behind him. 'I'm glad to see you. The city's swarming with SP men. Almost every block. And the patrols—'

'I know. I saw a couple at the spaceport.' Jennings sat down on the couch. 'It's good to be back, though.'

'I was afraid they might stop all the Intercity flights and check through the passengers.'

'They have no reason to assume I'd be coming into the city.'

'I didn't think of that.' Kelly sat down across from him. 'Now, what comes next? Now that you have got away with the material, what are you going to do?'

'Next I meet Rethrick and spring the news on him. The news that the person who escaped from the Plant was myself. He knows that someone got away, but he doesn't know who it was. Undoubtedly, he assumes it was an SP man.'

'Couldn't he use the time mirror to find out?'

A shadow crossed Jennings' face. 'That's so. I didn't think of that.' He rubbed his jaw, frowning. 'In any case, I have the material. Or, you have the material.'

Kelly nodded.

'All right. We'll go ahead with our plans. Tomorrow we'll see Rethrick. We'll see him here, in New York. Can you get him down to the Office? Will he come if you send for him?'

'Yes. We have a code. If I ask him to come, he'll come.'

'Fine. I'll meet him there. When he realizes that we have the picture and schematics he'll have to agree to my demands. He'll have to let me into Rethrick Construction, on my own terms. It's either that, or face the possibility of having the material turned over to the Security Police.'

'And once you're in? Once Rethrick agrees to your demands?'

'I saw enough at the Plant to convince me that Rethrick is far bigger than I had realized. How big, I don't know. No wonder *he* was so interested!'

'You're going to demand equal control of the Company?'

Jennings nodded.

'You would never be satisfied to go back as a mechanic, would you? The way you were before.'

'No. To get booted out again?' Jennings smiled. 'Anyhow, I know *he* intended better things than that. *He* laid careful plans. The trinkets. He must have planned everything long in advance. No, I'm not going back as a mechanic. I saw a lot there, level after level of machines and men. They're doing something. And I want to be in on it.'

Kelly was silent.

'See?' Jennings said.

'I see.'

He left the apartment, hurrying along the dark street. He had stayed there too long. If the SP found the two of them together it would be all up with Rethrick Construction. He could take no chances, with the end almost in sight.

He looked at his watch. It was past midnight. He would meet Rethrick this morning, and present him with the proposition. His spirits rose as he walked. He would be safe. More than safe. Rethrick Construction was aiming at something far larger than mere industrial power. What he had seen had convinced him that a revolution was brewing. Down in the many levels below the ground, down under the fortress of concrete, guarded by guns and armed men, Rethrick was planning a war. Machines were being turned out. The time scoop and the mirror were hard at work, watching, dipping, extracting.

No wonder *he* had worked out such careful plans. *He* had seen all this and understood, begun to ponder. The problem of the mind cleaning. His memory would be gone when he was released. Destruction of all the plans. Destruction? There was the alternate clause in the contract. Others had seen it, used it. But not the way *he* intended!

He was after much more than anyone who had come before. *He* was the first to understand, to plan. The seven trinkets were a bridge to something beyond anything that—

At the end of the block an SP cruiser pulled up to the curb. Its doors slid open.

Jennings stopped, his heart constricting. The night patrol, roaming through the city. It was after eleven, after curfew. He looked quickly around. Everything was dark. The stores and houses were shut up tight, locked for the night. Silent apartment houses, buildings. Even the bars were dark.

He looked back the way he had come. Behind him, a second SP cruiser had stopped. Two SP officers had stepped out onto the curb. They had seen him. They were coming toward him. He stood frozen, looking up and down the street.

Across from him was the entrance of a swank hotel, its neon sign glimmering. He began to walk toward it, his heels echoing against the pavement.

'Stop!' one of the SP men called. 'Come back here. What are you doing out? What's your—'

Jennings went up the stairs, into the hotel. He crossed the lobby. The clerk was staring at him. No one else was around. The lobby was deserted. His heart sank. He didn't have a chance. He began to run aimlessly, past the desk, along a carpeted hall. Maybe it led out some back way. Behind him, the SP men had already entered the lobby.

Jennings turned a corner. Two men stepped out, blocking his way.

'Where are you going?'

He stopped, wary. 'Let me by.' He reached into his coat for the Boris gun. At once the men moved.

'Get him.'

His arms were pinned to his sides. Professional hoods. Past them he could see light. Light and sound. Some kind of activity. People.

'All right,' one of the hoods said. They dragged him back along the corridor, toward the lobby. Jennings struggled futilely. He had entered a blind alley. Hoods, a joint. The city was dotted with them, hidden in the darkness. The swank hotel a front. They would toss him out, into the hands of the SP.

Some people came along the halls, a man and a woman. Older people. Well dressed. They gazed curiously at Jennings, suspended between the two men.

Suddenly Jennings understood. A wave of relief hit him, blinding him. 'Wait,' he said thickly. 'My pocket.'

'Come on.'

'Wait. Look. My right pocket. Look for yourselves.'

He relaxed, waiting. The hood on his right reached, dipping cautiously into the pocket. Jennings smiled. It was over. *He* had seen even this. There was no possibility of failure. This solved one problem: where to stay until it was time to meet Rethrick. He could stay here.

The hood brought out the half poker chip, examining the serrated edges. 'Just a second.' From his own coat he took a matching chip, fitting on a gold chain. He touched the edges together.

'All right?' Jennings said.

'Sure.' They let him go. He brushed off his coat automatically. 'Sure, mister. Sorry. Say, you should have—'

'Take me in the back,' Jennings said, wiping his face. 'Some people are looking for me. I don't particularly want them to find me.'

'Sure.' They led him back, into the gambling rooms. The half chip had turned what might have been a disaster into an asset. A gambling and girl joint. One of the few institutions the Police left alone. He was safe. No question of that. Only one thing remained. The struggle with Rethrick!

Rethrick's face was hard. He gazed at Jennings, swallowing rapidly.

'No,' he said. 'I didn't know it was you. We thought it was the SP.'

There was silence. Kelly sat at the chair by her desk, her legs crossed, a cigarette between her fingers. Jennings leaned against the door, his arms folded.

'Why didn't you use the mirror?' he said.

Rethrick's face flickered. 'The mirror? You did a good job, my friend. We *tried* to use the mirror.'

'Tried?'

'Before you finished your term with us you changed a few leads inside the mirror. When we tried to operate it nothing happened. I left the plant half an hour ago. They were still working on it.'

'I did that before I finished my two years?'

'Apparently you had worked out your plans in detail. You know that with the mirror we would have no trouble tracking you down. You're a good mechanic, Jennings. The best we ever had. We'd like to have you back, sometime. Working for us again. There's not one of us that can operate the mirror the way you could. And right now, we can't use it at all.'

Jennings smiled. 'I had no idea *he* did anything like that. I underestimated him. *His* protection was even—'

'Who are you talking about?'

'Myself. During the two years. I use the objective. It's easier.'

'Well, Jennings. So the two of you worked out an elaborate plan to steal our schematics. Why? What's the purpose? You haven't turned them over to the Police.'

'No.'

'Then I can assume it's blackmail.'

'That's right.'

'What for? What do you want?' Rethrick seemed to have aged. He slumped, his eyes small and glassy, rubbing his chin nervously. 'You went to a lot of trouble to get us into this position. I'm curious why. While you were working for us you laid the groundwork. Now you've completed it, in spite of our precautions.'

'Precautions?'

'Erasing your mind. Concealing the Plant.'

'Tell him,' Kelly said. 'Tell him why you did it.'

Jennings took a deep breath. 'Rethrick, I did it to get back in. Back to the Company. That's the only reason. No other.'

Rethrick stared at him. 'To get back into the Company? You can come back in. I told you that.' His voice was thin and sharp, edged with strain. 'What's the matter with you? You can come back in. For as long as you want to stay.'

'As a mechanic.'

'Yes. As a mechanic. We employ many—'

'I don't want to come back as a mechanic. I'm not interested in working for you. Listen, Rethrick. The SP picked me up as soon as I left this Office. If it hadn't been for *him* I'd be dead.'

'They picked you up?'

'They wanted to know what Rethrick Construction does. They wanted me to tell them.'

Rethrick nodded. 'That's bad. We didn't know that.'

'No, Rethrick. I'm not coming in as an employee you can toss out any time it pleases you. I'm coming in with you, not for you.'

'With me?' Rethrick stared at him. Slowly a film settled over his face, an ugly hard film. 'I don't understand what you mean.'

'You and I are going to run Rethrick Construction together. That'll be the way, from now on. And no one will be burning my memory out, for their own safety.'

'That's what you want?'

'Yes.'

'And if we don't cut you in?'

'Then the schematics and films go to the SP. It's as simple as that. But I don't want to. I don't want to destroy the Company. I want to get into the Company! I want to be safe. You don't know what it's like, being out there, with no place to go. An individual has no place to turn to, anymore. No one to help him. He's caught between two ruthless forces, a pawn between political and economic powers. And I'm tired of being a pawn.'

For a long time Rethrick said nothing. He stared down at the floor, his face dull and blank. At last he looked up. 'I know it's that way. That's something I've known for a long time. Longer than you have. I'm a lot older than you. I've seen it come, grow that way, year after year. That's why Rethrick Construction exists. Someday, it'll be all different. Someday, when we have the scoop and the mirror finished. When the weapons are finished.'

Jennings said nothing.

'I know very well how it is! I'm an old man. I've been working a long time. When they told me someone had got out of the Plant with schematics, I thought the end had come. We already knew you had damaged the mirror. We knew there was a connection, but we had parts figured wrong.

'We thought, of course, that Security had planted you with us, to find out what we were doing. Then, when you realized you couldn't carry out your information, you damaged the mirror. With the mirror damaged, SP could go ahead and—'

He stopped, rubbing his cheek.

'Go on,' Jennings said.

'So you did this alone . . . Blackmail. To get into the Company. You don't know what the Company is for, Jennings! How dare you try to come in! We've been working and building for a long time. You'd wreck us, to save your hide. You'd destroy us, just to save yourself.'

'I'm not wrecking you. I can be a lot of help.'

'I run the Company alone. It's my Company. I made it, put it together. It's mine.'

Jennings laughed. 'And what happens when you die? Or is the revolution going to come in your own lifetime?'

Rethrick's head jerked up.

'You'll die, and there won't be anyone to go on. You know I'm a good mechanic. You said so yourself. You're a fool, Rethrick. You want to manage it all yourself. Do everything, decide everything. But you'll die, someday. And then what will happen?'

There was silence.

'You better let me in – for the Company's good, as well as my own. I can do a lot for you. When you're gone the Company will survive in my hands. And maybe the revolution will work.'

'You should be glad you're alive at all! If we hadn't allowed you to take your trinkets out with you—'

'What else could you do? How could you let men service your mirror, see their own futures, and not let them lift a finger to help themselves. It's easy to see why you were forced to insert the alternate-payment clause. You had no choice.'

'You don't even know what we are doing. Why we exist.'

'I have a good idea. After all, I worked for you two years.'

Time passed. Rethrick moistened his lips again and again, rubbing his cheek. Perspiration stood out on his forehead. At last he looked up.

'No,' he said. 'It's no deal. No one will ever run the Company but me. If I die, it dies with me. It's my property.'

Jennings became instantly alert. 'Then the papers go to the Police.'

Rethrick said nothing, but a peculiar expression moved across his face, an expression that gave Jennings a sudden chill.

'Kelly,' Jennings said. 'Do you have the papers with you?'

Kelly stirred, standing up. She put out her cigarette, her face pale. 'No.'

'Where are they? Where did you put them?'

'Sorry,' Kelly said softly. 'I'm not going to tell you.'

He stared at her. 'What?'

'I'm sorry,' Kelly said again. Her voice was small and faint. 'They're safe. The SP won't ever get them. But neither will you. When it's convenient, I'll turn them back to my father.'

'Your father!'

'Kelly is my daughter,' Rethrick said. 'That was one thing you didn't count on, Jennings. *He* didn't count on it, either. No one knew that but the two of us. I wanted to keep all positions of trust in the family. I see now that it was a good idea. But it had to be kept secret. If the SP had guessed they would have picked her up at once. Her life wouldn't have been safe.'

Jennings let his breath out slowly. 'I see.'

'It seemed like a good idea to go along with you,' Kelly said. 'Otherwise you'd have done it alone, anyhow. And you would have had the papers on you. As you said, if the SP caught you with the papers it would be the end of us. So I went along with you. As soon as you gave me the papers I put them in a good safe place.' She smiled a little. 'No one will find them but me. I'm sorry.'

'Jennings, you can come in with us,' Rethrick said. 'You can work for us forever, if you want. You can have anything you want. Anything except—'

'Except that no one runs the Company but you.'

'That's right. Jennings, the Company is old. Older than I am. I didn't bring it into existence. It was – you might say, *willed* to me. I took the burden on. The job of managing it, making it grow, moving it toward the day. The day of revolution, as you put it.

'My grandfather founded the Company, back in the twentieth century. The Company has always been in the family. And it will always be. Someday, when Kelly marries, there'll be an heir to carry it on after me. So that's taken care of. The Company was founded up in Maine, in a small New England town. My grandfather was a little old New Englander, frugal, honest, passionately independent. He had a little repair business of some sort, a little tool and fix-it place. And plenty of knack.

'When he saw government and big business closing in on everyone, he went underground. Rethrick Construction disappeared from the map. It took government quite a while to organize Maine, longer than most places. When the rest of the world had been divided up between international cartels and world-states, there was New England, still alive. Still free. And my grandfather and Rethrick Construction.

'He brought in a few men, mechanics, doctors, lawyers, little once-a-week newspapermen from the Middle West. The Company grew. Weapons appeared, weapons and knowledge. The time scoop and mirror! The Plant was built, secretly, at great cost, over a long period of time. The Plant is big. Big and deep. It goes down many more levels than you saw. *He* saw them, your alter ego. There's a lot of power there. Power, and men who've disappeared, purged all over the world, in fact. We got them first, the best of them.

'Someday, Jennings, we're going to break out. You see, conditions like this can't go one. People can't live this way, tossed back and forth by political and economic powers. Masses of people shoved this way and that according to the needs of this government or that cartel. There's going to be resistance, someday. A strong, desperate resistance. Not by big people, powerful people, but by little people. Bus drivers. Grocers. Vidscreen operators. Waiters. And that's where the Company comes in.

'We're going to provide them with the help they'll need, the tools, weapons, the knowledge. We're going to "sell" them our services. They'll be able to hire us. And they'll need someone they can hire. They'll have a lot lined up against them. A lot of wealth and power.'

There was silence.

'Do you see?' Kelly said. 'That's why you mustn't interfere. It's Dad's Company. It's always been that way. That's the way Maine people are. It's part of the family. The Company belongs to the family. It's ours.'

'Come in with us,' Rethrick said. 'As a mechanic. I'm sorry, but that's our limited outlook showing through. Maybe it's narrow, but we've always done things this way.'

Jennings said nothing. He walked slowly across the office, his hands in his pockets. After a time he raised the blind and stared out at the street, far below.

Down below, like a tiny black bug, a Security cruiser moved along, drifting silently with the traffic that flowed up and down the street. It joined a second cruiser, already parked. Four SP men were standing by it in their green uniforms, and even as he watched some more could be seen coming from across the street. He let the blind down.

'It's a hard decision to make,' he said.

'If you go out there they'll get you,' Rethrick said. 'They're out there all the time. You haven't got a chance.'

'Please—' Kelly said, looking up at him.

Suddenly Jennings smiled. 'So you won't tell me where the papers are. Where you put them.'

Kelly shook her head.

'Wait.' Jennings reached into his pocket. He brought out a small piece of paper. He unfolded it slowly, scanning it. 'By any chance did you deposit them with the Dunne National Bank, about three o'clock yesterday afternoon? For safekeeping in their storage vaults?'

Kelly gasped. She grabbed her handbag, unsnapping it. Jennings put the slip of paper, the parcel receipt, back in his pocket. 'So *he* saw even that,' he murmured. 'The last of the trinkets. I wondered what it was for.'

Kelly groped frantically in her purse, her face wild. She brought out a slip of paper, waving it.

'You're wrong! Here it is! It's still here.' She relaxed a little. 'I don't know what *you* have, but this is—'

In the air above them something moved. A dark space formed, a circle. The space stirred. Kelly and Rethrick stared up, frozen.

From the dark circle a claw appeared, a metal claw, joined to a shimmering rod. The claw dropped, swinging in a wide arc. The claw swept the paper from Kelly's fingers. It hesitated for a second. Then it drew itself up again, disappearing with the paper, into the circle of black. Then, silently, the claw and the rod and the circle blinked out. There was nothing. Nothing at all.

'Where – where did it go?' Kelly whispered. 'The paper. What was that?'

Jennings patted his pocket. 'It's safe. It's safe, right here. I wondered when *he* would show up. I was beginning to worry.'

Rethrick and his daughter stood, shocked into silence.

'Don't look so unhappy,' Jennings said. He folded his arms. 'The paper's safe – and the Company's safe. When the time comes it'll be there, strong and very glad to help out the revolution. We'll see to that, all of us, you, me and your daughter.'

He glanced at Kelly, his eyes twinkling. 'All three of us. And maybe by that time there'll be even *more* members to the family!'

Nanny

'When I look back,' Mary Fields said, 'I marvel that we ever could have grown up without a Nanny to take care of us.'

There was no doubt that Nanny had changed the whole life of the Fields' house since she had come. From the time the children opened their eyes in the morning to their last sleepy nod at night, Nanny was in there with them, watching them, hovering about them, seeing that all their wants were taken care of.

Mr Fields knew, when he went to the office, that his kids were safe, perfectly safe. And Mary was relieved of a countless procession of chores and worries. She did not have to wake the children up, dress them, see that they were washed, ate their meals, or anything else. She did not even have to take them to school. And after school, if they did not come right home, she did not have to pace back and forth in anxiety, worried that something had happened to them.

Not that Nanny spoiled them, of course. When they demanded something absurd or harmful (a whole storeful of candy, or a policeman's motorcycle) Nanny's will was like iron. Like a good shepherd she knew when to refuse the flock its wishes.

Both children loved her. Once, when Nanny had to be sent to the repair shop, they cried and cried without stopping. Neither their mother nor their father could console them. But at last Nanny was back again, and everything was all right. And just in time! Mrs Fields was exhausted.

'Lord,' she said, throwing herself down. 'What would we do without her?'

Mr Fields looked up. 'Without who?'

'Without Nanny.'

'Heaven only knows,' Mr Fields said.

After Nanny had aroused the children from sleep – by emitting a soft, musical whirr a few feet from their heads – she made certain that they were dressed and down at the breakfast table promptly, with faces clean and dispositions unclouded. If they were cross Nanny allowed them the pleasure of riding downstairs on her back.

Coveted pleasure! Almost like a roller coaster, with Bobby and Jean hanging on for dear life and Nanny flowing down step by step in the funny rolling way she had.

Nanny did not prepare breakfast, of course. That was all done by the kitchen. But she remained to see that the children ate properly and then, when breakfast was over, she supervised their preparations for school. And after they had got their books together and were all brushed and neat, her most important job: seeing that they were safe on the busy streets.

There were many hazards in the city, quite enough to keep Nanny watchful. The swift rocket cruisers that swept along, carrying businessmen to work. The time a bully had tried to hurt Bobby. One quick push from Nanny's starboard grapple and away he went, howling for all he was worth. And the time a drunk started talking to Jean, with heaven knows *what* in mind. Nanny tipped him into the gutter with one nudge of her powerful metal side.

Sometimes the children would linger in front of a store. Nanny would have to prod them gently, urging them on. Or if (as sometimes happened) the children were late to school, Nanny would put them on her back and fairly speed along the sidewalk, her treads buzzing and flapping at a great rate.

After school Nanny was with them constantly, supervising their play, watching over them, protecting them, and at last, when it began to get dark and late, dragging them away from their games and turned in the direction of home.

Sure enough, just as dinner was being set on the table, there was Nanny, herding Bobby and Jean in through the front door, clicking and whirring admonishingly at them. Just in time for dinner! A quick run to the bathroom to wash their faces and hands.

And at night—

Mrs Fields was silent, frowning just a little. At night . . . 'Tom?' she said.

Her husband looked up from his paper. 'What?'

'I've been meaning to talk to you about something. It's very odd, something I don't understand. Of course, I don't know anything about mechanical things. But Tom, at night when we're all sleep and the house is quiet, Nanny—'

There was a sound.

'Mommy!' Jean and Bobby came scampering into the living room, their faces flushed with pleasure. 'Mommy, we raced Nanny all the way home, and we won!'

'We won,' Bobby said. 'We beat her.'

'We ran a lot faster than she did,' Jean said.

'Where is Nanny, children?' Mrs Fields asked.

'She's coming. Hello, Daddy.'

'Hello, kids,' Tom Fields said. He cocked his head to one side, listening. From the front porch came an odd scraping sound, an unusual whirr and scrape. He smiled.

'That's Nanny,' Bobby said.

And into the room came Nanny.

Mr Fields watched her. She had always intrigued him. The only sound in the room was her metal treads, scraping against the hardwood floor, a peculiar rhythmic sound. Nanny came to a halt in front of him, stopping a few feet away. Two unwinking photocell eyes appraised him, eyes on flexible wire stalks. The stalks moved speculatively, weaving slightly. Then they withdrew.

Nanny was built in the shape of a sphere, a large metal

sphere, flattened on the bottom. Her surface had been sprayed with a dull green enamel, which had become chipped and gouged through wear. There was not much visible in addition to the eye stalks. The treads could not be seen. On each side of the hull was the outline of a door. From these the magnetic grapples came, when they were needed. The front of the hull came to a point, and there the metal was reinforced. The extra plates welded both fore and aft made her look almost like a weapon of war. A tank of some kind. Or a ship, a rounded metal ship that had come up on land. Or like an insect. A sowbug, as they are called.

'Come on!' Bobby shouted.

Abruptly Nanny moved, spinning slightly as her treads gripped the floor and turned her around. One of her side doors opened. A long metal rod shot out. Playfully, Nanny caught Bobby's arm with her grapple and drew him to her. She perched him on her back. Bobby's leg straddled the metal hull. He kicked with his heels excitedly, jumping up and down.

'Race you around the block!' Jean shouted.

'Giddup!' Bobby cried. Nanny moved away, out of the room with him. A great round bug of whirring metal and relays, clicking photocells and tubes. Jean ran beside her.

There was silence. The parents were alone again.

'Isn't she amazing?' Mrs Fields said. 'Of course, robots are a common sight these days. Certainly more so than a few years ago. You see them everywhere you go, behind counters in stores, driving buses, digging ditches—'

'But Nanny is different,' Tom Fields murmured.

'She's – she's not like a machine. She's like a person. A living person. But after all, she's much more complex than any other kind. She has to be. They say she's even more intricate than the kitchen.'

'We certainly paid enough for her,' Tom said.

'Yes,' Mary Fields murmured. 'She's very much like a living creature.' There was a strange note in her voice. 'Very much so.'

'She sure takes care of the kids,' Tom said, returning to his newspaper.

'But I'm worried.' Mary put her coffee cup down, frowning. They were eating dinner. It was late. The two children had been sent up to bed. Mary touched her mouth with her napkin. 'Tom, I'm worried. I wish you'd listen to me.'

Tom Fields blinked. 'Worried? What about?'

'About her. About Nanny.'

'Why?'

'I – I don't know.'

'You mean we're going to have to repair her again? We just got through fixing her. What is it this time? If those kids didn't get her to—'

'It's not that.'

'What, then?'

For a long time his wife did not answer. Abruptly she got up from the table and walked across the room to the stairs. She peered up, staring into the darkness. Tom watched her, puzzled.

'What's the matter?'

'I want to be sure she can't hear us.'

'She? Nanny?'

Mary came toward him. 'Tom, I woke up last night again. Because of the sounds. I heard them again, the same sounds, the sounds I heard before. And you told me it didn't mean anything!'

Tom gestured. 'It doesn't. What does it mean?'

'I don't know. That's what worries me. But after we're all asleep she comes downstairs. She leaves their room. She slips down the stairs as quietly as she can, as soon as she's sure we're all asleep.'

'But why?'

'I don't know! Last night I heard her going down, slithering down the stairs, quiet as a mouse. I heard her moving around down here. And then—'

'Then what?'

'Tom, then I heard her go out the back door. Out,

outside the house. She went into the back yard. That was all I heard for a while.'

Tom rubbed his jaw. 'Go on.'

'I listened. I sat up in bed. You were asleep, of course. Sound asleep. No use trying to wake you. I got up and went to the window. I lifted the shade and looked out. She was out there, out in the back yard.'

'What was she doing?'

'I don't know.' Mary Fields's face was lined with worry. 'I don't know! What in the world *would* a Nanny be doing outside at night, in the back yard?'

It was dark. Terribly dark. But the infrared filter clicked into place, and the darkness vanished. The metal shape moved forward, easing through the kitchen, its treads half-retracted for greatest quiet. It came to the back door and halted, listening.

There was no sound. The house was still. They were all asleep upstairs. Sound asleep.

The Nanny pushed, and the back door opened. It moved out onto the porch, letting the door close gently behind it. The night air was thin and cold. And full of smells, all the strange, tingling smells of the night, when spring has begun to change into summer, when the ground is still moist and the hot July sun has not had a chance to kill all the little growing things.

The Nanny went down the steps, onto the cement path. Then it moved cautiously onto the lawn, the wet blades of grass slapping its sides. After a time it stopped, rising up on its back treads. Its front part jutted up into the air. Its eye stalks stretched, rigid and taut, waving very slightly. Then it settled back down and continued its motion forward.

It was just going around the peach tree, coming back toward the house, when the noise came.

It stopped instantly, alert. Its side doors fell away and its grapples ran out their full lengths, lithe and wary. On the other side of the board fence, beyond the row of shasta

daisies, something had stirred. The Nanny peered, clicking
filters rapidly. Only a few faint stars winked in the sky
overhead. But it saw, and that was enough.

On the other side of the fence a second Nanny was
moving, making its way softly through the flowers, coming
toward the fence. It was trying to make as little noise
as possible. Both Nannies stopped, suddenly unmoving,
regarding each other – the green Nanny waiting in its own
yard, the blue prowler that had been coming toward the
fence.

The blue prowler was a larger Nanny, built to manage
two young boys: Its sides were dented and warped from use,
but its grapples were still strong and powerful. In addition
to the usual reinforced plates across its nose there was a
gouge of tough steel, a jutting jaw that was already sliding
into position, ready and able.

Mecho-Products, its manufacturer, had lavished attention on this jaw-construction. It was their trademark, their
unique feature. Their ads, their brochures, stressed the
massive frontal scoop mounted on all their models. And
there was an optional assist: a cutting edge, power-driven,
that at extra cost could easily be installed in their 'Luxury-
line' models.

This blue Nanny was so equipped.

Moving cautiously ahead, the blue Nanny reached the
fence. It stopped and carefully inspected the boards. They
were thin and rotted, put up a long time ago. It pushed its
hard head against the wood. The fence gave, splintering and
ripping. At once the green Nanny rose on its back treads, its
grapples leaping out. A fierce joy filled it, a bursting excitement. The wild frenzy of battle.

The two closed, rolling silently on the ground, their
grapples locked. Neither made any noise, the blue Mecho-
Products Nanny nor the smaller, lighter, pale-green Service
Industries, Inc., Nanny. On and on they fought, hugged
tightly together, the great jaw trying to push underneath,
into the soft treads. And the green Nanny trying to hook its

metal point into the eyes that gleamed fitfully against its side. The green Nanny had the disadvantage of being a medium-priced model; it was outclassed and outweighed. But it fought grimly, furiously.

On and on they struggled, rolling in the wet soil. Without sound of any kind. Performing the wrathful, ultimate task for which each had been designed.

'I can't imagine,' Mary Fields murmured, shaking her head. 'I just don't know.'

'Do you suppose some animal did it?' Tom conjectured. 'Are there any big dogs in the neighborhood?'

'No. There was a big red Irish setter, but they moved away, to the country. That was Mr Petty's dog.'

The two of them watched, troubled and disturbed. Nanny lay at rest by the bathroom door, watching Bobby to make sure he brushed his teeth. The green hull was twisted and bent. One eye had been shattered, the glass knocked out, splintered. One grapple no longer retracted completely; it hung forlornly out of its little door, dragging uselessly.

'I just don't understand,' Mary repeated. 'I'll call the repair place and see what they say. Tom, it must have happened sometime during the night. While we were asleep. The noises I heard—'

'Shhh,' Tom muttered warningly. Nanny was coming toward them, away from the bathroom. Clicking and whirring raggedly, she passed them, a limping green tub of metal that emitted an unrhythmic, grating sound. Tom and Mary Fields unhappily watched her as she lumbered slowly into the living room.

'I wonder,' Mary murmured.

'Wonder what?'

'I wonder if this will happen again.' She glanced up suddenly at her husband, eyes full of worry. 'You know how the children love her . . . and they need her so. They just wouldn't be safe without her. Would they?'

'Maybe it won't happen again,' Tom said soothingly. 'Maybe it was an accident.' But he didn't believe it; he knew better. What had happened was no accident.

From the garage he backed his surface cruiser, maneuvered it until its loading entrance was locked against the rear door of the house. It took only a moment to load the sagging, dented Nanny inside; within ten minutes he was on his way across town to the repair and maintenance department of Service Industries, Inc.

The serviceman, in grease-stained white overalls, met him at the entrance. 'Troubles?' he asked wearily; behind him, in the depths of the block-long building, stood rows of battered Nannies, in various stages of disassembly. 'What seems to be the matter this time?'

Tom said nothing. He ordered the Nanny out of the cruiser and waited while the serviceman examined it for himself.

Shaking his head, the serviceman crawled to his feet and wiped grease from his hands. 'That's going to run into money,' he said. 'The whole neural transmission's out.'

His throat dry, Tom demanded: 'Ever see anything like this before? It didn't break; you know that. It was demolished.'

'Sure,' the serviceman agreed tonelessly. 'It pretty much got taken down a peg. On the basis of those missing chunks—' He indicated the dented anterior hull-sections. 'I'd guess it was one of Mecho's new jaw-models.'

Tom Fields's blood stopped moving in his veins. 'Then this isn't new to you,' he said softly, his chest constricting. 'This goes on all the time.'

'Well, Mecho just put out that jaw-model. It's not half bad . . . costs about twice what this model ran. Of course,' the serviceman added thoughtfully, 'we have an equivalent. We can match their best, and for less money.'

Keeping his voice as calm as possible, Tom said: 'I want this one fixed. I'm not getting another.'

'I'll do what I can. But it won't be the same as it was. The damage goes pretty deep. I'd advise you to trade it in – you can get damn near what you paid. With the new models coming out in a month or so, the salesmen are eager as hell to—'

'Let me get this straight.' Shakily, Tom Fields lit up a cigarette. 'You people really don't want to fix these, do you? You want to sell brand-new ones, when these break down.' He eyed the repairman intently. 'Break down, or are *knocked* down.'

The repairman shrugged. 'It seems like a waste of time to fix it up. It's going to get finished off, anyhow, soon.' He kicked the misshapen green hull with his boot. 'This model is around three years old. Mister, it's obsolete.'

'Fix it up,' Tom grated. He was beginning to see the whole picture; his self-control was about to snap. 'I'm not getting a new one! I want this one fixed!'

'Sure,' the serviceman said, resigned. He began making out a work-order sheet. 'We'll do our best. But don't expect miracles.'

While Tom Fields was jerkily signing his name to the sheet, two more damaged Nannies were brought into the repair building.

'When can I get it back?' he demanded.

'It'll take a couple of days,' the mechanic said, nodding toward the rows of semi-repaired Nannies behind him. 'As you can see,' he added leisurely, 'we're pretty well full-up.'

'I'll wait,' Tom said tautly. 'Even if it takes a month.'

'Let's go to the park!' Jean cried.

So they went to the park.

It was a lovely day, with the sun shining down hotly and the grass and flowers blowing in the wind. The two children strolled along the gravel path, breathing the warm-scented air, taking deep breaths and holding the presence of roses and hydrangeas and orange blossoms inside them as long as possible. They passed through a swaying grove of dark, rich cedars. The ground was soft with mold underfoot, the velvet, moist fur of a living world beneath their feet. Beyond the cedars, where the sun returned and the blue sky flashed back into being, a great green lawn stretched out.

Behind them Nanny came, trudging slowly, her treads clicking noisily. The dragging grapple had been repaired, and a new optic unit had been installed in place of the damaged one. But the smooth coordination of the old days was lacking; and the clean-cut lines of her hull had not been restored. Occasionally she halted, and the two children halted, too, waiting impatiently for her to catch up with them.

'What's the matter, Nanny?' Bobby asked her.

'Something's wrong with her,' Jean complained. 'She's been all funny since last Wednesday. Real slow and funny. And she was gone, for a while.'

'She was in the repair shop,' Bobby announced. 'I guess she got sort of tired. She's old, Daddy says. I heard him and Mommy talking.'

A little sadly they continued on, with Nanny painfully following. Now they had come to benches placed here and there on the lawn, with people languidly dozing in the sun. On the grass lay a young man, a newspaper over his face, his coat rolled up under his head. They crossed carefully around him, so as not to step on him.

'There's the lake!' Jean shouted, her spirits returning.

The great field of grass sloped gradually down, lower and lower. At the far end, the lowest end, lay a path, a gravel trail, and beyond that, a blue lake. The two children scampered excitedly, filled with anticipation. They hurried faster and faster down the carefully graded slope, Nanny struggling miserably to keep up with them.

'The lake!'

'Last one there's a dead Martian stinko-bug!'

Breathlessly, they rushed across the path, onto the tiny strip of green bank against which the water lapped. Bobby threw himself down on his hands and knees, laughing and panting and peering down into the water. Jean settled down beside him, smoothing her dress tidily into place. Deep in the cloudy-blue water some tadpoles and minnows moved, minute artificial fish too small to catch.

At one end of the lake some children were floating boats with flapping white sails. At a bench a fat man sat laboriously reading a book, a pipe jammed in his mouth. A young man and woman strolled along the edge of the lake together, arm in arm, intent on each other, oblivious of the world around them.

'I wish we had a boat,' Bobby said wistfully.

Grinding and clashing, Nanny managed to make her way across the path and up to them. She stopped, settling down, retracting her treads. She did not stir. One eye, the good eye, reflected the sunlight. The other had not been synchronized; it gaped with futile emptiness. She had managed to shift most of her weight on her less-damaged side, but her motion was bad and uneven, and slow. There was a smell about her, an odor of burning oil and friction.

Jean studied her. Faintly she patted the bent green side sympathetically. 'Poor Nanny! What did you do, Nanny? What happened to you? Were you in a wreck?'

'Let's push Nanny in,' Bobby said lazily. 'And see if she can swim. Can a Nanny swim?'

Jean said no, because she was too heavy. She would sink to the bottom and they would never see her again.

'Then we won't push her in,' Bobby agreed.

For a time there was silence. Overhead a few birds fluttered past, plump specks streaking swiftly across the sky. A small boy on a bicycle came riding hesitantly along the gravel path, his front wheel wobbling.

'I wish I had a bicycle,' Bobby murmured.

The boy careened on past. Across the lake the fat man stood up and knocked his pipe against the bench. He closed his book and sauntered off along the path, wiping his perspiring forehead with a vast red handkerchief.

'What happens to Nannies when they get old?' Bobby asked wonderingly. 'What do they do? Where do they go?'

'They go to heaven.' Jean lovingly thumped the green dented hull with her hand. 'Just like everybody else.'

'Are Nannies born? Were there always Nannies?' Bobby had begun to conjecture on ultimate cosmic mysteries. 'Maybe there was a time before there were Nannies. I wonder what the world was like in the days before Nannies lived.'

'Of course there were always Nannies,' Jean said impatiently. 'If there weren't, where did they come from?'

Bobby couldn't answer that. He meditated for a time, but presently he became sleepy . . . he was really too young to solve such problems. His eyelids became heavy and he yawned. Both he and Jean lay on the warm grass by the edge of the lake, watching the sky and the clouds, listening to the wind moving through the grove of cedar trees. Beside them the battered green Nanny rested and recuperated her meager strength.

A little girl came slowly across the field of grass, a pretty child in a blue dress with a bright ribbon in her long dark hair. She was coming toward the lake.

'Look,' Jean said. 'There's Phyllis Casworthy. She has an *orange* Nanny.'

They watched, interested. 'Who ever heard of an orange Nanny?' Bobby said, disgusted. The girl and her Nanny crossed the path a short distance down, and reached the edge of the lake. She and her orange Nanny halted, gazing around at the water and the white sails of toy boats, the mechanical fish.

'Her Nanny is bigger than ours,' Jean observed.

'That's true,' Bobby admitted. He thumped the green side loyally. 'But ours is nicer. Isn't she?'

Their Nanny did not move. Surprised, he turned to look. The green Nanny stood rigid, taut. Its better eye stalk was far out, staring at the orange Nanny fixedly, unwinkingly.

'What's the matter?' Bobby asked uncomfortably.

'Nanny, what's the matter?' Jean echoed.

The green Nanny whirred, as its gears meshed. Its treads

dropped and locked into place with a sharp metallic snap. Slowly its doors retracted and its grapples slithered out.

'Nanny, what are you doing?' Jean scrambled nervously to her feet. Bobby leaped up, too.

'Nanny! What's going on?'

'Let's go,' Jean said, frightened. 'Let's go home.'

'Come on, Nanny,' Bobby ordered. 'We're going home, now.'

The green Nanny moved away from them; it was totally unaware of their existence. Down the lake-side the other Nanny, the great orange Nanny, detached itself from the little girl and began to flow.

'Nanny, you come back!' the little girl's voice came, shrill and apprehensive.

Jean and Bobby rushed up the sloping lawn, away from the lake. 'She'll come!' Bobby said. 'Nanny! Please come!'

But the Nanny did not come.

The orange Nanny neared. It was huge, much more immense than the blue Mecho jaw-model that had come into the back yard that night. That one now lay scattered in pieces on the far side of the fence, hull ripped open, its parts strewn everywhere.

This Nanny was the largest the green Nanny had ever seen. The green Nanny moved awkwardly to meet it, raising its grapples and preparing its internal shields. But the orange Nanny was unbending a square arm of metal, mounted on a long cable. The metal arm whipped out, rising high in the air. It began to whirl in a circle, gathering ominous velocity, faster and faster.

The green Nanny hesitated. It retreated, moving uncertainly away from the swinging mace of metal. And as it rested warily, unhappily, trying to make up its mind, the other leaped.

'Nanny!' Jean screamed.

'Nanny! Nanny!'

The two metal bodies rolled furiously in the grass, fighting and struggling desperately. Again and again the metal

mace came, bashing wildly into the green side. The warm
sun shone benignly down on them. The surface of the lake
eddied gently in the wind.

'Nanny!' Bobby screamed, helplessly jumping up and
down.

But there was no response from the frenzied, twisting
mass of crashing orange and green.

'What are you going to do?' Mary Fields asked, tight-lipped
and pale.

'You stay here.' Tom grabbed up his coat and threw it on;
he yanked his hat down from the closet shelf and strode
toward the front door.

'Where are you going?'

'Is the cruiser out front?' Tom pulled open the front door
and made his way out onto the porch. The two children,
miserable and trembling, watched him fearfully.

'Yes,' Mary murmured, 'it's out front. But where—'

Tom turned abruptly to the children. 'You're sure she's –
dead?'

Bobby nodded. His face was streaked with grimy tears.
'Pieces . . . all over the lawn.'

Tom nodded grimly. 'I'll be right back. And don't worry
at all. You three stay here.'

He strode down the front steps, down the walk, to the
parked cruiser. A moment later they heard him drive furiously away.

He had to go to several agencies before he found what
he wanted. Service Industries had nothing he could use;
he was through with them. It was at Allied Domestic that he
saw exactly what he was looking for, displayed in their
luxurious, well-lighted window. They were just closing, but
the clerk let him inside when he saw the expression on his
face.

'I'll take it,' Tom said, reaching into his coat for his
checkbook.

'Which one, sir?' the clerk faltered.

'The big one. The big black one in the window. With the four arms and the ram in front.'

The clerk beamed, his face aglow with pleasure. 'Yes sir!' he cried, whipping out his order pad. 'The Imperator Deluxe, with power-beam focus. Did you want the optional high-velocity grapple-lock and the remote-control feed-back? At moderate cost, we can equip her with a visual report screen; you can follow the situation from the comfort of your own living room.'

'The situation?' Tom said thickly.

'As she goes into action.' The clerk began writing rapidly. 'And I mean *action* – this model warms up and closes in on its adversary within fifteen seconds of the time it's activated. You can't find faster reaction in any single-unit models, ours or anybody else's. Six months ago, they said fifteen seconds closing was a pipe dream.' The clerk laughed excitedly. 'But science goes on.'

A strange cold numbness settled over Tom Fields. 'Listen,' he said hoarsely. Grabbing the clerk by the lapel he yanked him closer. The order pad fluttered away; the clerk gulped with surprise and fright. 'Listen to me,' Tom grated, 'you're building these things bigger all the time – *aren't you*? Every year, new models, new weapons. You and all the other companies – building them with improved equipment to destroy each other.'

'Oh,' the clerk squeaked indignantly. 'Allied Domestic's models are *never* destroyed. Banged up a little now and then, perhaps, but you show me one of our models that's been put out of commission.' With dignity, he retrieved his order pad and smoothed down his coat. 'No, sir,' he said emphatically, 'our models survive. Why, I saw a seven-year-old Allied running around, an old Model 3-S. Dented a bit, perhaps, but plenty of fire left. I'd like to see one of those cheap Protecto-Corp. models try to tangle with *that*.'

Controlling himself with an effort, Tom asked: 'But why? What's it all for? What's the purpose in this – competition between them?'

The clerk hesitated. Uncertainly, he began again with his order pad. 'Yes, sir,' he said. 'Competition; you put your finger right on it. Successful competition, to be exact. Allied Domestic doesn't meet competition – it *demolishes* it.'

It took a second for Tom Fields to react. Then understanding came. 'I see,' he said. 'In other words, every year these things are obsolete. No good, not large enough. Not powerful enough. And if they're not replaced, if I don't get a new one, a more advanced model—'

'Your present Nanny was, ah, the loser?' The clerk smiled knowingly. 'Your present model was, perhaps, slightly anachronistic? It failed to meet present-day standards of competition? It, ah, failed to come out at the end of the day?'

'It never came home,' Tom said thickly.

'Yes, it was demolished . . . I fully understand. Very common. You see, sir, you don't have a choice. It's nobody's fault, sir. Don't blame us; don't blame Allied Domestic.'

'But,' Tom said harshly, 'when one is destroyed, that means you sell another one. That means a sale for you. Money in the cash register.'

'True. But we all have to meet contemporary standards of excellence. We can't let ourselves fall behind . . . As you saw, sir, if you don't mind my saying so, you saw the unfortunate consequences of falling behind.'

'Yes,' Tom agreed, in an almost inaudible voice. 'They told me not to have her repaired. They said I should replace her.'

The clerk's confident, smugly beaming face seemed to expand. Like a miniature sun, it glowed happily, exaltedly. 'But now you're all set up, sir. With this model you're right up there in the front. Your worries are over, Mr . . .' He halted expectantly. 'Your name, sir? To whom shall I make out this purchase order?'

*

Bobby and Jean watched with fascination as the delivery men lugged the enormous crate into the living room. Grunting and sweating, they set it down and straightened gratefully up.

'All right,' Tom said crisply. 'Thanks.'

'Not at all, mister.' The delivery men stalked out, noisily closing the door after them.

'Daddy, what is it?' Jean whispered. The two children came cautiously around the crate, wide-eyed and awed.

'You'll see in a minute.'

'Tom, it's past their bedtime,' Mary protested. 'Can't they look at it tomorrow?'

'I want them to look at it *now*.' Tom disappeared downstairs into the basement and returned with a screwdriver. Kneeling on the floor beside the crate he began rapidly unscrewing the bolts that held it together. 'They can go to bed a little late, for once.'

He removed the boards, one by one, working expertly and calmly. At last the final board was gone, propped up against the wall with the others. He unclipped the book of instructions and the 90-day warranty and handed them to Mary. 'Hold onto these.'

'It's a Nanny!' Bobby cried.

'It's a huge, huge Nanny!'

In the crate the great black shape lay quietly, like an enormous metal tortoise, encased in a coating of grease. Carefully checked, oiled, and fully guaranteed. Tom nodded. 'That's right. It's a Nanny, a new Nanny. To take the place of the old one.'

'For *us*?'

'Yes.' Tom sat down in a nearby chair and it a cigarette. 'Tomorrow morning we'll turn her on and warm her up. See how she runs.'

The children's eyes were like saucers. Neither of them could breathe or speak.

'But this time,' Mary said, 'you must stay away from the park. Don't take her near the park. You hear?'

'No,' Tom contradicted. 'They can go in the park.'

Mary glanced uncertainly at him. 'But that orange thing might—'

Tom smiled grimly. 'It's fine with me if they go into the park.' He leaned toward Bobby and Jean. 'You kids go into the park anytime you want. And don't be afraid of anything. Of anything or anyone. Remember that.'

He kicked the end of the massive crate with his toe.

'There isn't anything in the world you have to be afraid of. Not anymore.'

Bobby and Jean nodded, still gazing fixedly into the crate.

'All right, Daddy,' Jean breathed.

'Boy, look at her!' Bobby whispered. 'Just look at her! I can hardly wait till tomorrow!'

Mrs Andrew Casworthy greeted her husband on the front steps of their attractive three-story house, wringing her hands anxiously.

'What's the matter?' Casworthy grunted, taking off his hat. With his pocket handkerchief he wiped sweat from his florid face. 'Lord, it was hot today. What's wrong? What is it?'

'Andrew, I'm afraid—'

'What the hell happened?'

'Phyllis came home from the park today without her Nanny. She was bent and scratched yesterday when Phyllis brought her home, and Phyllis is so upset I can't make out—'

'*Without her Nanny?*'

'She came home alone. By herself. All alone.'

Slow rage suffused the man's heavy features. 'What happened?'

'Something in the park, like yesterday. Something attacked her Nanny. Destroyed her! I can't get the story exactly straight, but something black, something huge and black . . . It must have been another Nanny.'

Casworthy's jaw slowly jutted out. His thickset face turned ugly dark red, a deep unwholesome flush that rose ominously and settled in place. Abruptly, he turned on his heel.

'Where are you going?' his wife fluttered nervously.

The paunchy, red-faced man stalked rapidly down the walk toward his sleek surface cruiser, already reaching for the door handle.

'I'm going to shop for another Nanny,' he muttered. 'The best damn Nanny I can get. Even if have to go to a hundred stores. I want the best – and the biggest.'

'But, dear,' his wife began, hurrying apprehensively after him, 'can we really afford it?' Wringing her hands together anxiously, she raced on: 'I mean, wouldn't it be better to wait? Until you've had time to think it over, perhaps. Maybe later on, when you're a little more – calm.'

But Andrew Casworthy wasn't listening. Already the surface cruiser boiled with quick, eager life, ready to leap forward. 'Nobody's going to get ahead of me,' he said grimly, his heavy lips twitching. 'I'll show them, all of them. Even if I have to get a new size designed. Even if I have to get one of those manufacturers to turn out a new model for me!'

And, oddly, he knew one of them would.

Jon's World

Kastner walked around the ship without speaking. He climbed the ramp and entered, disappearing cautiously inside. For a time his outline could be seen, stirring around. He appeared again, his broad face dimly alight.

'Well?' Caleb Ryan said. 'What do you think?'

Kastner came down the ramp. 'Is it ready to go? Nothing left to work out?'

'It's almost ready. Workmen are finishing up the remaining sections. Relay connections and feed lines. But no major problems exist. None we can predict, at least.'

The two men stood together, looking up at the squat metal box with its ports and screens and observation grills. The ship was not lovely. There were no trim lines, no chrome and rexcroid struts to ease the hull into a gradually tapering tear-drop. The ship was square and knobby, with turrets and projections rising up everywhere.

'What will they think when we emerge from that?' Kastner murmured.

'We had no time to beautify it. Of course, if you want to wait another two months—'

'Couldn't you take off a few of the knobs? What are they for? What do they do?'

'Valves. You can examine the plans. They drain off the power load when it peaks too far up. Time travel is going to be dangerous. A vast load is collected as the ship moves back. It has to be leaked off gradually – or we'll be an immense bomb charged with millions of volts.'

'I'll take your word on it.' Kastner picked up his

briefcase. He moved toward one of the exits. League Guards stepped out of his way. 'I'll tell the Directors it's almost ready. By the way, I have something to reveal.'

'What is it?'

'We've decided who's going along with you.'

'Who?'

'I'm going. I've always wanted to know what things were like before the war. You see the history spools, but it isn't the same. I want to *be* there. Walk around. You know, they say there was no ash before the war. The surface was fertile. You could walk for miles without seeing ruins. This I would like to see.'

'I didn't know you were interested in the past.'

'Oh, yes. My family preserved some illustrated books showing how it was. No wonder USIC wants to get hold of Schonerman's papers. If reconstruction could begin—'

'That's what we all want.'

'And maybe we'll get it. I'll see you later.'

Ryan watched the plump little businessman depart, his briefcase clutched tightly. The row of League Guards stepped aside for him to pass, filling in behind him as he disappeared through the doorway.

Ryan returned his attention to the ship. So Kastner was to be his companion. USIC – United Synthetic Industries Combine – had held out for equal representation on the trip. One man from the League, one from USIC. USIC had been the source of supply, both commercial and financial, for Project Clock. Without its help the Project would never have got out of the paper stage. Ryan sat down at the bench and sent the blueprints racing through the scanner. They had worked a long time. There was not much left to be done. Only a few finishing touches here and there.

The vidscreen clicked. Ryan halted the scanner and swung to catch the call.

'Ryan.'

The League monitor appeared on the screen. The call was coming through League cables. 'Emergency call.'

Ryan froze. 'Put it through.'

The monitor faded. After a moment an old face appeared, florid and lined. 'Ryan—'

'What's happened?'

'You had better come home. As soon as you can.'

'What is it?'

'Jon.'

Ryan forced himself to be calm. 'Another attack?' His voice was thick.

'Yes.'

'Like the others?'

'Exactly like the others.'

Ryan's hand jerked to the cut-off switch. 'All right. I'll be home at once. Don't let anyone in. Try to keep him quiet. Don't let him out of his room. Double the guard, if necessary.'

Ryan broke the circuit. A moment later he was on his way to the roof, toward his inter-city ship parked above him, at the roof field of the building.

His inter-city ship rushed above the unending gray ash, automatic grapples guiding it toward City Four. Ryan stared blankly out the port, only half-seeing the sight below.

He was between cities. The surface was wasted, endless heaps of slag and ash as far as the eye could see. Cities rose up like occasional toadstools, separated by miles of gray. Toadstools here and there, towers and buildings, men and women working. Gradually the surface was being reclaimed. Supplies and equipment were being brought down from the Lunar Base.

During the war human beings had left Terra and gone to the moon. Terra was devasted. Nothing but a globe of ruin and ash. Men had come back gradually, when the war was over.

Actually there had been two wars. The first was man against man. The second was man against the claws –

complex robots that had been created as a war weapon. The claws had turned on their makers, designing their own new types and equipment.

Ryan's ship began to descend. He was over City Four. Presently the ship came to rest on the roof of his massive private residence at the center of the city. Ryan leaped quickly out and crossed the roof to the lift.

A moment later he entered his quarters and made his way toward Jon's room.

He found the old man watching Jon through the glass side of the room, his face grave. Jon's room was partly in darkness. Jon was sitting on the edge of his bed, his hands clasped tightly together. His eyes were shut. His mouth was open a little, and from time to time his tongue came out, stiff and rigid.

'How long has he been like that?' Ryan said to the old man beside him.

'About an hour.'

'The other attacks followed the same pattern?'

'This is more severe. Each has been more severe.'

'No one has seen him but you?'

'Just the two of us. I called you when I was certain. It's almost over. He's coming out of it.'

On the other side of the glass Jon stood up and walked away from his bed, his arms folded. His blond hair hung down raggedly in his face. His eyes were still shut. His face was pale and set. His lips twitched.

'He was completely unconscious at first. I had left him alone for awhile. I was in another part of the building. When I came back I found him lying on the floor. He had been reading. The spools were scattered all around him. His face was blue. His breathing was irregular. There were repeated muscular spasms, as before.'

'What did you do?'

'I entered the room and carried him to the bed. He was rigid at first, but after a few minutes he began to relax. His body became limp. I tested his pulse. It was

very slow. Breathing was coming more easily. And then it
began.'

'It?'

'The talk.'

'Oh.' Ryan nodded.

'I wish you could have been here. He talked more than
ever before. On and on. Streams of it. Without pause. As if
he couldn't stop.'

'Was – was it the same talk as before?'

'Exactly the same as it's always been. And his face was lit
up. Glowing. As before.'

Ryan considered. 'Is it all right for me to go into the
room?'

'Yes. It's almost over.'

Ryan moved to the door. His fingers pressed against the
code lock and the door slid back into the wall.

Jon did not notice him as he came quietly into the room.
He paced back and forth, eyes shut, his arms wrapped
around his body. He swayed a little, rocking from side to
side. Ryan came to the center of the room and stopped.

'Jon!'

The boy blinked. His eyes opened. He shook his head
rapidly. 'Ryan? What – what did you want?'

'Better sit down.'

Jon nodded. 'Yes. Thank you.' He sat down on the bed
uncertainly. His eyes were wide and blue. He pushed his
hair back out of his face, smiling a little at Ryan.

'How do you feel?'

'I feel all right.'

Ryan sat down across from him, drawing a chair over. He
crossed his legs, leaning back. For a long time he studied
the boy. Neither of them spoke. 'Grant says you had a little
attack,' Ryan said finally.

Jon nodded.

'You're over it now?'

'Oh, yes. How is the time ship coming?'

'Fine.'

'You promised I could see it, when it's ready.'

'You can. When it's completely done.'

'When will that be?'

'Soon. A few more days.'

'I want to see it very much. I've been thinking about it. Imagine going into time. You could go back to Greece. You could go back and see Pericles and Xenophon and – and Epictetus. You could go back to Egypt and talk to Ikhnation.' He grinned. 'I can't wait to see it.'

Ryan shifted. 'Jon, do you really think you're well enough to go outside? Maybe—'

'Well enough? What do you mean?'

'Your attacks. You really think you should go out? Are you strong enough?'

Jon's face clouded. 'They're not attacks. Not really. I wish you wouldn't call them attacks.'

'Not attacks? What are they?'

Jon hesitated. 'I – I shouldn't tell you, Ryan. You wouldn't understand.'

Ryan stood up. 'All right, Jon. If you feel you can't talk to me I'll go back to the lab.' He crossed the room to the door. 'It's a shame you can't see the ship. I think you'd like it.'

Jon followed him plaintively. 'Can't I see it?'

'Maybe if I knew more about your – your attacks I'd know whether you're well enough to go out.'

Jon's face flickered. Ryan watched him intently. He could see thoughts crossing Jon's mind, written on his features. He struggled inwardly.

'Don't you want to tell me?'

Jon took a deep breath. 'They're *visions*.'

'What?'

'They're visions.' Jon's face was alive with radiance. 'I've known it a long time. Grant says they're not, but they are. If you could see them you'd know, too. They're not like anything else. More real than, well, than this.' He thumped the wall. 'More real than that.'

Ryan lit a cigarette slowly. 'Go on.'

It all came with a rush. 'More real than *anything* else! Like looking through a window. A window into another world. A real world. Much more real than this. It makes all this just a shadow world. Only dim shadows. Shapes. Images.'

'Shadows of an ultimate reality?'

'Yes! Exactly. The world behind all this.' Jon paced back and forth, animated by excitement. 'This, all these things. What we see here. Buildings. The sky. The cities. The endless ash. None is quite real. It's so dim and vague! I don't really feel it, not like the other. And it's becoming less real, all the time. The other is growing, Ryan. Growing more and more vivid! Grant told me it's only my imagination. But it's not. It's real. More real than any of these things here, these things in this room.'

'Then why can't we all see it?'

'I don't know. I wish you could. You ought to see it, Ryan. It's beautiful. You'd like it, after you got used to it. It takes time to adjust.'

Ryan considered. 'Tell me,' he said at last. 'I want to know exactly what you see. Do you always see the same thing?'

'Yes. Always the same. But more intensely.'

'What is it? What do you see that's so real?'

Jon did not answer for awhile. He seemed to have withdrawn. Ryan waited, watching his son. What was going on in his mind? What was he thinking? The boy's eyes were shut again. His hands were pressed together, the fingers white. He was off again, off in his private world.

'Go on,' Ryan said aloud.

So it was *visions* the boy saw. Visions of ultimate reality. Like the Middle Ages. His own son. There was a grim irony in it. Just when it seemed they had finally licked that proclivity in man, his eternal inability to face reality. His eternal dreaming. Would science never be able to realize its ideal? Would man always go on preferring illusion to reality?

His own son. Retrogression. A thousand years lost. Ghosts and gods and devils and the secret inner world. The world of ultimate reality. All the fables and fictions and metaphysics that man had used for centuries to compensate for his fear, his terror of the world. All the dreams he had made up to hide the truth, the harsh world of reality. Myths, religions, fairy tales. A better land, beyond and above. Paradise. All coming back, reappearing again, and in his own son.

'Go on,' Ryan said impatiently. 'What do you see?'

'I see fields,' Jon said. 'Yellow fields as bright as the sun. Fields and parks. Endless parks. Green, mixed in with the yellow. Paths, for people to walk.'

'What else?'

'Men and women. In robes. Walking along the paths, among the trees. The air fresh and sweet. The sky bright blue. Birds. Animals. Animals moving through the parks. Butterflies. Oceans. Lapping oceans of clear water.'

'No cities?'

'Not like our cities. Not the same. People living in the parks. Little wood houses here and there. Among the trees.'

'Roads?'

'Only paths. No ships or anything. Only walking.'

'What else do you see?'

'That's all.' Jon opened his eyes. His cheeks were flushed. His eyes sparkled and danced. 'That's all, Ryan. Parks and yellow fields. Men and women in robes. And so many animals. The wonderful animals.'

'How do they live?'

'What?'

'How do the people live? What keeps them alive?'

'They grow things. In the fields.'

'Is that all? Don't they build? Don't they have factories?'

'I don't think so.'

'An agrarian society. Primitive.' Ryan frowned. 'No business or commerce.'

'They work in the fields. And discuss things.'

'Can you *hear* them?'

'Very faintly. Sometimes I can hear them a little, if I listen very hard. I can't make out any words, though.'

'What are they discussing?'

'Things.'

'What kind of things?'

Jon gestured vaguely. 'Great things. The world. The universe.'

There was silence. Ryan grunted. He did not say anything. Finally he put out his cigarette. 'Jon—'

'Yes?'

'You think what you see is *real*?'

Jon smiled. 'I know it's real.'

Ryan's gaze was sharp. 'What do you mean, real? In what way is this world of yours real?'

'It exists.'

'Where does it exist?'

'I don't know.'

'Here? Does it exist here?'

'No. It's not here.'

'Some place else? A long way off? Some other part of the universe beyond our range of experience?'

'Not another part of the universe. It has nothing to do with space. It's here.' Jon waved around him. 'Close by. It's very close. I see it all around me.'

'Do you see it now?'

'No. It comes and goes.'

'It ceases to exist? It only exists sometimes?'

'No, it's always there. But I can't always make contact with it.'

'How do you know it's always there?'

'I just know.'

'Why can't *I* see it? Why are you the only one who can see it?'

'I don't know.' Jon rubbed his forehead wearily. 'I don't know why I'm the only one who can see it. I wish you could see it. I wish everybody could see it.'

'How can you demonstrate it isn't an hallucination? You have no objective validation of it. You have only your own inner sense, your state of consciousness. How could it be presented for empirical analysis?'

'Maybe it can't. I don't know. I don't care. I don't *want* to present it for empirical analysis.'

There was silence. Jon's face was set and grim, his jaw tight. Ryan sighed. Impasse.

'All right, Jon.' He moved slowly toward the door. 'I'll see you later.'

Jon said nothing.

At the door Ryan halted, looking back. 'Then your visions are getting stronger, aren't they? Progressively more vivid.'

Jon nodded curtly.

Ryan considered awhile. Finally he raised his hand. The door slid away and he passed outside the room, into the hall.

Grant came up to him. 'I was watching through the window. He's quite withdrawn, isn't he?'

'It's difficult to talk to him. He seems to believe these attacks are some kind of vision.'

'I know. He's told me.'

'Why didn't you let me know?'

'I didn't want to alarm you more. I know you've been worried about him.'

'The attacks are getting worse. He says they're more vivid. More convincing.'

Grant nodded.

Ryan moved along the corridor, deep in thought, Grant a little behind. 'It's difficult to be certain of the best course of action. The attacks absorb him more and more. He's beginning to take them seriously. They're usurping the place of the outside world. And in addition—'

'And in addition you're leaving soon.'

'I wish we knew more about time travel. A great number of things may happen to us.' Ryan rubbed his jaw. 'We might not come back. Time is a potent force. No real exploration has been done. We have no idea what we may run into.'

He came to the lift and stopped.

'I'll have to make my decision right away. It has to be made before we leave.'

'Your decision?'

Ryan entered the lift. 'You'll know about it later. Watch Jon constantly from now on. Don't be away from him for even a moment. Do you understand?'

Grant nodded. 'I understand. You want to be sure he doesn't leave his room.'

'You'll hear from me either tonight or tomorrow.' Ryan ascended to the roof and entered his inter-city ship.

As soon as he was in the sky he clicked on the vidscreen and dialed the League Offices. The face of the League Monitor appeared. 'Offices.'

'Give me the medical center.'

The monitor faded. Presently Walter Timmer, the medical director, appeared on the screen. His eyes flickered as he recognized Ryan. 'What can I do for you, Caleb?'

'I want you to get out a medical car and a few good men and come over here to City Four.'

'Why?'

'It's a matter I discussed with you several months ago. You recall, I think.'

Timmer's expression changed. 'Your son?'

'I've decided. I can't wait any longer. He's getting worse, and we'll be leaving soon on the time trip. I want it performed before I leave.'

'All right.' Timmer made a note. 'We'll make immediate arrangements here. And we'll send a ship over to pick him up at once.'

Ryan hesitated. 'You'll do a good job?'

'Of course. We'll have James Pryor perform the actual operation.' Timmer reached up to cut the vidscreen circuit.

'Don't worry, Caleb. He'll do a good job. Pryor is the best lobotomist the center has.'

Ryan laid out the map, stretching the corners flat against the table. 'This is a time map, drawn up in the form of a space projection. So we can see where we're going.'

Kastner peered over his shoulder. 'Will we be confined to the one Project – getting Schonerman's papers? Or can we move around?'

'Only the one Project is contemplated. But to be certain of success we should make several stops on this side of Schonerman's continuum. Our time map may be inaccurate, or the drive itself may act with some bias.'

The work was finished. All the final sections were put in place.

In a corner of the room Jon sat watching, his face expressionless. Ryan glanced toward him. 'How does it look to you?'

'Fine.'

The time ship was like some stubby insect, overgrown with warts and knobs. A square box with windows and endless turrets. Not really a ship at all.

'I guess you wish you could come,' Kastner said to Jon. 'Right?'

Jon nodded faintly.

'How are you feeling?' Ryan asked him.

'Fine.'

Ryan studied his son. The boy's color had come back. He had regained most of his original vitality. The visions, of course, no longer existed.

'Maybe you can come next time,' Kastner said.

Ryan returned to the map. 'Schonerman did most of his work between 2030 and 2037. The results were not put to any use until several years later. The decision to use his work in the war was reached only after long consideration. The Governments seemed to have been aware of the dangers.'

'But not sufficiently so.'

'No.' Ryan hesitated. 'And we may be getting ourselves into the same situation.'

'How do you mean?'

'Schonerman's discovery of the artificial brain was lost when the last claw was destroyed. None of us have been able to duplicate his work. If we bring his papers we may put society back in jeopardy. We may bring back the claws.'

Kastner shook his head. 'No. Schonerman's work was not implicitly related to the claws. The development of an artificial brain does not imply lethal usage. Any scientific discovery can be used for destruction. Even the wheel was used in the Assyrian war chariots.'

'I suppose so.' Ryan glanced up at Kastner. 'Are you certain USIC doesn't intend to use Schonerman's work along military lines?'

'USIC is an industrial combine. Not a government.'

'It would ensure its advantage for a long time.'

'USIC is strong enough as it is.'

'Let it go.' Ryan rolled up the map. 'We can start any minute. I'm anxious to get going. We've worked a long time on this.'

'I agree.'

Ryan crossed the room to his soon. 'We're leaving, Jon. We should be back fairly soon. Wish us luck.'

Jon nodded. 'I wish you luck.'

'You're feeling all right?'

'Yes.'

'Jon – you feel better now, don't you? Better than before?'

'Yes.'

'Aren't you glad they're gone? All the troubles you were having?'

'Yes.'

Ryan put his hand awkwardly on the boy's shoulder. 'We'll see you later.'

Ryan and Kastner made their way up the ramp to the

hatch of the time ship. From the corner, Jon watched them silently. A few League Guards lounged at the entrances to the work lab, watching with idle interest.

Ryan paused at the hatch. He called one of the guards over. 'Tell Timmer I want him.'

The guard went off, pushing through the exit.

'What is it?' Kastner said.

'I have some final instructions to give him.'

Kastner shot him a sharp glance. 'Final? What's the matter? You think something's going to happen to us?'

'No. Just a precaution.'

Timmer came striding in. 'You're leaving, Ryan?'

'Everything's ready. There's no reason to hold back any longer.'

Timmer came up the ramp. 'What did you want me for?'

'This may be unnecessary. But there's always the possibility something might go wrong. In case the ship doesn't reappear according to schedule I've filed with the League members—'

'You want me to name a protector for Jon.'

'That's right.'

'There's nothing to worry about.'

'I know. But I'd feel better. Someone should watch out for him.'

They both glanced at the silent, expressionless boy sitting in the corner of the room. Jon stared straight ahead. His face was blank. His eyes were dull, listless. There was nothing there.

'Good luck,' Timmer said. He and Ryan shook hands. 'I hope everything works out.'

Kastner climbed inside the ship, setting down his briefcase. Ryan followed him, lowering the hatch into place and bolting it into position. He sealed the inner lock. A bank of automatic lighting came on. Controlled atmosphere began to hiss into the cabin of the ship.

'Air, light, heat,' Kastner said. He peered out the port at the League Guards outside. 'It's hard to believe. In a few minutes all this will disappear. This building. These guards. Everything.'

Ryan seated himself at the control board of the ship, spreading out the time map. He fastened the map into position, crossing the surface with the cable leads from the board before him. 'It's my plan to make several observation stops along the way, so we can view some of the past events relevant to our work.'

'The war?'

'Mainly. I'm interested in seeing the claws in actual operation. At one time they were in complete control of Terra, according to the War Office records.'

'Let's not get too close, Ryan.'

Ryan laughed. 'We won't land. We'll make our observations from the air. The only actual contact we'll make will be with Schonerman.'

Ryan closed the power circuit. Energy flowed through the ship around them, flooding into the meters and indicators on the control board. Needles jumped, registering the load.

'The main thing we have to watch is our energy peak,' Ryan explained. 'If we build up too much of a load of time ergs the ship won't be able to come out of the time stream. We'll keep moving back into the past, building up a greater and greater charge.'

'An enormous bomb.'

'That's right.' Ryan adjusted the switches before him. The meter readings changed. 'Here we go. Better hang on.'

He released the controls. The ship shuddered as it polarized into position, easing into the time flow. The vanes and knobs changed their settings, adjusting themselves to the stress. Relays closed, braking the ship against the current sweeping around them.

'Like the ocean,' Ryan murmured. 'The most potent energy in the universe. The great dynamic behind all motion. The Prime Mover.'

'Maybe this is what they used to mean by God.'

Ryan nodded. The ship was vibrating around them. They were in the grip of a giant hand, an immense fist closing silently. They were in motion. Through the port the men and walls had begun to waver, fading out of existence as the ship slipped out of phase with the present, drifting farther and farther into the flow of the time stream.

'It won't be long,' Ryan murmured.

All at once the scene beyond the port winked out. There was nothing there. Nothing beyond them.

'We've not phased with any space-time objects,' Ryan explained. 'We're out of focus with the universe itself. At this moment we exist in non-time. There's no continuum in which we're operating.'

'I hope we can get back again.' Kastner sat down nervously, his eyes on the blank port. 'I feel like the first man who went down in a submarine.'

'That was during the American Revolution. The submarine was propelled by a crank which the pilot turned. The other end of the crank was a propeller.'

'How could he go very far?'

'He didn't. He cranked his ship under a British frigate and then bored a hole in the frigate's hull.'

Kastner glanced up at the hull of the time ship, vibrating and rattling from stress. 'What would happen if this ship should break open?'

'We'd be atomized. Dissolved into the stream around us.' Ryan lit a cigarette. 'We'd become a part of the time flow. We'd move back and forth endlessly, from one end of the universe to the other.'

'End?'

'The time ends. Time flows both ways. Right now we're moving back. But energy must move both ways to keep a balance. Otherwise time ergs in vast amounts would collect at one particular continuum and the result would be catastrophic.'

'Do you suppose there's some purpose behind all of this? I wonder how the time flow ever got started.'

'Your question is meaningless. Questions of purpose have no objective validity. They can't be subjected to any form of empirical investigation.'

Kastner lapsed into silence. He picked at his sleeve nervously, watching the port.

Across the time map the cable arms moved, tracing a line from the present back into the past. Ryan studied the motion of the arms. 'We're reaching the latter part of the war. The final stages. I'm going to rephase the ship and bring it out of the time flow.'

'Then we'll be back in the universe again?'

'Among objects. In a specific continuum.'

Ryan gripped the power switch. He took a deep breath. The first great test of the ship had passed. They had entered the time stream without accident. Could they leave it as easily? He opened the switch.

The ship leaped. Kastner staggered, catching hold of the wall support. Outside the port a gray sky twisted and wavered. Adjustments fell into place, leveling the ship in the air. Down below them Terra circled and tilted as the ship gained equilibrium.

Kastner hurried to the port to peer out. They were a few hundred feet above the surface, rushing parallel to the ground. Gray ash stretched out in all directions, broken by the occasional mounds of rubbish. Ruins of towns, buildings, walls. Wrecks of military equipment. Clouds of ash blew across the sky, darkening the sun.

'Is the war still on?' Kastner asked.

'The claws still possess Terra. We should be able to see them.'

Ryan raised the time ship, increasing the scope of their view. Kastner scanned the ground. 'What if they fire at us?'

'We can always escape into time.'

'They might capture the ship and use it to come to the present.'

'I doubt it. At this stage in the war the claws were busy fighting among themselves.'

To their right ran a winding road, disappearing into the ash and reappearing again later on. Bomb craters gaped here and there, breaking the road up. Something was coming slowly along it.

'There,' Kastner said. 'On the road. A column of some sort.'

Ryan maneuvered the ship. They hung above the road, the two of them peering out. The column was dark brown, a marching file making its way steadily along. Men, a column of men, marching silently through the landscape of ash.

Suddenly Kastner gasped. 'They're identical! All of them are the same!'

They were seeing a column of claws. Like lead toys, the robots marched along, tramping through the gray ash. Ryan caught his breath. He had expected such a sight, of course. There were only four types of claws. These he saw now had all been turned out in the same underground plant, from the same dies and stampers. Fifty or sixty robots, shaped like young men, marched calmly along. They moved very slowly. Each had only one leg.

'They must have been fighting among themselves,' Kastner murmured.

'No. This type was made this way. The Wounded Soldier Type. Originally they were designed to trick human sentries to gain entrance into regular bunkers.'

It was weird, watching the silent column of men, identical men, each the same as the next, plodding along the road. Each soldier supported himself with a crutch. Even the crutches were identical. Kastner opened and closed his mouth in revulsion.

'Not very pleasant, is it?' Ryan said. 'We're lucky the human race got away to Luna.'

'Didn't any of these follow?'

'A few, but by the time we had identified the four types and were ready for them.' Ryan took hold of the power switch. 'Let's go on.'

'Wait.' Kastner raised his hand. 'Something's going to happen.'

To the right of the road a group of figures were slipping rapidly down the side of a rise, through the ash. Ryan let go of the power switch, watching. The figures were identical. Women. The women, in uniforms and boots, advanced quietly toward the column on the road.

'Another variety,' Kastner said.

Suddenly the column of soldiers halted. They scattered, hobbling awkwardly in all directions. Some of them fell, stumbling and dropping their crutches. The women rushed out on the road. They were slender and young, with dark hair and eyes. One of the Wounded Soldiers began to fire. A woman fumbled at her belt. She made a throwing motion.

'What ' Kastner muttered. There was a sudden flash. A cloud of white light rose from the center of the road, billowing in all directions.

'Some kind of concussion bomb,' Ryan said.

'Maybe we better get out of here.'

Ryan threw the switch. The scene below them began to waver. Abruptly it faded. It winked out.

'Thank God that's over,' Kastner said. 'So that's what the war was like.'

'The second part. The major part. Claw against claw. It's a good thing they started fighting with each other. Good for us, I mean.'

'Where to now?'

'We'll make one more observation stop. During the early part of the war. Before claws came into use.'

'And then Schonerman?'

Ryan set his jaw. 'That's right. One more stop and then Schonerman.'

Ryan adjusted the controls. The meters moved slightly. Across the map the cable arms traced their path. 'It won't be long,' Ryan murmured. He gripped the switch, setting the relays in place. 'This time we have to be more careful. There'll be more war activity.'

'Maybe we shouldn't even—'

'I want to see. This was man against man. The Soviet region against the United Nations. I'm curious to see what it was like.'

'What if we're spotted?'

'We can get away quickly.'

Kastner said nothing. Ryan manipulated the controls. Time passed. At the edge of the board Ryan's cigarette burned to an ash. At last he straightened up.

'Here we go. Get set.' He opened the switch.

Below them green and brown plains stretched out, pocked with bomb craters. Part of a city swept past. It was burning. Towering columns of smoke rose up, drifting into the sky. Along the roads black dots moved, vehicles and people streaming away.

'A bombing,' Kastner said. 'Recent.'

The city fell behind. They were over open country. Military trucks rushed along. Most of the land was still intact. They could see a few farmers working the fields. The farmers dropped down as the time ship moved over them.

Ryan studied the sky. 'Watch out.'

'Air craft?'

'I'm not sure where we are. I don't know the location of the sides in this part of the war. We may be over UN territory, or Soviet territory.' Ryan held on tight to the switch.

From the blue sky two dots appeared. The dots grew. Ryan watched them intently. Beside him Kastner gave a nervous grunt. 'Ryan, we better—'

The dots separated. Ryan's hand closed over the power switch. He yanked it closed. As the scene dissolved the dots swept past. Then there was nothing but grayness outside.

In their ears the roar of the two planes still echoed.

'That was close,' Kastner said.

'Very. They didn't waste any time.'

'I hope you don't want to stop any more.'

'No. No more observation stops. The Project itself comes next. We're close to Schonerman's time area. I can begin to slow down the velocity of the ship. This is going to be critical.'

'Critical?'

'There are going to be problems getting to Schonerman. We must hit his continuum exactly, both in space as well as time. He may be guarded. In any case they won't give us much time to explain who we are.' Ryan tapped the time map. 'And there's always the chance the information given here is incorrect.'

'How long before we rephase with a continuum? Schonerman's continuum?'

Ryan looked at his wristwatch. 'About five or ten minutes. Get ready to leave the ship. Part of this is going to be on foot.'

It was night. There was no sound, only unending silence. Kastner strained to hear, his ear against the hull of the ship. 'Nothing.'

'No. I don't hear anything either.' Carefully, Ryan unbolted the hatch, sliding the locks back. He pushed the hatch open, his gun gripped tight. He peered out into the darkness.

The air was fresh and cold. Full of smells of growing things. Trees and flowers. He took a deep breath. He could see nothing. It was pitch black. Far off, a long way off, a cricket chirruped.

'Hear that?' Ryan said.

'What is it?'

'A beetle.' Ryan stepped gingerly down. The ground was soft underfoot. He was beginning to adjust to the darkness. Above him a few stars glinted. He could make out trees, a field of trees. And beyond the trees a high fence.

Kastner stepped down beside him. 'What now?'

'Keep your voice down.' Ryan indicated the fence. 'We're going that way. Some kind of building.'

They crossed the field to the fence. At the fence Ryan aimed his gun, setting the charge at minimum. The fence charred and sank, the wire glowed red.

Ryan and Kastner stepped over the fence. The side of the building rose, concrete and iron. Ryan nodded to Kastner. 'We'll have to move quickly. And low.'

He crouched, taking a breath. Then he ran, bent over, Kastner beside him. They crossed the ground to the building. A window loomed up in front of them. Then a door. Ryan threw his weight against the door.

The door opened. Ryan fell inside, staggering. He caught a quick glimpse of startled faces, men leaping to their feet.

Ryan fired, sweeping the interior of the room with his gun. Flame rushed out, crackling around him. Kastner fired past his shoulder. Shapes moved in the flame, dim outlines falling and rolling.

The flames died. Ryan advanced, stepping over charred heaps on the floor. A barracks. Bunks, remains of a table. An overturned lamp and radio.

By the rays of the lamp Ryan studied a battle map pinned on the wall. He traced the map with his finger, deep in thought.

'Are we far?' Kastner asked, standing by the door with his gun ready.

'No. Only a few miles.'

'How do we get there?'

'We'll move the time ship. It's safer. We're lucky. It might have been on the other side of the world.'

'Will there be many guards?'

'I'll tell you the facts when we get there.' Ryan moved to the door. 'Come on. Someone may have seen us.'

Kastner grabbed up a handful of newspapers from the remains of the table. 'I'll bring these. Maybe they'll tell us something.'

'Good idea.'

*

Ryan set the ship down in a hollow between two hills. He
spread the newspapers out, studying them intently. 'We're
earlier than I thought. By a few months. Assuming these
are new.' He fingered the newsprint. 'Not turned yellow.
Probably only a day or so old.'

'What is the date?'

'Autumn, 2030. September 21.'

Kastner peered out the port. 'The sun is going to be
coming up soon. The sky is beginning to turn gray.'

'We'll have to work fast.'

'I'm a little uncertain. What am I supposed to do?'

'Schonerman is in a small village beyond this hill. We're
in the United States. In Kansas. This area is surrounded
by troops, a circle of pillboxes and dugouts. We're inside
the periphery. Schonerman is virtually unknown at this
continuum. His research has never been published. At this
time he's working as part of a large Government research
project.'

'Then he's not especially protected.'

'Only later on, when his work has been turned over to the
Government will he be protected day and night. Kept in an
underground laboratory and never let up to the surface.
The Government's most valuable research worker. But
right now—'

'How will we know him?'

Ryan handed Kastner a sheaf of photographs. 'This is
Schonerman. All the pictures that survived up to our own
time.'

Kastner studied the pictures. Schonerman was a small
man with horn-rimmed glasses. He smiled feebly at the
camera, a thin nervous man with a prominent forehead.
His hands were slender, the fingers long and tapered. In
one photograph he sat at his desk, a pipe beside him, his
thin chest covered by a sleeveless wool sweater. In another
he sat with his legs crossed, a tabby cat in his lap, a mug of
beer in front of him. An old German enamel mug with
hunting scenes and Gothic letters.

'So that's the man who invented the claws. Or did the research work.'

'That's the man who worked out the principles for the first workable artificial brain.'

'Did he know they were going to use his work to make the claws?'

'Not at first. According to reports, Schonerman first learned about it only when the initial batch of claws was released. The United Nations were losing the war. The Soviets gained an original advantage, due to their opening surprise attacks. The claws were hailed as a triumph of Western development. For a time they seemed to have turned the tide of the war.'

'And then—'

'And then the claws began to manufacture their own varieties and attack Soviets and Westerners alike. The only humans that survived were those at the UN base on Luna. A few dozen million.'

'It was a good thing the claws finally turned on each other.'

'Schonerman saw the whole development of his work to the last stages. They say he became greatly embittered.'

Kastner passed the pictures back. 'And you say he's not especially well guarded?'

'Not at this continuum. No more than any other research worker. He's young. In this continuum he's only twenty-five. Remember that.'

'Where'll we find him?'

'The Government Project is located in what was once a school house. Most of the work is done on the surface. No big underground development has begun yet. The research workers have barracks about a quarter mile from their labs.' Ryan glanced at his watch. 'Our best chance is to nab him as he begins work at his bench in the lab.'

'Not in the barracks?'

'The papers are all in the lab. The Government doesn't allow any written work to be taken out. Each worker is

searched as he leaves.' Ryan touched his coat gingerly. 'We
have to be careful. Schonerman must not be harmed. We
only want his papers.'

'We won't use our blasters?'

'No. We don't dare take the chance of injuring him.'

'His papers will definitely be at his bench?'

'He's not allowed to remove them for any reason. We
know exactly where we'll find what we want. There's only
one place the papers can be.'

'Their security precautions play right into our hands.'

'Exactly,' Ryan murmured.

Ryan and Kastner slipped down the hillside, running between the trees. The ground was hard and cold underfoot.
They emerged at the edge of the town. A few people were
already up, moving slowly along the street. The town had
not been bombed. There was no damage, as yet. The
windows of the stores had been boarded up and huge
arrows pointed to the underground shelters.

'What do they have on?' Kastner said. 'Some of them
have something on their faces.'

'Bacteria masks. Come on.' Ryan gripped his blast pistol
as he and Kastner made their way through the town. None
of the people paid any attention to them.

'Just two more uniformed people,' Kastner said.

'Our main hope is surprise. We're inside the wall of
defense. The sky is patrolled against Soviet craft. No
Soviet agents could be landed here. And in any case, this
is a minor research lab, in the center of the United
States. There would be no reason for Soviet agents to
come here.'

'But there will be guards.'

'Everything is guarded. All science. All kinds of research
work.'

The school house loomed up ahead of them. A few men
were milling around the doorway. Ryan's heart constricted.
Was Schonerman one of them?

The men were going inside, one by one. A guard in helmet and uniform was checking their badges. A few of the men wore bacteria masks, only their eyes visible. Would he recognize Schonerman? What if he wore a mask? Fear gripped Ryan suddenly. In a mask Schonerman would look like anyone else.

Ryan slipped his blast pistol away, motioning Kastner to do the same. His fingers closed over the lining of his coat pocket. Sleep-gas crystals. No one this early would have been immunized against sleep-gas. It had not been developed until a year or so later. The gas would put everyone for several hundred feet around into varying periods of sleep. It was a tricky and unpredictable weapon – but perfect for this situation.

'I'm ready,' Kastner murmured.

'Wait. We have to wait for *him*.'

They waited. The sun rose, warming the cold sky. More research workers appeared, filing up the path and inside the building. They puffed white clouds of frozen moisture and slapped their hands together. Ryan began to become nervous. One of the guards was watching him and Kastner. If they became suspicious—

A small man in a heavy overcoat and horn-rimmed glasses came up the path, hurrying toward the building.

Ryan tensed. Schonerman! Schonerman flashed his badge to the guard. He stamped his feet and went inside the building, stripping off his mittens. It was over in a second. A brisk young man, hurrying to get to his work. To his papers.

'Come on,' Ryan said.

He and Kastner moved forward. Ryan pulled the gas crystals loose from the lining of his pocket. The crystals were cold and hard in his hand. Like diamonds. The guard was watching them coming, his gun alert. His face was set. Studying them. He had never seen them before. Ryan, watching the guard's face, could read his thoughts without trouble.

Ryan and Kastner halted at the doorway. 'We're from the FBI,' Ryan said calmly.

'Identify yourselves.' The guard did not move.

'Here are our credentials,' Ryan said. He drew his hand out from his coat pocket. And crushed the gas crystals in his fist.

The guard sagged. His face relaxed. Limply, his body slid to the ground. The gas spread. Kastner stepped through the door, peering around, his eyes bright.

The building was small. Lab benches and equipment stretched out on all sides of them. The workers lay where they had been standing, inert heaps on the floor, their arms and legs out, their mouths open.

'Quick.' Ryan passed Kastner, hurrying across the lab. At the far end of the room Schonerman lay slumped over his bench, his head resting against the metal surface. His glasses had fallen off. His eyes were open, staring. He had taken his papers out of the drawer. The padlock and key were still on the bench. The papers were under his head and between his hands.

Kastner ran to Schonerman and snatched the papers up, stuffing them into his briefcase.

'Get them all!'

'I have them all.' Kastner pulled open the drawer. He grabbed the remaining papers in the drawer. 'Every one of them.'

'Let's go. The gas will dissipate rapidly.'

They ran back outside. A few sprawled bodies lay across the entrance, workers who had come into the area.

'Hurry.'

They ran through the town, along the single main street. People gaped at them in astonishment. Kastner gasped for breath, holding on tight to his briefcase as he ran. 'I'm – winded.'

'Don't stop.'

They reached the edge of the town and started up the hillside. Ryan ran between the trees, his body bent forward, not looking back. Some of the workers would be reviving. And other guards would be coming into the area. It would not be long before the alarm would be out.

Behind them a siren whirred into life.

'Here they come.' Ryan paused at the top of the hill, waiting for Kastner. Behind them men were swelling rapidly into the street, coming up out of underground bunkers. More sirens wailed, a dismal echoing sound.

'Down!' Ryan ran down the hillside toward the time ship, sliding and slipping on the dry earth. Kastner hurried after him, sobbing for breath. They could hear orders being shouted. Soldiers swarming up the hillside after them.

Ryan reached the ship. He grabbed Kastner and pulled him inside. 'Get the hatch shut. Get it closed!'

Ryan ran to the control board. Kastner dropped his briefcase and tugged at the rim of the hatch. At the top of the hill a line of soldiers appeared. They made their way down the hillside, aiming and firing as they ran.

'Get down,' Ryan barked. Shells crashed against the hull of the ship. 'Down!'

Kastner fired back with his blast pistol. A wave of flame rolled up the hillside at the soldiers. The hatch came shut with a bang. Kastner spun the bolts and slid the inner lock into place. 'Ready. All ready.'

Ryan threw the power switch. Outside, the remaining soldiers fought through the flame to the side of the ship. Ryan could see their faces through the port, seared and scorched by the blast.

One man raised his gun awkwardly. Most of them were down, rolling and struggling to rise. As the scene dimmed and faded he saw one of them crawling to his knees. The man's clothing was on fire. Smoke billowed from him, from his arms and shoulders. His face was contorted with pain. He reached out, toward the ship, reaching up at Ryan, his hands shaking, his body bent.

Suddenly Ryan froze.

He was still staring fixedly when the scene winked out

and there was nothing. Nothing at all. The meters changed reading. Across the time map the arms moved calmly, tracing their lines.

In the last moment Ryan had looked directly into the man's face. The pain-contorted face. The features had been twisted, screwed up out of shape. And the horn-rimmed glasses were gone. But there was no doubt – It was Schonerman.

Ryan sat down. He ran a shaking hand through his hair.

'You're certain?' Kastner said.

'Yes. He must have come out of the sleep very quickly. It reacts differently on each person. And he was at the far end of the room. He must have come out of it and followed after us.'

'Was he badly injured?'

'I don't know,'

Kasner opened his briefcase. 'Anyhow, we have the papers.'

Ryan nodded, only half hearing. Schonerman injured, blasted, his clothing on fire. That had not been part of the plan.

But more important – *had it been part of history?*

For the first time the ramification of what they had done was beginning to emerge in his mind. Their own concern had been to obtain Schonerman's papers, so that USIC could make use of the artificial brain. Properly used, Schonerman's discovery could have great value in aiding the restoration of demolished Terra. Armies of worker-robots replanting and rebuilding. A mechanical army to make Terra fertile again. Robots could do in a generation what humans would toil at for years. Terra could be reborn.

But in returning to the past had they introduced new factors? Had a new past been created? Had some kind of balance been upset?

Ryan stood up and paced back and forth.

'What is it?' Kastner said. 'We got the papers.'

'I know.'

'USIC will be pleased. The League can expect aid from now on. Whatever it wants. This will set up USIC forever. After all, USIC will manufacture the robots. Worker-robots. The end of human labor. Machines instead of men to work the ground.'

Ryan nodded. 'Fine.'

'Then what's wrong?'

'I'm worried about our continuum.'

'What are you worried about?'

Ryan crossed to the control board and studied the time map. The ship was moving back toward the present, the arms tracing a path back. 'I'm worried about new factors we may have introduced into past continuums. There's no record of Schonerman being injured. There's no record of this event. It may have set a different causal chain into motion.'

'Like what?'

'I don't know. But I intend to find out. We're going to make a stop right away and discover what new factors we've set into motion.'

Ryan moved the ship into a continuum immediately following the Schonerman incident. It was early October, a little over a week later. He landed the ship in a farmer's field outside of Des Moines, Iowa, at sunset. A cold autumn night with the ground hard and brittle underfoot.

Ryan and Kastner walked into town, Kastner holding tightly onto his briefcase. Des Moines had been bombed by Russian guided missiles. Most of the industrial sections were gone. Only military men and construction workers still remained in the city. The civilian population had been evacuated.

Animals roamed around the deserted streets, looking for food. Glass and debris lay everywhere. The city was cold and desolate. The streets were gutted and wrecked from the fires following the bombing. The autumn air was heavy with the decaying smells of vast heaps of rubble and bodies mixed together in mounds at intersections and open lots.

From a boarded-up newsstand Ryan stole a copy of a news magazine, *Week Review*. The magazine was damp and covered with mold. Kastner put it into his briefcase and they returned to the time ship. Occasional soldiers passed them, moving weapons and equipment out of the city. No one challenged them.

They reached the time ship and entered, locking the hatch behind them. The fields around them were deserted. The farm building had been burned down, and the crops were withered and dead. In the driveway the remains of a ruined automobile lay on its side, a charred wreck. A group of ugly pigs nosed around the remains of the farmhouse, searching for something to eat.

Ryan sat down, opened the magazine. He studied it for a long time, turning the damp pages slowly.

'What do you see?' Kastner asked.

'All about the war. It's still in the opening stages. Soviet guided missiles dropping down. American disc bombs showering all over Russia.'

'Any mention of Schonerman?'

'Nothing I can find. Too much else going on.' Ryan went on studying the magazine. Finally, on one of the back pages, he found what he was looking for. A small item, only a paragraph long.

SOVIET AGENTS SURPRISED

A group of Soviet agents, attempting to demolish a Government research station at Harristown, Kansas, were fired on by guards and quickly routed. The agents escaped, after attempting to slip past the guards into the work offices of the station. Passing themselves off as FBI men, the Soviet agents tried to gain entry as the early morning shift was beginning work. Alert guards intercepted them and gave chase. No damage was done to the research labs or equipment. Two guards and one worker were killed in the encounter. The names of the guards

Ryan clutched the magazine.

'What is it?' Kastner hurried over.

Ryan read the rest of the article. He laid down the magazine, pushing it slowly toward Kastner.

'What is it?' Kastner searched the page.

'Schonerman died. Killed by the blast. We killed him. We've changed the past.'

Ryan stood up and walked to the port. He lit a cigarette, some of his composure returning. 'We set up new factors and started a new line of events. There's no telling where it will end.'

'What do you mean?'

'Someone else may discover the artificial brain. Maybe the shift will rectify itself. The time flow will resume its regular course.'

'Why should it?'

'I don't know. As it stands, we killed him and stole his papers. There's no way the Government can get hold of his work. They won't even know it ever existed. Unless someone else does the same work, covers the same material—'

'How will we know?'

'We'll have to take more looks. It's the only way to find out.'

Ryan selected the year 2051.

In 2051 the first claws had begun to appear. The Soviets had almost won the war. The UN was beginning to bring out the claws in the last desperate attempt to turn the tide of the war.

Ryan landed the time ship at the top of a ridge. Below them a level plain stretched out, criss-crossed with ruins and barbed wire and the remains of weapons.

Kastner unscrewed the hatch and stepped gingerly out onto the ground.

'Be careful,' Ryan said. 'Remember the claws.'

Kastner drew his blast gun. 'I'll remember.'

'At this stage they were small. About a foot long. Metal.

They hid down in the ash. The humanoid types hadn't come into existence, yet.'

The sun was high in the sky. It was about noon. The air was warm and thick. Clouds of ash rolled across the ground, blown by the wind.

Suddenly Kastner tensed. 'Look. What's that? Coming along the road.'

A truck bumped slowly toward them, a heavy brown truck, loaded with soldiers. The truck made its way along the road to the base of the ridge. Ryan drew his blast gun. He and Kastner stood ready.

The truck stopped. Some of the soldiers leaped down and started up the side of the ridge, striding through the ash.

'Get set,' Ryan murmured.

The soldiers reached them, halted a few feet away. Ryan and Kastner stood silently, their blast guns up.

One of the soldiers laughed. 'Put them away. Don't you know the war's over?'

'Over?'

The soldiers relaxed. Their leader, a big man with a red face, wiped sweat from his forehead and pushed his way up to Ryan. His uniform was ragged and dirty. He wore boots, split and caked with ash. 'That war's been over for a week. Come on! There's a lot to do. We'll take you on back.'

'Back?'

'We're rounding up all the outposts. You were cut off? No communications?'

'No,' Ryan said.

'Be months before everyone knows the war's over. Come along. No time to stand here jawing.'

Ryan shifted. 'Tell me. You say the war is really over? But—'

'Good thing, too. We couldn't have lasted much longer.' The officer tapped his belt. 'You don't by any chance have a cigarette, do you?'

Ryan brought out his pack slowly. He took the cigarettes

from it and handed them to the officer, crumpling the pack carefully and restoring it to his pocket.

'Thanks.' The officer passed the cigarettes around to his men. They lit up. 'Yes, it's a good thing. We were almost finished.'

Kastner's mouth opened. 'The claws. What about the claws?'

The officer scowled. 'What?'

'Why did the war end so – so suddenly?'

'Counter-revolution in the Soviet Union. We had been dropping agents and material for months. Never thought anything would come of it, though. They were a lot weaker than anyone realized.'

'Then the war's really ended?'

'Of course.' The officer grabbed Ryan by the arm. 'Let's go. We have work to do. We're trying to clear this god damn ash away and get things planted.'

'Planted? Crops?'

'Of course. What would *you* plant?'

Ryan pulled away. 'Let me get this straight. The war is over. No more fighting. And you know nothing about any claws? Any kind of weapon called claws?'

The officer's face wrinkled. 'What do you mean?'

'Mechanical killers. Robots. As a weapon.'

The circle of soldiers drew back a little. 'What the hell is he talking about?'

'You better explain,' the officer said, his face suddenly hard. 'What's this about claws?'

'No weapon was ever developed along those lines?' Kastner asked.

There was silence. Finally one of the soldiers grunted. 'I think I know what he means. He means Dowling's mine.'

Ryan turned. 'What?'

'An English physicist. He's been experimenting with artificial mines, self-governing. Robot mines. But the mines couldn't repair themselves. So the Government abandoned the project and increased its propaganda work instead.'

'That's why the war's over,' the officer said. He started off. 'Let's go.'

The soldiers trailed after him, down the side of the ridge.

'Coming?' The officer halted, looking back at Ryan and Kastner.

'We'll be along later,' Ryan said. 'We have to get our equipment together.'

'All right. The camp is down the road about half a mile. There's a settlement there. People coming back from the moon.'

'From the moon?'

'We had started moving units to Luna, but now there isn't any need. Maybe it's a good thing. Who the hell wants to leave Terra?'

'Thanks for the cigarettes,' one of the soldiers called back. The soldiers piled in the back of the truck. The officer slid behind the wheel. The truck started up and continued on its way, rumbling along the road.

Ryan and Kastner watched it go.

'Then Schonerman's death was never balanced,' Ryan murmured. 'A whole new past —'

'I wonder how far the change carries. I wonder if it carries up to our own time.'

'There's only one way to find out.'

Kastner nodded. 'I want to know right away. The sooner the better. Let's get started.'

Ryan nodded, deep in thought. 'The sooner the better.'

They entered the time ship. Kastner sat down with his briefcase. Ryan adjusted the controls. Outside the port the scene winked out of existence. They were in the time flow again, moving toward the present.

Ryan's face was grim. 'I can't believe it. The whole structure of the past changed. An entire new chain set in motion. Expanding through every continuum. Altering more and more of our stream.'

'Then it won't be our present, when we get back. There's no telling how different it will be. All stemming from Schonerman's death. A whole new history set in motion from one incident.'

'Not from Schonerman's death,' Ryan corrected.

'What do you mean?'

'Not from his death but from the loss of his papers. Because Schonerman died the Government didn't obtain a successful methodology by which they could build an artificial brain. Therefore the claws never came into existence.'

'It's the same thing.'

'Is it?'

Kastner looked up quickly. 'Explain.'

'Schonerman's death is of no importance. The loss of his papers to the Government is the determining factor.' Ryan pointed at Kastner's briefcase. 'Where are the papers? In there. We have them.'

Kastner nodded. 'That's true.'

'We can restore the situation by moving back into the past and delivering the papers to some agency of the Government. Schonerman is unimportant. It's his papers that matter.'

Ryan's hand moved toward the power switch.

'Wait!' Kastner said. 'Don't we want to see the present? We should see what changes carry down to our own time.'

Ryan hesitated. 'True.'

'Then we can decide what we want to do. Whether we want to restore the papers.'

'All right. We'll continue to the present and then make up our minds.'

The fingers crossing the time map had returned almost to their original position. Ryan studied them for a long time, his hand on the power switch. Kastner held on tightly to the briefcase, his arms wrapped around it, the heavy leather bundle resting in his lap.

'We're almost there,' Ryan said.

'To our own time?'

'In another few moments.' Ryan stood up, gripping the switch. 'I wonder what we'll see.'

'Probably very little we'll recognize.'

Ryan took a deep breath, feeling the cold metal under his fingers. How different would their world be? Would they recognize anything? Had they swept everything familiar out of existence?

A vast chain had been started in motion. A tidal wave moving through time, altering each continuum, echoing down through all the ages to come. The second part of the war had never happened. Before the claws could be invented the war had ended. The concept of the artificial brain had never been transformed into workable practice. The most potent engine of war had never come into existence. Human energies had turned from war to rebuilding of the planet.

Around Ryan the meters and dials vibrated. In a few seconds they would be back. What would Terra be like? Would anything be the same?

The Fifty Cities. Probably they would not exist. Jon, his son, sitting quietly in his room reading. USIC. The Government. The League and its labs and offices, its buildings and roof fields and guards. The whole complicated social structure. Would it all be gone without a trace? Probably.

And what would he find instead?

'We'll know in a minute,' Ryan murmured.

'It won't be long,' Kastner got to his feet and moved to the port. 'I want to see it. It should be a very unfamiliar world.'

Ryan threw the power switch. The ship jerked, pulling out of the time flow. Outside the port something drifted and turned, as the ship righted itself. Automatic gravity controls slipped into place. The ship was rushing above the surface of the ground.

Kastner gasped.

'What do you see?' Ryan demanded, adjusting the velocity of the ship. 'What's out there?'

Kastner said nothing.

'What do you see?'

After a long time Kastner turned away from the port. 'Very interesting. Look for yourself.'

'What's out there?'

Kastner sat down slowly, picking up his briefcase. 'This opens up a whole new line of thought.'

Ryan made his way to the port and gazed out. Below the ship lay Terra. But not the Terra they had left.

Fields, endless yellow fields. And parks. Parks and yellow fields. Squares of green among the yellow, as far as the eye could see. Nothing else.

'No cities,' Ryan said thickly.

'No. Don't you remember? The people are all out in the fields. Or walking in the parks. Discussing the nature of the universe.'

'This is what Jon saw.'

'Your son was extremely accurate.'

Ryan moved back to the controls, his face blank. His mind was numb. He sat down and adjusted the landing grapples. The ship sank lower and lower until it was coasting over the flat fields. Men and women glanced up at the ship, startled. Men and women in robes.

They passed over a park. A herd of animals rushed frantically away. Some kind of deer.

This was the world his son had seen. This was his vision. Fields and parks and men and women in long flowing robes. Walking along the paths. Discussing the problems of the universe.

And the other world, his world, no longer existed. The League was gone. His whole life's work destroyed. In this world it did not exist. Jon. His son. Snuffed out. He would never see him again. His work, his son, everything he had known had winked out of existence.

'We have to go back,' Ryan said suddenly.

Kastner blinked. 'Beg pardon?'

'We have to take the papers back to the continuum where they belong. We can't recreate the situation exactly, but we can place the papers in the Government's hands. That will restore all the relevant factors.'

'Are you serious?'

Ryan stood up unsteadily, moving toward Kastner. 'Give me the papers. This is a very serious situation. We must work quickly. Things have to be put back in place.'

Kastner stepped back, whipping out his blaster. Ryan lunged. His shoulder caught Kastner, bowling the little businessman over. The blaster skidded across the floor of the ship, clattering against the wall. The papers fluttered in all directions.

'You damn fool!' Ryan grabbed at the papers, dropping down to his knees.

Kastner chased after the blaster. He scooped it up, his round face set with owlish determination. Ryan saw him out of the corner of his eye. For a moment the temptation to laugh almost overcame him. Kastner's face was flushed, his cheeks burning red. He fumbled with the blaster, trying to aim it.

'Kastner, for God's sake—'

The little businessman's fingers tightened around the trigger. Abrupt fear chilled Ryan. He scrambled to his feet. The blaster roared, flame crackling across the time ship. Ryan leaped out of the way, singed by the trail of fire.

Schonerman's papers flared up, glowing where they lay scattered over the floor. For a brief second they burned. Then the glow died out, flickering into charred ash. The thin acrid smell of the blast drifted to Ryan, tickling his nose and making his eyes water.

'Sorry,' Kastner murmured. He laid the blaster down on the control board. 'Don't you think you better get us down? We're quite close to the surface.'

Ryan moved mechanically to the control board. After a

moment he took his seat and began to adjust the controls, decreasing the velocity of the ship. He said nothing.

'I'm beginning to understand about Jon,' Kastner murmured. 'He must have had some kind of parallel time sense. Awareness of other possible futures. As work progressed on the time ship his visions increased, didn't they? Every day his visions become more real. Every day the time ship became more actual.'

Ryan nodded.

'This opens up whole new lines of speculation. The mystical visions of medieval saints. Perhaps they were of other futures, other time flows. Visions of hell would be worse time flows. Visions of heaven would be better time flows. Ours must stand some place in the middle. And the vision of the eternal unchanging world. Perhaps that's an awareness of non-time. Not another world but this world, seen outside of time. We'll have to think more about that, too.'

The ship landed, coming to rest at the edge of one of the parks. Kastner crossed to the port and gazed out at the trees beyond the ship.

'In the books my family saved there were some pictures of trees,' he said thoughtfully. 'These trees here, by us. They're pepper trees. Those over there are what they call evergreen trees. They stay that way all year around. That's why the name.'

Kastner picked up his briefcase, gripping it tightly. He moved toward the hatch.

'Let's go find some of the people. So we can begin discussing things. Metaphysical things.' He grinned at Ryan. 'I always did like metaphysical things.'

Breakfast at Twilight

'Dad?' Earl asked, hurrying out of the bathroom, 'you going to drive us to school today?'

Tim McLean poured himself a second cup of coffee. 'You kids can walk for a change. The car's in the garage.'

Judy pouted. 'It's raining.'

'No it isn't,' Virginia corrected her sister. She drew the shade back. 'It's all foggy, but it isn't raining.'

'Let me look.' Mary McLean dried her hands and came over from the sink. 'What an odd day. Is that fog? It looks more like smoke. I can't make out a thing. What did the weatherman say?'

'I couldn't get anything on the radio,' Earl said. 'Nothing but static.'

Tim stirred angrily. 'That darn thing on the blink again? Seems like I just had it fixed.' He got up and moved sleepily over to the radio. He fiddled idly with the dials. The three children hurried back and forth, getting ready for school. 'Strange,' Tim said.

'I'm going.' Earl opened the front door.

'Wait for your sisters,' Mary ordered absently.

'I'm ready,' Virginia said. 'Do I look all right?'

'You look fine,' Mary said, kissing her.

'I'll call the radio repair place from the office,' Tim said.

He broke off. Earl stood at the kitchen door, pale and silent, his eyes wide with terror.

'What is it?'

'I – I came back.'

'What is it? Are you sick?'

'I can't go to school.'

They stared at him. 'What is wrong?' Tim grabbed his son's arm. 'Why can't you go to school?'

'They – they won't let me.'

'*Who?*'

'The soldiers.' It came tumbling out with a rush. 'They're all over. Soldiers and guns. And they're coming here.'

'Coming? Coming here?' Tim echoed, dazed.

'They're coming here and they're going to—' Earl broke off, terrified. From the front porch came the sound of heavy boots. A crash. Splintering wood. Voices.

'Good Lord,' Mary gasped. 'What is it, Tim?'

Tim entered the living room, his heart laboring painfully. Three men stood inside the door. Men in gray-green uniforms, weighted with guns and complex tangles of equipment. Tubes and hoses. Meters on thick cords. Boxes and leather straps and antennas. Elaborate masks locked over their heads. Behind the masks Tim saw tired, whisker-stubbled faces, red-rimmed eyes that gazed at him in brutal displeasure.

One of the soldiers jerked up his gun, aiming at McLean's middle. Tim peered at it dumbly. *The gun.* Long and thin. Like a needle. Attached to a coil of tubes.

'What in the name of—' he began, but the soldier cut him off savagely.

'Who are you?' His voice was harsh, guttural. 'What are you doing here?' He pushed his mask aside. His skin was dirty. Cuts and pocks lined his sallow flesh. His teeth were broken and missing.

'Answer!' a second soldier demanded. 'What are you doing here?'

'Show your blue card,' the third said. 'Let's see your Sector number.' His eyes strayed to the children and Mary standing mutely at the dining room door. His mouth fell open.

'*A woman!*'

The three soldiers gazed in disbelief.

'What the hell is this?' the first demanded. 'How long has this woman been here?'

Tim found his voice. 'She's my wife. What is this? What—'

'Your *wife*?' They were incredulous.

'My wife and children. For God's sake—'

'Your wife? And you'd bring her here? You must be out of your head!'

'He's got ash sickness,' one said. He lowered his gun and strode across the living room to Mary. 'Come on, sister. You're coming with us.'

Tim lunged.

A wall of force hit him. He sprawled, clouds of darkness rolling around him. His ears sang. His head throbbed. Everything receded. Dimly, he was aware of shapes moving. Voices. The room. He concentrated.

The soldiers were herding the children back. One of them grabbed Mary by the arm. He tore her dress away, ripping it from her shoulders. 'Gee,' he snarled. 'He'd bring her here, and she's not even strung!'

'Take her along.'

'OK, Captain.' The soldier dragged Mary toward the front door. 'We'll do what we can with her.'

'The kids.' The captain waved the other soldier over with the children. 'Take them along. I don't get it. No masks. No cards. How'd this house miss getting hit? Last night was the worst in months!'

Tim struggled painfully to his feet. His mouth was bleeding. His vision blurred. He hung on tight to the wall. 'Look,' he muttered. 'For God's sake—'

The captain was staring into the kitchen. 'Is that – is that *food*?' He advanced slowly through the dining room. 'Look!'

The other soldiers came after him, Mary and the children forgotten. They stood around the table, amazed.

'Look at it!'

'Coffee.' One grabbed up the pot and drank it greedily

down. He choked, black coffee dripping down his tunic. 'Hot. Jeeze. Hot coffee.'

'Cream!' Another soldier tore open the refrigerator. 'Look. Milk. Eggs. Butter. Meat.' His voice broke. 'It's full of food.'

The captain disappeared into the pantry. He came out, lugging a case of canned peas. 'Get the rest. Get it all. We'll load it in the snake.'

He dropped the case on the table with a crash. Watching Tim intently, he fumbled in his dirty tunic until he found a cigarette. He lit it slowly, not taking his eyes from Tim. 'All right,' he said. 'Let's hear what you have to say.'

Tim's mouth opened and closed. No words came. His mind was blank. Dead. He couldn't think.

'This food. Where'd you get it? And these things.' The captain waved around the kitchen. 'Dishes. Furniture. How come this house hasn't been hit? How did you survive last night's attack?'

'I—' Tim gasped.

The captain came toward him ominously. 'The woman. And the kids. All of you. What are you doing here?' His voice was hard. 'You better be able to explain, mister. You better be able to explain what you're doing here – or we'll have to burn the whole damn lot of you.'

Tim sat down at the table. He took a deep, shuddering breath, trying to focus his mind. His body ached. He rubbed blood from his mouth, conscious of a broken molar and bits of loose tooth. He got out a handkerchief and spat the bits into it. His hands were shaking.

'Come on,' the captain said.

Mary and the children slipped into the room. Judy was crying. Virginia's face was blank with shock. Earl stared wide-eyed at the soldiers, his face white.

'Tim,' Mary said, putting her hand on his arm. 'Are you all right?'

Tim nodded. 'I'm all right.'

Mary pulled her dress around her. 'Tim, they can't get

away with it. Somebody'll come. The mailman. The neigh-bors. They can't just—'

'Shut up,' the captain snapped. His eyes flickered oddly. 'The mailman? What are you talking about?' He held out his hand. 'Let's see your yellow slip, sister.'

'Yellow slip?' Mary faltered.

The captain rubbed his jaw. 'No yellow slip. No masks. No cards.'

'They're geeps,' a soldier said.

'Maybe. And maybe not.'

'They're geeps, Captain. We better burn 'em. We can't take any chances.'

'There's something funny going on here,' the captain said. He plucked at his neck, lifting up a small box on a cord. 'I'm getting a polic here.'

'A polic?' A shiver moved through the soldiers. 'Wait, Captain. We can handle this. Don't get a polic. He'll put us on 4 and then we'll never—'

The captain spoke into the box. 'Give me Web B.'

Tim looked up at Mary. 'Listen, honey. I—'

'Shut up.' A soldier prodded him. Tim lapsed into silence.

The box squawked. 'Web B.'

'Can you spare a polic? We've run into something strange. Group of five. Man, woman, three kids. No masks, no cards, the woman not strung, dwelling com-pletely intact. Furniture, fixtures, about two hundred pounds of food.'

The box hesitated. 'All right. Polic on the way. Stay there. Don't let them escape.'

'I won't.' The captain dropped the box back in his shirt. 'A polic will be here any minute. Meanwhile, let's get the food loaded.'

From outside came a deep thundering roar. It shook the house, rattling the dishes in the cupboard.

'Jeez,' a soldier said. 'That was close.'

'I hope the screens hold until nightfall.' The captain

grabbed up the case of canned peas. 'Get the rest. We want it loaded before the polic comes.'

The two soldiers filled their arms and followed him through the house, out the front door. Their voices diminished as they strode down the path.

Tim got to his feet. 'Stay here,' he said thickly.

'What are you doing?' Mary asked nervously.

'Maybe I can get out.' He ran to the back door and unlatched it, hands shaking. He pulled the door wide and stepped out on the back porch. 'I don't see any of them. If we can only . . .'

He stopped.

Around him gray clouds blew. Gray ash, billowing as far as he could see. Dim shapes were visible. Broken shapes, silent and unmoving in the grayness.

Ruins.

Ruined buildings. Heaps of rubble. Debris everywhere. He walked slowly down the back steps. The concrete walk ended abruptly. Beyond it, slag and heaps of rubble were strewn. Nothing else. Nothing as far as the eye could see.

Nothing stirred. Nothing moved. In the gray silence there was no life. No motion. Only the clouds of drifting ash. The slag and the endless heaps.

The city was gone. The buildings were destroyed. Nothing remained. No people. No life. Jagged walls, empty and gaping. A few dark weeds growing among the debris. Tim bent down, touching a weed. Rough, thick stalk. And the slag. It was a metal slag. Melted metal. He straightened up—

'Come back inside,' a crisp voice said.

He turned numbly. A man stood on the porch, behind him, hands on his hips. A small man, hollow-cheeked. Eyes small and bright, like two black coals. He wore a uniform different from the soldiers'. His mask was pushed back, away from his face. His skin was yellow, faintly luminous, clinging to his cheekbones. A sick face, ravaged by fever and fatigue.

'Who are you?' Tim said.

'Douglas. Political Commissioner Douglas.'

'You're – you're the police,' Tim said.

'That's right. Now come inside. I expect to hear some answers from you. I have quite a few questions.

'The first thing I want to know,' Commissioner Douglas said, 'is how this house escaped destruction.'

Tim and Mary and the children sat together on the couch, silent and unmoving, faces blank with shock.

'Well?' Douglas demanded.

Tim found his voice. 'Look,' he said. 'I don't know. I don't know anything. We woke up this morning like every other morning. We dressed and ate breakfast—'

'It was foggy out,' Virginia said. 'We looked out and saw the fog.'

'And the radio wouldn't work,' Earl said.

'The radio?' Douglas's thin face twisted. 'There haven't been any audio signals in months. Except for government purposes. This house. All of you. I don't understand. If you were geeps—'

'Geeps. What does that mean?' Mary murmured.

'Soviet general-purpose troops.'

'Then the war has begun.'

'North America was attacked two years ago,' Douglas said. 'In 1978.'

Tim sagged. '1978. Then this is 1980.' He reached suddenly into his pocket. He pulled out his wallet and tossed it to Douglas. 'Look in there.'

Douglas opened the wallet suspiciously. 'Why?'

'The library card. The parcel receipts. Look at the dates.' Tim turned to Mary. 'I'm beginning to understand now. I had an idea when I saw the ruins.'

'Are we winning?' Earl piped.

Douglas studied Tim's wallet intently. 'Very interesting. These are all old. Seven and eight years.' His eyes flickered. 'What are you trying to say? That you came from the past? That you're time travelers?'

The captain came back inside. 'The snake is all loaded, sir.'

Douglas nodded curtly. 'All right. You can take off with your patrol.'

The captain glanced at Tim. 'Will you be—'

'I'll handle them.'

The captain saluted. 'Fine, sir.' He quickly disappeared through the door. Outside, he and his men climbed aboard a long thin truck, like a pipe mounted on treads. With a faint hum the truck leaped forward.

In a moment only gray clouds and the dim outline of ruined buildings remained.

Douglas paced back and forth, examining the living room, the wallpaper, the light fixture and chairs. He picked up some magazines and thumbed through them. 'From the past. But not far in the past.'

'Seven years?'

'Could it be? I suppose. A lot of things have happened in the last few months. Time travel.' Douglas grinned ironically. 'You picked a bad spot, McLean. You should have gone farther on.'

'I didn't pick it. It just happened.'

'You must have done *something*.'

Tim shook his head. 'No. Nothing. We got up. And we were – here.'

Douglas was deep in thought. 'Here. Seven years in the future. Moved forward through time. We know nothing about time travel. No work has been done with it. There seem to be evident military possibilities.'

'How did the war begin?' Mary asked faintly.

'Begin? It didn't begin. You remember. There was war seven years ago.'

'The real war. This.'

'There wasn't any point when it became – this. We fought in Korea. We fought in China. In Germany and Yugoslavia and Iran. It spread, farther and farther. Finally the bombs were falling here. It came like the plague. The war *grew*. It didn't begin.' Abruptly he put his notebook away. 'A report on you would be suspect. They might think that I had the ash sickness.'

'What's that?' Virginia asked.

'Radioactive particles in the air. Carried to the brain. Causes insanity. Everybody has a touch of it, even with the masks.'

'I'd sure like to know who's winning,' Earl repeated. 'What was that outside? That truck. Was it rocket propelled?'

'The snake? No. Turbines. Boring snout. Cuts through the debris.'

'Seven years,' Mary said. 'So much has changed. It doesn't seem possible.'

'So much?' Douglas shrugged. 'I suppose so. I remember what I was doing seven years ago. I was still in school. Learning. I had an apartment and a car. I went out dancing. I bought a TV set. But these things were there. The twilight. This. Only I didn't know. None of us knew. But they were there.'

'You're a Political Commissioner?' Tim asked.

'I supervise the troops. Watch for political deviation. In a total war we have to keep people under constant surveillance. One Commie down in the Webs could wreck the whole business. We can't take chances.'

Tim nodded. 'Yes. It was there. The twilight. Only we didn't understand it.'

Douglas examined the books in the bookcase. 'I'll take a couple of these along. I haven't seen fiction in months. Most of it disappeared. Burned back in '77.'

'Burned?'

Douglas helped himself. 'Shakespeare. Milton. Dryden. I'll take the old stuff. It's safer. None of the Steinbeck and Dos Passos. Even a polic can get in trouble. If you stay here, you better get rid of *that*.' He tapped a volume of Dostoevski, *The Brothers Karamazov*.

'If we stay! What else can we do?'

'You want to stay?'

'No,' Mary said quietly.

Douglas shot her a quick glance. 'No, I suppose not. If you stay you'll be separated, of course. Children to the Canadian Relocation Centers. Women are situated down in the undersurface factory-labor camps. Men are automatically a part of Military.'

'Like those there who left,' Tim said.

'Unless you can qualify for the id block.'

'What's that?'

'Industrial Designing and Technology. What training have you had? Anything along scientific lines?'

'No. Accounting.'

Douglas shrugged. 'Well, you'll be given a standard test. If your IQ is high enough you could go in the Political Service. We use a lot of men.' He paused thoughtfully, his arms loaded with books. 'You better go back, McLean. You'll have trouble getting accustomed to this. I'd go back, if I could. But I can't.'

'Back?' Mary echoed. 'How?'

'The way you came.'

'We just came.'

Douglas halted at the front door. 'Last night was the worst rom attack so far. They hit this whole area.'

'Rom?'

'Robot operated missiles. The Soviets are systemically destroying continental America, mile by mile. Roms are cheap. They make them by the million and fire them off. The whole process is automatic. Robot factories turn them out and fire them at us. Last night they came over here – waves of them. This morning the patrol came in and found nothing. Except you, of course.'

Tim nodded slowly. 'I'm beginning to see.'

'The concentrated energy must have tipped some unstable time fault. Like a rock fault. We're always starting earthquakes. But a *time quake* . . . Interesting. That's what happened, I think. The release of energy, the destruction of matter, sucked your house into the future. Carried the house seven years ahead. This street, everything here, this very spot, was pulverized. Your house, seven years back, was caught in the undertow. The blast must have lashed back through time.'

'Sucked into the future,' Tim said. 'During the night. While we were asleep.'

Douglas watched him carefully. 'Tonight,' he said, 'there will be another rom attack. It should finish off what is left.' He looked at his watch. 'It is now four in the afternoon. The attack will begin in a few hours. You should be under-surface. Nothing will survive up here. I can take you down with me, if you want. But if you want to take a chance, if you want to stay here—'

'You think it might tip us back?'

'Maybe. I don't know. It's a gamble. It might tip you back to your own time, or it might not. If not—'

'If not we wouldn't have a chance of survival.'

Douglas flicked out a pocket map and spread it open on the couch. 'A patrol will remain in this area another half-hour. If you decide to come undersurface with us, go down the street this way.' He traced a line on the map. 'To this open field here. The patrol is a Political unit. They'll take you the rest of the way down. You think you can find the field?'

'I think so,' Tim said, looking at the map. His lips twisted. 'That open field used to be the grammar school my kids went to. That's where they were going when the troops stopped them. Just a little while ago.'

'Seven years ago,' Douglas corrected. He snapped the map shut and restored it to his pocket. He pulled his mask down and moved out the front door onto the porch. 'Maybe I'll see you again. Maybe not. It's your decision. You'll have to decide one way or the other. In any case – good luck.'

He turned and walked briskly from the house.

'Dad,' Earl shouted, 'are you going in the Army? Are you

going to wear a mask and shoot one of those guns?' His eyes sparkled with excitement. 'Are you going to drive a *snake*?'

Tim McLean squatted down and pulled his son to him. 'You want that? *You want to stay here?* If I'm going to wear a mask and shoot one of those guns we can't go back.'

Earl looked doubtful. 'Couldn't we go back later?'

Tim shook his head. 'Afraid not. We've got to decide now, whether we're going back or not.'

'You heard Mr Douglas,' Virginia said disgustedly. 'The attack's going to start in a couple hours.'

Tim got to his feet and paced back and forth. 'If we stay in the house we'll get blown to bits. Let's face it. There's only a faint chance we'll be tipped back to our own time. A slim possibility – a long shot. Do we want to stay here with roms falling all around us, knowing any second it may be the end – hearing them come closer, hitting nearer – lying on the floor, waiting, listening—'

'Do you really want to go back?' Mary demanded.

'Of course, but the risk—'

'I'm not asking you about the risk. I'm asking you if you really want to go back. Maybe you want to stay here. Maybe Earl's right. You in a uniform and a mask, with one of those needle guns. Driving a snake.'

'With you in a factory-labor camp! And the kids in a Government Relocation Center! How do you think that would be? What do you think they'd teach them? What do you think they'd grow up like? And believe . . .'

'They'd probably teach them to be very useful.'

'Useful! To what? To themselves? To mankind? Or to the war effort . . .?'

'They'd be alive,' Mary said. 'They'd be safe. This way, if we stay in the house, wait for the attack to come—'

'Sure,' Tim grated. 'They would be alive. Probably quite healthy. Well fed. Well clothed and cared for.' He looked down at his children, his face hard. 'They'd stay alive, all right. They'd live to grow up and become adults. But what

kind of adults? You heard what he said! Book burnings in
'77. What'll they be taught from? What kind of ideas are
left, since '77? What kind of beliefs can they get from a
Government Relocation Center? What kind of values will
they have?'

'There's the id block,' Mary suggested.

'Industrial Designing and Technology. For the bright
ones. The clever ones with imagination. Busy slide rules
and pencils. Drawing and planning and making discoveries.
The girls could go into that. They could design the guns.
Earl could go into the Political Service. He could make
sure the guns were used. If any of the troops deviated,
didn't want to shoot, Earl could report them and have
them hauled off for reeducation. To have their political
faith strengthened – in a world where those *with* brains
design weapons and those *without* brains fire them.'

'But they'd be alive,' Mary repeated.

'You've got a strange idea of what being alive is! You
call that alive? Maybe it is.' Tim shook his head wearily.
'Maybe you're right. Maybe we should go undersurface
with Douglas. Stay in this world. Stay alive.'

'I didn't say that,' Mary said softly. 'Tim, I had to find
out if you *really* understood why it's worth it. Worth staying
in the house, taking the chance we won't be tipped back.'

'Then you want to take the chance?'

'Of course! We *have* to. We can't turn our children over
to them – to the Relocation Center. To be taught how to
hate and kill and destroy.' Mary smiled up wanly. 'Anyhow,
they've always gone to the Jefferson School. And here, in
this world, it's only an open field.'

'Are we going back?' Judy piped. She caught hold of
Tim's sleeve imploringly 'Are we going back now?'

Tim disengaged her arm. 'Very soon, honey.'

Mary opened the supply cupboards and rooted in them.
'Everything's here. What did they take?'

'The case of canned peas. Everything we had in the
refrigerator. And they smashed the front door.'

'I'll bet we're beating them!' Earl shouted. He ran to the window and peered out. The sight of the rolling ash disappointed him. 'I can't see anything! Just the fog!' He turned questioningly to Tim. 'Is it always like this, here?'

'Yes,' Tim answered.

Earl's face fell. 'Just fog? Nothing else. Doesn't the sun shine ever?'

'I'll fix some coffee,' Mary said.

'Good.' Tim went into the bathroom and examined himself in the mirror. His mouth was cut, caked with dried blood. His head ached. He felt sick at his stomach.

'It doesn't seem possible,' Mary said, as they sat down at the kitchen table.

Tim sipped his coffee. 'No. It doesn't.' Where he sat he could see out the window. The clouds of ash. The dim, jagged outline of ruined buildings.

'Is the man coming back?' Judy piped. 'He was all thin and funny-looking. He isn't coming back, is he?'

Tim looked at his watch. It read ten o'clock. He reset it, moving the hands to four-fifteen. 'Douglas said it would begin at nightfall. That won't be long.'

'Then we're really staying in the house,' Mary said.

'That's right.'

'Even though there's only a little chance?'

'Even though there's only a little chance we'll get back. Are you glad?'

'I'm glad,' Mary said, her eyes bright. 'It's worth it, Tim. You know it is. Anything's worth it, any chance. *To get back*. And something else. We'll all be here together . . . We can't be – broken up. Separated.'

Tim poured himself more coffee. 'We might as well make ourselves comfortable. We have maybe three hours to wait. We might as well try to enjoy them.'

At six-thirty the first rom fell. They felt the shock, a deep rolling wave of force that lapped over the house.

Judy came running in from the dining room, face white with fear. 'Daddy! What is it?'

'Nothing. Don't worry.'

'Come on back,' Virginia called impatiently. 'It's your turn.' They were playing Monopoly.

Earl leaped to his feet. 'I want to see.' He ran excitedly to the window. 'I can see where it hit!'

Tim lifted the shade and looked out. Far off, in the distance, a white glare burned fitfully. A towering column of luminous smoke rose from it.

A second shudder vibrated through the house. A dish crashed from the shelf, into the sink.

It was almost dark outside. Except for the two spots of white Tim could make out nothing. The clouds of ash were lost in the gloom. The ash and the ragged remains of buildings.

'That was closer,' Mary said.

A third rom fell. In the living room windows burst, showering glass across the rug.

'We better get back,' Tim said.

'Where?'

'Down in the basement. Come on.' Tim unlocked the basement door and they trooped nervously downstairs.

'Food,' Mary said. 'We better bring the food that's left.'

'Good idea. You kids go on down. We'll come along in a minute.'

'I can carry something,' Earl said.

'Go on down.' The fourth rom hit, farther off than the last. 'And stay away from the window.'

'I'll move something over the window,' Earl said. 'The big piece of plywood we used for my train.'

'Good idea.' Tim and Mary returned to the kitchen. 'Food. Dishes. What else?'

'Books.' Mary looked nervously around. 'I don't know. Nothing else. Come on.'

A shattering roar drowned out her words. The kitchen window gave, showering glass over them. The dishes over the sink tumbled down in a torrent of breaking china. Tim grabbed Mary and pulled her down.

From the broken window rolling clouds of ominous gray drifted into the room. The evening air stank, a sour, rotten smell. Tim shuddered.

'Forget the food. Let's get back down.'

'But—'

'Forget it.' He grabbed her and pulled her down the basement stairs. They tumbled in a heap, Tim slamming the door after them.

'Where's the food?' Virginia demanded.

Tim wiped his forehead shakily. 'Forget it. We won't need it.'

'Help me,' Earl gasped. Tim helped him move the sheet of plywood over the window above the laundry tubs. The basement was cold and silent. The cement floor under them was faintly moist.

Two roms struck at once. Tim was hurled to the floor. The concrete hit him and he grunted. For a moment blackness swirled around him. Then he was on his knees, groping his way up.

'Everybody all right?' he muttered.

'I'm all right,' Mary said. Judy began to whimper. Earl was feeling his way across the room.

'I'm all right,' Virginia said. 'I guess.'

The lights flickered and dimmed. Abruptly they went out. The basement was pitch-black.

'Well,' Tim said. 'There they go.'

'I have my flashlight.' Earl winked the flashlight on. 'How's that?'

'Fine,' Tim said.

More roms hit. The ground leaped under them, bucking and heaving. A wave of force shuddering the whole house.

'We better lie down,' Mary said.

'Yes. Lie down.' Tim stretched himself out awkwardly. A few bits of plaster rained down around them.

'When will it stop?' Earl asked uneasily.

'Soon,' Tim said.

'Then we'll be back?'

'Yes. We'll be back.'

The next blast hit them almost at once. Tim felt the concrete rise under him. It grew, swelling higher and higher. He was going up. He shut his eyes, holding on tight. Higher and higher he went, carried up by the ballooning concrete. Around him beams and timbers cracked. Plaster poured down. He could hear glass breaking. And a long way off, the licking crackles of fire.

'Tim,' Mary's voice came faintly.

'Yes.'

'We're not going to – to make it.'

'I don't know.'

'We're not. I can tell.'

'Maybe not.' He grunted in pain as a board struck his back, settling over him. Boards and plaster, covering him, burying him. He could smell the sour smell, the night air and ash. It drifted and rolled into the cellar, through the broken window.

'Daddy,' Judy's voice came faintly.

'What?'

'Aren't we going back?'

He opened his mouth to answer. A shattering roar cut his words off. He jerked, tossed by the blast. Everything was moving around him. A vast wind tugged at him, a hot wind, licking at him, gnawing at him. He held on tight. The wind pulled, dragging him with it. He cried out as it seared his hands and face.

'Mary—'

Then silence. Only blackness and silence.

Cars.

Cars were stopping nearby. Then voices. And the noise of footsteps. Tim stirred, pushing the boards from him. He struggled to his feet.

'Mary.' He looked around. 'We're back.'

The basement was in ruins. The walls were broken and sagging. Great gaping holes showed a green line of grass beyond. A concrete walk. The small rose garden. The white stucco house next door.

Lines of telephone poles. Roofs. Houses. The city. As it had always been. Every morning.

'We're back!' Wild joy leaped through him. *Back*. Safe. It was over. Tim pushed quickly through the debris of his ruined house. 'Mary, are you all right?'

'Here.' Mary sat up, plaster dust raining from her. She was white all over, her hair, her skin, her clothing. Her face was cut and scratched. Her dress was torn. 'Are we really back?'

'Mr McLean! You all right?'

A blue-clad policeman leaped down into the cellar. Behind him two white-clad figures jumped. A group of neighbors collected outside, peering anxiously to see.

'I'm OK,' Tim said. He helped Judy and Virginia up. 'I think we're all OK.'

'What happened?' The policeman pushed boards aside, coming over. 'A bomb? Some kind of a bomb?'

'The house is a shambles,' one of the white-clad interns said. 'You sure nobody's hurt?'

'We were down here. In the basement.'

'You all right, Tim,' Mrs Hendricks called, stepping down gingerly into the cellar.

'What happened?' Frank Foley shouted. He leaped down with a crash. 'God, Tim! What the hell were you doing?'

The two white-clad interns poked suspiciously around the ruins. 'You're lucky, mister. Damn lucky. There's nothing left upstairs.'

Foley came over beside Tim. 'Damn it man! I *told* you to have that hot water heater looked at!'

'What?' Tim muttered.

'The hot water heater! I told you there was something wrong with the cut-off. It must've kept heating up, not turned off . . .' Foley winked nervously. 'But I won't say anything, Tim. The insurance. You can count on me.'

Tim opened his mouth. But the words didn't come.

What could he say? – No, it wasn't a defective hot water heater that I forgot to have repaired. No, it wasn't a faulty connection in the stove. It wasn't any of those things. It wasn't a leaky gas line, it wasn't a plugged furnace, it wasn't a pressure cooker we forgot to turn off.

It's war. Total war. And not just war for me. For my family. For my house.

It's for your house, too. Your house and my house and all the houses. Here and in the next block, in the next town, the next state and country and continent. The whole world, like this. Shambles and ruins. Fog and dank weeds growing in the rusting slag. War for all of us. For everybody crowding down into the basement, white-faced, frightened, somehow sensing something terrible.

And when it really came, when the five years were up, there'd be no escape. No going back, tipping back into the past, away from it. When it came for them all, it would have them for eternity; there would be no one climbing back out, as he had.

Mary was watching him. The policeman, the neighbors, the white-clad interns – all of them were watching him. Waiting for him to explain. To tell them what it was.

'Was it the hot water heater?' Mrs Hendricks asked timidly. 'That was it, wasn't it, Tim? Things like that do happen. You can't be sure . . .'

'Maybe it was home brew,' a neighbor suggested, in a feeble attempt at humor. 'Was that it?'

He couldn't tell them. They wouldn't understand, because they didn't want to understand. They didn't want to know. They needed reassurance. He could see it in their eyes. Pitiful, pathetic fear. They sensed something terrible – and they were afraid. They were searching his face, seeking his help. Words of comfort. Words to banish their fear.

'Yeah,' Tim said heavily. 'It was the hot water heater.'

'I thought so!' Foley breathed. A sigh of relief swept through them all. Murmurs, shaky laughs. Nods, grins.

'I should have got it fixed,' Tim went on. 'I should have

had it looked at a long time ago. Before it got in such bad shape.' Tim looked around at the circle of anxious people, hanging on his words. 'I should have had it looked at. Before it was too late.'

Small Town

Verne Haskel crept miserably up the front steps of his house, his overcoat dragging behind him. He was tired. Tired and discouraged. And his feet ached.

'My God,' Madge exclaimed, as he closed the door and peeled off his coat and hat. 'You home already?'

Haskel dumped his briefcase and began untying his shoes. His body sagged. His face was drawn and gray.

'Say something!'

'Dinner ready?'

'No, dinner isn't ready. What's wrong this time? Another fight with Larson?'

Haskel stumped into the kitchen and filled a glass with warm water and soda. 'Let's move,' he said.

'Move?'

'Away from Woodland. To San Francisco. Anywhere.' Haskel drank his soda, his middle-aged flabby body supported by the gleaming sink. 'I feel lousy. Maybe I ought to see Doc Barnes again. I wish this was Friday and tomorrow was Saturday.'

'What do you want for dinner?'

'Nothing. I don't know.' Haskel shook his head wearily. 'Anything.' He sank down at the kitchen table. 'All I want is rest. Open a can of stew. Pork and beans. Anything.'

'I suggest we go out to Don's Steakhouse. On Monday they have good sirloins.'

'No. I've seen enough human faces today.'

'I suppose you're too tired to drive me over to Helen Grant's.'

'The car's in the garage. Busted again.'

'If you took better care of it—'

'What the hell do you want me to do? Carry it around in a cellophane bag?'

'Don't shout at me, Verne Haskel!' Madge flushed with anger. 'Maybe you want to fix your own dinner.'

Haskel got wearily to his feet. He shuffled toward the cellar door. 'I'll see you.'

'Where are you going?'

'Downstairs in the basement.'

'Oh, Lord!' Madge cried wildly. 'Those trains! Those toys! How can a grown man, a middle-aged man—'

Haskel said nothing. He was already half way down the stairs, feeling around for the basement light.

The basement was cool and moist. Haskel took his engineer's cap from the hook and fitted it on his head. Excitement and a faint surge of renewed energy filled his tired body. He approached the great plywood table with eager steps.

Trains ran everywhere. Along the floor, under the coal bin, among the steam pipes of the furnace. The tracks converged at the table, rising up on carefully graded ramps. The table itself was littered with transformers and signals and switches and heaps of equipment and wiring. And—

And the town.

The detailed, painfully accurate model of Woodland. Every tree and house, every store and building and street and fireplug. A minute town, each facet in perfect order. Constructed with elaborate care throughout the years. As long as he could remember. Since he was a kid, building and glueing and working after school.

Haskel turned on the main transformer. All along the track signal lights glowed. He fed power to the heavy Lionel engine parked with its load of freight cars. The engine sped smoothly into life, gliding along the track. A flashing dark projectile of metal that made his breath catch in his throat. He opened an electric switch and the engine headed down the ramp, through a tunnel and off the table. It raced under the workbench.

His trains. And his town. Haskel bent over the miniature houses and streets, his heart glowing with pride. He had built it – himself. Every inch. Every perfect inch. The whole town. He touched the corner of Fred's Grocery Store. Not a detail lacking. Even the windows. The displays of food. The signs. The counters.

The Uptown Hotel. He ran his hand over its flat roof. The sofas and chairs in the lobby. He could see them through the window.

Green's Drugstore. Bunion pad displays. Magazines. Frazier's Auto Parts. Mexico City Dining. Sharpstein's Apparel. Bob's Liquor Store. Ace Billiard Parlor.

The whole town. He ran his hands over it. He had built it; the town was his.

The train came rushing back, out from under the workbench. Its wheels passed over an automatic switch and a drawbridge lowered itself obediently. The train swept over and beyond, dragging its cars behind it.

Haskel turned up the power. The train gained speed. Its whistle sounded. It turned a sharp curve and grated across a cross-track. More speed. Haskel's hands jerked convulsively at the transformer. The train leaped and shot ahead. It swayed and bucked as it shot around a curve. The transformer was turned up to maximum. The train was a clattering blur of speed, rushing along the track, across bridges and switches, behind the big pipes of the floor furnace.

It disappeared into the coal bin. A moment later it swept out the other side, rocking wildly.

Haskel slowed the train down. He was breathing hard, his chest rising painfully. He say down on the stool by the workbench and lit a cigarette with shaking fingers.

The train, the model town, gave him a strange feeling. It was hard to explain. He had always loved trains, model engines and signals and buildings. Since he was a little kid, maybe six or seven. His father had given him his first train. An engine and a few pieces of track. An old wind-up train. When he was nine he got his first real electric train. And two switches.

He added to it, year after year. Track, engines, switches, cars, signals. More powerful transformers. And the beginnings of the town.

He had built the town up carefully. Piece by piece. First, when he was in junior high, a model of the Southern Pacific Depot. Then the taxi stand next door. The cafe where the drivers ate. Broad Street.

And so on. More and more. Houses, buildings, stores. A whole town, growing under his hands, as the years went by. Every afternoon he came home from school and worked. Glued and cut and painted and sawed.

Now it was virtually complete. Almost done. He was forty-three years old and the town was almost done.

Haskel moved around the big plywood table, his hands extended reverently. He touched a miniature store here and there. The flower shop. The theater. The Telephone Company. Larson's Pump and Valve Works.

That, too. Where he worked. His place of business. A perfect miniature of the plant, down to the last detail.

Haskel scowled. Jim Larson. For twenty years he had worked there, slaved day after day. For what? To see others advanced over him. Younger men. Favorites of the boss. Yes-men with bright ties and pressed pants and wide, stupid grins.

Misery and hatred welled up in Haskel. All his life Woodland had got the better of him. He had never been happy. The town had always been against him. Miss Murphy in high school. The frats in college. Clerks in the snooty department stores. His neighbors. Cops and mailmen and bus drivers and delivery boys. Even his wife. Even Madge.

He had never meshed with the town. The rich, expensive

little suburb of San Francisco, down the peninsula beyond
the fog belt. Woodland was too damn upper-middle class.
Too many big houses and lawns and chrome cars and deck
chairs. Too stuffy and sleek. As long as he could remember.
In school. His job—

Larson. The Pump and Valve Works. Twenty years of
hard work.

Haskel's fingers closed over the tiny building, the model
of Larson's Pump and Valve Works. Savagely, he ripped it
loose and threw it to the floor. He crushed it underfoot,
grinding the bits of glass and metal and cardboard into a
shapeless mass.

God, he was shaking all over. He stared down at the
remains, his heart pounding wildly. Strange emotions,
crazy emotions, twisted through him. Thoughts he never
had had before. For a long time he gazed down at the
crumpled wad by his hose. What had once been the model
of Larson's Pump and Valve Works.

Abruptly he pulled away. In a trance he returned to his
workbench and sat stiffly down on the stool. He pulled his
tools and materials together, clicking the power drill on.

It took only a few moments. Working rapidly, with
quick, expert fingers, Haskel assembled a new model. He
painted, glued, fitted pieces together. He lettered a microscopic sign and sprayed a green lawn into place.

Then he carried the new model carefully over to the table
and glued it in the correct spot. The place where Larson's
Pump and Valve Works had been. The new building
gleamed in the overhead light, still moist and shiny.

WOODLAND MORTUARY

Haskel rubbed his hands in an ecstasy of satisfaction. The
Valve Works was gone. He had destroyed it. Obliterated it.
Removed it from the town. Below him was Woodland –
without the Valve Works. A mortuary instead.

His eyes gleamed. His lips twitched. His surging emotions swelled. He had got rid of it. In a brief flurry of action.

In a second. The whole thing was simple – amazingly easy.
  Odd he hadn't thought of it before.

Sipping a tall glass of ice-cold beer thoughtfully, Madge
Haskel said, 'There's something wrong with Verne. I noticed
it especially last night. When he came home from work.'
  Doctor Paul Tyler grunted absently. 'A highly neurotic
type. Sense of inferiority. Withdrawal and introversion.'
  'But he's getting worse. Him and his trains. Those damn
model trains. My God, Paul! Do you know he has a whole
town down there in the basement?'
  Tyler was curious. 'Really? I never knew that.'
  'All the time I've known him he's had them down there.
Started when he was a kid. Imagine a grown man playing
with trains! It's – it's disgusting. Every night the same
thing.'
  'Interesting.' Tyler rubbed his jaw. 'He keeps at them
continually? An unvarying pattern?'
  'Every night. Last night he didn't even eat dinner. He
just came home and went directly down.'
  Paul Tyler's polished features twisted into a frown.
Across from him Madge sat languidly sipping her beer.
It was two in the afternoon. The day was warm and
bright. The living room was attractive in a lazy, quiet way.
Abruptly Tyler got to his feet. 'Let's take a look at them.
The models. I didn't know it had gone so far.'
  'Do you really want to?' Madge slid back the sleeve of her
green silk lounge pajamas and consulted her wristwatch.
'He won't be home until five.' She jumped to her feet,
setting down her glass. 'All right. We have time.'
  'Fine. Let's go down.' Tyler caught hold of Madge's
arm and they hurried down into the basement, a strange
excitement flooding through them. Madge clicked on the
basement light and they approached the big plywood table,
giggling and nervous, like mischievous children.
  'See?' Madge said, squeezing Tyler's arm. 'Look at it.
Took years. All his life.'

Tyler nodded slowly. 'Must have.' There was awe in his voice. 'I've never seen anything like it. The detail . . . He has skill.'

'Yes, Verne is good with his hands.' Madge indicated the workbench. 'He buys tools all the time.'

Tyler walked slowly around the big table, bending over and peering. 'Amazing. Every building. The whole town is here. Look! There's my place.'

He indicated his luxurious apartment building, a few blocks from the Haskel residence.

'I guess it's all there,' Madge said. 'Imagine a grown man coming down here and playing with model trains!'

'Power.' Tyler pushed an engine along a track. 'That's why it appeals to boys. Trains are big things. Huge and noisy. Power-sex symbols. The boy sees the train rushing along the track. It's so huge and ruthless it scares him. Then he gets a toy train. A model, like these. He controls it. Makes it start, stop. Go slow. Fast. He runs it. It responds to him.'

Madge shivered. 'Let's go upstairs where it's warm. It's so cold down here.'

'But as the boy grows up, he gets bigger and stronger. He can shed the model-symbol. Master the real object, the real train. Get genuine control over things. Valid mastery.' Tyler shook his head. 'Not this substitute thing. Unusual, a grown person going to such lengths.' He frowned. 'I never noticed a mortuary on State Street.'

'A mortuary?'

'And this. Steuben Pet Shop. Next door to the radio repair shop. There's no pet shop there.' Tyler cudgeled his brain. 'What *is* there? Next to the radio repair place.'

'Paris Furs.' Madge clasped her arms. 'Brrrrr. Come on, Paul. Let's go upstairs before I freeze.'

Tyler laughed. 'Okay, sissy.' He headed toward the stairs, frowning again. 'I wonder why. Steuben Pets. Never heard of it. Everything is so detailed. He must know the town by heart. To put a shop there that isn't—' He clicked off the basement light. 'And the mortuary. What's supposed to be there? Isn't the—'

'Forget it,' Madge called back, hurrying past him, into the warm living room. 'You're practically as bad as he is. Men are such children.'

Tyler didn't respond. He was deep in thought. His suave confidence was gone; he looked nervous and shaken.

Madge pulled the venetian blinds down. The living room sank into amber gloom. She flopped down on the couch and pulled Tyler down beside her. 'Stop looking like that,' she ordered. 'I've never seen you this way.' Her slim arms circled his neck and her lips brushed close to his ear. 'I wouldn't have let you in if I thought you were going to worry about *him*.'

Tyler grunted, preoccupied. 'Why *did* you let me in?'

The pressure of Madge's arms increased. Her silk pajamas rustled as she moved against him. 'Silly,' she said.

Big red-headed Jim Larson gaped in disbelief. 'What do you mean? What's the matter with you?'

'I'm quitting.' Haskel shoveled the contents of his desk into his briefcase. 'Mail the check to my house.'

'But—'

'Get out of the way.' Haskel pushed past Larson, out into the hall. Larson was stunned with amazement. There was a fixed expression on Haskel's face. A glazed look. A rigid look Larson had never seen before.

'Are you – all right?' Larson asked.

'Sure.' Haskel opened the front door of the plant and disappeared outside. The door slammed after him. 'Sure I'm all right,' he muttered to himself. He made his way through the crowds of late-afternoon shoppers, his lips twitching. 'You're damn right I'm all right.'

'Watch it, buddy,' a laborer muttered ominously, as Haskel shoved past him.

'Sorry.' Haskel hurried on, gripping his briefcase. At the top of the hill he paused a moment to get his breath. Behind him was Larson's Pump and Valve Works. Haskel laughed shrilly. Twenty years – cut short in a second. It was over. No more Larson. No more dull, grinding job, day after day. Without promotion or future. Routine and boredom, months on end. It was over and done for. A new life and beginning.

He hurried on. The sun was setting. Cars streaked by him, businessmen going home from work. Tomorrow they would be going back – but not him. Not ever again.

He reached his own street. Ed Tildon's house rose up, a great stately structure of concrete and glass. Tildon's dog came rushing out to bark. Haskel hastened past. Tildon's dog. He laughed wildly.

'Better keep away!' he shouted at the dog.

He reached his own house and leaped up the front steps two at a time. He tore the door open. The living room was dark and silent. There was a sudden stir of motion. Shapes untangling themselves, getting quickly up from the couch.

'Verne!' Madge gasped. 'What are you doing home so early?'

Verne Haskel threw his briefcase down and dropped his hat and coat over a chair. His lined face was twisted with emotion, pulled out of shape by violent inner forces.

'What in the world!' Madge fluttered, hurrying toward him nervously, smoothing down her lounge pajamas. 'Has something happened? I didn't expect you so—' She broke off, blushing. 'I mean, I—'

Paul Tyler strolled leisurely toward Haskel. 'Hi there, Verne,' he murmured, embarrassed. 'Dropped by to say hello and return a book to your wife.'

Haskel nodded curtly. 'Afternoon.' He turned and headed toward the basement door, ignoring the two of them. 'I'll be downstairs.'

'But Verne!' Madge protested. 'What's happened?'

Verne halted briefly at the door. 'I quit my job.'

'You *what?*'

'I quit my job. I finished Larson off. There won't be any more of him.' The basement door slammed.

'Good Lord!' Madge shrieked, clutching at Tyler hysterically. 'He's gone out of his mind!'

Down in the basement, Verne Haskel snapped on the light impatiently. He put on his engineer's cap and pulled his stool up beside the great plywood table.

What next?

Morris Home Furnishings. The big plush store. Where the clerks all looked down their noses at him.

He rubbed his hands gleefully. No more of them. No more snooty clerks, lifting their eyebrows when he came in. Only hair and bow ties and folded handkerchiefs.

He removed the model of Morris Home Furnishings and disassembled it. He worked feverishly, with frantic haste. Now that he had really begun he wasted no time. A moment later he was gluing two small buildings in its place. Ritz Shoeshine. Pete's Bowling Alley.

Haskel giggled excitedly. Fitting extinction for the luxurious, exclusive furniture store. A shoeshine parlor and a bowling alley. Just what it deserved.

The California State Bank. He had always hated the Bank. They had once refused him a loan. He pulled the Bank loose.

Ed Tildon's mansion. His damn dog. The dog had bit him on the ankle one afternoon. He ripped the model off. His head spun. He could do anything.

Harrison Appliance. They had sold him a bum radio. Off came Harrison Appliance.

Joe's Cigar and Smoke Shop. Joe had given him a lead quarter in May, 1949. Off came Joe's.

The Ink Works. He loathed the smell of ink. Maybe a bread factory, instead. He loved baking bread. Off came the Ink Works.

Elm Street was too dark at night. A couple of times he had stumbled. A few more streetlights were in order.

Not enough bars along High Street. Too many dress

shops and expensive hat and fur shops and ladies' apparel. He ripped a whole handful loose and carried them to the workbench.

At the top of the stairs the door opened slowly. Madge peered down, pale and frightened. 'Verne?'

He scowled up impatiently. 'What do you want?'

Madge came downstairs hesitantly. Behind her Doctor Tyler followed, suave and handsome in his gray suit. 'Verne – is everything all right?'

'Of course.'

'Did – did you really quit your job?'

Haskel nodded. He began to disassemble the Ink Works, ignoring his wife and Doctor Tyler.

'But *why*?'

Haskel grunted impatiently. 'No time.'

Doctor Tyler had begun to look worried. 'Do I understand you're too busy for your job?'

'That's right.'

'Too busy doing *what*?' Tyler's voice rose; he was trembling nervously. 'Working down here on this town of yours? Changing things?'

'Go away,' Haskel muttered. His deft hands were assembling a lovely little Langendorf Bread Factory. He shaped it with loving care, sprayed it with white paint, brushed a gravel walk and shrubs in front of it. He put it aside and began on a park. A big green park. Woodland had always needed a park. It would go in place of State Street Hotel.

Tyler pulled Madge away from the table, off in a corner of the basement. 'Good God.' He lit a cigarette shakily. The cigarette flipped out of his hands and rolled away. He ignored it and fumbled for another. 'You see? You see what he's doing?'

Madge shook her head mutely. 'What is it? I don't—'

'How long has he been working on this? All his life?'

Madge nodded, white-faced. 'Yes, all his life.'

Tyler's features twisted. 'My God, Madge. It's enough to

drive you out of your mind. I can hardly believe it. We've got to do something.'

'What's happening?' Madge moaned. 'What—'

'He's losing himself into it.' Tyler's face was a mask of incredulous disbelief. 'Faster and faster.'

'He's always come down here,' Madge faltered. 'It's nothing new. He's always wanted to get away.'

'Yes. Get away.' Tyler shuddered, clenched his fists and pulled himself together. He advanced across the basement and stopped by Verne Haskel.

'What do you want?' Haskel muttered, noticing him.

Tyler licked his lips. 'You're adding some things, aren't you? New buildings.'

Haskel nodded.

Tyler touched the little bread factory with shaking fingers. 'What's this? Bread? Where does it go?' He moved around the table. 'I don't remember any bread factory in Woodland.' He whirled. 'You aren't by any chance *improving* on the town? Fixing it up here and there?'

'Get the hell out of here,' Haskel said, with ominous calm. 'Both of you.'

'Verne!' Madge squeaked.

'I've got a lot to do. You can bring sandwiches down about eleven. I hope to finish sometime tonight.'

'Finish?' Tyler asked.

'Finish,' Haskel answered, returning to his work.

'Come on, Madge.' Tyler grabbed her and pulled her to the stairs. 'Let's get out of here.' He strode ahead of her, up to the stairs and into the hall. 'Come on!' As soon as she was up he closed the door tightly after them.

Madge dabbed at her eyes hysterically. 'He's gone crazy, Paul! What'll we do?'

Tyler was in deep thought. 'Be quiet. I have to think this out.' He paced back and forth, a hard scowl on his features. 'It'll come soon. It won't be long, not at this rate. Sometime tonight.'

'*What?* What do you mean?'

'His withdrawal. Into his substitute world. The improved model he controls. Where he can get away.'

'Isn't there something we can do?'

'Do?' Tyler smiled faintly. 'Do we want to do something?'

Madge gasped. 'But we can't just—'

'Maybe this will solve our problem. This may be what we've been looking for.' Tyler eyed Mrs Haskel thoughtfully. 'This may be just the thing.'

It was after midnight, almost two o'clock in the morning, when he began to get things into final shape. He was tired – but alert. Things were happening fast. The job was almost done.

Virtually perfect.

He halted work a moment, surveying what he had accomplished. The town had been radically changed. About ten o'clock he had begun basic structural alterations in the lay-out of the streets. He had removed most of the public buildings, the civic center and the sprawling business district around it.

He had erected a new city hall, police station, and an immense park with fountains and indirect lighting. He had cleared the slum area, the old rundown stores and houses and streets. The streets were wider and well-lit. The houses were now small and clean. The stores modern and attractive – without being ostentatious.

All advertising signs had been removed. Most of the filling stations were gone. The immense factory area was gone, too. Rolling countryside took its place. Trees and hills and green grass.

The wealthy district had been altered. There were now only a few of the mansions left – belonging to persons he looked favorably on. The rest had been cut down, turned into uniform two-bedroom dwellings, one story, with a single garage each.

The city hall was no longer an elaborate, rococo

structure. Now it was low and simple, modeled after the Parthenon, a favorite of his.

There were ten or twelve persons who had done him special harm. He had altered their houses considerably. Given them war-time housing unit apartments, six to a building, at the far edge of town. Where the wind came off the bay, carrying the smell of decaying mud-flats.

Jim Larson's house was completely gone. He had erased Larson utterly. He no longer existed, not in this new Woodland – which was now almost complete.

Almost. Haskel studied his work intently. All the changes had to be made *now*. Not later. This was the time of creation. Later, when it had been finished, it could not be altered. He had to catch all the necessary changes now – or forget them.

The new Woodland looked pretty good. Clean and neat – and simple. The rich district had been toned down. The poor district had been improved. Glaring ads, signs, displays, had all been changed or removed. The business community was smaller. Parks and countryside took the place of factories. The civic center was lovely.

He added a couple of playgrounds for smaller kids. A small theater instead of the enormous Uptown with its flashing neon sign. After some consideration he removed most of the bars he had previously constructed. The new Woodland was going to be moral. Extremely moral. Few bars, no billiards, no red light district. And there was an especially fine jail for undesirables.

The most difficult part had been the microscopic lettering on the main office door of the city hall. He had left it until last, and then painted the words with agonizing care:

MAYOR
VERNON R. HASKEL

A few last changes. He gave the Edwardses a '39 Plymouth instead of a new Cadillac. He added more trees in the downtown district. One more fire department. One less dress shop. He had never liked taxis. On impulse, he removed the taxi stand and put in a flower shop.

Haskel rubbed his hands. Anything more? Or was it complete . . . Perfect . . . He studied each part intently. What had he overlooked?

The high school. He removed it and put in two smaller high schools, one at each end of town. Another hospital. That took almost half an hour. He was getting tired. His hands were less swift. He mopped his forehead shakily. Anything else? He sat down on his stool wearily, to rest and think.

All done. It was complete. Joy welled up in him. A bursting cry of happiness. His work was over.

'Finished!' Verne Haskel shouted.

He got unsteadily to his feet. He closed his eyes, held his arms out, and advanced toward the plywood table. Reaching, grasping, fingers extended, Haskel headed toward it, a look of radiant exaltation on his seamed, middle-aged face.

Upstairs, Tyler and Madge heard the shout. A distant booming that rolled through the house in waves. Madge winced in terror. 'What was that?'

Tyler listened intently. He heard Haskel moving below them, in the basement. Abruptly, he stubbed out his cigarette. 'I think it's happened. Sooner than I expected.'

'It? You mean he's—'

Tyler got quickly to his feet. 'He's gone, Madge. Into his other world. We're finally free.'

Madge caught his arm. 'Maybe we're making a mistake. It's so terrible. Shouldn't we – try to do something? Bring him out of it – try to pull him back.'

'Bring him back?' Tyler laughed nervously. 'I don't think we could, now. Even if we wanted to. It's too late.' He hurried toward the basement door. 'Come on.'

'It's horrible.' Madge shuddered and followed reluctantly. 'I wish we had never got started.'

Tyler halted briefly at the door. 'Horrible? He's happier, where he is, now. And you're happier. The way it was, nobody was happy. This is the best thing.'

He opened the basement door. Madge followed him. They moved cautiously down the stairs, into the dark, silent basement, damp with the faint night mists.

The basement was empty.

Tyler relaxed. He was overcome with dazed relief. 'He's gone. Everything's okay. It worked out exactly right.'

'But I don't understand,' Madge repeated hopelessly, as Tyler's Buick purred along the dark, deserted streets. 'Where did he go?'

'You know where he went,' Tyler answered. 'Into his substitute world, of course.' He screeched around a corner on two wheels. 'The rest should be fairly simple. A few routine forms. There really isn't much left, now.'

The night was frigid and bleak. No lights showed, except an occasional lonely streetlamp. Far off, a train whistle sounded mournfully, a dismal echo. Rows of silent houses flickered by on both sides of them.

'Where are we going?' Madge asked. She sat huddled against the door, face pale with shock and terror, shivering under her coat.

'To the police station.'

'Why?'

'To report him, naturally. So they'll know he's gone. We'll have to wait; it'll be several years before he'll be declared legally dead.' Tyler reached over and hugged her briefly. 'We'll make out in the meantime, I'm sure.'

'What if – they find him?'

Tyler shook his head angrily. He was still tense, on edge. 'Don't you understand? They'll never find him – he doesn't exist. As least, not in our world. He's in his own world. You saw it. The model. The improved substitute.'

'He's there?'

'All his life he's worked on it. Built it up. Made it real. He

brought that world into being – and now he's in it. That's
what he wanted. That's why he built it. He didn't merely
dream about an escape world. He actually constructed it –
every bit and piece. Now he's warped himself right out of
our world, into it. Out of our lives.'

Madge finally began to understand. 'Then he really *did*
lose himself in his substitute world. You meant that, what
you said about him – getting away.'

'It took me awhile to realize it. The mind constructs
reality. Frames it. Creates it. We all have a common reality,
a common dream. But Haskel turned his back on our
common reality and created his own. And he had a unique
capacity – far beyond the ordinary. He devoted his whole
life, his whole skill to building it. He's there now.'

Tyler hesitated and frowned. He gripped the wheel tightly
and increased speed. The Buick hissed along the dark street,
through the silent, unmoving bleakness that was the town.

'There's only one thing,' he continued presently. 'One
thing I don't understand.'

'What is it?'

'The model. It was also gone. I assumed he'd – shrink, I
suppose. Merge with it. But the model's gone, too.' Tyler
shrugged. 'It doesn't matter.' He peered into the darkness.
'We're almost there. This is Elm.'

It was then Madge screamed. '*Look!*'

To the right of the car was a small, neat building. And a
sign. The sign was easily visible in the darkness.

WOODLAND MORTUARY

Madge was sobbing in horror. The car roared forward,
automatically guided by Tyler's numb hands. Another sign
flashed by briefly, as they coasted up before the city hall.

STEUBEN PET SHOP

The city hall was lit by recessed, hidden illumination. A
low, simple building, a square of glowing white. Like a
marble Greek temple.

Tyler pulled the car to a halt. Then suddenly shrieked and started up again. But not soon enough.

The two shiny-black police cars came silently up around the Buick, one on each side. The four stern cops already had their hands on the door. Stepping out and coming toward him, grim and efficient.

The Father-Thing

'Dinner's ready,' commanded Mrs Walton. 'Go get your father and tell him to wash his hands. The same applies to you, young man.' She carried a steaming casserole to the neatly set table. 'You'll find him out in the garage.'

Charles hesitated. He was only eight years old, and the problem bothering him would have confounded Hillel. 'I—' he began uncertainly.

'What's wrong?' June Walton caught the uneasy tone in her son's voice and her matronly bosom fluttered with sudden alarm. 'Isn't Ted out in the garage? For heaven's sake, he was sharpening the hedge shears a minute ago. He didn't go over to the Andersons', did he? I told him dinner was practically on the table.'

'He's in the garage,' Charles said. 'But he's – talking to himself.'

'Talking to himself!' Mrs Walton removed her bright plastic apron and hung it over the doorknob. 'Ted? Why, he never talks to himself. Go tell him to come in here.' She poured boiling black coffee in the little blue-and-white china cups and began ladling out creamed corn. 'What's wrong with you? Go tell him!'

'I don't know which of them to tell.' Charles blurted out desperately. 'They both look alike.'

June Walton's fingers lost their hold on the aluminum pan; for a moment the creamed corn slushed dangerously. 'Young man—' she began angrily, but at that moment Ted Walton came striding into the kitchen, inhaling and sniffing and rubbing his hands together.

'Ah,' he cried happily. 'Lamb stew.'

'Beef stew,' June murmured. 'Ted, what were you doing out there?'

Ted threw himself down at his place and unfolded his napkin. 'I got the shears sharpened like a razor. Oiled and sharpened. Better not touch them – they'll cut your hand off.' He was a good-looking man in his early thirties; thick blond hair, strong arms, competent hands, square face and flashing brown eyes. 'Man, this stew looks good. Hard day at the office – Friday, you know. Stuff piles up and we have to get all the accounts out by five. Al McKinley claims the department could handle 20 per cent more stuff if we organized our lunch hours; staggered them so somebody was there all the time.' He beckoned Charles over. 'Sit down and let's go.'

Mrs Walton served the frozen peas. 'Ted,' she said, as she slowly took her seat, 'is there anything on your mind?'

'On my mind?' He blinked. 'No, nothing unusual. Just the regular stuff. Why?'

Uneasily, June Walton glanced over at her son. Charles was sitting bolt-upright at his place, face expressionless, white as chalk. He hadn't moved, hadn't unfolded his napkin or even touched his milk. A tension was in the air; she could feel it. Charles had pulled his chair away from his father's; he was huddled in a tense little bundle as far from his father as possible. His lips were moving, but she couldn't catch what he was saying.

'What is it?' she demanded, leaning toward him.

'*The other one*,' Charles was muttering under his breath. 'The other one came in.'

'What do you mean, dear?' June Walton asked out loud. 'What other one?'

Ted jerked. A strange expression flitted across his face. It vanished at once; but in the brief instant Ted Walton's face lost all familiarity. Something alien and cold gleamed out, a twisting, wriggling mass. The eyes blurred and receded, as an archaic sheen filmed over them. The ordinary look of a tired, middle-aged husband was gone.

And then it was back – or nearly back. Ted grinned and began to wolf down his stew and frozen peas and creamed corn. He laughed, stirred his coffee, kidded and ate. But something terrible was wrong.

'The other one,' Charles muttered, face white, hands beginning to tremble. Suddenly he leaped up and backed away from the table. 'Get away!' he shouted. 'Get out of here!'

'Hey,' Ted rumbled ominously. 'What's got into you?' He pointed sternly at the boy's chair. 'You sit down there and eat your dinner, young man. Your mother didn't fix it for nothing.'

Charles turned and ran out of the kitchen, upstairs to his room. June Walton gasped and fluttered in dismay. 'What in the world—'

Ted went on eating. His face was grim, his eyes were hard and dark. 'That kid,' he grated, 'is going to have to learn a few things. Maybe he and I need to have a little private conference together.'

Charles crouched and listened.

The father-thing was coming up the stairs, nearer and nearer. 'Charles!' it shouted angrily. 'Are you up there?'

He didn't answer. Soundlessly, he moved back into his room and pulled the door shut. His heart was pounding heavily. The father-thing had reached the landing; in a moment it would come in his room.

He hurried to the window. He was terrified; it was already fumbling in the dark hall for the knob. He lifted the window and climbed out on the roof. With a grunt he dropped into the flower garden that ran by the front door, staggered and gasped, then leaped to his feet and ran from the light that streamed out the window, a patch of yellow in the evening darkness.

He found the garage; it loomed up ahead, a black square against the skyline. Breathing quickly, he fumbled in his pocket for his flashlight, then cautiously slid the door up and entered.

The garage was empty. The car was parked out front. To the left was his father's workbench. Hammers and saws on the wooden walls. In the back were the lawnmower, rake, shovel, hoe. A drum of kerosene. License plates nailed up everywhere. Floor was concrete and dirt; a great oil slick stained the center, tufts of weeds greasy and black in the flickering beam of the flashlight.

Just inside the door was a big trash barrel. On top of the barrel were stacks of soggy newspapers and magazines, moldy and damp. A thick stench of decay issued from them as Charles began to move them around. Spiders dropped to the cement and scampered off; he crushed them with his foot and went on looking.

The sight made him shriek. He dropped the flashlight and leaped wildly back. The garage was plunged into instant gloom. He forced himself to kneel down, and for an ageless moment he groped in the darkness for the light, among the spiders and greasy weeds. Finally he had it again. He managed to turn the beam down into the barrel, down the well he had made by pushing back the piles of magazines.

The father-thing had stuffed it down in the very bottom of the barrel. Among the old leaves and torn-up cardboard, the rotting remains of magazines and curtains, rubbish from the attic his mother had lugged down here with the idea of burning someday. It still looked a little like his father enough for him to recognize. He had found it – and the sight made him sick at his stomach. He hung onto the barrel and shut his eyes until finally he was able to look again. In the barrel were the remains of his father, his real father. Bits the father-thing had no use for. Bits it had discarded.

He got the rake and pushed it down to stir the remains. They were dry. They cracked and broke at the touch of the rake. They were like a discarded snake skin, flaky and crumbling, rustling at the touch. *An empty skin.* The insides were gone. The important part. This was all that remained, just the brittle, cracking skin, wadded down at the bottom of the trash barrel in a little heap. This was all the father-thing had left; it had eaten the rest. Taken the insides – and his father's place.

A sound.

He dropped the rake and hurried to the door. The father-thing was coming down the path, toward the garage. Its shoes crushed the gravel; it felt its way along uncertainly. 'Charles!' it called angrily. 'Are you in there? Wait'll I get my hands on you, young man!'

His mother's ample, nervous shape was outlined in the bright doorway of the house. 'Ted, please don't hurt him. He's all upset about something.'

'I'm not going to hurt him,' the father-thing rasped; it halted to strike a match. 'I'm just going to have a little talk with him. He needs to learn better manners. Leaving the table like that and running out at night, climbing down the roof—'

Charles slipped from the garage; the glare of the match caught his moving shape, and with a bellow the father-thing lunged forward.

'*Come here!*'

Charles ran. He knew the ground better than the father-thing; it knew a lot, had taken a lot when it got his father's insides, but nobody knew the way like *he* did. He reached the fence, climbed it, leaped into the Andersons' yard, raced past their clothesline, down the path around the side of their house, and out on Maple Street.

He listened, crouched down and not breathing. The father-thing hadn't come after him. It had gone back. Or it was coming around the sidewalk.

He took a deep, shuddering breath. He had to keep moving. Sooner or later it would find him. He glanced right and left, made sure it wasn't watching, and then started off at a rapid dog-trot.

'What do you want?' Tony Peretti demanded belligerently. Tony was fourteen. He was sitting at the table in the oak-panelled Peretti dining room, books and pencils scattered around him, half a ham-and-peanut-butter sandwich and a Coke beside him. 'You're Walton, aren't you?'

Tony Peretti had a job uncrating stoves and refrigerators after school at Johnson's Appliance Shop, downtown. He was big and blunt-faced. Black hair, olive skin, white teeth. A couple of times he had beaten up Charles; he had beaten up every kid in the neighborhood.

Charles twisted. 'Say, Peretti. Do me a favor?'

'What do you want?' Peretti was annoyed. 'You looking for a bruise?'

Gazing unhappily down, his fists clenched, Charles explained what had happened in short, mumbled words.

When he had finished, Peretti let out a low whistle. 'No kidding.'

'It's true.' He nodded quickly. 'I'll show you. Come on and I'll show you.'

Peretti got slowly to his feet. 'Yeah, show me. I want to see.'

He got his b.b. gun from his room, and the two of them walked silently up the dark street, toward Charles' house. Neither of them said much. Peretti was deep in thought, serious and solemn-faced. Charles was still dazed; his mind was completely blank.

They turned down the Anderson driveway, cut through the back yard, climbed the fence, and lowered themselves cautiously into Charles' back yard. There was no movement. The yard was silent. The front door of the house was closed.

They peered through the living room window. The shades were down, but a narrow crack of yellow streamed out. Sitting on the couch was Mrs Walton, sewing a cotton T-shirt. There was a sad, troubled look on her large face. She worked listlessly, without interest. Opposite her was the father-thing. Leaning back in his father's easy chair, its shoes off, reading the evening newspaper. The TV was on, playing to itself in the corner. A can of beer rested on the arm of the easy chair. The father-thing sat exactly as his own father had sat; it had learned a lot.

'Looks just like him,' Peretti whispered suspiciously. 'You sure you're not bulling me?'

Charles led him to the garage and showed him the trash barrel. Peretti reached his long tanned arms down and carefully pulled up the dry, flaking remains. They spread out, unfolded, until the whole figure of his father was outlined. Peretti laid the remains on the floor and pieced broken parts back into place. The remains were colorless. Almost transparent. An amber yellow, thin as paper. Dry and utterly lifeless.

'That's all,' Charles said. Tears welled up in his eyes. 'That's all that's left of him. The thing has the insides.'

Peretti had turned pale. Shakily, he crammed the remains back in the trash barrel. 'This is really something,' he muttered. 'You say you saw the two of them together?'

'Talking. They looked exactly alike. I ran inside.' Charles wiped the tears away and sniveled; he couldn't hold it back any longer. 'It ate him while I was inside. Then it came in the house. It pretended it was him. But it isn't. It killed him and ate his insides.'

For a moment Peretti was silent. 'I'll tell you something,' he said suddenly. 'I've heard about this sort of thing. It's a bad business. You have to use your head and not get scared. You're not scared, are you?'

'No,' Charles managed to mutter.

'The first thing we have to do is figure out how to kill it.' He rattled his b.b. gun. 'I don't know if this'll work. It must be plenty tough to get hold of your father. He was a big man.' Peretti considered. 'Let's get out of here. It might come back. They say that's what a murderer does.'

They left the garage. Peretti crouched down and peeked through the window again. Mrs Walton had got to her feet. She was talking anxiously. Vague sounds filtered out.

The father-thing threw down its newspaper. They were arguing.

'For God's sake!' the father-thing shouted. 'Don't do anything stupid like that.'

'Something's wrong,' Mrs Walton moaned. 'Something terrible. Just let me call the hospital and see.'

'Don't call anybody. He's all right. Probably up the street playing.'

'He's never out this late. He never disobeys. He was terribly upset – afraid of you! I don't blame him.' Her voice broke with misery. 'What's wrong with you? You're so strange.' She moved out of the room, into the hall. 'I'm going to call some of the neighbors.'

The father-thing glared after her until she had disappeared. Then a terrifying thing happened. Charles gasped; even Peretti grunted under his breath.

'Look,' Charles muttered. 'What—'

'Golly,' Peretti said, black eyes wide.

As soon as Mrs Walton was gone from the room, the father-thing sagged in its chair. It became limp. Its mouth fell open. Its eyes peered vacantly. Its head fell forward, like a discarded rag doll.

Peretti moved away from the window. 'That's it,' he whispered. 'That's the whole thing.'

'What is it?' Charles demanded. He was shocked and bewildered. 'It looked like somebody turned off its power.'

'Exactly.' Peretti nodded slowly, grim and shaken. 'It's controlled from outside.'

Horror settled over Charles. 'You mean, something outside our world?'

Peretti shook his head with disgust. 'Outside the house! In the yard. You know how to find?'

'Not very well.' Charles pulled his mind together. 'But I know somebody who's good at finding.' He forced his mind to summon the name. 'Bobby Daniels.'

'That little black kid? Is he good at finding?'

'The best.'

'All right,' Peretti said. 'Let's go get him. We have to find the thing that's outside. That made *it* in there, and keeps it going . . .'

'It's near the garage,' Peretti said to the small, thin-faced Negro boy who crouched beside them in the darkness. 'When it got him, he was in the garage. So look there.'

'In the garage?' Daniels asked.

'*Around* the garage. Walton's already gone over the garage, inside. Look around outside. Nearby.'

There was a small bed of flowers growing by the garage, and a great tangle of bamboo and discarded debris between the garage and the back of the house. The moon had come out; a cold, misty light filtered down over everything. 'If we don't find it pretty soon,' Daniels said, 'I got to go back home. I can't stay up much later.' He wasn't any older than Charles. Perhaps nine.

'All right,' Peretti agreed. 'Then get looking.'

The three of them spread out and began to go over the ground with care. Daniels worked with incredible speed; his thin little body moved in a blur of motion as he crawled among the flowers, turned over rocks, peered under the house, separated stalks of plants, ran his expert hands over leaves and stems, in tangles of compost and weeds. No inch was missed.

Peretti halted after a short time. 'I'll guard. It might be dangerous. The father-thing might come and try to stop us.' He posted himself on the back step with his b.b. gun while Charles and Bobby Daniels searched. Charles worked slowly. He was tired, and his body was cold and numb. It seemed impossible, the father-thing and what had happened to his own father, his real father. But terror spurred him on; what if it happened to his mother, or to him? Or to everyone? Maybe the whole world.

'I found it!' Daniels called in a thin, high voice. 'You all come around here quick!'

Peretti raised his gun and got up cautiously. Charles

hurried over; he turned the flickering yellow beam of his flashlight where Daniels stood.

The Negro boy had raised a concrete stone. In the moist, rotting soil the light gleamed on a metallic body. A thin, jointed thing with endless crooked legs was digging frantically. Plated, like an ant; a red-brown bug that rapidly disappeared before their eyes. Its rows of legs scabbed and clutched. The ground gave rapidly under it. Its wicked-looking tail twisted furiously as it struggled down the tunnel it had made.

Peretti ran into the garage and grabbed up the rake. He pinned down the tail of the bug with it. 'Quick! Shoot it with the b.b. gun!'

Daniels snatched the gun and took aim. The first shot tore the tail of the bug loose. It writhed and twisted frantically; its tail dragged uselessly and some of its legs broke off. It was a foot long, like a great millipede. It struggled desperately to escape down its hole.

'Shoot again,' Peretti ordered.

Daniels fumbled with the gun. The bug slithered and hissed. Its head jerked back and forth; it twisted and bit at the rake holding it down. Its wicked specks of eyes gleamed with hatred. For a moment it struck futilely at the rake; then abruptly, without warning, it thrashed in a frantic convulsion that made them all draw away in fear.

Something buzzed through Charles' brain. A loud humming, metallic and harsh, a billion metal wires dancing and vibrating at once. He was tossed about violently by the force; the banging crash of metal made him deaf and confused. He stumbled to his feet and backed off; the others were doing the same, white-faced and shaken.

'If we can't kill it with the gun,' Peretti gasped, 'we can drown it. Or burn it. Or stick a pin through its brain.' He fought to hold onto the rake, to keep the bug pinned down.

'I have a jar of formaldehyde,' Daniels muttered. His fingers fumbled nervously with the b.b. gun. 'How do this thing work? I can't seem to—'

Charles grabbed the gun from him. 'I'll kill it.' He squatted down, one eye to the sight, and gripped the trigger. The bug lashed and struggled. Its force-field hammered in his ears, but he hung onto the gun. His finger tightened . . .

'All right, Charles,' the father-thing said. Powerful fingers gripped him, a paralyzing pressure around his wrists. The gun fell to the ground as he struggled futilely. The father-thing shoved against Peretti. The boy leaped away and the bug, free of the rake, slithered triumphantly down its tunnel.

'You have a spanking coming, Charles,' the father-thing droned on. 'What got into you? Your poor mother's out of her mind with worry.'

It had been there, hiding in the shadows. Crouched in the darkness watching them. Its calm, emotionless voice, a dreadful parody of his father's, rumbled close to his ear as it pulled him relentlessly toward the garage. Its cold breath blew in his face, an icy-sweet odor, like decaying soil. Its strength was immense; there was nothing he could do.

'Don't fight me,' it said calmly. 'Come along, into the garage. This is for your own good. I know best, Charles.'

'Did you find him?' his mother called anxiously, opening the back door.

'Yes, I found him.'

'What are you going to do?'

'A little spanking.' The father-thing pushed up the garage door. 'In the garage.' In the half-light a faint smile, humorless and utterly without emotion, touched its lips. 'You go back in the living room, June. I'll take care of this. It's more in my line. You never did like punishing him.'

The back door reluctantly closed. As the light cut off, Peretti bent down and groped for the b.b. gun. The father-thing instantly froze.

'Go on home, boys,' it rasped.

Peretti stood undecided, gripping the b.b. gun.

'Get going,' the father-thing repeated. 'Put down that toy and get out of here.' It moved slowly toward Peretti, gripping Charles with one hand, reaching toward Peretti with the other. 'No b.b. guns allowed in town, sonny. Your father know you have that? There's a city ordinance. I think you better give me that before—'

Peretti shot it in the eye.

The father-thing grunted and pawed at its ruined eye. Abruptly it slashed out at Peretti. Peretti moved down the driveway, trying to cock the gun. The father-thing lunged. Its powerful fingers snatched the gun from Peretti's hands. Silently, the father-thing mashed the gun against the wall of the house.

Charles broke away and ran numbly off. Where could he hide? It was between him and the house. Already, it was coming back toward him, a black shape creeping carefully, peering into the darkness, trying to make him out. Charles retreated. If there were only some place he could hide . . .

The bamboo.

He crept quickly into the bamboo. The stalks were huge and old. They closed after him with a faint rustle. The father-thing was fumbling in its pocket; it lit a match, then the whole pack flared up. 'Charles,' it said. 'I know you're here, someplace. There's no use hiding. You're only making it more difficult.'

His heart hammering, Charles crouched among the bamboo. Here, debris and filth rotted. Weeds, garbage, papers, boxes, old clothing, boards, tin cans, bottles. Spiders and salamanders squirmed around him. The bamboo swayed with the night wind. Insects and filth.

And something else.

A shape, a silent, unmoving shape that grew up from the mound of filth like some nocturnal mushroom. A white column, a pulpy mass that glistened moistly in the moonlight. Webs covered it, a moldy cocoon. It had vague arms and legs. An indistinct half-shaped head. As yet, the features hadn't formed. But he could tell what it was.

A mother-thing. Growing here in the filth and dampness, between the garage and the house. Behind the towering bamboo.

It was almost ready. Another few days and it would reach maturity. It was still a larva, white and soft and pulpy. But the sun would dry and warm it. Harden its shell. Turn it dark and strong. It would emerge from its cocoon, and one day when his mother came by the garage . . . Behind the mother-thing were other pulpy white larvae, recently laid by the bug. Small. Just coming into existence. He could see where the father-thing had broken off; the place where it had grown. It had matured here. And in the garage, his father had met it.

Charles began to move numbly away, past the rotting boards, the filth and debris, the pulpy mushroom larvae. Weakly, he reached out to take hold of the fence – and scrambled back.

Another one. Another larvae. He hadn't seen this one, at first. It wasn't white. It had already turned dark. The web, the pulpy softness, the moistness, were gone. It was ready. It stirred a little, moved its arm feebly.

The Charles-thing.

The bamboo separated, and the father-thing's hand clamped firmly around the boy's wrist. 'You stay right here,' it said. 'This is exactly the place for you. Don't move.' With its other hand it tore at the remains of the cocoon binding the Charles-thing. 'I'll help it out – it's still a little weak.'

The last shred of moist gray was stripped back, and the Charles-thing tottered out. It floundered uncertainly, as the father-thing cleared a path for it toward Charles.

'This way,' the father-thing grunted. 'I'll hold him for you. When you've fed you'll be stronger.'

The Charles-thing's mouth opened and closed. It reached greedily toward Charles. The boy struggled wildly, but the father-thing's immense hand held him down.

'Stop that, young man,' the father-thing commanded. 'It'll be a lot easier for you if you—'

It screamed and convulsed. It let go of Charles and staggered back. Its body twitched violently. It crashed against the garage, limbs jerking. For a time it rolled and flopped in a dance of agony. It whimpered, moaned, tried to crawl away. Gradually it became quiet. The Charles-thing settled down in a silent heap. It lay stupidly among the bamboo and rotting debris, body slack, face empty and blank.

At last the father-thing ceased to stir. There was only the faint rustle of the bamboo in the night wind.

Charles got up awkwardly. He stepped down onto the cement driveway. Peretti and Daniels approached, wide-eyed and cautious. 'Don't go near it,' Daniels ordered sharply. 'It ain't dead yet. Takes a little while.'

'What did you do?' Charles muttered.

Daniels set down the drum of kerosene with a gasp of relief. 'Found this in the garage. We Daniels always used kerosene on our mosquitoes, back in Virginia.'

'Daniels poured the kerosene down the bug's tunnel,' Peretti explained, still awed. 'It was his idea.'

Daniels kicked cautiously at the contorted body of the father-thing. 'It's dead, now. Died as soon as the bug died.'

'I guess the other'll die, too,' Peretti said. He pushed aside the bamboo to examine the larvae growing here and there among the debris. The Charles-thing didn't move at all, as Peretti jabbed the end of a stick into its chest. 'This one's dead.'

'We better make sure,' Daniels said grimly. He picked up the heavy drum of kerosene and lugged it to the edge of the bamboo. 'It dropped some matches in the driveway. You get them, Peretti.'

They looked at each other.

'Sure,' Peretti said softly.

'We better turn on the hose,' Charles said. 'To make sure it doesn't spread.'

'Let's get going,' Peretti said impatiently. He was already moving off. Charles quickly followed him and they began searching for the matches, in the moonlit darkness.

The Chromium Fence

Earth tilted toward six o'clock, the work-day almost over. Commute discs rose in dense swarms and billowed away from the industrial zone toward the surrounding residential rings. Like nocturnal moths, the thick clouds of discs darkened the evening sky. Silent, weightless, they whisked their passengers toward home and waiting families, hot meals and bed.

Don Walsh was the third man on his disc; he completed the load. As he dropped the coin in the slot the carpet rose impatiently. Walsh settled gratefully against the invisible safety-rail and unrolled the evening newspaper. Across from him the other two commuters were doing the same.

HORNEY AMENDMENT STIRS UP FIGHT

Walsh reflected on the significance of the headline. He lowered the paper from the steady windcurrents and perused the next column.

HUGE TURNOUT EXPECTED MONDAY

ENTIRE PLANET TO GO TO POLLS

On the back of the single sheet was the day's scandal.

WIFE MURDERS HUSBAND OVER POLITICAL TIFF

And an item that made strange chills up and down his spine. He had seen it crop up repeatedly, but it always made him feel uncomfortable.

PURIST MOB LYNCHES NATURALIST IN BOSTON

WINDOWS SMASHED — GREAT DAMAGE DONE

And in the next column:

NATURALIST MOB LYNCHES PURIST IN CHICAGO

BUILDINGS BURNED — GREAT DAMAGE DONE

Across from Walsh, one of his companions was beginning to mumble aloud. He was a big heavy-set man, middle-aged, with red hair and beer-swollen features. Suddenly he wadded up his newspaper and hurled it from the disc. 'They'll never pass it!' he shouted. 'They won't get away with it!'

Walsh buried his nose in his paper and desperately ignored the man. It was happening again, the thing he dreaded every hour of the day. A political argument. The other commuter had lowered his newspaper; briefly, he eyed the red-haired man and then continued reading.

The red-haired man addressed Walsh. 'You signed the Butte Petition?' He yanked a mentalfoil tablet from his pocket and pushed it in Walsh's face. 'Don't be afraid to put down your name for liberty.'

Walsh clutched his newspaper and peered frantically over the side of the disc. The Detroit residential units were spinning by; he was almost home. 'Sorry,' he muttered. 'Thanks, no thanks.'

'Leave him alone,' the other commuter said to the red-haired man. 'Can't you see he doesn't want to sign it?'

'Mind your own business.' The red-haired man moved close to Walsh, the tablet extended belligerently. 'Look, friend. You know what it'll mean to you and yours if this thing gets passed? You think you'll be safe? Wake up, friend. When the Horney Amendment comes in, freedom and liberty go out.'

The other commuter quietly put his newspaper away. He was slim, well-dressed, a gray-haired cosmopolitan. He removed his glasses and said, 'You smell like a Naturalist, to me.'

The red-haired man studied his opponent. He noticed the wide plutonium ring on the slender man's hand; a jaw-breaking band of heavy metal. 'What are you?' the red-haired man muttered, 'a sissy-kissing Purist? Agh.' He made a disgusting spitting motion and returned to Walsh. 'Look, friend, you know what these Purists are after. They want to make us degenerates. They'll turn us into a race of women. If God made the universe the way it is, it's good enough for me. They're going against God when they go against nature. This planet was built up by red-blooded *men*, who were proud of their bodies, proud of the way they looked and smelled.' He tapped his own heavy chest. 'By God, I'm proud of the way *I* smell!'

Walsh stalled desperately. 'I—' he muttered. 'No, I can't sign it.'

'You already signed?'

'No.'

Suspicion settled over the red-haired man's beefy features. 'You mean you're *for* the Horney Amendment?' His thick voice rose wrathfully. 'You want to see an end to the natural order of—'

'This is where I get off,' Walsh interrupted; he hurriedly yanked the stop-cord of the disc. It swept down toward the magnetic grapple at the end of his unit-section, a row of white squares set across the green and brown hill-side.

'Wait a minute, friend.' The red-haired man reached ominously for Walsh's sleeve, as the disc slid to a halt on the flat surface of the grapple. Surface cars were parked in rows; wives waiting to cart their husbands home. 'I don't like your attitude. You afraid to stand up and be counted? You ashamed to be a part of your race? By God, if you're not man enough to—'

The lean, gray-haired man smashed him with his plutonium ring, and the grip on Walsh's sleeve loosened. The petition clattered to the ground and the two of them fought furiously, silently.

Walsh pushed aside the safety-rail and jumped from the disc, down the three steps of the grapple and onto the ashes and cinders of the parking lot. In the gloom of early evening he could make out his wife's car; Betty sat watching the dashboard TV, oblivious of him and the silent struggle between the red-haired Naturalist and the gray-haired Purist.

'Beast,' the gray-haired man gasped, as he straightened up. 'Stinking animal!'

The red-haired man lay semi-conscious against the safety-rail. 'God damn – lily!' he grunted.

The gray-haired man pressed the release, and the disc rose above Walsh and on its way. Walsh waved gratefully. 'Thanks,' he called up. 'I appreciate that.'

'Not at all,' the gray-haired man answered, cheerfully examining a broken tooth. His voice dwindled, as the disc gained altitude. 'Always glad to help out a fellow . . . ' The final words came drifting to Walsh's ears. '. . . A fellow Purist.'

'I'm not!' Walsh shouted futilely. 'I'm not a Purist and I'm not a Naturalist! You hear me?'

Nobody heard him.

'I'm not,' Walsh repeated monotonously, as he sat at the dinner table spooning up creamed corn, potatoes, and rib steak. 'I'm not a Purist and I'm not a Naturalist. Why do I have to be one or the other? Isn't there any place for a man who has his *own* opinion?'

'Eat your food, dear,' Betty murmured.

Through the thin walls of the bright little dining room came the echoing clink of other families eating, other conversations in progress. The tinny blare of TV sets. The purr of stoves and freezers and air conditioners and wall-heaters. Across from Walsh his brother-in-law Carl was gulping down a second plateful of steaming food. Beside him, Walsh's fifteen-year-old son Jimmy was scanning a paperbound edition of *Finnegans Wake* he had bought in the downramp store that supplied the self-contained housing unit.

'Don't read at the table,' Walsh said angrily to his son.

Jimmy glanced up. 'Don't kid me. I know the unit rules; that one sure as hell isn't listed. And anyhow, I have to get this read before I leave.'

'Where are you going tonight, dear?' Betty asked.

'Official party business,' Jimmy answered obliquely. 'I can't tell you any more than that.'

Walsh concentrated on his food and tried to brake the tirade of thoughts screaming through his mind. 'On the way home from work,' he said, 'there was a fight.'

Jimmy was interested. 'Who won?'

'The Purist.'

A glow of pride slowly covered the boy's face; he was a sergeant in the Purist Youth League. 'Dad, you ought to get moving. Sign up now and you'll be eligible to vote next Monday.'

'I'm going to vote.'

'Not unless you're a member of one of the two parties.'

It was true. Walsh gazed unhappily past his son, into the days that lay ahead. He saw himself involved in endless wretched situations like the one today; sometimes it would be Naturalists who attacked him, and other times (like last week) it would be enraged Purists.

'You know,' his brother-in-law said, 'you're helping the Purists by just sitting around here doing nothing.' He belched contentedly and pushed his empty plate away. 'You're what *we* class as unconsciously pro-Purist.' He glared at Jimmy. 'You little squirt! If you were legal age I'd take you out and whale the tar out of you.'

'Please,' Betty sighed. 'No quarreling about politics at the table. Let's have peace and quiet, for a change. I'll certainly be glad when the election is over.'

Carl and Jimmy glared at each other and continued eating warily. 'You should eat in the kitchen—' Jimmy said to him. 'Under the stove. That's where you belong. Look at you – there's sweat all over you.' A nasty sneer interrupted his eating. 'When we get the Amendment passed, you better get rid of that, if you don't want to get hauled off to jail.'

Carl flushed. 'You creeps won't get it passed.' But his gruff voice lacked conviction. The Naturalists were scared; Purists had control of the Federal Council. If the election moved in their favor it was really possible the legislation to compel forced observation of the five-point Purist code might get on the books. 'Nobody is going to remove my sweat glands,' Carl muttered. 'Nobody is going to make me submit to breath-control and teeth-whitening and hair-restorer. It's part of life to get dirty and bald and fat and old.'

'Is it true?' Betty asked her husband. 'Are you really unconsciously pro-Purist?'

Don Walsh savagely speared a remnant of rib steak. 'Because I don't join either party I'm called unconsciously pro-Purist and unconsciously pro-Naturalist. I claim they balance. If I'm everybody's enemy then I'm nobody's enemy.' He added, 'Or friend.'

'You Naturalists have nothing to offer the future,' Jimmy said to Carl. 'What can you give the youth of the planet – like me? Caves and raw meat and a bestial existence. You're anti civilization.'

'Slogans,' Carl retorted.

'You want to carry us back to a primitive existence, away from social integration.' Jimmy waved an excited skinny finger in his uncle's face. 'You're thalamically oriented!'

'I'll break your head,' Carl snarled, half out of his chair. 'You Purist squirts have no respect for your elders.'

Jimmy giggled shrilly. 'I'd like to see you try. It's five years in prison for striking a minor. Go ahead – hit me.'

Don Walsh got heavily to his feet and left the dining room.

'Where are you going?' Betty called peevishly after him. 'You're not through eating.'

'The future belongs to youth,' Jimmy was informing Carl. 'And the youth of the planet is firmly Purist. You don't have a chance; the Purist revolution is coming.'

Don Walsh left the apartment and wandered down the common corridor toward the ramp. Closed doors extended in rows on both sides of him. Noise and light and activity radiated around him, the close presence of families and domestic interaction. He pushed past a boy and girl making love in the dark shadows and reached the ramp. For a moment he halted, then abruptly he moved forward and descended to the lowest level of the unit.

The level was deserted and cool and slightly moist. Above him the sounds of people had faded to dull echoes against the concrete ceiling. Conscious of his sudden plunge into isolation and silence he advanced thoughtfully between the dark grocery and dry goods stores, past the beauty shop and the liquor store, past the laundry and medical supply store, past the dentist and physical doctor, to the ante-room of the unit analyst.

He could see the analyst within the inner chamber. It sat immobile and silent, in the dark shadows of evening. Nobody was consulting it; the analyst was turned off. Walsh hesitated, then crossed the check-frame of the ante-room and knocked on the transparent inner door. The presence of his body closed relays and switches; abruptly the lights of the inner office winked on and the analyst itself sat up, smiled and half-rose to its feet.

'Don,' it called heartily. 'Come on in and sit down.'

He entered and wearily seated himself. 'I thought maybe I could talk to you, Charley,' he said.

'Sure, Don.' The robot leaned forward to see the clock on its wide mahogany desk. 'But, isn't it dinner time?'

'Yes,' Walsh admitted. 'I'm not hungry. Charley, you know what we were talking about last time . . . you remember what I was saying. You remember what's been bothering me.'

'Sure, Don.' The robot settled back in its swivel chair, rested its almost-convincing elbows on the desk, and regarded its patient kindly. 'How's it been going, the last couple of days?'

'Not so good. Charley, I've go to do something. You can help me; you're not biased.' He appealed to the quasi-human face of metal and plastic. 'You can see this undistorted, Charley. *How can I join one of the parties?* All their slogans and propaganda, it seems so damn – silly. How the hell can I get excited about clean teeth and underarm odor? People kill each other over these trifles . . . it doesn't make sense. There's going to be suicidal civil war, if that Amendment passes, and I'm supposed to join one side or the other.'

Charley nodded. 'I have the picture, Don.'

'Am I supposed to go out and knock some fellow over the head because he does or doesn't smell? Some man I never saw before? I won't do it. I refuse. Why can't they let me alone? Why can't I have my own opinions? Why do I have to get in on this – insanity?'

The analyst smiled tolerantly. 'That's a little harsh, Don. You're out of phase with your society, you know. So the cultural climate and mores seem a trifle unconvincing to you. But this is your society; you have to live in it. You can't withdraw.'

Walsh forced his hands to relax. 'Here's what I think. Any man who wants to smell should be allowed to smell. Any man who doesn't want to smell should go and get his glands removed. What's the matter with that?'

'Don, you're avoiding the issue.' The robot's voice was calm, dispassionate. 'What you're saying is that neither side is right. And that's foolish, isn't it? One side must be right.'

'Why?'

'Because the two sides exhaust the practical possibilities. Your position isn't really a position . . . it's a sort of description. You see, Don, you have a psychological inability to come to grips with an issue. You don't want to commit yourself for fear you'll lose your freedom and individuality. You're sort of an intellectual virgin; you want to stay pure.'

Walsh reflected. 'I want,' he said, 'to keep my integrity.'

'You're not an isolated individual, Don. You're a part of society . . . ideas don't exist in a vacuum.'

'I have a right to hold my own ideas.'

'No, Don,' the robot answered gently. 'They're not your ideas; you didn't create them. You can't turn them on and off when you feel like it. They operate through you . . .

they're conditionings deposited by your environment. What you believe is a reflection of certain social forces and pressures. In your case the two mutually exclusive social trends have produced a sort of stalemate. You're at war with yourself . . . You can't decide which side to join because elements of both exist in you.' The robot nodded wisely. 'But you've got to make a decision. You've got to resolve this conflict and act. You can't remain a spectator . . . you've got to be a participant. Nobody can be a spectator to life . . . and this is life.'

'You mean there's no other world but this business about sweat and teeth and hair?'

'Logically, there are other societies. But this is the one you were born into. This is your society . . . the only one you will ever have. You either live in it, or you don't live.'

Walsh got to his feet. 'In other words, *I* have to make the adjustment. Something has to give, and it's got to be me.'

'Afraid so, Don. It would be silly to expect everybody else to adjust to you, wouldn't it? Three and a half billion people would have to change just to please Don Walsh. You see, Don, you're not quite out of your infantile-selfish stage. You haven't quite got to the point of facing reality.' The robot smiled. 'But you will.'

Walsh started moodily from the office. 'I'll think it over.'

'It's for your own good, Don.'

At the door, Walsh turned to say something more. But the robot had clicked off; it was fading into darkness and silence, elbows still resting on the desk. The dimming overhead lights caught something he hadn't noticed before. The powercord that was the robot's umbilicus had a white plastic tag wired to it. In the semi-gloom he could make out the printed words.

PROPERTY OF THE FEDERAL COUNCIL
FOR PUBLIC USE ONLY

The robot, like everything else in the multi-family unit, was supplied by the controlling institutions of society. The analyst was a creature of the state, a bureaucrat with a desk

and job. Its function was to equate people like Don Walsh
with the world as it was.

But if he didn't listen to the unit analyst, who was he
supposed to listen to? Where else could he go?

Three days later the election took place. The glaring headline told him nothing he didn't already know; his office had
buzzed with the news all day. He put the paper away in his
coat pocket and didn't examine it until he got home.

PURISTS WIN BY LANDSLIDE
HORNEY AMENDMENT CERTAIN TO PASS

Walsh lay back wearily in his chair. In the kitchen Betty
was briskly preparing dinner. The pleasant clink of dishes
and the warm odor of cooking food drifted through the
bright little apartment.

'The Purists won,' Walsh said, when Betty appeared with
an armload of silver and cups. 'It's all over.'

'Jimmy will be happy,' Betty answered vaguely. 'I wonder
if Carl will be home in time for dinner.' She calculated
silently. 'Maybe I ought to run downramp for some more
coffee.'

'Don't you understand?' Walsh demanded. 'It's happened! The Purists have complete power!'

'I understand,' Betty answered peevishly. 'You don't have
to shout. Did you sign that petition thing? That Butte
Petition the Naturalists have been circulating?'

'No.'

'Thank God. I didn't think so; you never sign anything
anybody brings around.' She lingered at the kitchen door. 'I
hope Carl has sense enough to do something. I never did
like him sitting around guzzling beer and smelling like a pig
in summer.'

The door of the apartment opened and Carl hurried in,
flushed and scowling. 'Don't fix dinner for me, Betty. I'll be
at an emergency meeting.' He glanced briefly at Walsh.
'Now are you satisfied? If you'd put your back to the wheel,
maybe this wouldn't have happened.'

'How soon will they get the Amendment passed?' Walsh asked.

Carl bellowed with nervous laughter. 'They've already passed it.' He grabbed up an armload of papers from his desk and stuffed them in a waste-disposal slot. 'We've got informants at Purist headquarters. As soon as the new councilmen were sworn in they rammed the Amendment through. They want to catch us unawares.' He grinned starkly. 'But they won't.'

The door slammed and Carl's hurried footsteps diminished down the public hall.

'I've never seen him move so fast,' Betty remarked wonderingly.

Horror rose in Don Walsh as he listened to the rapid, lumbering footsteps of his brother-in-law. Outside the unit, Carl was climbing quickly into his surface car. The motor gunned, and Carl drove off. 'He's afraid,' Walsh said. 'He's in danger.'

'I guess he can take care of himself. He's pretty big.'

Walsh shakily lit a cigarette. 'Even your brother isn't that big. It doesn't seem possible they really mean this. Putting over an Amendment like this, forcing everybody to conform to their idea of what's right. But it's been in the cards for years . . . This is the last step on a large road.'

'I wish they'd get it over with, once and for all,' Betty complained. 'Was it always this way? I don't remember always hearing about politics when I was a child.'

'They didn't call it politics, back in those days. The industrialists hammered away at the people to buy and consume. It centered around this hair-sweat-teeth purity; the city people got it and developed an ideology around it.'

Betty set the table and brought in the dishes of food. 'You mean the Purist political movement was deliberately started?'

'They didn't realize what a hold it was getting on them.

They didn't know their children were growing up to take such things as underarm perspiration and white teeth and nice-looking hair as the most important things in the world. Things worth fighting and dying for. Things important enough to kill those who didn't agree.'

'The Naturalists were country people?'

'People who lived outside the cities and weren't conditioned by the stimuli.' Walsh shook his head irritably. 'Incredible, that one man will kill another over trivialities. All through history men murdering each other over verbal nonsense, meaningless slogans instilled in them by somebody else – who sits back and benefits.'

'It isn't meaningless if they believe in it.'

'It's meaningless to kill another man because he has halitosis! It's meaningless to beat up somebody because he hasn't had his sweat glands removed and artificial waste-excretion tubes installed. There's going to be senseless warfare; the Naturalists have weapons stored up at party headquarters. Men'll be just as dead as if they died for something real.'

'Time to eat, dear,' Betty said, indicating the table.

'I'm not hungry.'

'Stop sulking and eat. Or you'll have indigestion, and you know what that means.'

He knew what it meant, all right. It meant his life was in danger. One belch in the presence of a Purist and it was a life and death struggle. There was no room in the same world for men who belched and men who wouldn't tolerate men who belched. Something had to give . . . and it had already given. The Amendment had been passed: the Naturalists' days were numbered.

'Jimmy will be late tonight,' Betty said, as she helped herself to lamb chops, green peas, and creamed corn. 'There's some sort of Purist celebration. Speeches, parades, torch-light rallies.' She added wistfully, 'I guess we can't go down and watch, can we? It'll be pretty, all the lights and voices, and marching.'

'Go ahead.' Listlessly, Walsh spooned up his food. He ate without tasting. 'Enjoy yourself.'

They were still eating, when the door burst open and Carl entered briskly. 'Anything left for me?' he demanded.

Betty half-rose, astonished. 'Carl! You don't – smell any more.'

Carl seated himself and grabbed for the plate of lamb chops. Then he recollected, and daintily selected a small one, and a tiny portion of peas. 'I'm hungry,' he admitted, 'but not too hungry.' He ate carefully, quietly.

Walsh gazed at him dumbfounded. 'What the hell happened?' he demanded. 'Your hair – and your teeth and breath. *What did you do?*'

Without looking up, Carl answered, 'Party tactics. We're beating a strategical retreat. In the face of this Amendment, there's no point in doing something foolhardy. Hell, we don't intend to get slaughtered.' He sipped some luke-warm coffee. 'As a matter of fact, we've gone underground.'

Walsh slowly lowered his fork. 'You mean you're not going to fight?'

'Hell, no. It's suicide.' Carl glanced furtively around. 'Now listen to me. I'm completely in conformity with the provisions of the Horney Amendment; nobody can pin a thing on me. When the cops come snooping around, keep your mouths shut. The Amendment gives the right to recant, and that's technically what we've done. We're clean; they can't touch us. But let's just not say anything.' He displayed a small blue card. 'A Purist membership card. Backdated; we planned for any eventuality.'

'Oh, Carl!' Betty cried delightedly. 'I'm so glad. You look just – *wonderful*!'

Walsh said nothing.

'What's the matter?' Betty demanded. 'Isn't this what you wanted? You didn't want them to fight and kill each other—' Her voice rose shrilly. 'Won't anything satisfy you? This is what you wanted and you're still dissatisfied. What on earth more do you want?'

There was noise below the unit. Carl sat up straight, and for an instant color left his face. He would have begun sweating if it were still possible. 'That's the conformity police,' he said thickly. 'Just sit tight; they'll make a routine check and keep on going.'

'Oh dear,' Betty gasped. 'I hope they don't break anything. Maybe I better go and freshen up.'

'Just sit still,' Carl grated. 'There's no reason for them to suspect anything.'

When the door opened, Jimmy stood dwarfed by the green-tinted conformity police.

'There he is!' Jimmy shrilled, indicating Carl. 'He's a Naturalist official! *Smell* him!'

The police spread efficiently into the room. Standing around the immobile Carl, they examined him briefly, then moved away. 'No body odor,' the police sergeant disagreed. 'No halitosis. Hair thick and well-groomed.' He signalled, and Carl obediently opened his mouth. 'Teeth white, totally brushed. Nothing nonacceptable. No, this man is all right.'

Jimmy glared furiously at Carl. 'Pretty smart.'

Carl picked stoically at his plate of food and ignored the boy and the police.

'Apparently we've broken the core of Naturalist resistance,' the sergeant said into his neck-phone. 'At least in this area there's no organized opposition.'

'Good,' the phone answered. 'Your area was a stronghold. We'll go ahead and set up the compulsory purification machinery, though. It should be implemented as soon as possible.'

One of the cops turned his attention to Don Walsh. His nostrils twitched and then a harsh, oblique expression settled over his face. 'What's your name?' he demanded.

Walsh gave his name.

The police came cautiously around him. 'Body odor,' one noted. 'But hair fully restored and groomed. Open your mouth.'

Walsh opened his mouth.

'Teeth clean and white. But—' The cop sniffed. 'Faint halitosis . . . stomach variety. I don't get it. Is he a Naturalist or isn't he?'

'He's not a Purist,' the sergeant said. 'No Purist would have body odor. So he must be a Naturalist.'

Jimmy pushed forward. 'This man,' he explained, 'is only a fellow hiker. He's not a party member.'

'You know him?'

'He's – related to me,' Jimmy admitted.

The police took notes. 'He's been playing around with Naturalists, but he hasn't gone the whole way?'

'He's on the fence,' Jimmy agreed. 'A quasi-Naturalist. He can be salvaged; this shouldn't be a criminal case.'

'Remedial action,' the sergeant noted. 'All right, Walsh,' he addressed Walsh. 'Get your things and let's go. The Amendment provides compulsory purification for your type of person; let's not waste time.'

Walsh hit the sergeant in the jaw.

The sergeant sprawled foolishly, arms flapping, dazed with disbelief. The cops drew their guns hysterically and milled around the room shouting and knocking into each other. Betty began to scream wildly. Jimmy's shrill voice was lost in the general uproar.

Walsh grabbed up a table lamp and smashed it over a cop's head. The lights in the apartment flickered and died out; the room was a chaos of yelling blackness. Walsh encountered a body; he kicked with his knee and with a groan of pain the body settled down. For a moment he was lost in the seething din; then his fingers found the door. He pried it open and scrambled out into the public corridor.

One shape followed, as Walsh reached the descent lift. '*Why?*' Jimmy wailed unhappily. 'I had it all fixed – you didn't have to worry!'

His thin, metallic voice faded as the lift plunged down the well to the ground floor. Behind Walsh, the police were coming cautiously out into the hall; the sound of their boots echoed dismally after him.

He examined his watch. Probably, he had fifteen or twenty minutes. They'd get him, then; it was inevitable. Taking a deep breath, he stepped from the lift and as calmly as possible walked down the dark, deserted commercial corridor, between the rows of black store-entrances.

Charley was lit up and animate when Walsh entered the ante-chamber. Two men were waiting, and a third was being interviewed. But at the sight of the expression on Walsh's face the robot waved him instantly in.

'What is it, Don?' it asked seriously, indicating a chair. 'Sit down and tell me what's on your mind.'

Walsh told it.

When he was finished, the analyst sat back and gave a low, soundless whistle. 'That's a felony, Don. They'll freeze you for that; it's a provision of the new Amendment.'

'I know,' Walsh agreed. He felt no emotion. For the first time in years the ceaseless swirl of feelings and thoughts had been purged from his mind. He was a little tired and that was all.

The robot shook its head. 'Well, Don, you're finally off the fence. That's something, at least; you're finally moving.' It reached thoughtfully into the top drawer of its desk and got out a pad. 'Is the police pick-up van here, yet?'

'I heard sirens as I came in the ante-room. It's on its way.'

The robot's metal fingers drummed restlessly on the surface of the big mahogany desk. 'Your sudden release of inhibition marks the moment of psychological integration. You're not undecided anymore, are you?'

'No,' Walsh said.

'Good. Well, it had to come sooner or later. I'm sorry it had to come this way, though.'

'I'm not,' Walsh said. 'This was the only way possible. It's clear to me, now. Being undecided isn't necessarily a negative thing. Not seeing anything in slogans and organized parties and beliefs and dying can be a belief worth dying for, in itself. I thought I was without a creed . . . now I realize I have a very strong creed.'

The robot wasn't listening. It scribbled something on its pad, signed it, and then expertly tore it off. 'Here.' It handed the paper briskly to Walsh.

'What's this?' Walsh demanded.

'I don't want anything to interfere with your therapy. You're finally coming around – and we want to keep moving.' The robot got quickly to its feet. 'Good luck, Don. Show that to the police; if there's any trouble have them call me.'

The slip was a voucher from the Federal Psychiatric Board. Walsh turned it over numbly. 'You mean this'll get me off?'

'You were acting compulsively; you weren't responsible. There'll be a cursory examination, of course, but nothing to worry about.' The robot slapped him good-naturedly on the back. 'It was your final neurotic act . . . now you're free. That was the pent-up stuff; strictly a symbolic assertion of libido – with no political significance.'

'I see,' Walsh said.

The robot propelled him firmly toward the external exit. 'Now go on out there and give the slip to them.' From its metal chest the robot popped a small bottle. 'And take one of these capsules before you go to sleep. Nothing serious, just a mild sedative to quiet your nerves. Everything will be all right; I'll expect to see you again, soon. And keep this in mind: we're finally making some real progress.'

Walsh found himself outside in the night darkness. A police van was pulled up at the entrance of the unit, a vast ominous black shape against the dead sky. A crowd of curious people had collected at a safe distance, trying to make out what was going on.

Walsh automatically put the bottle of pills away in his coat pocket. He stood for a time breathing the chill night air, the cold clear smell of darkness and evening. Above his head a few bright pale stars glittered remotely.

'Hey,' one of the policemen shouted. He flashed his light suspiciously in Walsh's face. 'Come over here.'

'That looks like him,' another said. 'Come on, buddy. Make it snappy.'

Walsh brought out the voucher Charley had given him. 'I'm coming,' he answered. As he walked up to the policeman he carefully tore the paper to shreds and tossed the shreds to the night wind. The wind picked the shreds up and scattered them away.

'What the hell did you do?' one of the cops demanded.

'Nothing,' Walsh answered. 'I just threw away some waste paper. Something I won't be needing.'

'What a strange one this one is,' a cop muttered, as they froze Walsh with their cold beams. 'He gives me the creeps.'

'Be glad we don't get more like him,' another said. 'Except for a few guys like this, everything's going fine.'

Walsh's inert body was tossed in the van and the doors slammed shut. Disposal machinery immediately began consuming his body and reducing it to basic mineral elements. A moment later, the van was on its way to the next call.

Autofac

I

Tension hung over the three waiting men. They smoked, paced back and forth, kicked aimlessly at weeds growing by the side of the road. A hot noonday sun glared down on brown fields, rows of neat plastic houses, the distant line of mountains to the west.

'Almost time,' Earl Perine said, knotting his skinny hands together. 'It varies according to the load, a half second for every additional pound.'

Bitterly, Morrison answered, 'You've got it plotted? You're as bad as it is. Let's pretend it just *happens* to be late.'

The third man said nothing. O'Neill was visiting from another settlement; he didn't know Perine and Morrison well enough to argue with them. Instead, he crouched down and arranged the papers clipped to his aluminum checkboard. In the blazing sun, O'Neill's arms were tanned, furry, glistening with sweat. Wiry, with tangled gray hair, horn-rimmed glasses, he was older than the other two. He wore slacks, a sports shirt and crepe-soled shoes. Between his fingers, his fountain pen glittered, metallic and efficient.

'What're you writing?' Perine grumbled.

'I'm laying out the procedure we're going to employ,' O'Neill said mildly. 'Better to systemize it now, instead of trying at random. We want to know what we tried and what didn't work. Otherwise we'll go around in a circle. The problem we have here is one of communication; that's how I see it.'

'Communication,' Morrison agreed in his deep, chesty voice. 'Yes, we can't get in touch with the damn thing. It comes, leaves off its load and goes on – there's no contact between us and it.'

'It's a machine,' Perine said excitedly. 'It's dead – blind and deaf.'

'But it's in contact with the outside world,' O'Neill pointed out. 'There has to be some way to get to it. Specific semantic signals are meaningful to it; all we have to do is find those signals. Rediscover, actually. Maybe half a dozen out of a billion possibilities.'

A low rumble interrupted the three men. They glanced up, wary and alert. The time had come.

'Here it is,' Perine said. 'Okay, wise guy, let's see you make one single change in its routine.'

The truck was massive, rumbling under its tightly packed load. In many ways, it resembled conventional human-operated transportation vehicles, but with one exception – there was no driver's cabin. The horizontal surface was a loading stage, and the part that would normally be the headlights and radiator grill was a fibrous spongelike mass of receptors, the limited sensory apparatus of this mobile utility extension.

Aware of the three men, the truck slowed to a halt, shifted gears and pulled on its emergency brake. A moment passed as relays moved into action; then a portion of the loading surface tilted and a cascade of heavy cartons spilled down onto the roadway. With the objects fluttered a detailed inventory sheet.

'You know what to do,' O'Neill said rapidly. 'Hurry up, before it gets out of here.'

Expertly, grimly, the three men grabbed up the deposited cartons and ripped the protective wrappers from them. Objects gleamed: a binocular microscope, a portable radio, heaps of plastic dishes, medical supplies, razor blades, clothing, food. Most of the shipment, as usual, was food. The three men systematically began smashing objects. In a few minutes, there was nothing but a chaos of debris littered around them.

'That's that,' O'Neill panted, stepping back. He fumbled for his checksheet. 'Now let's see what it does.'

The truck had begun to move away; abruptly it stopped and backed toward them. Its receptors had taken in the fact that the three men had demolished the dropped-off portion of the load. It spun in a grinding half circle and came around to face its receptor bank in their direction. Up went its antenna; it had begun communicating with the factory. Instructions were on the way.

A second, identical load was tilted and shoved off the truck.

'We failed,' Perine groaned as a duplicate inventory sheet fluttered after the new load. 'We destroyed all that stuff for nothing.'

'What now?' Morrison asked O'Neill. 'What's the next stratagem on our board?'

'Give me a hand.' O'Neill grabbed up a carton and lugged it back to the truck. Sliding the carton onto the platform, he turned for another. The other two men followed clumsily after him. They put the load back onto the truck. As the truck started forward, the last square box was again in place.

The truck hesitated. Its receptors registered the return of its load. From within its works came a low sustained buzzing.

'This may drive it crazy,' O'Neill commented, sweating. 'It went through its operation and accomplished nothing.'

The truck made a short, abortive move toward going on. Then it swung purposefully around and, in a blur of speed, again dumped the load onto the road.

'Get them!' O'Neill yelled. The three men grabbed up the cartons and feverishly reloaded them. But as fast as the cartons were shoved back on the horizontal stage, the truck's grapples tilted them down its far-side ramps and onto the road.

'No use,' Morrison said, breathing hard. 'Water through a sieve.'

'We're licked,' Perine gasped in wretched agreement, 'like always. We humans lose every time.'

The truck regarded them calmly, its receptors blank and impassive. It was doing its job. The planetwide network of automatic factories was smoothly performing the task imposed on it five years before, in the early days of the Total Global Conflict.

'There it goes,' Morrison observed dismally. The truck's antenna had come down; it shifted into low gear and released its parking brake.

'One last try,' O'Neill said. He swept up one of the cartons and ripped it open. From it he dragged a ten-gallon milk tank and unscrewed the lid. 'Silly as it seems.'

'This is absurd,' Perine protested. Reluctantly, he found a cup among the littered debris and dipped it into the milk. 'A kid's game!'

The truck had paused to observe them.

'Do it,' O'Neill ordered sharply. 'Exactly the way we practiced it.'

The three of them drank quickly from the milk tank, visibly allowing the milk to spill down their chins; there had to be no mistaking what they were doing.

As planned, O'Neill was the first. His face twisting in revulsion, he hurled the cup away and violently spat the milk into the road.

'God's sake!' he choked.

The other two did the same; stamping and loudly cursing, they kicked over the milk tank and glared accusingly at the truck.

'It's no good!' Morrison roared.

Curious, the truck came slowly back. Electronic synapses clicked and whirred, responding to the situation; its antenna shot up like a flagpole.

'I think this is it,' O'Neill said, trembling. As the truck watched, he dragged out a second milk tank, unscrewed its lid and tasted the contents. 'The same!' he shouted at the truck. 'It's just as bad!'

From the truck popped a metal cylinder. The cylinder dropped at Morrison's feet; he quickly snatched it up and tore it open.

STATE NATURE OF DEFECT

The instruction sheets listed rows of possible defects, with neat boxes by each; a punch-stick was included to indicate the particular deficiency of the product.

'What'll I check?' Morrison asked. 'Contaminated? Bacterial? Sour? Rancid? Incorrectly labeled? Broken? Crushed? Cracked? Bent? Soiled?'

Thinking rapidly, O'Neill said, 'Don't check any of them. The factory's undoubtedly ready to test and re-sample. It'll make its own analysis and then ignore us.' His face glowed as frantic inspiration came. 'Write in that blank at the bottom. It's an open space for further data.'

'Write what?'

O'Neill said, 'Write: *the product is thoroughly pizzled.*'

'What's that?' Perine demanded, baffled.

'Write it! It's a semantic garble – the factory won't be able to understand it. Maybe we can jam the works.'

With O'Neill's pen, Morrison carefully wrote that the milk was pizzled. Shaking his head, he resealed the cylinder and returned it to the truck. The truck swept up the milk tanks and slammed its railing tidily into place. With a shriek of tires, it hurtled off. From its slot, a final cylinder bounced; the truck hurriedly departed, leaving the cylinder lying in the dust.

O'Neill got it open and held up the paper for the others to see.

A FACTORY REPRESENTATIVE
WILL BE SENT OUT.
BE PREPARED TO SUPPLY COMPLETE DATA
ON PRODUCT DEFICIENCY.

For a moment, the three men were silent. Then Perine began to giggle. 'We did it. We contacted it. We got across.'

'We sure did,' O'Neill agreed. 'It never heard of a product being pizzled.'

Cut into the base of the mountains lay the vast metallic cube of the Kansas City factory. Its surface was corroded, pitted with radiation pox, cracked and scarred from the five years of war that had swept over it. Most of the factory was buried subsurface, only its entrance stages visible. The truck was a speck rumbling at high speed toward the expanse of black metal. Presently an opening formed in the uniform surface; the truck plunged into it and disappeared inside. The entrance snapped shut.

'Now the big job remains,' O'Neill said. 'Now we have to persuade it to close down operations – to shut itself off.'

II

Judith O'Neill served hot black coffee to the people sitting around the living room. Her husband talked while the others listened. O'Neill was as close to being an authority on the autofac system as could still be found.

In his own area, the Chicago region, he had shorted out the protective fence of the local factory long enough to get away with data tapes stored in its posterior brain. The factory, of course, had immediately reconstructed a better type of fence. But he had shown that the factories were not infallible.

'The Institute of Applied Cybernetics,' O'Neill explained, 'had complete control over the network. Blame the war. Blame the big noise along the lines of communication that wiped out the knowledge we need. In any case, the Institute failed to transmit its information to us, so we can't transmit our information to the factories – the news that the war is over and we're ready to resume control of industrial operations.'

'And meanwhile,' Morrison added sourly, 'the damn

network expands and consumes more of our natural resources all the time.'

'I get the feeling,' Judith said, 'that if I stamped hard enough, I'd fall right down into a factory tunnel. They must have mines everywhere by now.'

'Isn't there some limiting injunction?' Perine asked nervously. 'Were they set up to expand indefinitely?'

'Each factory is limited to its own operational area,' O'Neill said, 'but the network itself is unbounded. It can go on scooping up our resources forever. The Institute decided it gets top priority; we mere people come second.'

'Will there be *anything* left for us?' Morrison wanted to know.

'Not unless we can stop the network's operations. It's already used up half a dozen basic minerals. Its search teams are out all the time, from every factory, looking everywhere for some last scrap to drag home.'

'What would happen if tunnels from two factories crossed each other?'

O'Neill shrugged. 'Normally, that won't happen. Each factory has its own special section of our planet, its own private cut of the pie for its exclusive use.'

'But it *could* happen.'

'Well, they're raw material-tropic; as long as there's anything left, they'll hunt it down.' O'Neill pondered the idea with growing interest. 'It's something to consider. I suppose as things get scarcer—'

He stopped talking. A figure had come into the room; it stood silently by the door, surveying them all.

In the dull shadows, the figure looked almost human. For a brief moment, O'Neill thought it was a settlement late-comer. Then, as it moved forward, he realized that it was only quasi-human: a functional upright biped chassis, with data-receptors mounted at the top, effectors and proprioceptors mounted in a downward worm that ended in floor-grippers. Its resemblance to a human being was testimony to nature's efficiency; no sentimental imitation was intended.

The factory representative had arrived.

It began without preamble. 'This is a data-collecting machine capable of communicating on an oral basis. It contains both broadcasting and receiving apparatus and can integrate facts relevant to its line of inquiry.'

The voice was pleasant, confident. Obviously it was a tape, recorded by some Institute technician before the war. Coming from the quasi-human shape, it sounded grotesque; O'Neill could vividly imagine the dead young man whose cheerful voice now issued from the mechanical mouth of this upright construction of steel and wiring.

'One word of caution,' the pleasant voice continued. 'It is fruitless to consider this receptor human and to engage it in discussions for which it is not equipped. Although purposeful, it is not capable of conceptual thought; it can only reassemble material already available to it.'

The optimistic voice clicked out and a second voice came on. It resembled the first, but now there were no intonations or personal mannerisms. The machine was utilizing the dead man's phonetic speech-pattern for its own communication.

'Analysis of the rejected product,' it stated, 'shows no foreign elements or noticeable deterioration. The product meets the continual testing-standards employed throughout the network. Rejection is therefore on a basis outside the test area; standards not available to the network are being employed.'

'That's right,' O'Neill agreed. Weighing his words with care, he continued, 'We found the milk substandard. We want nothing to do with it. We insist on more careful output.'

The machine responded presently. 'The semantic content of the term "pizzled" is unfamiliar to the network. It does not exist in the taped vocabulary. Can you present a factual analysis of the milk in terms of specific elements present or absent?'

'No,' O'Neill said warily; the game he was playing was

intricate and dangerous. ' "Pizzled" is an overall term. It can't be reduced to chemical constituents.'

'What does "pizzled" signify?' the machine asked. 'Can you define it in terms of alternate semantic symbols?'

O'Neill hesitated. The representative had to be steered from its special inquiry to more general regions, to the ultimate problem of closing down the network. If he could pry it open at any point, get the theoretical discussion started . . .

' "Pizzled," ' he stated, 'means the condition of a product that is manufactured when no need exists. It indicates the rejection of objects on the grounds that they are no longer wanted.'

The representative said, 'Network analysis shows a need of high-grade pasteurized milk-substitute in this area. There is no alternate source; the network controls all the synthetic mammary-type equipment in existence.' It added, 'Original taped instructions describe milk as an essential to human diet.'

O'Neill was being outwitted; the machine was returning the discussion to the specific. 'We've decided,' he said desperately, 'that we don't *want* any more milk. We'd prefer to go without it, at least until we can locate cows.'

'That is contrary to the network tapes,' the representative objected. 'There are no cows. All milk is produced synthetically.'

'Then we'll produce it synthetically ourselves,' Morrison broke in impatiently. 'Why can't we take over the machines? My God, we're not children! We can run our own lives!'

The factory representative moved toward the door. 'Until such time as your community finds other sources of milk supply, the network will continue to supply you. Analytical and evaluating apparatus will remain in this area, conducting the customary random sampling.'

Perine shouted futilely, 'How can we find other sources? You have the whole setup! You're running the whole show!'

Following after it, he bellowed, 'You say we're not ready to run things – you claim we're not capable. How do you know? You don't give us a chance! We'll never have a chance!'

O'Neill was petrified. The machine was leaving; its one-track mind had completely triumphed.

'Look,' he said hoarsely, blocking its way. 'We want you to shut down, understand. We want to take over your equipment and run it ourselves. The war's over with. Damn it, you're not needed anymore!'

The factory representative paused briefly at the door. 'The inoperative cycle,' it said, 'is not geared to begin until network production merely duplicates outside production. There is at this time, according to our continual sampling, no outside production. Therefore network production continues.'

Without warning, Morrison swung the steel pipe in his hand. It slashed against the machine's shoulder and burst through the elaborate network of sensory apparatus that made up its chest. The tank of receptors shattered; bits of glass, wiring and minute parts showered everywhere.

'It's a paradox!' Morrison yelled. 'A word game – a semantic game they're pulling on us. The Cyberneticists have it rigged.' He raised the pipe and again brought it down savagely on the unprotesting machine. 'They've got us hamstrung. We're completely helpless.'

The room was in uproar. 'It's the only way,' Perine gasped as he pushed past O'Neill. 'We'll have to destroy them – it's the network or us.' Grabbing down a lamp, he hurled it in the 'face' of the factory representative. The lamp and the intricate surface of plastic burst; Perine waded in, groping blindly for the machine. Now all the people in the room were closing furiously around the upright cylinder, their impotent resentment boiling over. The machine sank down and disappeared as they dragged it to the floor.

Trembling, O'Neill turned away. His wife caught hold of his arm and led him to the side of the room.

'The idiots,' he said dejectedly. 'They can't destroy it; they'll only teach it to build more defenses. They're making the whole problem worse.'

Into the living room rolled a network repair team. Expertly, the mechanical units detached themselves from the half-track mother-bug and scurried toward the mound of struggling humans. They slid between people and rapidly burrowed. A moment later, the inert carcass of the factory representative was dragged into the hopper of the mother-bug. Parts were collected, torn remnants gathered up and carried off. The plastic strut and gear was located. Then the units restationed themselves on the bug and the team departed.

Through the open door came a second factory representative, an exact duplicate of the first. And outside in the hall stood two more upright machines. The settlement had been combed at random by a corps of representatives. Like a horde of ants, the mobile data-collecting machines had filtered through the town until, by chance, one of them had come across O'Neill.

'Destruction of network mobile data-gathering equipment is detrimental to best human interests,' the factory representative informed the roomful of people. 'Raw material intake is at a dangerously low ebb; what basic materials still exist should be utilized in the manufacture of consumer commodities.'

O'Neill and the machine stood facing each other.

'Oh?' O'Neill said softly. 'That's interesting. I wonder what you're lowest on – and what you'd really be willing to fight for.'

Helicopter rotors whined tinnily above O'Neill's head; he ignored them and peered through the cabin window at the ground not far below.

Slag and ruins stretched everywhere. Weeds poked their way up, sickly stalks among which insects scuttled. Here and there, rat colonies were visible: matted hovels con-

structed of bone and rubble. Radiation had mutated the
rats, along with most insects and animals. A little farther,
O'Neill identified a squadron of birds pursuing a ground
squirrel. The squirrel dived into a carefully prepared crack
in the surface of slag and the birds turned, thwarted.

'You think we'll ever have it rebuilt?' Morrison asked. 'It
makes me sick to look at it.'

'In time,' O'Neill answered. 'Assuming, of course, that
we get industrial control back. And assuming that anything
remains to work with. At best, it'll be slow. We'll have to
inch out from the settlements.'

To the right was a human colony, tattered scarecrows,
gaunt and emaciated, living among the ruins of what had
once been a town. A few acres of barren soil had been
cleared; drooping vegetables wilted in the sun, chickens
wandered listlessly here and there, and a fly-bothered
horse lay panting in the shade of a crude shed.

'Ruins-squatters,' O'Neill said gloomily. 'Too far from
the network – not tangent to any of the factories.'

'It's their own fault,' Morrison told him angrily. 'They
could come into one of the settlements.'

'That was their town. They're trying to do what *we're*
trying to do – build up things again on their own. But
they're starting now, without tools or machines, with their
bare hands, nailing together bits of rubble. And it won't
work. We need machines. We can't repair ruins; we've got
to start industrial production.'

Ahead lay a series of broken hills, chipped remains that
had once been a ridge. Beyond stretched out the titanic ugly
sore of an H-bomb crater, half filled with stagnant water
and slime, a disease-ridden inland sea.

And beyond that – a glitter of busy motion.

'There,' O'Neill said tensely. He lowered the helicopter
rapidly. 'Can you tell which factory they're from?'

'They all look alike to me,' Morrison muttered, leaning
over to see. 'We'll have to wait and follow them back, when
they get a load.'

'*If* they get a load,' O'Neill corrected.

The autofac exploring crew ignored the helicopter buzz-ing overhead and concentrated on its job. Ahead of the main truck scuttled two tractors; they made their way up mounds of rubble, probes burgeoning like quills, shot down the far slope and disappeared into a blanket of ash that lay spread over the slag. The two scouts burrowed until only their antennas were visible. They burst up to the surface and scuttled on, their treads whirring and clanking.

'What are they after?' Morrison asked.

'God knows.' O'Neill leafed intently through the papers on his clipboard. 'We'll have to analyze all our back-order slips.'

Below them, the autofac exploring crew disappeared behind. The helicopter passed over a deserted stretch of sand and slag on which nothing moved. A grove of scrub-brush appeared and then, far to the right, a series of tiny moving dots.

A procession of automatic ore carts was racing over the bleak slag, a string of rapidly moving metal trucks that followed one another nose to tail. O'Neill turned the heli-copter toward them and a few minutes later it hovered above the mine itself.

Masses of squat mining equipment had made their way to the operations. Shafts had been sunk; empty carts waited in patient rows. A steady stream of loaded carts hurled toward the horizon, dribbling ore after them. Activity and the noise of machines hung over the area, an abrupt center of industry in the bleak wastes of slag.

'Here comes that exploring crew,' Morrison observed, peering back the way they had come. 'You think maybe they'll tangle?' He grinned. 'No, I guess it's too much to hope for.'

'It is this time,' O'Neill answered. 'They're looking for different substances, probably. And they're normally con-ditioned to ignore each other.'

The first of the exploring bugs reached the line of ore

carts. it veered slightly and continued its search; the carts traveled in their inexorable line as if nothing had happened.

Disappointed, Morrison turned away from the window and swore. 'No use. It's like each doesn't exist for the other.'

Gradually the exploring crew moved away from the line of carts, past the mining operations and over a ridge beyond. There was no special hurry; they departed without having reacted to the ore-gathering syndrome.

'Maybe they're from the same factory,' Morrison said hopefully.

O'Neill pointed to the antennas visible on the major mining equipment. 'Their vanes are turned at a different vector, so these represent two factories. It's going to be hard; we'll have to get it exactly right or there won't be any reaction.' He clicked on the radio and got hold of the monitor at the settlement. 'Any results on the consolidated back-order sheets?'

The operator put him through to the settlement governing offices.

'They're starting to come in,' Perine told him. 'As soon as we get sufficient samplings, we'll try to determine which raw materials which factories lack. It's going to be risky, trying to extrapolate from complex products. There may be a number of basic elements common to the various sublots.'

'What happens when we've identified the missing element?' Morrison asked O'Neill. 'What happens when we've got two tangent factories short on the same material?'

'Then,' O'Neill said grimly, 'we start collecting the material ourselves – even if we have to melt down every object in the settlements.'

III

In the moth-ridden darkness of night, a dim wind stirred, chill and faint. Dense underbrush rattled metallically. Here and there a nocturnal rodent prowled, its senses hyper-alert, peering, planning, seeking food.

The area was wild. No human settlements existed for miles; the entire region had been seared flat, cauterized by repeated H-bomb blasts. Somewhere in the murky darkness, a sluggish trickle of water made its way among slag and weeds, dripping thickly into what had once been an elaborate labyrinth of sewer mains. The pipes lay cracked and broken, jutting up into the night darkness, overgrown with creeping vegetation. The wind raised clouds of black ash that swirled and danced among the weeds. Once an enormous mutant wren stirred sleepily, pulled its crude protective night coat of rags around it and dozed off.

For a time, there was no movement. A streak of stars showed in the sky overhead, glowing starkly, remotely. Earl Perine shivered, peered up and huddled closer to the pulsing heat-element placed on the ground between the three men.

'Well?' Morrison challenged, teeth chattering.

O'Neill didn't answer. He finished his cigarette, crushed it against a mound of decaying slag and, getting out his lighter, lit another. The mass of tungsten – the bait – lay a hundred yards directly ahead of them.

During the last few days, both the Detroit and Pittsburgh factories had run short of tungsten. And in at least one sector, their apparatus overlapped. This sluggish heap represented precision cutting tools, parts ripped from electrical switches, high-quality surgical equipment, sections of permanent magnets, measuring devices – tungsten from every possible source, gathered feverishly from all the settlements.

Dark mist lay spread over the tungsten mound. Occasionally, a night moth fluttered down, attracted by the glow of reflected starlight. The moth hung momentarily, beat its elongated wings futilely against the interwoven tangle of metal and then drifted off, into the shadows of the thick-packed vines that rose up from the stumps of sewer pipes.

'Not a very damn pretty spot,' Perine said wryly.

'Don't kid yourself,' O'Neill retorted. 'This is the prettiest spot on Earth. This is the spot that marks the grave of the autofac network. People are going to come around here looking for it someday. There's going to be a plaque here a mile high.'

'You're trying to keep your morale up,' Morrison snorted. 'You don't believe they're going to slaughter themselves over a heap of surgical tools and light-bulb filaments. They've probably got a machine down in the bottom level that sucks tungsten out of rock.'

'Maybe,' O'Neill said, slapping at a mosquito. The insect dodged cannily and then buzzed over to annoy Perine. Perine swung viciously at it and squatted sullenly down against the damp vegetation.

And there was what they had come to see.

O'Neill realized with a start that he had been looking at it for several minutes without recognizing it. The search-bug lay absolutely still. It rested at the crest of a small rise of slag, its anterior end slightly raised, receptors fully extended. It might have been an abandoned hulk; there was no activity of any kind, no sign of life or consciousness. The search-bug fitted perfectly into the wasted, fire-drenched landscape. A vague tub of metal sheets and gears and flat treads, it rested and waited. And watched.

It was examining the heap of tungsten. The bait had drawn its first bite.

'Fish,' Perine said thickly. 'The line moved. I think the sinker dropped.'

'What the hell are you mumbling about?' Morrison grunted. And then he, too, saw the search-bug. 'Jesus,' he whispered. He half rose to his feet, massive body arched forward. 'Well, there's *one* of them. Now all we need is a unit from the other factory. Which do you suppose it is?'

O'Neill located the communication vane and traced its angle. 'Pittsburgh, so pray for Detroit . . . pray like mad.'

Satisfied, the search-bug detached itself and rolled

forward. Cautiously approaching the mound, it began a series of intricate maneuvers, rolling first one way and then another. The three watching men were mystified – until they glimpsed the first probing stalks of other search-bugs.

'Communication,' O'Neill said softly. 'Like bees.'

Now five Pittsburgh search-bugs were approaching the mound of tungsten products. Receptors waving excitedly, they increased their pace, scurrying in a sudden burst of discovery up the side of the mound to the top. A bug burrowed and rapidly disappeared. The whole mound shuddered; the bug was down inside, exploring the extent of the find.

Ten minutes later, the first Pittsburgh ore carts appeared and began industriously hurrying off with their haul.

'Damn it!' O'Neill said, agonized. 'They'll have it all before Detroit shows up.'

'Can't we do anything to slow them down?' Perine demanded helplessly. Leaping to his feet, he grabbed up a rock and heaved it at the nearest cart. The rock bounced off and the cart continued its work, unperturbed.

O'Neill got to his feet and prowled around, body rigid with impotent fury. Where were they? The autofacs were equal in all respects and the spot was the exact same linear distance from each center. Theoretically, the parties should have arrived simultaneously. Yet there was no sign of Detroit – and the final pieces of tungsten were being loaded before his eyes.

But then something streaked past him.

He didn't recognize it, for the object moved too quickly. It shot like a bullet among the tangled vines, raced up the side of the hill-crest, poised for an instant to aim itself and hurtled down the far side. It smashed directly into the lead cart. Projectile and victim shattered in an abrupt burst of sound.

Morrison leaped up. 'What the hell?'

'That's it!' Perine screamed, dancing around and waving his skinny arms. 'It's Detroit!'

A second Detroit search-bug appeared, hesitated as it took in the situation, and then flung itself furiously at the retreating Pittsburgh carts. Fragments of tungsten scattered everywhere – parts, wiring, broken plates, gears and springs and bolts of the two antagonists flew in all directions. The remaining carts wheeled screechingly; one of them dumped its load and rattled off at top speed. A second followed, still weighed down with tungsten. A Detroit search-bug caught up with it, spun directly in its path and neatly overturned it. Bug and cart rolled down a shallow trench, into a stagnant pool of water. Dripping and glistening, the two of them struggled, half submerged.

'Well,' O'Neill said unsteadily, 'we did it. We can start back home.' His legs felt weak. 'Where's our vehicle?'

As he gunned the truck motor, something flashed a long way off, something large and metallic, moving over the dead slag and ash. It was a dense clot of carts, a solid expanse of heavy-duty ore carriers racing to the scene. Which factory were they from?

It didn't matter, for out of the thick tangle of black dripping vines, a web of counter-extensions was creeping to meet them. Both factories were assembling their mobile units. From all directions, bugs slithered and crept, closing in around the remaining heap of tungsten. Neither factory was going to let needed raw material get away; neither was going to give up its find. Blindly, mechanically, in the grip of inflexible directives, the two opponents labored to assemble superior forces.

'Come on,' Morrison said urgently. 'Let's get out of here. All hell is bursting loose.'

O'Neill hastily turned the truck in the direction of the settlement. They began rumbling through the darkness on their way back. Every now and then, a metallic shape shot by them, going in the opposite direction.

'Did you see the load in that last cart?' Perine asked, worried. 'It wasn't empty.'

Neither were the carts that followed it, a whole

procession of bulging supply carriers directed by an elaborate high-level surveying unit.

'Guns,' Morrison said, eyes wide with apprehension. 'They're taking in weapons. But who's going to use them?'

'They are,' O'Neill answered. He indicated a movement to their right. 'Look over there. This is something we hadn't expected.'

They were seeing the first factory representative move into action.

As the truck pulled into the Kansas City settlement, Judith hurried breathlessly toward them. Fluttering in her hand was a strip of metal-foil paper.

'What is it?' O'Neill demanded, grabbing it from her.

'Just come.' His wife struggled to catch her breath. 'A mobile car – raced up, dropped it off – and left. Big excitement. Golly, the factory's – a blaze of lights. You can see it for miles.'

O'Neill scanned the paper. It was a factory certification for the last group of settlement-placed orders, a total tabulation of requested and factory-analyzed needs. Stamped across the list in heavy black type were six foreboding words:

ALL SHIPMENTS SUSPENDED UNTIL FURTHER NOTICE

Letting out his breath harshly, O'Neill handed the paper over to Perine. 'No more consumer goods,' he said ironically, a nervous grin twitching across his face. 'The network's going on a wartime footing.'

'Then we did it?' Morrison asked haltingly.

'That's right,' O'Neill said. Now that the conflict had been sparked, he felt a growing, frigid terror. 'Pittsburgh and Detroit are in it to the finish. It's too late for us to change our minds, now – they're lining up allies.'

IV

Cool morning sunlight lay across the ruined plain of black metallic ash. The ash smoldered a dull, unhealthy red; it was still warm.

'Watch your step,' O'Neill cautioned. Grabbing hold of his wife's arm, he led her from the rusty, sagging truck, up onto the top of a pile of strewn concrete blocks, the scattered remains of a pillbox installation. Earl Perine followed, making his way carefully, hesitantly.

Behind them, the dilapidated settlement lay spread out, a disorderly checkerboard of houses, buildings and streets. Since the autofac network had closed down its supply and maintenance, the human settlements had fallen into semi-barbarism. The commodities that remained were broken and only partly usable. It had been over a year since the last mobile factory truck had appeared, loaded with food, tools, clothing and repair parts. From the flat expanse of dark concrete and metal at the foot of the mountains, nothing had emerged in their direction.

Their wish had been granted – they were cut off, detached from the network.

On their own.

Around the settlement grew ragged fields of wheat and tattered stalks of sun-baked vegetables. Crude handmade tools had been distributed, primitive artifacts hammered out with great labor by the various settlements. The settlements were linked only by horsedrawn carts and by the slow stutter of the telegraph key.

They had managed to keep their organization, though. Goods and services were exchanged on a slow, steady basis. Basic commodities were produced and distributed. The clothing that O'Neill and his wife and Earl Perine wore was coarse and unbleached, but sturdy. And they had managed to convert a few of the trucks from gasoline to wood.

'Here we are,' O'Neill said. 'We can see from here.'

'Is it worth it?' Judith asked, exhausted. Bending down, she plucked aimlessly at her shoe, trying to dig a pebble from the soft hide sole. 'It's a long way to come, to see something we've seen every day for thirteen months.'

'True,' O'Neill admitted, his hand briefly resting on his wife's limp shoulder. 'But this may be the last. And that's what we want to see.'

In the gray sky above them, a swift circling dot of opaque black moved. High, remote, the dot spun and darted, following an intricate and wary course. Gradually, its gyrations moved it toward the mountains and the bleak expanse of bomb-rubbled structure sunk in their base.

'San Francisco,' O'Neill explained. 'One of those long-range hawk projectiles, all the way from the West Coast.'

'And you think it's the last?' Perine asked.

'It's the only one we've seen this month.' O'Neill seated himself and began sprinkling dried bits of tobacco into a trench of brown paper. 'And we used to see hundreds.'

'Maybe they have something better,' Judith suggested. She found a smooth rock and tiredly seated herself. 'Could it be?'

Her husband smiled ironically. 'No. They don't have anything better.'

The three of them were tensely silent. Above them, the circling dot of black drew closer. There was no sign of activity from the flat surface of metal and concrete; the Kansas City factory remained inert, totally unresponsive. A few billows of warm ash drifted across it and one end was partly submerged in rubble. The factory had taken numerous direct hits. Across the plain, the furrows of its subsurface tunnels lay exposed, clogged with debris and the dark, water-seeking tendrils of tough vines.

'Those damn vines,' Perine grumbled, picking at an old sore on his unshaven chin. 'They're taking over the world.'

Here and there around the factory, the demolished ruin of a mobile extension rusted in the morning dew. Carts, trucks, search-bugs, factory representatives, weapons carriers, guns, supply trains, subsurface projectiles, indiscriminate parts of machinery mixed and fused together in shapeless piles. Some had been destroyed returning to the factory; others had been contacted as they emerged, fully loaded, heavy with equipment. The factory itself – what remained of it – seemed to have settled more deeply into the earth. Its upper surface was barely visible, almost lost in drifting ash.

In four days, there had been no known activity, no visible movement of any sort.

'It's dead,' Perine said. 'You can see it's dead.'

O'Neill didn't answer. Squatting down, he made himself comfortable and prepared to wait. In his own mind, he was sure that some fragment of automation remained in the eroded factory. Time would tell. He examined his wristwatch, it was eight thirty. In the old days, the factory would be starting its daily routine. Processions of trucks and varied mobile units would be coming to the surface, loaded with supplies, to begin their expeditions to the human settlements.

Off to the right, something stirred. He quickly turned his attention to it.

A single battered ore-gathering cart was creeping clumsily toward the factory. One last damaged mobile unit trying to complete its task. The cart was virtually empty; a few meager scraps of metal lay strewn in its hold. A scavenger . . . the metal was sections ripped from destroyed equipment encountered on the way. Feebly, like a blind metallic insect, the cart approached the factory. Its progress was incredibly jerky. Every now and then, it halted, bucked and quivered, and wandered aimlessly off the path.

'Control is bad,' Judith said, with a touch of horror in her voice. 'The factory's having trouble guiding it back.'

Yes, he had seen that. Around New York, the factory had lost its high-frequency transmitter completely. Its mobile units had floundered in crazy gyrations, racing in random circles, crashing against rocks and trees, sliding into gullies, overturning, finally unwinding and becoming reluctantly inanimate.

The ore cart reached the edge of the ruined plain and halted briefly. Above it, the dot of black still circled the sky. For a time, the cart remained frozen.

'The factory's trying to decide,' Perine said. 'It needs the material, but it's afraid of that hawk up there.'

The factory debated and nothing stirred. Then the ore cart again resumed its unsteady crawl. It left the tangle of vines and started out across the blasted open plain. Painfully, with infinite caution, it headed toward the slab of dark concrete and metal at the base of the mountains.

The hawk stopped circling.

'Get down!' O'Neill said sharply. 'They've got those rigged with the new bombs.'

His wife and Perine crouched down beside him and the three of them peered warily at the plain and the metal insect crawling laboriously across it. In the sky, the hawk swept in a straight line until it hung directly over the cart. Then, without a sound or warning, it came down in a straight dive. Hands to her face, Judith shrieked, 'I can't watch! It's awful! Like wild animals!'

'It's not after the cart,' O'Neill grated.

As the airborne projectile dropped, the cart put on a burst of desperate speed. It raced noisily toward the factory, clanking and rattling, trying in a last futile attempt to reach safely. Forgetting the menace above, the frantically eager factory opened up and guided its mobile unit directly inside. And the hawk had what it wanted.

Before the barrier could close, the hawk swooped down in a long glide parallel with the ground. As the cart disappeared into the depths of the factory, the hawk shot after it, a swift shimmer of metal that hurtled past the clanking cart. Suddenly aware, the factory snapped the barrier shut. Grotesquely, the cart struggled; it was caught fast in the half-closed entrance.

But whether it freed itself didn't matter. There was a dull

rumbling stir. The ground moved, billowed, then settled back. A deep shock wave passed beneath the three watching human beings. From the factory rose a single column of black smoke. The surface of concrete split like a dried pod; it shriveled and broke, and dribbled shattered bits of itself in a shower of ruin. The smoke hung for a while, drifting aimlessly away with the morning wind.

The factory was a fused, gutted wreck. It had been penetrated and destroyed.

O'Neill got stiffly to his feet. 'That's all. All over with. We've got what we set out after – we've destroyed the autofac network.' He glanced at Perine. 'Or was that what we were after?'

They looked toward the settlement that lay behind them. Little remained of the orderly rows of houses and streets of the previous years. Without the network, the settlement had rapidly decayed. The original prosperous neatness had dissipated; the settlement was shabby, ill-kept.

'Of course,' Perine said haltingly. 'Once we get into the factories and start setting up our own assembly lines . . .'

'Is there anything left?' Judith inquired.

'There must be something left. My God, there were levels going down miles!'

'Some of those bombs they developed toward the end were awfully big,' Judith pointed out. 'Better than anything we had in our war.'

'Remember that camp we saw? The ruins-squatters?'

'I wasn't along,' Perine said.

'They were like wild animals. Eating roots and larvae. Sharpening rocks, tanning hides. Savagery, bestiality.'

'But that's what people like that want,' Perine answered defensively

'Do they? Do we want this?' O'Neill indicated the straggling settlement. 'Is this what we set out looking for, that day we collected the tungsten? Or that day we told the factory truck its milk was—' He couldn't remember the word.

'Pizzled,' Judith supplied.

'Come on,' O'Neill said. 'Let's get started. Let's see what's left of that factory – left for us.'

They approached the ruined factory late in the afternoon. Four trucks rumbled shakily up to the rim of the gutted pit and halted, motors steaming, tailpipes dripping. Wary and alert, workmen scrambled down and stepped gingerly across the hot ash.

'Maybe it's too soon,' one of them objected.

O'Neill had no intention of waiting. 'Come on,' he ordered. Grabbing up a flashlight, he stepped down into the crater.

The sheltered hull of the Kansas City factory lay directly ahead. In its gutted mouth, the ore cart still hung caught, but it was no longer struggling. Beyond the cart was an ominous pool of gloom. O'Neill flashed his light through the entrance; the tangled, jagged remains of upright supports were visible.

'We want to get down deep,' he said to Morrison, who prowled cautiously beside him. 'If there's anything left, it's at the bottom.'

Morrison grunted. 'Those boring moles from Atlanta got most of the deep layers.'

'Until the others got their mines sunk.' O'Neill stepped carefully through the sagging entrance, climbed a heap of debris that had been tossed against the slit from inside, and found himself within the factory – an expanse of confused wreckage, without pattern or meaning.

'Entropy,' Morrison breathed, oppressed. 'The thing it always hated. The thing it was built to fight. Random particles everywhere. No purpose to it.'

'Down underneath,' O'Neill said stubbornly, 'we may find some sealed enclaves. I know they got so they were dividing up into autonomous sections, trying to preserve repair units intact, to re-form the composite factory.'

'The moles got most of them, too,' Morrison observed, but he lumbered after O'Neill.

Behind them, the workmen came slowly. A section of wreckage shifted ominously and a shower of hot fragments cascaded down.

'You men get back to the trucks,' O'Neill said. 'No sense endangering any more of us than we have to. If Morrison and I don't come back, forget us – don't risk sending a rescue party.' As they left, he pointed out to Morrison a descending ramp still partially intact. 'Let's get below.'

Silently, the two men passed one dead level after another. Endless miles of dark ruin stretched out, without sound or activity. The vague shapes of darkened machinery, unmoving belts and conveyer equipment were partially visible, and the partially completed husks of war projectiles, bent and twisted by the final blast.

'We can salvage some of that,' O'Neill said, but he didn't actually believe it. The machinery was fused, shapeless. Everything in the factory had run together, molten slag without form or use. 'Once we get it to the surface . . .'

'We can't,' Morrison contradicted bitterly. 'We don't have hoists or winches.' He kicked at a heap of charred supplies that had stopped along its broken belt and spilled halfway across the ramp.

'It seemed like a good idea at the time,' O'Neill said as the two of them continued past vacant levels of machines. 'But now that I look back, I'm not so sure.'

They had penetrated a long way into the factory. The final level lap spread out ahead of them. O'Neill flashed the light here and there, trying to locate undestroyed sections, portions of the assembly process still intact.

It was Morrison who felt it first. He suddenly dropped to his hands and knees; heavy body pressed against the floor, he lay listening, face hard, eyes wide. 'For God's sake—'

'What is it?' O'Neill cried. Then he, too, felt it. Beneath them, a faint, insistent vibration hummed through the floor, a steady hum of activity. They had been wrong; the hawk had not been totally successful. Below, in a deeper level, the factory was still alive. Closed, limited operations still went on.

'On its own,' O'Neill muttered, searching for an extension of the descent lift. 'Autonomous activity, set to continue after the rest is gone. How do we get down?'

The descent lift was broken off, sealed by a thick section of metal. The still-living layer beneath their feet was completely cut off; there was no entrance.

Racing back the way they had come, O'Neill reached the surface and hailed the first truck. 'Where the hell's the torch? Give it here!'

The precious blowtorch was passed to him and he hurried back, puffing, into the depths of the ruined factory where Morrison waited. Together, the two of them began frantically cutting through the warped metal flooring, burning apart the sealed layers of protective mesh.

'It's coming,' Morrison gasped, squinting in the glare of the torch. The plate fell with a clang, disappearing into the level below. A blaze of white light burst up around them and the two men leaped back.

In the sealed chamber, furious activity boomed and echoed, a steady process of moving belts, whirring machine-tools, fast-moving mechanical supervisors. At one end, a steady flow of raw materials entered the line; at the far end, the final product was whipped off, inspected and crammed into a conveyer tube.

All this was visible for a split second; then the intrusion was discovered. Robot relays came into play. The blaze of lights flickered and dimmed. The assembly line froze to a halt, stopped in its furious activity.

The machines clicked off and became silent.

At one end, a mobile unit detached itself and sped up the wall toward the hole O'Neill and Morrison had cut. It slammed an emergency seal in place and expertly welded it tight. The scene below was gone. A moment later the floor shivered as activity resumed.

Morrison, white-faced and shaking, turned to O'Neill. 'What are they doing? What are they making?'

'Not weapons,' O'Neill said.

'That stuff is being sent up' – Morrison gestured convulsively – 'to the surface.'

Shakily, O'Neill climbed to his feet. 'Can we locate the spot?'

'I – think so.'

'We better.' O'Neill swept up the flashlight and started toward the ascent ramp. 'We're going to have to see what those pellets are that they're shooting up.'

The exit valve of the conveyor tube was concealed in a tangle of vines and ruins a quarter of a mile beyond the factory. In a slot of rock at the base of the mountains the valve poked up like a nozzle. From ten yards away, it was invisible; the two men were almost on top of it before they noticed it.

Every few moments, a pellet burst from the valve and shot up into the sky. The nozzle revolved and altered its angle of deflection; each pellet was launched in a slightly varied trajectory.

'How far are they going?' Morrison wondered.

'Probably varies. It's distributing them at random.' O'Neill advanced cautiously, but the mechanism took no note of him. Plastered against the towering wall of rock was a crumpled pellet; by accident, the nozzle had released it directly at the mountainside. O'Neill climbed up, got it and jumped down.

The pellet was a smashed container of machinery, tiny metallic elements too minute to be analyzed without a microscope.

'Not a weapon,' O'Neill said.

The cylinder had split. At first he couldn't tell if it had been the impact or deliberate internal mechanisms at work. From the rent, an ooze of metal bits was sliding. Squatting down, O'Neill examined them.

The bits were in motion. Microscopic machinery, smaller than ants, smaller than pins, working energetically, purposefully – constructing something that looked like a tiny rectangle of steel.

'They're building,' O'Neill said, awed. He got up and prowled on. Off to the side, at the far edge of the gully, he came across a downed pellet far advanced on its construction. Apparently it had been released some time ago.

This one had made great enough progress to be identified. Minute as it was, the structure was familiar. The machinery was building a miniature replica of the demolished factory.

'Well,' O'Neill said thoughtfully, 'we're back where we started from. For better or worse . . . I don't know.'

'I guess they must be all over Earth by now,' Morrison said, 'landing everywhere and going to work.'

A thought struck O'Neill. 'Maybe some of them are geared to escape velocity. That would be neat – autofac networks throughout the whole universe.'

Behind him, the nozzle continued to spurt out its torrent of metal seeds.

The Days of Perky Pat

At ten in the morning a terrific horn, familiar to him, hooted Sam Regan out of his sleep, and he cursed the careboy upstairs; he knew the racket was deliberate. The careboy, circling, wanted to be certain that flukers – and not merely wild animals – got the care parcels that were to be dropped.

We'll get them, we'll get them, Sam Regan said to himself as he zipped his dust-proof overalls, put his feet into boots and then grumpily sauntered as slowly as possible toward the ramp. Several other flukers joined him, all showing similar irritation.

'He's early today,' Tod Morrison complained. 'And I'll bet it's all staples, sugar and flour and lard – nothing interesting like say candy.'

'We ought to be grateful,' Norman Schein said.

'Grateful!' Tod halted to stare at him. 'GRATEFUL?'

'Yes,' Schein said. 'What do you think we'd be eating without them: If they hadn't seen the clouds ten years ago.'

'Well,' Tod said sullenly, 'I just don't like them to come *early*; I actually don't exactly mind their coming, as such.'

As he put his shoulders against the lid at the top of the ramp, Schein said genially, 'That's mighty tolerant of you, Tod boy. I'm sure the careboys would be pleased to hear your sentiments.'

Of the three of them, Sam Regan was the last to reach the surface; he did not like the upstairs at all, and he did not care who knew it. And anyhow, no one could compel him to leave the safety of the Pinole Fluke-pit; it was entirely his business, and he noted now that a number of his fellow flukers had elected to remain below in their quarters, confident that those who did answer the horn would bring them back something.

'It's bright,' Tod murmured, blinking in the sun.

The care ship sparkled close overhead, set against the gray sky as if hanging from an uneasy thread. Good pilot, this drop, Tod decided. He, or rather *it*, just lazily handles it, in no hurry. Tod waved at the care ship, and once more the huge horn burst out its din, making him clap his hands to his ears. Hey, a joke's a joke, he said to himself. And then the horn ceased; the careboy had relented.

'Wave to him to drop,' Norm Schein said to Tod. 'You've got the wigwag.'

'Sure,' Tod said, and began laboriously flapping the red flag, which the Martian creatures had long ago provided, back and forth, back and forth.

A projectile slid from the underpart of the ship, tossed out stabilizers, spiraled toward the ground.

'Sheoot,' Sam Regan said with disgust. 'It is staples; they don't have the parachute.' He turned away, not interested.

How miserable the upstairs looked today, he thought as he surveyed the scene surrounding him. There, to the right, the uncompleted house which someone – not far from their pit – had begun to build out of lumber salvaged from Vallejo, ten miles to the north. Animals or radiation dust had gotten the builder, and so his work remained where it was; it would never be put to use. And, Sam Regan saw, an unusually heavy precipitate had formed since last he had been up here, Thursday morning or perhaps Friday; he had lost exact track. The darn dust, he thought. Just rocks, pieces of rubble, and the dust. World's becoming a dusty object with no one to whisk it off regularly. How about you? he asked silently of the Martian careboy flying in slow circles overhead. Isn't your technology limitless? Can't you appear some morning with a dust rag a million miles in surface area and restore our planet to pristine newness?

Or rather, he thought, to pristine *oldness*, the way it was in the 'ol-days', as the children call it. We'd like that. While you're looking for something to give to us in the way of further aid, try that.

The careboy circled once more, searching for signs of writing in the dust: a message from the flukers below. I'll write that, Sam thought. BRING DUST RAG, RESTORE OUR CIVILIZATION. Okay, careboy?

All at once the care ship shot off, no doubt on its way back home to its base on Luna or perhaps all the way to Mars.

From the open fluke-pit hole, up which the three of them had come, a further head poked, a woman. Jean Regan, Sam's wife, appeared, shielded by a bonnet against the gray, blinding sun, frowning and saying, 'Anything important? Anything *new*?'

''Fraid not,' Sam said. The care parcel projectile had landed and he walked toward it, scuffing his boots in the dust. The hull of the projectile had cracked open from the impact and he could see the canisters already It looked to be five thousand pounds of salt – might as well leave it up here so the animals wouldn't starve, he decided. He felt despondent.

How peculiarly anxious the careboys were. Concerned all the time that the mainstays of existence be ferried from their own planet to Earth. They must think we eat all day long, Sam thought. My God . . . the pit was filled to capacity with stored foods. But of course it had been one of the smallest public shelters in Northern California.

'Hey,' Schein said, stooping down by the projectile and peering into the crack opened along its side. 'I believe I see something we can use.' He found a rusted metal pole – once it had helped reinforce the concrete side of an ol-days public building – and poked at the projectile, stirring its release mechanism into action. The mechanism, triggered off, popped the rear half of the projectile open . . . and there lay the contents.

'Looks like radios in that box,' Tod said. 'Transistor radios.' Thoughtfully stroking his short black beard he said, 'Maybe we can use them for something new in our layouts.'

'Mine's already got a radio,' Schein pointed out.

'Well, build an electronic self-directing lawn mower with the parts,' Tod said. 'You don't have that, do you?' He knew the Scheins' Perky Pat layout fairly well; the two couples, he and his wife with Schein and his, had played together a good deal, being almost evenly matched.

Sam Regan said, 'Dibs on the radios, because I can use them.' His layout lacked the automatic garage-door opener that both Schein and Tod had; he was considerably behind them.

'Let's get to work,' Schein agreed. 'We'll leave the staples here and just cart back the radios. If anybody wants the staples, let them come here and get them. Before the do-cats do.'

Nodding, the other two men fell to the job of carting the useful contents of the projectile to the entrance of their fluke-pit ramp. For use in their precious, elaborate Perky Pat layouts.

Seated cross-legged with his whetstone, Timothy Schein, ten years old and aware of his many responsibilities, sharp-ened his knife, slowly and expertly. Meanwhile, disturbing him, his mother and father noisily quarreled with Mr and Mrs Morrison, on the far side of the partition. They were playing Perky Pat again. As usual.

How many times today they have to play that dumb game? Timothy asked himself. Forever, I guess. He could see nothing in it, but his parents played on anyhow. And they weren't the only ones; he knew from what other kids said, even from other fluke-pits, that their parents, too, played Perky Pat most of the day, and sometimes even on into the night.

His mother said loudly, 'Perky Pat's going to the grocery

store and it's got one of those electric eyes that opens the door. Look.' A pause. 'See, it opened for her, and now she's inside.'

'She pushes a cart,' Timothy's dad added, in support.

'No, she doesn't,' Mrs Morrison contradicted. 'That's wrong. She gives her list to the grocer and he fills it.'

'That's only in little neighborhood stores,' his mother explained. 'And this is a supermarket, you can tell because of the electric eye door.'

'I'm sure all grocery stores had electric eye doors,' Mrs Morrison said stubbornly, and her husband chimed in with his agreement. Now the voices rose in anger; another squabble had broken out. As usual.

Aw, cung to them, Timothy said to himself, using the strongest word which he and his friends knew. What's a supermarket anyhow? He tested the blade of his knife – he had made it himself, originally, out of a heavy metal pan – and then hopped to his feet. A moment later he had sprinted silently down the hall and was rapping his special rap on the door of the Chamberlains' quarters.

Fred, also ten years old, answered. 'Hi. Ready to go? I see you got that ol' knife of yours sharpened; what do you think we'll catch?'

'Not a do-cat,' Timothy said. 'A lot better than that; I'm tired of eating do-cat. Too peppery.'

'Your parents playing Perky Pat?'

'Yeah.'

Fred said, 'My mom and dad have been gone for a long time, off playing with the Benteleys.' He glanced sideways at Timothy, and in an instant they had shared their mute disappointment regarding their parents. Gosh, and maybe the darn game was all over the world, by now; that would not have surprised either of them.

'How come your parents play it?' Timothy asked.

'Same reason yours do,' Fred said.

Hesitating, Timothy said, 'Well, why? I don't know why they do; I'm asking you, can't you say?'

'It's because—' Fred broke off. 'Ask them. Come on; let's get upstairs and start hunting.' His eyes shone. 'Let's see what we can catch and kill today.'

Shortly, they had ascended the ramp, popped open the lid, and were crouching amidst the dust and rocks, searching the horizon. Timothy's heart pounded; this moment always overwhelmed him, the first instant of reaching the upstairs. The thrilling initial sight of the expanse. Because it was never the same. The dust, heavier today, had a darker gray color to it than before; it seemed denser, more mysterious.

Here and there, covered by many layers of dust, lay parcels dropped from past relief ships – dropped and left to deteriorate. Never to be claimed. And, Timothy saw, an additional new projectile which had arrived that morning. Most of its cargo could be seen within; the grownups had not had any use for the majority of the contents, today.

'Look,' Fred said softly.

Two do-cats – mutant dogs or cats; no one knew for sure – could be seen, lightly sniffing at the projectile. Attracted by the unclaimed contents.

'We don't want them,' Timothy said.

'That one's sure nice and fat,' Fred said longingly. But it was Timothy that had the knife; all he himself had was a string with a metal bolt on the end, a bull-roarer that could kill a bird or a small animal at a distance – but useless against a do-cat, which generally weighed fifteen to twenty pounds and sometimes more.

High up in the sky a dot moved at immense speed, and Timothy knew that it was a care ship heading for another fluke-pit, bringing supplies to it. Sure are busy, he thought to himself. Those careboys always coming and going; they never stop, because if they did, the grownups would die. Wouldn't that be too bad? he thought ironically. Sure be sad.

Fred said, 'Wave to it and maybe it'll drop something.'

He grinned at Timothy, and then they both broke out laughing.

'Sure,' Timothy said. 'Let's see; what do I want?' Again the two of them laughed at the idea of them wanting something. The two boys had the entire upstairs, as far as the eye could see . . . they had even more than the careboys had, and that was plenty, more than plenty.

'Do you think they know,' Fred said, 'that our parents play Perky Pat with furniture made out of what they drop? I bet they don't know about Perky Pat; they never have seen a Perky Pat doll, and if they did they'd be really mad.'

'You're right,' Timothy said. 'They'd be so sore they'd probably stop dropping stuff.' He glanced at Fred, catching his eye.

'Aw no,' Fred said. 'We shouldn't tell them; your dad would beat you again if you did that, and probably me, too.'

Even so, it was an interesting idea. He could imagine first the surprise and then the anger of the careboys; it would be fun to see that, see the reaction of the eight-legged Martian creatures who had so much charity inside their warty bodies, the cephalopodic univalve mollusk-like organisms who had voluntarily taken it upon themselves to supply succor to the waning remnants of the human race . . . This was how they got paid back for their charity, this utterly wasteful, stupid purpose to which their goods were being put. This stupid Perky Pat game that all the adults played.

And anyhow it would be very hard to tell them; there was almost no communication between humans and careboys. They were too different. Acts, deeds, could be done, conveying something . . . but not mere words, not mere *signs*. And anyhow—'

A great brown rabbit bounded by to the right, past the half-completed house. Timothy whipped out his knife. 'Oh boy!' he said aloud in excitement. 'Let's go!' He set off across the rubbly ground, Fred a little behind him. Gradually they gained on the rabbit; swift running came easy to the two boys: they had done much practicing.

'Throw the knife!' Fred panted, and Timothy, skidding to a halt, raised his right arm, paused to take aim, and then hurled the sharpened, weighted knife. His most valuable, self-made possession.

It cleaved the rabbit straight through its vitals. The rabbit tumbled, slid, raising a cloud of dust.

'I bet we can get a dollar for that!' Fred exclaimed, leaping up and down. 'The hide alone – I bet we can get fifty cents just for the darn hide!'

Together, they hurried toward the dead rabbit, wanting to get there before a red-tailed hawk or a day-owl swooped on it from the gray sky above.

Bending, Norman Schein picked up his Perky Pat doll and said sullenly, 'I'm quitting; I don't want to play any more.'

Distressed, his wife protested, 'But we've got Perky Pat all the way downtown in her new Ford hardtop convertible and parked and a dime in the meter and she's shopped and now she's in the analyst's office reading *Fortune* – we're way ahead of the Morrisons! Why do you want to quit, Norm?'

'We just don't agree,' Norman grumbled. 'You say analysts charged twenty dollars an hour and I distinctly remember them charging only ten; nobody could charge twenty. So you're penalizing our side, and for what? The Morrisons agree it was only ten. Don't you?' he said to Mr and Mrs Morrison, who squatted on the far side of the layout which combined both couples' Perky Pat sets.

Helen Morrison said to her husband, 'You went to the analyst more than I did; are you sure he charged only ten?'

'Well, I went mostly to group therapy,' Tod said. 'At the Berkeley State Mental Hygiene Clinic, and they charged according to your ability to pay. And Perky Pat is at a *private* psychoanalyst.'

'We'll have to ask someone else,' Helen said to Norman Schein. 'I guess all we can do now this minute is suspend the game.' He found himself being glared at by her, too, now, because by his insistence on the one point he had put an end to their game for the whole afternoon.

'Shall we leave it all set up?' Fran Schein asked. 'We might as well; maybe we can finish tonight after dinner.'

Norman Schein gazed down at their combined layout, the swanky shops, the well-lit streets with the parked new-model cars, all of them shiny, the split-level house itself, where Perky Pat lived and where she entertained Leonard, her boy friend. It was the *house* that he perpetually yearned for; the house was the real focus of the layout – of all the Perky Pat layouts, however much they might otherwise differ.

Perky Pat's wardrobe, for instance, there in the closet of the house, the big bedroom closet. Her capri pants, her white cotton short-shorts, her two-piece polka dot swimsuit, her fuzzy sweaters . . . and there, in her bedroom, her hi-fi set, her collection of long playing records . . .

It had been this way, once, really been like this in the ol-days. Norm Schein could remember his own l-p record collection, and he had once had clothes almost as swanky as Perky Pat's boy friend Leonard, cashmere jackets and tweed suits and Italian sportshirts and shoes made in England. He hadn't owned a Jaguar XKE sports car, like Leonard did, but he had owned a fine-looking old 1963 Mercedes-Benz, which he had used to drive to work.

We lived then, Norm Schein said to himself, *like Perky Pat and Leonard do now*. This is how it actually was.

To his wife he said, pointing to the clock radio which Perky Pat kept beside her bed, 'Remember our GE clock radio? How it used to wake us up in the morning with classical music from that FM station, KSFR? The "Wolf-gangers", the program was called. From six A.M. to nine every morning.'

'Yes,' Fran said, nodding soberly. 'And you used to get up before me; I knew I should have gotten up and fixed bacon and hot coffee for you, but it was so much fun just indulging myself, not stirring for half an hour longer, until the kids woke up.'

'Woke up, hell; they were awake before we were,' Norm said. 'Don't you remember? They were in the back watching "The Three Stooges" on TV until eight. Then I got up and fixed hot cereal for them, and then I went on to my job at Ampex down at Redwood City.'

'Oh yes,' Fran said. 'The TV.' Their Perky Pat did not have a TV set; they had lost it to the Regans in a game a week ago, and Norm had not yet been able to fashion another one realistic-looking enough to substitute. So, in a game, they pretended now that 'the TV repairman had come for it'. That was how they explained their Perky Pat not having something she really would have had.

Norm thought, Playing this game . . . it's like being back there, back in the world before the war. That's why we play it, I suppose. He felt shame, but only fleetingly; the shame, almost at once, was replaced by the desire to play a little longer.

'Let's not quit,' he said suddenly. 'I'll agree the psychoanalyst would have charged Perky Pat twenty dollars. Okay?'

'Okay,' both the Morrisons said together, and they settled back down once more to resume the game.

Tod Morrison had picked up their Perky Pat; he held it, stroking its blonde hair – theirs was blonde, whereas the Scheins' was a brunette – and fiddling with the snaps of its skirt.

'Whatever are you doing?' his wife inquired.

'Nice skirt she has,' Tod said. 'You did a good job sewing it.'

Norm said, 'Ever know a girl, back in the ol-days, that looked like Perky Pat?'

'No,' Tod Morrison said somberly. 'Wish I had, though. I *saw* girls like Perky Pat, especially when I was living in Los Angeles during the Korean War. But I just could never manage to know them personally. And of course there were really terrific girl singers, like Peggy Lee and Julie London . . . they looked a lot like Perky Pat.'

'Play,' Fran said vigorously. And Norm, whose turn it was, picked up the spinner and spun.

'Eleven,' he said. 'That gets my Leonard out of the sports car repair garage and on his way to the race track.' He moved the Leonard doll ahead.

Thoughtfully, Tod Morrison said, 'You know, I was out the other day hauling in perishables which the careboys had dropped . . . Bill Ferner was there, and he told me something interesting. He met a fluker from a fluke-pit down where Oakland used to be. And at that fluke-pit you know what they play? Not Perky Pat. They never have heard of Perky Pat.'

'Well, what do they play, then?' Helen asked.

'They have another doll entirely.' Frowning, Tod continued, 'Bill says the Oakland fluker called it a Connie Companion doll. Ever hear of that?'

'A "Connie Companion" doll,' Fran said thoughtfully. 'How strange. I wonder what she's like. Does she have a boy friend?'

'Oh sure,' Tod said. 'His name is Paul. Connie and Paul. You know, we ought to hike down there to that Oakland Fluke-pit one of these days and see what Connie and Paul look like and how they live. Maybe we could learn a few things to add to our own layouts.'

Norm said, 'Maybe we could play them.'

Puzzled, Fran said, 'Could a Perky Pat play a Connie Companion? Is that possible? I wonder what would happen?'

There was no answer from any of the others. Because none of them knew.

As they skinned the rabbit, Fred said to Timothy, 'Where did the name "fluker" come from? It's sure an ugly word; why do they use it?'

'A fluker is a person who lived through the hydrogen war,' Timothy explained. 'You know, by a fluke. A fluke of fate? See? Because almost everyone was killed; there used to be thousands of people.'

'But what's a "fluke", then? When you say a "fluke of fate—"'

'A fluke is when fate has decided to spare you,' Timothy said, and that was all he had to say on the subject. That was all he knew.

Fred said thoughtfully, 'But you and I, we're not flukers because we weren't alive when the war broke out. We were born after.'

'Right,' Timothy said.

'So anybody who calls me a fluker,' Fred said, 'is going to get hit in the eye with my bull-roarer.'

'And "careboy",' Timothy said, 'that's a made-up word, too. It's from when stuff was dumped from jet planes and ships to people in a disaster area. They were called "care parcels" because they came from people who cared.'

'I know that,' Fred said. 'I didn't ask that.'

'Well, I told you anyhow,' Timothy said.

The two boys continued skinning the rabbit.

Jean Regan said to her husband, 'Have you heard about the Connie Companion doll?' She glanced down the long rough-board table to make sure none of the other families was listening. 'Sam,' she said, 'I heard it from Helen Morrison; she heard it from Tod and he heard it from Bill Ferner, I think. So it's probably true.'

'What's true?' Sam said.

'That in the Oakland Fluke-pit they don't have Perky Pat; they have Connie Companion . . . and it occurred to me that maybe some of this – you know, this sort of emptiness, this boredom we feel now and then – maybe if we saw the Connie Companion doll and how she lives, maybe we could add enough to our own layout to—' She paused, reflecting. 'To make it more complete.'

'I don't care for the name,' Sam Regan said. 'Connie Companion; it sounds cheap.' He spooned up some of the plain, utilitarian grain-mash which the careboys had been dropping, of late. And, as he ate a mouthful, he thought, I'll bet Connie Companion doesn't eat slop like this; I'll bet she eats cheeseburgers with all the trimmings, at a high type drive-in.

'Could we make a trek down there?' Jean asked.

'To Oakland Fluke-pit?' Sam stared at her. 'It's *fifteen miles*, all the way on the other side of the Berkeley Fluke-pit!'

'But this is important,' Jean said stubbornly. 'And Bill says that a fluker from Oakland came all the way up here, in search of electronic parts or something . . . so if he can do it, we can. We've got the dust suits they dropped us. I know we could do it.'

Little Timothy Schein, sitting with his family, had overheard her; now he spoke up. 'Mrs Regan, Fred Chamberlain and I, we could trek down that far, if you pay us. What do you say?' He nudged Fred, who sat beside him. 'Couldn't we? For maybe five dollars.'

Fred, his face serious, turned to Mrs Regan and said, 'We could get you a Connie Companion doll. For five dollars for *each* of us.'

'Good grief,' Jean Regan said, outraged. And dropped the subject.

But later, after dinner, she brought it up again when she and Sam were alone in their quarters.

'Sam, I've got to see it,' she burst out. Sam, in a galvanized tub, was taking his weekly bath, so he had to listen to her. 'Now that we know it exists we have to play against someone in the Oakland Fluke-pit; at least we can do that. Can't we? Please.' She paced back and forth in the small room, her hands clasped tensely. 'Connie Companion may have a Standard Station and an airport terminal with jet landing strip and color TV and a French restaurant where they serve escargot, like the one you and I went to when we were first married . . . I just have to see her layout.'

'I don't know,' Sam said hesitantly. 'There's something about Connie Companion doll that – makes me uneasy.'

'What could it possibly be?'

'I don't know.'

Jean said bitterly, 'It's because you know her layout is so much better than ours and she's so much more than Perky Pat.'

'Maybe that's it,' Sam murmured.

'If you don't go, if you don't try to make contact with them down at the Oakland Fluke-pit, someone else will – someone with more ambition will get ahead of you. Like Norman Schein. He's not afraid the way you are.'

Sam said nothing; he continued with his bath. But his hands shook.

A careboy had recently dropped complicated pieces of machinery which were, evidently, a form of mechanical computer. For several weeks the computers – if that was what they were – had sat about the pit in their cartons, unused, but now Norman Schein was finding something to do with one. At the moment he was busy adapting some of its gears, the smallest ones, to form a garbage disposal unit for his Perky Pat's kitchen.

Using the tiny special tools – designed and built by inhabitants of the fluke-pit – which were necessary in fashioning environmental items for Perky Pat, he was busy at his hobby bench. Thoroughly engrossed in what he was doing, he all at once realized that Fran was standing directly behind him, watching.

'I get nervous when I'm watched,' Norm said, holding a tiny gear with a pair of tweezers.

'Listen,' Fran said, 'I've thought of something. Does this suggest anything to you?' She placed before him one of the transistor radios which had been dropped the day before.

'It suggests that garage-door opener already thought of,'

Norm said irritably. He continued with his work, expertly fitting the miniature pieces together in the sink drain of Pat's kitchen; such delicate work demanded maximum concentration.

Fran said, 'It suggests that there must be radio *transmitters* on Earth somewhere, or the careboys wouldn't have dropped these.'

'So?' Norm said, uninterested.

'Maybe our Mayor has one,' Fran said. 'Maybe there's one right here in our own pit, and we could use it to call the Oakland Fluke-pit. Representatives from there could meet us halfway . . . say at the Berkeley Fluke-pit. And we could play there. So we wouldn't have that long fifteen-mile trip.'

Norman hesitated in his work; he set the tweezers down and said slowly, 'I think possibly you're right.' But if their Mayor Hooker Glebe had a radio transmitter, would he let them use it? And if he did—

'We can try,' Fran urged. 'It wouldn't hurt to try.'

'Okay,' Norm said, rising from his hobby bench.

The short, sly-faced man in Army uniform, the Mayor of the Pinole Fluke-pit, listened in silence as Norm Schein spoke. Then he smiled a wise, cunning smile. 'Sure, I have a radio transmitter. Had it all the time. Fifty watt output. But why would you want to get in touch with the Oakland Fluke-pit?'

Guardedly, Norm said, 'That's my business.'

Hooker Glebe said thoughtfully, 'I'll let you use it for fifteen dollars.'

It was a nasty shock, and Norm recoiled. Good Lord; all the money he and his wife had – they needed every bill of it for use in playing Perky Pat. Money was the tender in the game; there was no other criterion by which one could tell if he had won or lost. 'That's too much,' he said aloud.

'Well, say ten,' the Mayor said, shrugging.

In the end they settled for six dollars and a fifty-cent piece.

'I'll make the radio contact for you,' Hooker Glebe said. 'Because you don't know how. It will take time.' He began turning a crank at the side of the generator of the transmitter. 'I'll notify you when I've made contact with them. But give me the money now.' He held out his hand for it, and, with great reluctance, Norm paid him.

It was not until late that evening that Hooker managed to establish contact with Oakland. Pleased with himself, beaming in self-satisfaction, he appeared at the Scheins' quarters during their dinner hour. 'All set,' he announced. 'Say, you know there are actually *nine* fluke-pits in Oakland? I didn't know that. Which you want? I've got one with the radio code of Red Vanilla.' He chuckled. 'They're tough and suspicious down there; it was hard to get any of them to answer.'

Leaving his evening meal, Norman hurried to the Mayor's quarters, Hooker puffing along after him.

The transmitter, sure enough, was on, and static wheezed from the speaker of its monitoring unit. Awkwardly, Norm seated himself at the microphone. 'Do I just talk?' he asked Hooker Glebe.

'Just say, This is Pinole Fluke-pit calling. Repeat that a couple of times and then when they acknowledge, you say what you want to say.' The Mayor fiddled with controls of the transmitter, fussing in an important fashion.

'This is Pinole Fluke-pit,' Norm said loudly into the microphone.

Almost at once a clear voice from the monitor said, 'This is Red Vanilla Three answering.' The voice was cold and harsh; it struck him forcefully as distinctly alien. Hooker was right. 'Do you have Connie Companion down there where you are?'

'Yes we do,' the Oakland fluker answered.

'Well, I challenge you,' Norman said, feeling the veins in his throat pulse with the tension of what he was saying. 'We're Perky Pat in this area; we'll play Perky Pat against your Connie Companion. Where can we meet?'

'Perky Pat,' the Oakland fluker echoed. 'Yeah, I know about her. What would the stakes be, in your mind?'

'Up here we play for paper money mostly,' Norman said, feeling that his response was somehow lame.

'We've got lots of paper money,' the Oakland fluker said cuttingly. 'That wouldn't interest any of us. What else?'

'I don't know.' He felt hampered, talking to someone he could not see; he was not used to that. People should, he thought, be face to face, then you can see the other person's expression. This was not natural. 'Let's meet halfway,' he said, 'and discuss it. Maybe we could meet at the Berkeley Fluke-it; how about that?'

The Oakland fluker said, 'That's too far. You mean lug our Connie Companion layout all that way? It's too heavy and something might happen to it.'

'No, just to discuss rules and stakes,' Norman said.

Dubiously, the Oakland fluker said, 'Well, I guess we could do that. But you better understand – we take Connie Companion doll pretty damn seriously; you better be prepared to talk terms.'

'We will,' Norm assured him.

All this time Mayor Hooker Glebe had been cranking the handle of the generator; perspiring, his face bloated with exertion, he motioned angrily for Norm to conclude his palaver.

'At the Berkeley Fluke-pit,' Norm finished. 'In three days. And send your best player, the one who has the biggest and most authentic layout. Our Perky Pat layouts are works of art, you understand.'

The Oakland fluker said, 'We'll believe that when we see them. After all, we've got carpenters and electricians and plasterers here, building our layouts; I'll bet you're all unskilled.'

'Not as much as you think,' Norm said hotly, and laid down the microphone. To Hooker Glebe – who had immediately stopped cranking – he said, 'We'll beat them. Wait'll they see the garbage disposal unit I'm making for my Perky Pat; did you know there were people back in the ol-days, I mean real alive human beings, who didn't have garbage disposal units?'

'I remember,' Hooker said peevishly. 'Say, you got a lot of cranking for your money; I think you gypped me, talking so long.' He eyed Norm with such hostility that Norm began to feel uneasy. After all, the Mayor of the pit had the authority to evict any fluker he wished; that was their law.

'I'll give you the fire alarm box I just finished the other day,' Norm said. 'In my layout it goes at the corner of the block where Perky Pat's boy friend Leonard lives.'

'Good enough,' Hooker agreed, and his hostility faded. It was replaced, at once, by desire. 'Let's see it, Norm. I bet it'll go good in my layout; a fire alarm box is just what I need to complete my first block where I have the mailbox. Thank you.'

'You're welcome,' Norm sighed, philosophically.

When he returned from the two-day trek to the Berkeley Fluke-pit his face was so grim that his wife knew at once that the parley with the Oakland people had not gone well.

That morning a careboy had dropped cartons of a synthetic tea-like drink; she fixed a cup of it for Norman, waiting to hear what had taken place eight miles to the south.

'We haggled,' Norm said, seated wearily on the bed which he and his wife and child all shared. 'They don't want money; they don't want goods – naturally not goods, because the darn careboys are dropping regularly down there, too.'

'What will they accept, then?'

Norm said, 'Perky Pat herself.' He was silent, then.

'Oh good Lord,' she said, appalled.

'But if we win,' Norm pointed out, 'we win Connie Companion.'

'And the layouts? What about them?'

'We keep our own. It's just Perky Pat herself, not Leonard, not anything else.'

'But,' she protested, 'what'll we *do* if we lose Perky Pat?'

'I can make another one,' Norm said. 'Given time. There's still a big supply of thermoplastics and artificial hair, here in the pit. And I have plenty of different paints; it would take at least a month, but I could do it. I don't look forward to the job, I admit. But—' His eyes glinted. 'Don't look on the dark side; *imagine what it would be like to win Connie Companion doll.* I think we may well win; their delegate seemed smart and, as Hooker said, tough . . . but the one I talked to didn't strike me as being very flukey. You know, on good terms with luck.'

And, after all, the element of luck, of chance, entered into each stage of the game through the agency of the spinner.

'It seems wrong,' Fran said, 'to put up Perky Pat herself. But if you say so—' She managed to smile a little. 'I'll go along with it. And if you won Connie Companion – who knows? You might be elected Mayor when Hooker dies. Imagine, to have won somebody else's *doll* – not just the game, the money, but the *doll itself.*'

'I can win,' Norm said soberly. 'Because I'm very flukey.' He could feel it in him, the same flukeyness that had got him through the hydrogen war alive, that had kept him alive ever since. You either have it or you don't, he realized. And I do.

His wife said, 'Shouldn't we ask Hooker to call a meeting of everyone in the pit, and send the best player out of our entire group. So as to be the surest of winning.'

'Listen,' Norm Schein said emphatically. 'I'm the best player. I'm going. And so are you; we made a good team, and we don't want to break it up. Anyhow, we'll need at least two people to carry Perky Pat's layout.' All in all, he judged, their layout weighed sixty pounds.

His plan seemed to him to be satisfactory. But when he mentioned it to the others living in the Pinole Fluke-pit he found himself facing sharp disagreement. The whole next day was filled with argument.

'You can't lug your layout all that way yourselves,' Sam Regan said. 'Either take more people with you or carry your layout in a vehicle of some sort. Such as a cart.' He scowled at Norm.

'Where'd I get a cart?' Norm demanded.

'Maybe something could be adapted,' Sam said. 'I'll give you every bit of help I can. Personally, I'd go along but as I told my wife this whole idea worries me.' He thumped Norm on the back. 'I admire your courage, you and Fran, setting off this way. I wish I had what it takes.' He looked unhappy.

In the end, Norm settled on a wheelbarrow. He and Fran would take turns pushing it. That way neither of them would have to carry any load above and beyond their food and water, and of course knives by which to protect them from the do-cats.

As they were carefully placing the elements of their layout in the wheelbarrow, Norm Schein's boy Timothy came sidling up to them. 'Take me along, Dad,' he pleaded. 'For fifty cents I'll go as guide and scout, and also I'll help you catch food along the way.'

'We'll manage fine,' Norm said. 'You stay here in the fluke-pit; you'll be safer here.' It annoyed him, the idea of his son tagging along on an important venture such as this. It was almost – sacrilegious.

'Kiss us goodbye,' Fran said to Timothy, smiling at him briefly; then her attention returned to the layout within the wheelbarrow. 'I hope it doesn't tip over,' she said fearfully to Norm.

'Not a chance,' Norm said. 'If we're careful.' He felt confident.

A few moments later they began wheeling the wheelbarrow up the ramp to the lid at the top, to upstairs. Their journey to the Berkeley Fluke-pit had begun.

*

A mile outside the Berkeley Fluke-pit he and Fran began to stumble over empty drop-canisters and some only partly empty: remains of past care parcels such as littered the surface near their own pit. Norm Schein breathed a sigh of relief; the journey had not been so bad after all, except that his hands had become blistered from gripping the metal handles of the wheelbarrow, and Fran had turned her ankle so that now she walked with a painful limp. But it had taken them less time than he had anticipated, and his mood was one of buoyancy.

Ahead, a figure appeared, crouching low in the ash. A boy. Norm waved at him and called, 'Hey, sonny – we're from the Pinole pit; we're supposed to meet a party from Oakland here . . . Do you remember me?'

The boy, without answering, turned and scampered off.

'Nothing to be afraid of,' Norm said to his wife. 'He's going to tell their Mayor. A nice old fellow named Ben Fennimore.'

Soon several adults appeared, approaching warily.

With relief, Norm set the legs of the wheelbarrow down into the ash, letting go and wiping his face with his handkerchief. 'Has the Oakland team arrived yet?' he called.

'Not yet,' a tall, elderly man with a white armband and ornate cap answered. 'It's you Schein, isn't it?' he said, peering. This was Ben Fennimore. 'Back already with your layout.' Now the Berkeley flukers had begun crowding around the wheelbarrow, inspecting the Scheins' layout. Their faces showed admiration.

'They have Perky Pat here,' Norm explained to his wife. 'But—' He lowered his voice. 'Their layouts are only basic. Just a house, wardrobe and car . . . they've built almost nothing. No imagination.'

One Berkeley fluker, a woman, said wonderingly to Fran, 'And you made each of the pieces of furniture yourselves?' Marveling, she turned to the man beside her. 'See what they've accomplished, Ed?'

'Yes,' the man answered, nodding. 'Say,' he said to Fran

and Norm, 'can we see it all set up? You're going to set it up in our pit, aren't you?'

'We are indeed,' Norm said.

The Berkeley flukers helped push the wheelbarrow the last mile. And before long they were descending the ramp, to the pit below the surface.

'It's a big pit,' Norm said knowingly to Fran. 'Must be two thousand people here. This is where the University of California was.'

'I see,' Fran said, a little timid at entering a strange pit; it was the first time in years – since the war, in fact – that she had seen any strangers. And so many at once. It was almost too much for her; Norm felt her shrink back, pressing against him in fright.

When they had reached the first level and were starting to unload the wheelbarrow, Ben Fennimore came up to them and said softly, 'I think the Oakland people have been spotted; we just got a report of activity upstairs. So be prepared.' He added, 'We're rooting for you, of course, because you're Perky Pat, the same as us.'

'Have you ever seen Connie Companion doll?' Fran asked him.

'No ma'am,' Fennimore answered courteously. 'But naturally we've heard about it, being neighbors to Oakland and all. I'll tell you one thing . . . we hear that Connie Companion doll is a bit older than Perky Pat. You know – more, um, *mature*.' He explained, 'I just wanted to prepare you.'

Norm and Fran glanced at each other. 'Thanks,' Norm said slowly. 'Yes, we should be as much prepared as possible. How about Paul?'

'Oh, he's not much,' Fennimore said. 'Connie runs things; I don't even think Paul has a real apartment of his own. But you better wait until the Oakland flukers get here; I don't want to mislead you – my knowledge is all hearsay, you understand.'

Another Berkeley fluker, standing nearby, spoke up. 'I saw Connie once, and she's much more grown up than Perky Pat.'

'How old do you figure Perky Pat is?' Norm asked him.

'Oh, I'd say seventeen or eighteen,' Norm was told.

'And Connie?' He waited tensely.

'Oh, she might be twenty-five, even.'

From the ramp behind them they heard noises. More Berkeley flukers appeared, and, after them, two men carrying between them a platform on which, spread out, Norm saw a great, spectacular layout.

This was the Oakland team, and they weren't a couple, a man and wife; they were both men, and they were hard-faced with stern, remote eyes. They jerked their heads briefly at him and Fran, acknowledging their presence. And then, with enormous care, they set down the platform on which their layout rested.

Behind them came a third Oakland fluker carrying a metal box, much like a lunch pail. Norm, watching, knew instinctively that in the box lay Connie Companion doll. The Oakland fluker produced a key and began unlocking the box.

'We're ready to begin playing any time,' the taller of the Oakland men said. 'As we agreed in our discussion, we'll use a numbered spinner instead of dice. Less chance of cheating that way.'

'Agreed,' Norm said. Hesitantly he held out his hand. 'I'm Norman Schein and this is my wife and play-partner Fran.'

The Oakland man, evidently the leader, said, 'I'm Walter R. Wynn. This is my partner here, Charley Dowd, and the man with the box, that's Peter Foster. He isn't going to play; he just guards out layout.' Wynn glanced about, at the Berkeley flukers, as if saying, I know you're all partial to Perky Pat, in here. But we don't care; we're not scared.

Fran said, 'We're ready to play, Mr Wynn.' He voice was low but controlled.

'What about money?' Fennimore asked.

'I think both teams have plenty of money,' Wynn said. He laid out several thousand dollars in greenbacks, and now Norm did the same. 'The money of course is not a factor in this, except as a means of conducting the game.'

Norm nodded; he understood perfectly. Only the dolls themselves mattered. And now, for the first time, he saw Connie Companion doll.

She was being placed in her bedroom by Mr Foster who evidently was in charge of her. And the sight of her took his breath away. Yes, she was older. A grown woman, not a girl at all . . . the difference between her and Perky Pat was acute. And so life-like. Carved, not poured; she obviously had been whittled out of wood and then painted – she was not a thermoplastic. And her hair. It appeared to be genuine hair.

He was deeply impressed.

'What do you think of her?' Walter Wynn asked, with a faint grin.

'Very – impressive,' Norm conceded.

Now the Oaklanders were studying Perky Pat. 'Poured thermoplastic,' one of them said. 'Artificial hair. Nice clothes, though; all stitched by hand, you can see that. Interesting; what we heard was correct. Perky Pat isn't a grownup, she's just a teenager.'

Now the male companion to Connie appeared; he was set down in the bedroom beside Connie.

'Wait a minute,' Norm said. 'You're putting Paul or whatever his name is, in her bedroom with her? Doesn't he have his own apartment?'

Wynn said, 'They're married.'

'*Married!*' Norman and Fran stared at him, dumbfounded.

'Why sure,' Wynn said. 'So naturally they live together. Your dolls, they're not, are they?'

'N-no,' Fran said. 'Leonard is Perky Pat's boy friend . . .'

Her voice trailed off. 'Norm,' she said, clutching his arm, 'I don't believe him; I think he's just saying they're married to get the advantage. Because if they both start out from the same room—'

Norm said aloud, 'You fellows, look here. It's not fair, calling them married.'

Wynn said, 'We're not "calling" them married; they are married. Their names are Connie and Paul Lathrope, of 24 Arden Place, Piedmont. They've been married for a year, most players will tell you.' He sounded calm.

Maybe, Norm thought, it's true. He was truly shaken.

'Look at them together,' Fran said, kneeling down to examine the Oaklanders' layout. 'In the same bedroom, in the same house. Why, Norm; do you see? There's just the one bed. A big double bed.' Wild-eyed, she appealed to him. 'How can Perky Pat and Leonard play against them?' Her voice shook. 'It's not morally *right*.'

'This is another type of layout entirely,' Norm said to Walter Wynn. 'This, that you have. Utterly different from what we're used to, as you can see.' He pointed to his own layout. 'I insist that in this game Connie and Paul *not* live together and *not* be considered married.'

'But they are,' Foster spoke up. 'It's a fact. Look – their clothes are in the same closet.' He showed them the closet. 'And in the same bureau drawers.' He showed them that, too. 'And look in the bathroom. Two toothbrushes. His and hers, in the same rack. So you can see we're not making it up.'

There was silence.

Then Fran said in a choked voice, 'And if they're married – you mean they've been – intimate?'

Wynn raised an eyebrow, then nodded. 'Sure, since they're married. Is there anything wrong with that?'

'Perky Pat and Leonard have never—' Fran began, and then ceased.

'Naturally not,' Wynn agreed. 'Because they're only going together. We understand that.'

Fran said, 'We just can't play. We can't.' She caught hold

of her husband's arm. 'Let's go back to Pinole pit – please, Norman.'

'Wait,' Wynn said, at once. 'If you don't play, you're conceding; you have to give up Perky Pat.'

The three Oaklanders all nodded. And, Norm saw, many of the Berkeley flukers were nodding, too, including Ben Fennimore.

'They're right,' Norm said heavily to his wife. 'We'd have to give her up. We better play, dear.'

'Yes,' Fran said, in a dead, flat voice. 'We'll play.' She bent down and listlessly spun the needle of the spinner. It stopped at six.

Smiling, Walter Wynn knelt down and spun. He obtained a four.

The game had begun.

Crouching behind the strewn, decayed contents of a care parcel that had been dropped long ago, Timothy Schein saw coming across the surface of ash his mother and father, pushing the wheelbarrow ahead of them. They looked tired and worn.

'Hi,' Timothy yelled, leaping out at them in joy at seeing them again; he had missed them very much.

'Hi, son,' his father murmured, nodding. He let go of the handles of the wheelbarrow, then halted and wiped his face with his handkerchief.

Now Fred Chamberlain raced up, panting. 'Hi, Mr Schein; hi, Mrs Schein. Hey, did you win? Did you beat the Oakland flukers? I bet you did, didn't you?' He looked from one of them to the other and then back.

In a low voice Fran said, 'Yes, Freddy. We won.'

Norm said, 'Look in the wheelbarrow.'

The two boys looked. And, there among Perky Pat's furnishings, lay another doll. Larger, fuller-figured, much older than Pat . . . They stared at her and she stared up sightlessly at the gray sky overhead. So this is Connie Companion doll, Timothy said to himself. Gee.

'We were lucky,' Norm said. Now several people had emerged from the pit and were gathering around them, listening. Jean and Sam Regan, Tod Morrison and his wife Helen, and now their Mayor, Hooker Glebe himself, waddling up excited and nervous, his face flushed, gasping for breath from the labor – unusual for him – of ascending the ramp.

Fran said, 'We got a cancellation of debts card, just when we were most behind. We owed fifty thousand, and it made us even with the Oakland flukers. And then, after that, we got an advance ten squares card, and that put us right on the jackpot square, at least in our layout. We had a very bitter squabble, because the Oaklanders showed us that on their layout it was a tax lien slapped on real estate holdings square, but we had spun an odd number so that put us back on our own board.' She sighed. 'I'm glad to be back. It was hard, Hooker; it was a tough game.'

Hooker Glebe wheezed, 'Let's all get a look at the Connie Companion doll, folks.' To Fran and Norm he said, 'Can I lift her up and show them?'

'Sure,' Norm said, nodding.

Hooker picked up Connie Companion doll. 'She sure is realistic,' he said, scrutinizing her. 'Clothes aren't as nice as ours generally are; they look machine-made.'

'They are,' Norm agreed. 'But she's carved, not poured.'

'Yes, so I see.' Hooker turned the doll about, inspecting her from all angles. 'A nice job. She's – um, more filled-out than Perky Pat. What's this outfit she has on? Tweed suit of some sort.'

'A business suit,' Fran said. 'We won that with her; they had agreed on that in advance.'

'You see, she has a job,' Norm explained. 'She's a psychology consultant for a business firm doing marketing research. In consumer preferences. A high-paying position . . . she earns twenty thousand a year, I believe Wynn said.'

'Golly,' Hooker said. 'And Pat's just going to college; she's still in school.' He looked troubled. 'Well, I guess they were bound to be ahead of us in some ways. What matters is that you won.' His jovial smile returned. 'Perky Pat came out ahead.' He held the Connie Companion doll up high, where everyone could see her. 'Look what Norm and Fran came back with, folks!'

Norm said, 'Be careful with her, Hooker.' His voice was firm.

'Eh?' Hooker said, pausing. 'Why, Norm?'

'Because,' Norm said, 'she's going to have a baby.'

There was a sudden chill silence. The ash around them stirred faintly; that was the only sound.

'How do you know?' Hooker asked.

'They told us. The Oaklanders told us. And we won that, too – after a bitter argument that Fennimore had to settle.' Reaching into the wheelbarrow he brought out a little leather pouch, from it he carefully took a carved pink new-born baby. 'We won this too because Fennimore agreed that from a technical standpoint it's literally part of Connie Companion doll at this point.'

Hooker stared a long, long time.

'She's married,' Fran explained. 'To Paul. They're not just going together. She's three months pregnant, Mr Wynn said. He didn't tell us until after we won; he didn't want to, then, but they felt they had to. I think they were right; it wouldn't have done not to say.'

Norm said, 'And in addition there's actually an embryo outfit—'

'Yes,' Fran said. 'You have to open Connie up, of course, to see—'

'No,' Jean Regan said. 'Please, no.'

Hooker said, 'No, Mrs Schein, don't.' He backed away.

Fran said, 'It shocked us of course at first, but—'

'You see,' Norm put in, 'it's logical; you have to follow the logic. Why, eventually Perky Pat—'

'No,' Hooker said violently. He bent down, picked up a

rock from the ash at his feet. 'No,' he said, and raised his arm. 'You stop, you two. Don't say any more.'

Now the Regans, too, had picked up rocks. No one spoke.

Fran said, at last, 'Norm, we've got to get out of here.'

'You're right,' Tod Morrison told them. His wife nodded in grim agreement.

'You two go back down to Oakland,' Hooker told Norman and Fran Schein. 'You don't live here any more. You're different than you were. You – changed.'

'Yes,' Sam Regan said slowly, half to himself. 'I was right; there was something to fear.' To Norm Schein he said, 'How difficult a trip is it to Oakland?'

'We just went to Berkeley,' Norm said. 'To the Berkeley Fluke-pit.' He seemed baffled and stunned by what was happening. 'My God,' he said, 'we can't turn around and push this wheelbarrow back all the way to Berkeley again – we're worn out, we need rest!'

Sam Regan said, 'What if somebody else pushed?' He walked up to the Scheins, then, and stood with them. 'I'll push the darn thing. You lead the way, Schein.' He looked toward his own wife, but Jean did not stir. And she did not put down her handful of rocks.

Timothy Schein plucked at his father's arm. 'Can I come this time, Dad? Please let me come.'

'Okay,' Norm said, half to himself. Now he drew himself together. 'So we're not wanted here.' He turned to Fran. 'Let's go. Sam's going to push the wheelbarrow; I think we can make it back there before nightfall. If not, we can sleep out in the open; Timothy'll help protect us against the do-cats.'

Fran said, 'I guess we have no choice.' Her face was pale.

'And take this,' Hooker said. He held out the tiny carved baby. Fran Schein accepted it and put it tenderly back in its leather pouch. Norm laid Connie Companion back down in the wheelbarrow, where she had been. They were ready to start back.

'It'll happen up here eventually,' Norm said to the group of people, to the Pinole flukers. 'Oakland is just more advanced; that's all.'

'Go on,' Hooker Glebe said. 'Get started.'

Nodding, Norm started to pick up the handles of the wheelbarrow, but Sam Regan moved him aside and took them himself. 'Let's go,' he said.

The three adults, with Timothy Schein going ahead of them with his knife ready – in case a do-cat attacked – started into motion, in the direction of Oakland and the south. No one spoke. There was nothing to say.

'It's a shame this had to happen,' Norm said at last, when they had gone almost a mile and there was no further sign of the Pinole flukers behind them.

'Maybe not,' Sam Regan said. 'Maybe it's for the good.' He did not seem downcast. And after all, he had lost his wife; he had given up more than anyone else, and yet – he had survived.

'Glad you feel that way,' Norm said somberly.

They continued on, each with his own thoughts.

After a while, Timothy said to his father, 'All these big fluke-pits to the south . . . there's lots more things to do there, isn't there? I mean, you don't just sit around playing that game.' He certainly hoped not.

His father said, 'That's true, I guess.'

Overhead, a care ship whistled at great velocity and then was gone again almost at once; Timothy watched it go but he was not really interested in it, because there was so much more to look forward to, on the ground and below the ground, ahead of them to the south.

His father murmured, 'Those Oaklanders; their game, their particular doll, it taught them something. Connie had to grow and it forced them all to grow along with her. Our flukers never learned about that, not from Perky Pat. I wonder if they ever will. She'd have to grow up the way Connie did. Connie must have been like Perky Pat, once. A long time ago.'

Not interested in what his father was saying – who really cared about dolls and games with dolls? – Timothy scampered ahead, peering to see what lay before them, the opportunities and possibilities, for him and for his mother and dad, for Mr Regan also.

'I can't wait,' he yelled back at his father, and Norm Schein managed a faint, fatigued smile in answer.

Stand-By

An hour before his morning program on channel six, ranking news clown Jim Briskin sat in his private office with his production staff, conferring on the report of an unknown possibly hostile flotilla detected at eight hundred astronomical units from the sun. It was big news, of course. But how should it be presented to his several billion viewers scattered over three planets and seven moons?

Peggy Jones, his secretary, lit a cigarette and said, 'Don't alarm them, Jim-Jam. Do it folksy-style.' She leaned back, riffled the dispatches received by their commercial station from Unicephalon 40-D's teletypers.

It had been the homeostatic problem-solving structure Unicephalon 40-D at the White House in Washington, DC which had detected this possible external enemy; in its capacity as President of the United States it had at once dispatched ships of the line to stand picket duty. The flotilla appeared to be entering from another solar system entirely, but that fact of course would have to be determined by the picket ships.

'Folksy-style,' Jim Briskin said glumly. 'I grin and say, Hey look comrades – it's happened at last, the thing we all feared, ha ha.' He eyed her. 'That'll get baskets full of laughs all over Earth and Mars but just possibly not on the far-out moons.' Because if there were some kind of attack it would be the farther colonists who would be hit first.

'No, they won't be amused,' his continuity advisor Ed Fineberg agreed. He, too, looked worried; he had a family on Ganymede.

'Is there any lighter piece of news?' Peggy asked. 'By which you could open your program? The sponsor would like that.' She passed the armload of news dispatches to Briskin. 'See what you can do. Mutant cow obtains voting franchise in court case in Alabama . . . you know.'

'I know,' Briskin agreed as he began to inspect the dispatches. One such as his quaint account – it had touched the hearts of millions – of the mutant blue jay which learned, by great trial and effort, to sew. It had sewn itself and its progeny a nest, one April morning, in Bismark, North Dakota, in front of the TV cameras of Briskin's network.

One piece of news stood out; he knew intuitively, as soon as he saw it, that here he had what he wanted to lighten the dire tone of the day's news. Seeing it, he relaxed. The worlds went on with business as usual, despite this great news-break from eight hundred AUs out.

'Look,' he said, grinning. 'Old Gus Schatz is dead. Finally.'

'Who's Gus Schatz?' Peggy asked, puzzled. 'That name . . . it does sound familiar.'

'The union man,' Jim Briskin said. 'You remember. The stand-by President, sent over to Washington by the union twenty-two years ago. He's dead, and the union—' He tossed her the dispatch: it was lucid and brief. 'Now it's sending a new stand-by President over to take Schatz's place. I think I'll interview him. Assuming he can talk.'

'That's right,' Peggy said. 'I keep forgetting. There still is a human stand-by in case Unicephalon fails. Has it ever failed?'

'No,' Ed Fineberg said. 'And it never will. So we have one more case of union featherbedding. The plague of our society.'

'But still,' Jim Briskin said, 'people would be amused. The home life of the top stand-by in the country . . . why the union picked him, what his hobbies are. What this man, whoever he is, plans to do during his term to keep from going mad with boredom. Old Gus learned to bind books;

he collected rare old motor magazines and bound them in vellum with gold-stamped lettering.'

Both Ed and Peggy nodded in agreement. 'Do that,' Peggy urged him. 'You can make it interesting, Jim-Jam; you can make anything interesting. I'll place a call to the White House, or is the new man there yet?'

'Probably still at union headquarters in Chicago,' Ed said. 'Try a line there. Government Civil Servants' Union, East Division.'

Picking up the phone, Peggy quickly dialed.

At seven o'clock in the morning Maximilian Fischer sleepily heard noises; he lifted his head from the pillow, heard the confusion growing in the kitchen, the landlady's shrill voice, then men's voices which were unfamiliar to him. Groggily, he managed to sit up, shifting his bulk with care. He did not hurry; the doc had said not to overexert, because of the strain on his already-enlarged heart. So he took his time dressing.

Must be after a contribution to one of the funds, Max said to himself. *It sounds like some of the fellas. Pretty early, though.* He did not feel alarmed. *I'm in good standing*, he thought firmly. *Nuthin' to fear.*

With care, he buttoned a fine pink and green-striped silk shirt, one of his favorites. *Gives me class*, he thought as with labored effort he managed to bend far enough over to slip on his authentic simulated deerskin pumps. *Be ready to meet them on an equality level*, he thought as he smoothed his thinning hair before the mirror. *If they shake me down too much I'll squawk directly to Pat Noble at the Noo York hiring hall; I mean, I don't have to stand for any stuff. I been in the union too long.*

From the other room a voice bawled, 'Fischer – get your clothes on and come out. We got a job for you and it begins today.'

A job, Max thought with mixed feelings; he did not know whether to be glad or sorry. For over a year now he had been drawing from the union fund, as were most of his friends. Well what do you know. *Cripes*, he thought; *suppose it's a hard job, like maybe I got to bend over all the time or move around.* He felt anger. *What a dirty deal. I mean, who do they think they are?* Opening the door, he faced them. 'Listen,' he began, but one of the union officials cut him off.

'Pack your things, Fischer. Gus Schatz kicked the bucket and you got to go down to Washington, DC and take over the number one stand-by; we want you there before they abolish the position or something and we have to go out on strike or go to court. Mainly, we want to get someone right in clean and easy with no trouble; you understand? Make the transition so smooth that no one hardly takes notice.'

At once, Max said, 'What's it pay?'

Witheringly, the union official said, 'You got no decision to make in this; *you're picked.* You want your freeloader fund-money cut off? You want to have to get out at your age and look for work?'

'Aw come on,' Max protested. 'I can pick up the phone and dial Pat Noble—'

The union officials were grabbing up objects here and there in the apartment. 'We'll help you pack. Pat wants you in the White House by ten o'clock this morning.'

'Pat!' Max echoed. He had been sold out.

The union officials, dragging suitcases from the closet, grinned.

Shortly, they were on their way across the flatlands of the Midwest by monorail. Moodily, Maximilian Fischer watched the countryside flash past; he said nothing to the officials flanking him, preferring to mull the matter over and over in his mind. What could he recall about the number one stand-by job? It began at eight A.M. – he recalled reading that. And there always were a lot of tourists flocking through the White House to catch a glimpse of Unicephalon 40-D, especially the school kids . . . and he disliked kids because they always jeered at him due to his weight. Cripes, he'd have a million of them filing by, because he had to be on the premises. By law, he had to be within a hundred yards of Unicephalon 40-D at all times, day and night, or was it fifty yards? Anyhow it practically was right on top, so if the homeostatic problem-solving system failed – *Maybe I better bone up on this*, he decided. *Take a TV educational course on government administration, just in case*.

To the union official on his right, Max asked, 'Listen, goodmember, do I have any powers in this job you guys got me? I mean, can I—'

'It's a union job like every other union job,' the official answered wearily. 'You sit. You stand by. Have you been out of work that long, you don't remember?' He laughed, nudging his companion. 'Listen, Fischer here wants to know what authority the job entails.' Now both men laughed. 'I tell you what, Fischer,' the official drawled. 'When you're all set up there in the White House, when you got your chair and bed and made all your arrangements for meals and laundry and TV viewing time, why don't you amble over to Unicephalon 40-D and just sort of whine around there, you know, scratch and whine, until it notices you.'

'Lay off,' Max muttered.

'And then,' the official continued, 'you sort of say, Hey Unicephalon, listen. I'm your buddy. How about a little "I scratch your back, you scratch mine." You pass an ordinance for me—'

'But what can he do in exchange?' the other union official asked.

'Amuse it. He can tell it the story of his life, how he rose out of poverty and obscurity and educated himself by watching TV seven days a week until finally, guess what, he rose all the way to the top; he got the job—' The official snickered. 'Of stand-by President.'

Maximilian, flushing, said nothing; he stared woodenly out of the monorail window.

*

When they reached Washington, DC and the White House, Maximilian Fischer was shown a little room. It had belonged to Gus, and although the faded old motor magazines had been cleared out, a few prints remained tacked on the walls: a 1963 Volvo S-122, a 1957 Peugeot 403 and other antique classics of a bygone age. And, on a bookcase, Max saw a hand-carved plastic model of a 1950 Studebaker Starlight coupe, with each detail perfect.

'He was making that when he croaked,' one of the union officials said as he set down Max's suitcase. 'He could tell you any fact there is about those old preturbine cars – any useless bit of car knowledge.'

Max nodded.

'You got any idea what you're going to do?' the official asked him.

'Aw hell,' Max said. 'How could I decide so soon? Give me time.' Moodily, he picked up the Studebaker Starlight coupe and examined its underside. The desire to smash the model car came to him; he put the car down, then, turning away.

'Make a rubber band ball,' the official said.

'What?' Max said.

'The stand-by before Gus. Louis somebody-or-other . . . he collected rubber bands, made a huge ball, big as a house, by the time he died. I forget his name, but the rubber band ball is at the Smithsonian now.'

There was a stir in the hallway. A White House receptionist, a middle-aged woman severely dressed, put her head in the room and said, 'Mr President, there's a TV news clown here to interview you. Please try to finish with him as quickly as possible because we have quite a few tours passing through the building today and some may want to look at you.'

'Okay,' Max said. He turned to face the TV news clown. It was Jim-Jam Briskin, he saw, the ranking clown just now. 'You want to see me?' he asked Briskin haltingly. 'I mean, you're sure it's *me* you want to interview?' He could not imagine what Briskin could find of interest about him. Holding out his hand he added, 'This is my room, but these model cars and pics aren't mine; they were Gus's. I can't tell you nuthin' about them.'

On Briskin's head the familiar flaming-red clown wig glowed, giving him in real life the same bizarre cast that the TV cameras picked up so well. He was older, however, than the TV image indicated, but he had the friendly, natural smile that everyone looked for: it was his badge of informality, a really nice guy, even-tempered but with a caustic wit when occasion demanded. Briskin was the sort of man who . . . *well*, Max thought, *the sort of fella you'd like to see marry into your family.*

They shook hands. Briskin said, 'You're on camera, Mr Max Fischer. Or rather, Mr President, I should say. This is Jim-Jam talking. For our literally billions of viewers located in every niche and corner of this far-flung solar system of ours, let me ask you this. How does it feel, sir, to know that if Unicephalon 40-D should fail, even momentarily, you would be catapulted into the most important post that has ever fallen onto the shoulders of a human being, that of actual, not merely stand-by, President of the United States? Does it worry you at night?' He smiled. Behind him the camera technicians swung their mobile lenses back and forth; lights burned Max's eyes and he felt the heat beginning to make him sweat under his arms and on his neck and upper lip. 'What emotions grip you at this instant?' Briskin asked. 'As you stand on the threshold of this new task for perhaps the balance of your life? What thoughts run through your mind, now that you're actually here in the White House?'

After a pause, Max said, 'It's – a big responsibility.' And then he realized, he saw, that Briskin was laughing at him, laughing silently as he stood there. Because it was all a gag Briskin was pulling. Out in the planets and moons his audience knew it, too; they knew Jim-Jam's humor.

'You're a large man, Mr Fischer,' Briskin said. 'If I may

say so, a stout man. Do you get much exercise? I ask this because with your new job you pretty well will be confined to this room, and I wondered what change in your life this would bring about.'

'Well,' Max said, 'I feel of course that a Government employee should always be at his post. Yes, what you say is true; I have to be right here day and night, but that doesn't bother me. I'm prepared for it.'

'Tell me,' Jim Briskin said, 'do you—' And then he ceased. Turning to the video technicians behind him he said in an odd voice, 'We're off the air.'

A man wearing headphones squeezed forward past the cameras. 'On the monitor, listen.' He hurriedly handed the headphones to Briskin. 'We've been pre-empted by Unicephalon; it's broadcasting a news bulletin.'

Briskin held the phones to his ear. His face writhed and he said, 'Those ships at eight hundred AUs. They are hostile, it says.' He glanced up sharply at his technicians, the red clown's wig sliding askew. 'They've begun to attack.'

Within the following twenty-four hours the aliens had managed not only to penetrate the Sol System but also to knock out Unicephalon 40-D.

News of this reached Maximilian Fischer in an indirect manner as he sat in the White House Cafeteria having his supper.

'Mr Maximilian Fischer?'

'Yeah,' Max said, glancing up at the group of Secret Servicemen who had surrounded his table.

'You're President of the United States.'

'Naw,' Max said. 'I'm the stand-by President; that's different.'

The Secret Serviceman said, 'Unicephalon 40-D is out of commission for perhaps as long as a month. So according to the amended Constitution, you're President and also Commander-in-Chief of the armed forces. We're here to guard

you.' The Secret Serviceman grinned ludicrously. Max
grinned back. 'Do you understand?' the Secret Serviceman
asked. 'I mean, does it penetrate?'

'Sure,' Max said. Now he understood the buzz of con-
versation he had overheard while waiting in the cafeteria
line with his tray. It explained why White House personnel
had looked at him strangely. He set down his coffee cup,
wiped his mouth with his napkin, slowly and deliberately,
pretended to be absorbed in solemn thought. But actually
his mind was empty.

'We've been told,' the Secret Serviceman said, 'that
you're needed at once at the National Security Council
bunker. They want your participation in finalization of
strategy deliberations.'

They walked from the cafeteria to the elevator.

'Strategy policy,' Max said, as they descended. 'I got a few
opinions about that. I guess it's time to deal harshly with
these alien ships, don't you agree?'

The Secret Servicemen nodded.

'Yes, we got to show we're not afraid,' Max said. 'Sure,
we'll get finalization; we'll blast the buggers.'

The Secret Servicemen laughed good-naturedly.

Pleased, Max nudged the leader of the group. 'I think
we're pretty goddam strong; I mean, the USA has got
teeth.'

'You tell 'em, Max,' one of the Secret Servicemen said,
and they all laughed aloud. Max included.

As they stepped from the elevator they were stopped by a
tall, well-dressed man who said urgently, 'Mr President, I'm
Jonathan Kirk, White House press secretary; I think before
you go in there to confer with the NSC people you should
address the nation in this hour of gravest peril. The public
wants to see what their new leader is like.' He held out
a paper. 'Here's a statement drawn up by the Political
Advisory Board; it codifies your—'

'Nuts,' Max said, handing it back without looking at it.
'I'm the President, not you. Kirk? Burke? Shirk? Never

heard of you. Show me the microphone and I'll make my own speech. Or get me Pat Noble; maybe he's got some ideas.' And then he remembered that Pat had sold him out in the first place; Pat had gotten him into this. 'Not him either,' Max said. 'Just give me the microphone.'

'This is a time of crisis,' Kirk grated.

'Sure,' Max said, 'so leave me alone; you keep out of my way and I'll keep out of yours. Ain't that right?' He slapped Kirk good-naturedly on the back. 'And we'll both be better off.'

A group of people with portable TV cameras and lighting appeared, and among them Max saw Jim-Jam Briskin, in the middle, with his staff.

'Hey, Jim-Jam,' he yelled. 'Look, I'm President now!'

Stolidly, Jim Briskin came toward him.

'I'm not going to be winding no ball of string,' Max said. 'Or making model boats, nuthin' like that.' He shook hands warmly with Briskin. 'I thank you,' Max said. 'For your congratulations.'

'Congratulations,' Briskin said, then, in a low voice.

'Thanks,' Max said, squeezing the man's hand until the knuckles creaked. 'Of course, sooner or later they'll get that noise-box patched up and I'll just be stand-by again. But—' He grinned gleefully around at all of them; the corridor was full of people now, from TV to White House staff members to Army officers and Secret Servicemen.

Briskin said, 'You have a big task, Mr Fischer.'

'Yeah,' Max agreed.

Something in Briskin's eyes said: *And I wonder if you can handle it. I wonder if you're the man to hold such power.*

'Surely I can do it,' Max declared, into Briskin's microphone, for all the vast audience to hear.

'Possibly you can,' Jim Briskin said, and on his face was dubiousness.

'Hey, you don't like me any more,' Max said. 'How come?'

Briskin said nothing, but his eyes flickered.

'Listen,' Max said, 'I'm President now; I can close down your silly network – I can send FBI men in any time I want. For your information I'm firing the Attorney General right now, whatever his name is, and putting in a man I know, a man I can trust.'

Briskin said, 'I see.' And now he looked less dubious; conviction, of a sort which Max could not fathom, began to appear instead. 'Yes,' Jim Briskin said, 'you have the authority to order that, don't you? *If* you're really President . . .'

'Watch out,' Max said. 'You're nothing compared to me, Briskin, even if you do have that great big audience.' Then, turning his back on the cameras, he strode through the open door, into the NSC bunker.

Hours later, in the early morning, down in the National Security Council subsurface bunker, Maximilian Fischer listened sleepily to the TV set in the background as it yammered out the latest news. By now, intelligence sources had plotted the arrival of thirty more alien ships in the Sol System. It was believed that seventy in all had entered. Each was being continually tracked.

But that was not enough, Max knew. Sooner or later he would have to give the order to attack the alien ships. He hesitated. After all, who were they? Nobody at CIA knew. How strong were they? Not known either. And – would the attack be successful?

And then there were domestic problems. Unicephalon had continually tinkered with the economy, priming it when necessary, cutting taxes, lowering interest rates . . . That had ceased with the problem-solver's destruction. *Jeez*, Max thought dismally. *What do I know about unemployment? I mean, how can I tell what factories to reopen and where?*

He turned to General Tompkins, Chairman of the Joint Chiefs of Staff, who sat beside him examining a report on the scrambling of the tactical defensive ships protecting Earth. 'They got all them ships distributed right?' he asked Tompkins.

'Yes, Mr President,' General Tompkins answered.

Max winced. But the general did not seem to have spoken ironically; his tone had been respectful. 'Okay,' Max murmured. 'Glad to hear that. And you got all that missile cloud up so there're no leaks, like you let in that ship to blast Unicephalon. I don't want that to happen again.'

'We're under Defcon one,' General Tompkins said. 'Full war footing, as of six o'clock, our time.'

'How about those strategic ships?' That, he had learned, was the euphemism for their offensive strike-force.

'We can mount an attack at any time,' General Tompkins said, glancing down at the long table to obtain the assenting nods of his co-workers. 'We can take care of each of the seventy invaders now within our system.'

With a groan, Max said, 'Anybody got any bicarb?' The whole business depressed him. *What a lot of work and sweat,* he thought. *All this goddam agitation – why don't the buggers just leave our system? I mean, do we have to get into a war? No telling what their home system will do in retaliation; you never can tell about unhuman life forms – they're unreliable.*

'That's what bothers me,' he said aloud. 'Retaliation.' He sighed.

General Tompkins said, 'Negotiation with them evidently is impossible.'

'Go ahead, then,' Max said. 'Go give it to them.' He looked about for the bicarb.

'I think you're making a wise choice,' General Tompkins said, and, across the table, the civilian advisors nodded in agreement.

'Here's an odd piece of news,' one of the advisors said to Max. He held out a teletype dispatch. 'James Briskin has just filed a writ of *mandamus* against you in a Federal Court in California, claiming you're not legally President because you didn't run for office.'

'You mean because I didn't get *voted* in?' Max said. 'Just because of that?'

'Yes sir. Briskin is asking the Federal Courts to rule on

this, and meanwhile he has announced his own candidacy.'

'WHAT?'

'Briskin claims not only that you must run for office and be voted in, but you must run against him. And with his popularity he evidently feels—'

'Aw nuts,' Max said in despair. 'How do you like that.'

No one answered.

'Well anyhow,' Max said, 'it's all decided; you military fellas go ahead and knock out those alien ships. And meanwhile—' He decided there and then. 'We'll put economic pressure on Jim-Jam's sponsors, that Reinlander Beer and Calbest Electronics, to get him not to run.'

The men at the long table nodded. Papers rattled as briefcases were put away; the meeting – temporarily – was at an end.

He's got an unfair advantage, Max said to himself. *How can I run when it's not equal, him a famous TV personality and me not? That's not right; I can't allow that.*

Jim-Jam can run, he decided, *but it won't do him any good.* He's not going to beat me because he's not going to be alive that long.

A week before the election, Telscan, the interplanetary public-opinion sampling agency, published its latest findings. Reading them, Maximilian Fischer felt more gloomy than ever.

'Look at this,' he said to his cousin Leon Lait, the lawyer whom he had recently made Attorney General. He tossed the report to him.

His own showing of course was negligible. In the election, Briskin would easily, and most definitely, win.

'Why is that?' Lait asked. Like Max, he was a large, paunchy man who for years now had held a stand-by job; he was not used to physical activity of any sort and his new position was proving difficult for him. However, out of family loyalty to Max, he remained. 'Is that because he's got all those TV stations?' he asked, sipping from his can of beer.

Max said cuttingly, 'Naw, it's because his navel glows in the dark. Of course it's because of his TV stations, you jerk – he's got them pounding away night and day, creatin' an *image.*' He paused, moodily. 'He's a clown. It's that red wig, it's fine for a newscaster, but not for a President.' Too morose to speak, he lapsed into silence.

And worse was to follow.

At nine P.M. that night, Jim-Jam Briskin began a seventy-two-hour marathon TV program over all his stations, a great final drive to bring his popularity over the top and ensure his victory.

In his special bedroom at the White House, Max Fischer sat with a tray of food before him, in bed, gloomily facing the TV set.

That Briskin, he thought furiously for the millionth time. 'Look,' he said to his cousin; the Attorney General sat in the easy chair across from him. 'There's the nerd now.' He pointed to the TV screen.

Leon Lait, munching on his cheeseburger, said, 'It's abominable.'

'You know where he's broadcasting from? Way out in deep space, out past Pluto. At their farthest-out transmitter, which your FBI guys will never in a million years manage to get to.'

'They will,' Leon assured him. 'I told them they *have* to get him – the President, my cousin, personally says so.'

'But they won't get him for a while,' Max said. 'Leon, you're just too damn slow. I'll tell you something. I got a ship of the line out there, the *Dwight D. Eisenhower*. It's all ready to lay an egg on them, you know, a big bang, just as soon as I pass on the word.'

'Right, Max.'

'And I hate to,' Max said.

*

The telecast had begun to pick up momentum already. Here came the Spotlights, and sauntering out onto the stage pretty Peggy Jones, wearing a glittery bare-shoulder gown, her hair radiant. *Now we get a top-flight striptease*, Max realized, *by a real fine-looking girl*. Even he sat up and took notice. Well, maybe not a true striptease, but certainly the opposition, Briskin and his staff, had sex working for them, here. Across the room his cousin the Attorney General had stopped munching his cheeseburger; the noise came to a halt, then picked up slowly once more.

On the screen, Peggy sang:

> *It's Jim-Jam, for whom I am,*
> *America's best-loved guy.*
> *It's Jim-Jam, the best one that am,*
> *The candidate for you and I.*

'Oh God,' Max groaned. And yet, the way she delivered it, with every part of her slim, long body . . . it was okay. 'I guess I got to inform the *Dwight D. Eisenhower* to go ahead,' he said, watching.

'If you say so, Max,' Leon said. 'I assure you, I'll rule that you acted legally; don't worry none about that.'

'Gimme the red phone,' Max said. 'That's the armored connection that only the Commander-in-Chief uses for top-secret instructions. Not bad, huh?' He accepted the phone from the Attorney General. 'I'm calling General Tompkins and he'll relay the order to the ship. Too bad, Briskin,' he added, with one last look at the screen. 'But it's your own fault; you didn't have to do what you did, opposing me and all.'

The girl in the silvery dress had gone now, and Jim-Jam Briskin had appeared in her place. Momentarily, Max waited.

'Hi, beloved comrades,' Briskin said, raising his hands for silence; the canned applause – Max knew that no audience existed in that remote spot – lowered, then rose again. Briskin grinned amiably, waiting for it to die.

'It's a fake,' Max grunted. 'Fake audience. They're smart, him and his staff. His rating's already way up.'

'Right, Max,' the Attorney General agreed. 'I noticed that.'

'Comrades,' Jim Briskin was saying soberly on the TV screen, 'as you may know, originally President Maximilian Fischer and I got along very well.'

His hand on the red phone, Max thought to himself that what Jim-Jam said was true.

'Where we broke,' Briskin continued, 'was over the issue of force – of the use of naked, raw power. To Max Fischer, the office of President is merely a machine, an instrument, which he can use as an extension of his own desires, to fulfill his own needs. I honestly believe that in many respects his aims are good; he is trying to carry out Unicephalon's fine policies. But as to the means. That's a different matter.'

Max said, 'Listen to him, Leon.' And he thought, *No matter what he says I'm going to keep on; nobody is going to stand in my way, because it's my duty; it's the job of the office, and if you got to be President like I am you'd do it, too.*

'Even the President,' Briskin was saying, 'must obey the law; he doesn't stand outside it, however powerful he is.' He was silent for a moment and then he said slowly, 'I know that at this moment the FBI, under direct orders from Max Fischer's appointee, Leon Lait, is attempting to close down these stations, to still my voice. Here again Max Fischer is making use of power, of the police agency, for his own ends, making it an extension—'

Max picked up the red phone. At once a voice said from it, 'Yes, Mr President. This is General Tompkins' C of C.'

'What's that?' Max said.

'Chief of Communications, Army 600-1000, sir. Aboard the *Dwight D. Eisenhower*, accepting relay through the transmitter at the Pluto Station.'

'Oh yeah,' Max said, nodding. 'Listen, you fellas stand by, you understand? Be ready to receive instructions.' He put his hand over the mouthpiece of the phone. 'Leon,' he said to his cousin, who had now finished his cheeseburger and was starting on a strawberry shake. 'How can I do it? I mean, Briskin is telling the truth.'

Leon said, 'Give Tompkins the word.' He belched, then tapped himself on the chest with the side of his fist. 'Pardon me.'

On the screen Jim Briskin said, 'I think very possibly I'm risking my life to speak to you, because this we must face: we have a President who would not mind employing murder to obtain his objectives. This is the political tactic of a tyranny, and that's what we're seeing, a tyranny coming into existence in our society, replacing the rational, disinterested rule of the homeostatic problem-solving Unicephalon 40-D which was designed, built and put into operation by some of the finest minds we have ever seen, minds dedicated to the preservation of all that's worthy in our tradition. And the transformation from this to a one-man tyranny is melancholy, to say the least.'

Quietly, Max said, 'Now I can't go ahead.'

'Why not?' Leon said.

'Didn't you hear him? He's talking about *me*. I'm the tyrant he has reference to. Keerist.' Max hung up the red phone. 'I waited too long.

'It's hard for me to say it,' Max said, 'but – well, hell, it would prove he's right.' *I know he's right anyhow*, Max thought. *But do they know it? Does the public know it? I can't let them find out about me*, he realized. *They should look up to their President, respect him. Honor him. No wonder I show up so bad in the Telscan poll. No wonder Jim Briskin decided to run against me the moment he heard I was in office. They really do know about me; they sense it, sense that Jim-Jam is speaking the truth. I'm just not Presidential caliber.*

I'm not fit, he thought, *to hold this office.*

'Listen, Leon,' he said, 'I'm going to give it to that Briskin anyhow and then step down. It'll be my last official act.' Once more he picked up the red phone. 'I'm going to order them to wipe out Briskin and then someone else can be President. Anyone the people want. Even Pat Noble or you; I don't care.' He jiggled the phone. 'Hey, C of C,' he said loudly. 'Come on, answer.' To his cousin he said, 'Leave me some of that shake; it's actually half mine.'

'Sure, Max,' Leon said loyally.

'Isn't no one there?' Max said into the phone. He waited. The phone remained dead. 'Something's gone wrong,' he said to Leon. 'Communications have busted down. It must be those aliens again.'

And then he saw the TV screen. It was blank.

'What's happening?' Max said. 'What are they doing to me? *Who's* doing it?' He looked around, frightened. 'I don't get it.'

Leon stoically drank the milkshake, shrugging to show that he had no answer. But his beefy face had paled.

'It's too late,' Max said. 'For some reason it's just too late.' Slowly, he hung up the phone. 'I've got enemies, Leon, more powerful than you or me. And I don't even know who they are.' He sat in silence, before the dark, soundless TV screen. Waiting.

The speaker of the TV set said abruptly, 'Psuedo-autonomic news bulletin. Stand by, please.' Then again there was silence.

Jim Briskin, glancing at Ed Fineberg and Peggy, waited.

'Comrade citizens of the United States,' the flat, unmodulated voice from the TV speaker said, all at once. 'The interregnum is over, the situation has returned to normal.' As it spoke, words appeared on the monitor screen, a ribbon of printed tape passing slowly across, before the TV cameras in Washington, DC Unicephalon 40-D had spliced itself into the co-ax in its usual fashion; it had pre-empted the program in progress: that was its traditional right.

The voice was the synthetic verbalizing-organ of the homeostatic structure itself.

'The election campaign is nullified,' Unicephalon 40-D said. 'That is item one. The stand-by President Maximilian

Fischer is cancelled out; that is item two. Item three: we are at war with the aliens who have invaded our system. Item four. James Briskin, who has been speaking to you—'

This is it, Jim Briskin realized.

In his earphones the impersonal, plateau-like voice continued, 'Item four. James Briskin, who has been speaking to you on these facilities, is hereby ordered to cease and desist, and a writ of *mandamus* is issued forthwith requiring him to show just cause why he should be free to pursue any further political activity. In the public interest we instruct him to become politically silent.'

Grinning starkly at Peggy and Ed Fineberg, Briskin said, 'That's it. It's over. I'm to politically shut up.'

'You can fight it in the courts,' Peggy said at once. 'You can take it all the way up to the Supreme Court; they've set aside decisions of Unicephalon in the past.' She put her hand on his shoulder, but he moved away. 'Or do you want to fight it?'

'At least I'm not cancelled out,' Briskin said. He felt tired. 'I'm glad to see that machine back in operation,' he said, to reassure Peggy. 'It means a return to stability. *That* we can use.'

'What'll you do, Jim-Jam?' Ed asked. 'Go back to Reinlander Beer and Calbest Electronics and try to get your old job back?'

'No,' Briskin murmured. Certainly not that. But – he could not really become politically silent; he could not do what the problem-solver said. It simply was not biologically possible for him; sooner or later he would begin to talk again, for better or worse. *And*, he thought, *I'll bet Max can't do what it says either . . . neither of us can.*

Maybe, he thought, *I'll answer the writ of* mandamus; *maybe I'll contest it. A counter suit . . . I'll sue Unicephalon 40-D in a court of law. Jim-Jam Briskin the plaintiff, Unicephalon 40-D the defendant.* He smiled. *I'll need a good lawyer for that. Someone quite a bit better than Max Fischer's top legal mind, cousin Leon Lait.*

Going to the closet of the small studio in which they had been broadcasting, he got his coat and began to put it on. A long trip lay ahead of them back to Earth from this remote spot, and he wanted to get started.

Peggy, following after him, said, 'You're not going back on the air *at all*? Not even to finish the program?'

'No,' he said.

'But Unicephalon will be cutting back out again, and what'll that leave? Just dead air. That's not right, is it, Jim? Just to walk out like this . . . I can't believe you'd do it, it's not like you.'

He halted at the door of the studio. 'You heard what it said. The instructions it handed out to me.'

'Nobody leaves dead air going,' Peggy said. 'It's a vacuum, Jim, the thing nature abhors. *And if you don't fill it, someone else will*. Look, Unicephalon is going back off right now.' She pointed at the TV monitor. The ribbon of words had ceased; once more the screen was dark, empty of motion and light. 'It's your responsibility,' Peggy said, 'and you know it.'

'Are we back on the air?' he asked Ed.

'Yes. It's definitely out of the circuit, at least for a while.' Ed gestured toward the vacant stage on which the TV cameras and lights focussed. He said nothing more; he did not have to.

With his coat still on, Jim Briskin walked that way. Hands in his pockets he stepped back into the range of the cameras, smiled and said, 'I think, beloved comrades, the interruption is over. For the time being, anyhow. So . . . let's continue.'

The noise of canned applause – manipulated by Ed Fineberg – swelled up, and Jim Briskin raised his hands and signalled the nonexistent studio audience for silence.

'Does any of you know a good lawyer?' Jim-Jam asked caustically. 'And if you do, phone us and tell us right away – before the FBI finally manages to reach us out here.'

*

In his bedroom at the White House, as Unicephalon's message ended, Maximilian Fischer turned to his cousin Leon and said, 'Well, I'm out of office.'

'Yeah, Max,' Leon said heavily. 'I guess you are.'

'And you, too,' Max pointed out. 'It's going to be a clean sweep; you can count on that. Cancelled.' He gritted his teeth. 'That's sort of insulting. It could have said *retired.*'

'I guess that's just its way of expressing itself,' Leon said. 'Don't get upset, Max; remember your heart trouble. You still got the job of stand-by, and that's the top stand-by position there is, Stand-by President of the United States, I want to remind you. And now you've got all this worry and effort off your back; you're lucky.'

'I wonder if I'm allowed to finish this meal,' Max said, picking at the food in the tray before him. His appetite, now that he was retired, began almost at once to improve; he selected a chicken salad sandwich and took a big bite from it. 'It's still mine,' he decided, his mouth full. 'I still get to live here and eat regularly – right?'

'Right,' Leon agreed, his legal mind active. 'That's in the contract the union signed with Congress; remember back to that? We didn't go out on strike for nothing.'

'Those were the days,' Max said. He finished the chicken salad sandwich and returned to the eggnog. It felt good not to have to make big decisions; he let out a long, heartfelt sigh and settled back into the pile of pillows propping him up.

But then he thought, *In some respects I sort of enjoyed making decisions. I mean, it was—* He searched for the thought. *It was different from being a stand-by or drawing unemployment. It had—*

Satisfaction, he thought. *That's what it gave me. Like I was accomplishing something.* He missed that already; he felt suddenly hollow, as if things had all at once become purposeless.

'Leon,' he said, 'I could have gone on as President

another whole month. And enjoyed the job. You know what
I mean?'

'Yeah, I guess I get your meaning,' Leon mumbled.

'No you don't,' Max said.

'I'm trying, Max,' his cousin said. 'Honest.'

With bitterness, Max said, 'I shouldn't have had them
go ahead and let those engineer-fellas patch up that Unicephalon; I should have buried the project, at least for six
months.'

'Too late to think about that now,' Leon said.

Is it? Max asked himself. *You know, something could* happen
to Unicephalon 40-D. An accident.

He pondered that as he ate a piece of green-apple pie
with a wide slice of longhorn cheese. A number of persons
whom he knew could pull off such tasks . . . and did so,
now and then.

A big, nearly-fatal accident, he thought. *Late some night,
when everyone's asleep and it's just me and it awake here in the
White House. I mean, let's face it; the aliens showed us how.*

'Look, Jim-Jam Briskin's back on the air,' Leon said,
gesturing at the TV set. Sure enough, there was the
famous, familiar red wig, and Briskin was saying something
witty and yet profound, something that made one stop to
ponder. 'Hey listen,' Leon said. 'He's poking fun at the
FBI; can you imagine him doing that *now*? He's not scared
of anything.'

'Don't bother me,' Max said. 'I'm thinking.' He reached
over and carefully turned the sound of the TV set off.

For thoughts such as he was having he wanted no dis-
tractions.

A Little Something
for us Tempunauts

Wearily, Addison Doug plodded up the long path of synthetic redwood rounds, step by step, his head down a little, moving as if he were in actual physical pain. The girl watched him, wanting to help him, hurt within her to see how worn and unhappy he was, but at the same time she rejoiced that he was there at all. On and on, toward her, without glancing up, going by feel . . . like he's done this many times, she thought suddenly. Knows the way too well. Why?

'Addi,' she called, and ran toward him. 'They said on the TV you were dead. All of you were killed!'

He paused, wiping back his dark hair, which was no longer long; just before the launch they had cropped it. But he had evidently forgotten. 'You believe everything you see on TV?' he said, and came on again, haltingly, but smiling now. And reaching up for her.

God, it felt good to hold him, and to have him clutch at her again, with more strength than she had expected. 'I was going to find somebody else,' she gasped. 'To replace you.'

'I'll knock your head off if you do,' he said. 'Anyhow, that isn't possible; nobody could replace me.'

'But what about the implosion?' she said. 'On reentry; they said—'

'I forget,' Addison said, in the tone he used when he meant, I'm not going to discuss it. The tone had always angered her before, but not now. This time she sensed how awful the memory was. 'I'm going to stay at your place a couple of days,' he said, as together they moved up the path

toward the open front door of the tilted A-frame house. 'If
that's okay. And Benz and Crayne will be joining me, later
on; maybe even as soon as tonight. We've got a lot to talk
over and figure out.'

'Then all three of you survived.' She gazed up into his
careworn face. 'Everything they said on TV . . .' She
understood, then. Or believed she did. 'It was a cover
story. For – political purposes, to fool the Russians. Right?
I mean, the Soviet Union'll think the launch was a failure
because on reentry—'

'No,' he said. 'A chrononaut will be joining us, most
likely. To help figure out what happened. General Toad
said one of them is already on his way here; they got
clearance already. Because of the gravity of the situation.'

'Jesus,' the girl said, stricken. 'Then who's the cover story
for?'

'Let's have something to drink,' Addison said. 'And then
I'll outline it all for you.'

'Only thing I've got at the moment is California brandy.'

Addison Doug said, 'I'd drink anything right now, the
way I feel.' He dropped to the couch, leaned back, and
sighed a ragged, distressed sigh, as the girl hurriedly began
fixing both of them a drink.

The FM-radio in the car yammered, '. . . grieves at the
stricken turn of events precipitating out of an un-
heralded . . .'

'Official nonsense babble,' Crayne said, shutting off the
radio. He and Benz were having trouble finding the house,
having been there only once before. It struck Crayne that
this was somewhat informal a way of convening a conference of this importance, meeting at Addison's chick's pad
out here in the boondocks of Ojai. On the other hand, they
wouldn't be pestered by the curious. And they probably
didn't have much time. But that was hard to say; about that
no one knew for sure.

The hills on both sides of the road had once been forests,

Crayne observed. Now housing tracts and their melted, irregular, plastic roads marred every rise in sight. 'I'll bet this was nice once,' he said to Benz, who was driving.

'The Los Padres National Forest is near here,' Benz said. 'I got lost in there when I was eight. For hours I was sure a rattler would get me. Every stick was a snake.'

'The rattler's got you now,' Crayne said.

'All of us,' Benz said.

'You know,' Crayne said, 'it's a hell of an experience to be dead.'

'Speak for yourself.'

'But technically—'

'If you listen to the radio and TV.' Benz turned toward him, his big gnome face bleak with admonishing sternness. 'We're no more dead than anyone else on the planet. The difference for us is that our death date is in the past, whereas everyone else's is set somewhere at an uncertain time in the future. Actually, some people have it pretty damn well set, like people in cancer wards; they're as certain as we are. More so. For example, how long can we stay here before we go back? We have a margin, a latitude that a terminal cancer victim doesn't have.'

Crayne said cheerfully, 'The next thing you'll be telling us to cheer us up is that we're in no pain.'

'Addi is. I watched him lurch off earlier today. He's got it psychosomatically – made it into a physical complaint. Like God's kneeling on his neck; you know, carrying a much-too-great burden that's unfair, only he won't complain out loud . . . just points now and then at the nail hole in his hand.' He grinned.

'Addi has got more to live for than we do.'

'Everyman has more to live for than any other man. I don't have a cute chick to sleep with, but I'd like to see the semis rolling along Riverside Freeway at sunset a few more times. It's not what you have to live for; it's that you want to live to see it, to be there – that's what is so damn sad.'

They rode on in silence.

*

In the quiet living room of the girl's house the three tempunauts sat around smoking, taking it easy; Addison Doug thought to himself that the girl looked unusually foxy and desirable in her stretched-tight white sweater and micro-skirt and he wished, wistfully, that she looked a little less interesting. He could not really afford to get embroiled in such stuff, at this point. He was too tired.

'Does she know,' Benz said, indicating the girl, 'what this is all about? I mean, can we talk openly? It won't wipe her out?'

'I haven't explained it to her yet,' Addison said.

'You goddam well better,' Crayne said.

'What is it?' the girl said, stricken, sitting upright with one hand directly between her breasts. As if clutching at a religious artifact that isn't there, Addison thought.

'We got snuffed on reentry,' Benz said. He was, really, the cruelest of the three. Or at least the most blunt. 'You see, Miss . . .'

'Hawkins,' the girl whispered.

'Glad to meet you, Miss Hawkins.' Benz surveyed her in his cold, lazy fashion. 'You have a first name?'

'Merry Lou.'

'Okay, Merry Lou,' Benz said. To the other two men he observed, 'Sounds like the name a waitress has stitched on her blouse. Merry Lou's my name and I'll be serving you dinner and breakfast and lunch and dinner and breakfast for the next few days or however long it is before you all give up and go back to your own time; that'll be fifty-three dollars and eight cents, please, not including tip And I hope y'all never come back, y'hear?' His voice had begun to shake; his cigarette, too. 'Sorry, Miss Hawkins,' he said then. 'We're all screwed up by the implosion at reentry. As soon as we got here in ETA we learned about it. We've known longer than anyone else; we knew as soon as we hit Emergence Time.'

'But there's nothing we could do,' Crayne said.

'There's nothing anyone can do,' Addison said to her, and put his arm around her. It felt like a déjà vu thing but then it hit him. We're in a closed time loop, he thought, we keep going through this again and again, trying to solve the reentry problem, each time imagining it's the first time, the only time . . . and never succeeding. Which attempt is this? Maybe the millionth; we have sat here a million times, raking the same facts over and over again and getting nowhere. He felt bone-weary, thinking that. And he felt a sort of vast philosophical hate toward all other men, who did not have this enigma to deal with. We all go to one place, he thought, as the Bible says. But . . . for the three of us, we have been there already. Are lying there now. So it's wrong to ask us to stand around on the surface of Earth afterward and argue and worry about it and try to figure out what malfunctioned. That should be, rightly, for our heirs to do. We've had enough already.

He did not say this aloud, though – for their sake.

'Maybe you bumped into something,' the girl said.

Glancing at the others, Benz said sardonically, 'Maybe we "bumped into something".'

'The TV commentators kept saying that,' Merry Lou said, 'about the hazard in reentry of being out of phase spatially and colliding right down to the molecular level with tangent objects, any one of which—' She gestured. 'You know. "No two objects can occupy the same space at the same time." So everything blew up, for that reason.' She glanced around questioningly.

'That is the major risk factor,' Crayne acknowledged. 'At least theoretically, as Dr Fein at Planning calculated when they got into the hazard question. But we had a variety of safety locking devices provided that functioned automatically. Reentry couldn't occur unless these assists had stabilized us spatially so we would not overlap. Of course, all those devices, in sequence, might have failed. One after the other. I was watching my feedback metric scopes on launch, and they agreed, every one of them, that we were phased properly at that time. And I heard no warning tones. Saw none, neither.' He grimaced. 'At least it didn't happen then.'

Suddenly Benz said, 'Do you realize that our next of kin are now rich? All our Federal and commercial life-insurance payoff. Our "next of kin" – God forbid, that's us, I guess. We can apply for tens of thousands of dollars, cash on the line. Walk into our brokers' offices and say, "I'm dead; lay the heavy bread on me." '

Addison Doug was thinking, The public memorial services. That they have planned, after the autopsies. That long line of black-draped Cads going down Pennsylvania Avenue, with all the government dignitaries and double-domed scientist types – *and we'll be there*. Not once but twice. Once in the oak hand-rubbed brass-fitted flag-draped caskets, but also . . . maybe riding in open limos, waving at the crowds of mourners.

'The ceremonies,' he said aloud.

The others stared at him, angrily, not comprehending. And then, one by one, they understood; he saw it on their faces.

'No,' Benz grated. 'That's – impossible.'

Crayne shook his head emphatically. 'They'll order us to be there, and we will be. Obeying orders.'

'Will we have to *smile*?' Addison said. 'To fucking *smile*?'

'No,' General Toad said slowly, his great wattled head shivering about on his broomstick neck, the color of his skin dirty and mottled, as if the mass of decorations on his stiff-board collar had started part of him decaying away. 'You are not to smile, but on the contrary are to adopt a properly grief-stricken manner. In keeping with the national mood of sorrow at this time.'

'That'll be hard to do,' Crayne said.

The Russian chrononaut showed no response; his thin

beaked face, narrow within his translating earphones, remained strained with concern.

'The nation,' General Toad said, 'will become aware of your presence among us once more for this brief interval; cameras of all major TV networks will pan up to you without warning, and at the same time, the various commentators have been instructed to tell their audiences something like the following.' He got out a piece of typed material, put on his glasses, cleared his throat and said, ' "We seem to be focusing on three figures riding together. Can't quite make them out. Can you?" ' General Toad lowered the paper. 'At this point they'll interrogate their colleagues extempore. Finally they'll exclaim, "Why, Roger," or Walter or Ned, as the case may be, according to the individual network—'

'Or Bill,' Crayne said. 'In case it's the Bufonidae network, down there in the swamp.'

General Toad ignored him. 'They will severally exclaim, "Why Roger I believe we're seeing the three tempunauts themselves! Does this indeed mean that somehow the difficulty—?" And then the colleague commentator says in his somewhat more somber voice, "What we're seeing at this time, I think, David," or Henry or Pete or Ralph, whichever it is, "consists of mankind's first verified glimpse of what the technical people refer to as Emergence Time Activity or ETA. Contrary to what might seem to be the case at first sight, these are *not* – repeat, not – our three valiant tempunauts as such, as we would ordinarily experience them, but more likely picked up by our cameras as the three of them are temporarily suspended in their voyage to the future, which we initially had reason to hope would take place in a time continuum roughly a hundred years from now . . . but it would seem that they somehow undershot and arc here now, at this moment, which of course is, as we know, our present." '

Addison Doug closed his eyes and thought, Crayne will ask him if he can be panned up on by the TV cameras

holding a balloon and eating cotton candy. I think we're all
going nuts from this, all of us. And then he wondered, How
many times have we gone through this idiotic exchange?

I can't prove it, he thought wearily. But I know it's true.
We've sat here, done this minuscule scrabbling, listened to
and said all this crap, many times. He shuddered. Each
rinky-dink word . . .

'What's the matter?' Benz said acutely.

The Soviet chrononaut spoke up for the first time. 'What
is the maximum interval of ETA possible to your three-
man team? And how large a per cent has been exhausted by
now?'

After a pause Crayne said, 'They briefed us on that before
we came in here today. We've consumed approximately one
half of our maximum total ETA interval.'

'However,' General Toad rumbled, 'we have scheduled
the Day of National Mourning to fall within the expected
period remaining to them of ETA time. This required us to
speed up the autopsy and other forensic findings, but in
view of public sentiment, it was felt . . .'

The autopsy, Addison Doug thought, and again he
shuddered; this time he could not keep his thoughts within
himself and he said, 'Why don't we adjourn this nonsense
meeting and drop down to pathology and view a few tissue
sections enlarged and in color, and maybe we'll brainstorm
a couple of vital concepts that'll aid medical science in its
quest for explanations? Explanations – that's what we need.
Explanations for problems that don't exist yet; we can
develop the problems later.' He paused. 'Who agrees?'

'I'm not looking at my spleen up there on the screen,'
Benz said. 'I'll ride in the parade but I won't participate in
my own autopsy.'

'You could distribute microscopic purple-stained slices of
your own gut to the mourners along the way,' Crayne said.
'They could provide each of us with a doggy bag; right,
General? We can strew tissue sections like confetti. I still
think we should smile.'

'I have researched all the memoranda about smiling,' General Toad said, riffling the pages stacked before him, 'and the consensus at policy is that smiling is not in accord with national sentiment. So that issue must be ruled closed. As far as your participating in the autopsical procedures which are now in progress—'

'We're missing out as we sit here,' Crayne said to Addison Doug. 'I always miss out.'

Ignoring him, Addison addressed the Soviet chrononaut. 'Officer N. Gauki,' he said into his microphone, dangling on his chest, 'what in your mind is the greatest terror facing a time traveler? That there will be an implosion due to coincidence on reentry, such as has occurred in our launch? Or did other traumatic obsessions bother you and your comrade during your own brief but highly successful time flight?'

N. Gauki, after a pause, answered, 'R. Plenya and I exchanged views at several informal times. I believe I can speak for us both when I respond to your question by emphasizing our perpetual fear that we had inadvertently entered a closed time loop and would never break out.'

'You'd repeat it forever?' Addison Doug asked.

'Yes, Mr A. Doug,' the chrononaut said, nodding somberly.

A fear that he had never experienced before overcame Addison Doug. He turned helplessly to Benz and muttered, 'Shit.' They gazed at each other.

'I really don't believe this is what happened,' Benz said to him in a low voice, putting his hand on Doug's shoulder; he gripped hard, the grip of friendship. 'We just imploded on reentry, that's all. Take it easy.'

'Could we adjourn soon?' Addison Doug said in a hoarse, strangling voice, half rising from his chair. He felt the room and the people in it rushing in at him, suffocating him. Claustrophobia, he realized. Like when I was in grade school, when they flashed a surprise test on our teaching machines, and I saw I couldn't pass it. 'Please,' he said simply, standing. They were all looking at him, with different expressions. The Russian's face was especially sympathetic, and deeply lined with care. Addison wished – 'I want to go home,' he said to them all, and felt stupid.

He was drunk. It was late at night, at a bar on Hollywood Boulevard; fortunately, Merry Lou was with him, and he was having a good time. Everyone was telling him so, anyhow. He clung to Merry Lou and said, 'The great unity in life, the supreme unity and meaning, is man and woman. Their absolute unity; right?'

'I know,' Merry Lou said. 'We studied that in class.' Tonight, at his request, Merry Lou was a small blonde girl, wearing purple bellbottoms and high heels and an open midriff blouse. Earlier she had had a lapis lazuli in her navel, but during dinner at Ting Ho's it had popped out and been lost. The owner of the restaurant had promised to keep on searching for it, but Merry Lou had been gloomy ever since. It was, she said, symbolic. But of what she did not say. Or anyhow he could not remember; maybe that was it. She had told him what it meant, and he had forgotten.

An elegant young black at a nearby table, with an Afro and striped vest and overstuffed red tie, had been staring at Addison for some time. He obviously wanted to come over to their table but was afraid to; meanwhile, he kept on staring.

'Did you ever get the sensation,' Addison said to Merry Lou, 'that you knew exactly what was about to happen? What someone was going to say? Word for word? Down to the slightest detail. As if you had already lived through it once before?'

'Everybody gets into that space,' Merry Lou said. She sipped a Bloody Mary.

The black rose and walked toward them. He stood by Addison. 'I'm sorry to bother you, sir.'

Addison said to Merry Lou, 'He's going to say, "Don't I know you from somewhere? Didn't I see you on TV?"'

'That was precisely what I intended to say,' the black said.

Addison said, 'You undoubtedly saw my picture on page forty-six of the current issue of *Time*, the section on new medical discoveries. I'm the GP from a small town in Iowa catapulted to fame by my invention of a widespread, easily available cure for eternal life. Several of the big pharmaceutical houses are already bidding on my vaccine.'

'That might have been where I saw your picture,' the black said, but he did not appear convinced. Nor did he appear drunk; he eyed Addison Doug intensely. 'May I seat myself with you and the lady?'

'Sure,' Addison Doug said. He now saw, in the man's hand, the ID of the US security agency that had ridden herd on the project from the start.

'Mr Doug,' the security agent said as he seated himself beside Addison, 'you really shouldn't be here shooting off your mouth like this. If I recognized you some other dude might and break out. It's all classified until the Day of Mourning. Technically, you're in violation of a Federal Statute by being here; did you realize that? I should haul you in. But this is a difficult situation; we don't want to do something uncool and make a scene. Where are your two colleagues?'

'At my place,' Merry Lou said. She had obviously not seen the ID. 'Listen,' she said sharply to the agent, 'why don't you get lost? My husband here has been through a grueling ordeal, and this is his only chance to unwind.'

Addison looked at the man. 'I knew what you were going to say before you came over here.' Word for word, he thought. I am right, and Benz is wrong and this will keep happening, this replay.

'Maybe,' the security agent said, 'I can induce you to go back to Miss Hawkins' place voluntarily. Some info arrived' – he tapped the tiny earphone in his right ear – 'just a few minutes ago, to all of us, to deliver to you, marked urgent, if we located you. At the launch site ruins . . . they've been combing through the rubble, you know?'

'I know,' Addison said.

'They think they have their first clue. Something was brought back by one of you. From ETA, over and above what you took, in violation of all your prelaunch training.'

'Let me ask you this,' Addison Doug said. 'Suppose somebody does see me? Suppose somebody does recognize me? So what?'

'The public believes that even though reentry failed, the flight into time, the first American time-travel launch, was successful. Three US tempunauts were thrust a hundred years into the future – roughly twice as far as the Soviet launch of last year. That you only went a *week* will be less of a shock if it's believed that you three chose deliberately to remanifest at this continuum because you wished to attend, in fact felt compelled to attend—'

'We wanted to be in the parade,' Addison interrupted. 'Twice.'

'You were drawn to the dramatic and somber spectacle of your own funeral procession, and will be glimpsed there by the alert camera crews of all major networks. Mr Doug, really, an awful lot of high-level planning and expense have gone into this to help correct a dreadful situation; trust us, believe me. It'll be easier on the public, and that's vital, if there's ever to be another US time shot. And that is, after all, what we all want.'

Addison Doug stared at him. 'We want what?'

Uneasily, the security agent said, 'To take further trips into time. As you have done. Unfortunately, you yourself cannot ever do so again, because of the tragic implosion and death of the three of you. But other tempunauts—'

'We want what? Is that what we want?' Addison's voice rose; people at nearby tables were watching now. Nervously.

'Certainly,' the agent said. 'And keep your voice down.'

'I don't want that,' Addison said. 'I want to stop. To stop

forever. To just lie in the ground, in the dust, with everyone else. To see no more summers – the *same* summer.'

'Seen one, you've seen them all,' Merry Lou said hysterically. 'I think he's right, Addi; we should get out of here. You've had too many drinks, and it's late, and this news about the—'

Addison broke in, 'What was brought back? How much extra mass?'

The security agent said, 'Preliminary analysis shows that machinery weighing about one hundred pounds was lugged back into the time-field of the module and picked up along with you. This much mass—' The agent gestured. 'That blew up the pad right on the spot. It couldn't begin to compensate for that much more than had occupied its open area at launch time.'

'Wow!' Merry Lou said, eyes wide. 'Maybe somebody sold one of you a quadraphonic phono for a dollar ninety-eight including fifteen-inch air-suspension speakers and a lifetime supply of Neil Diamond records.' She tried to laugh, but failed; her eyes dimmed over. 'Addi,' she whispered, 'I'm sorry. But it's sort of – weird. I mean, it's absurd; you all were briefed, weren't you, about your return weight? You weren't even to add so much as a piece of paper to what you took. I even saw Dr Fein demonstrating the reasons on TV. And one of you hoisted a hundred pounds of machinery into that field? You must have been trying to self-destruct, to do that!' Tears slid from her eyes; one tear rolled out onto her nose and hung there. He reached reflexively to wipe it away, as if helping a little girl rather than a grown one.

'I'll fly you to the analysis site,' the security agent said, standing up. He and Addison helped Merry Lou to her feet; she trembled as she stood a moment, finishing her Bloody Mary. Addison felt acute sorrow for her, but then, almost at once, it passed. He wondered why. One can weary even of that, he conjectured. Of caring for someone. If it goes on too long – on and on. Forever. And, at last, even after that, into something no one before, not God Himself, maybe, had ever had to suffer and in the end, for all His great heart, succumb to.

As they walked through the crowded bar toward the street, Addison Doug said to the security agent, 'Which one of us—'

'They know which one,' the agent said as he held the door to the street open for Merry Lou. The agent stood, now, behind Addison, signaling for a gray Federal car to land at the red parking area. Two other security agents, in uniform, hurried toward them.

'Was it me?' Addison Doug asked.

'You better believe it,' the security agent said.

The funeral procession moved with aching solemnity down Pennsylvania Avenue, three flag-draped caskets and dozens of black limousines passing between rows of heavily coated, shivering mourners. A low haze hung over the day, gray outlines of buildings faded into the rain-drenched murk of the Washington March day.

Scrutinizing the lead Cadillac through prismatic binoculars, TV's top news and public-events commentator, Henry Cassidy, droned on at his vast unseen audience, '. . . sad recollections of that earlier train among the wheatfields carrying the coffin of Abraham Lincoln back to burial and the nation's capital. And what a sad day this is, and what appropriate weather, with its dour overcast and sprinkles!' In his monitor he saw the zoomar lens pan up on the fourth Cadillac, as it followed those with the caskets of the dead tempunauts.

His engineer tapped him on the arm.

'We appear to be focusing on three unfamiliar figures so far not identified, riding together,' Henry Cassidy said into his neck mike, nodding agreement. 'So far I'm unable to quite make them out. Are your location and vision any better from where you're placed, Everett?' he inquired of his colleague and pressed the button that notified Everett Branton to replace him on the air.

'Why, Henry,' Branton said in a voice of growing excite-ment, 'I believe we're actually eyewitness to the three American tempunauts as they remanifest themselves on their historic journey into the future!'

'Does this signify,' Cassidy said, 'that somehow they have managed to solve and overcome the—'

'Afraid not, Henry,' Branton said in his slow, regretful voice. 'What we're eyewitnessing to our complete surprise consists of the Western world's first verified glimpse of what the technical people refer to as Emergence Time Activity.'

'Ah, yes, ETA,' Cassidy said brightly, reading it off the official script the Federal authorities had handed to him before air time.

'Right, Henry. Contrary to what *might* seem to be the case at first sight, these are not – repeat *not* – our three brave tempunauts as such, as we would ordinarily experience them—'

'I grasp it now, Everett,' Cassidy broke in excitedly, since his authorized script read CASS BREAKS IN EXCITEDLY. 'Our three tempunauts have momentarily suspended in their historic voyage to the future, which we believe will span across a time-continuum roughly a century from now . . . It would seem that the overwhelming grief and drama of this unanticipated day of mourning has caused them to—'

'Sorry to interrupt, Henry,' Everett Branton said, 'but I think, since the procession has momentarily halted on its slow march forward, that we might be able to—'

'No!' Cassidy said, as a note was handed him in a swift scribble, reading: *Do not interview nauts. Urgent. Dis. previous inst.* 'I don't think we're going to be able to . . .' he continued, '. . . to speak briefly with tempunauts Benz, Crayne, and Doug, as you had hoped, Everett. As we had all briefly hoped to.' He wildly waved the boom-mike back; it had already begun to swing out expectantly toward the stopped Cadillac. Cassidy shook his head violently at the mike technician and his engineer.

Perceiving the boom-mike swinging at them Addison Doug stood up in the back of the open Cadillac. Cassidy groaned. He wants to speak, he realized. Didn't they reinstruct *him*? Why am I the only one they get across to? Other boom-mikes representing other networks plus radio station interviewers on foot now were rushing out to thrust up their microphones into the faces of the three tempunauts, especially Addison Doug's. Doug was already beginning to speak, in response to a question shouted up to him by a reporter. With his boom-mike off, Cassidy couldn't hear the question, nor Doug's answer. With reluctance, he signaled for his own boom-mike to trigger on.

'. . . before,' Doug was saying loudly.

'In what manner, "All this has happened before"?' the radio reporter, standing close to the car, was saying.

'I mean,' US tempunaut Addison Doug declared, his face red and strained, 'that I have stood here in this spot and said again and again, and all of you have viewed this parade and our deaths at reentry endless times, a closed cycle of trapped time which must be broken.'

'Are you seeking,' another reporter jabbered up at Addison Doug, 'for a solution to the reentry implosion disaster which can be applied in retrospect so that when you do return to the past you will be able to correct the malfunction and avoid the tragedy which cost – or for you three, will cost – your lives?'

Tempunaut Benz said, 'We are doing that, yes.'

'Trying to ascertain the cause of the violent implosion and eliminate the cause before we return,' tempunaut Crayne added, nodding. 'We have learned already that, for reasons unknown, a mass of nearly one hundred pounds of miscellaneous Volkswagen motor parts, including cylinders, the head . . .'

This is awful, Cassidy thought. 'This is amazing!' he said aloud, into his neck mike. 'The already tragically deceased US tempunauts, with a determination that could emerge

only from the rigorous training and discipline to which they
were subjected – and we wondered why at the time but can
clearly see why now – have already analyzed the mechanical
slip-up responsible, evidently, for their own deaths, and
have begun the laborious process of shifting through and
eliminating causes of that slip-up so that they can return to
their original launch site and reenter without mishap.'

'One wonders,' Branton mumbled onto the air and into
his feedback earphone, 'what the consequences of this
alteration of the near past will be. If in reentry they do *not*
implode and are *not* killed, then they will not – well, it's too
complex for me, Henry, these time paradoxes that Dr Fein
at the Time Extrusion Labs in Pasadena has so frequently
and eloquently brought to our attention.'

Into all the microphones available, of all sorts, tempunaut
Addison Doug was saying, more quietly now, 'We must not
eliminate the cause of reentry implosion. The only way out
of this trip is for us to die. Death is the only solution for
this. For the three of us.' He was interrupted as the procession of Cadillacs began to move forward.

Shutting off his mike momentarily, Henry Cassidy said
to his engineer, 'Is he nuts?'

'Only time will tell,' his engineer said in a hard-to-hear
voice.

'An extraordinary moment in the history of the United
States' involvement in time travel,' Cassidy said, then, into
his now live mike. 'Only time will tell – if you will pardon
the inadvertent pun – whether tempunaut Doug's cryptic
remarks, uttered impromptu at this moment of supreme
suffering for him, as in a sense to a lesser degree it is for
all of us, are the words of a man deranged by grief or an
accurate insight into the macabre dilemma that in theoretical terms we knew all along might eventually confront –
confront and strike down with its lethal blow – a time-travel
launch, either ours or the Russians'.'

He segued, then, to a commercial.

'You know,' Branton's voice muttered in his ear, not on

the air but just to the control room and to him, 'if he's right they ought to let the poor bastards die.'

'They ought to release them,' Cassidy agreed. 'My God, the way Doug looked and talked, you'd imagine he'd gone through this for a thousand years and then some! I wouldn't be in his shoes for anything.'

'I'll bet you fifty bucks,' Branton said, 'they have gone through this before. Many times.'

'Then we have, too,' Cassidy said.

Rain fell now, making all the lined-up mourners shiny. Their faces, their eyes, even their clothes – everything glistened in wet reflections of broken, fractured light, bent and sparkling, as, from gathering gray formless layers above them, the day darkened.

'Are we on the air?' Branton asked.

Who knows? Cassidy thought. He wished the day would end.

The Soviet chrononaut N. Gauki lifted both hands impassionedly and spoke to the Americans across the table from him in a voice of extreme urgency. 'It is the opinion of myself and my colleague R. Plenya, who for his pioneering achievements in time travel has been certified a Hero of the Soviet People, and rightly so, that based on our own experience and on theoretical material developed both in your own academic circles and in the Soviet Academy of Sciences of the USSR, we believe that tempunaut A. Doug's fears may be justified. And his deliberate destruction of himself and his teammates at reentry, by hauling a huge mass of auto back with him from ETA, in violation of his orders, should be regarded as the act of a desperate man with no other means of escape. Of course, the decision is up to you. We have only an advisory position in this matter.'

Addison Doug played with his cigarette lighter on the table and did not look up. His ears hummed, and he wondered what that meant. It had an electronic quality. Maybe we're within the module again, he thought. But he didn't perceive it; he felt the reality of the people around him, the table, the blue plastic lighter between his fingers. No smoking in the module during reentry, he thought. He put the lighter carefully away in his pocket.

'We've developed no concrete evidence whatsoever,' General Toad said, 'that a closed time loop has been set up. There's only the subjective feelings of fatigue on the part of Mr Doug. Just his belief that he's done all this repeatedly. As he says, it is very probably psychological in nature.' He rooted, piglike, among the papers before him. 'I have a report, not disclosed to the media, from four psychiatrists at Yale on his psychological makeup. Although unusually stable, there is a tendency toward cyclothymia on his part, culminating in acute depression. This naturally was taken into account long before the launch, but it was calculated that the joyful qualities of the two others in the team would offset this functionally. Anyhow, that depressive tendency in him is exceptionally high, now.' He held the paper out, but no one at the table accepted it. 'Isn't it true, Dr Fein,' he said, 'that an acutely depressed person experiences time in a peculiar way, that is, circular time, time repeating itself, getting nowhere, around and around? The person gets so psychotic that he refuses to let go of the past. Reruns it in his head constantly.'

'But you see,' Dr Fein said, 'this subjective sensation of being trapped is perhaps all we would have.' This was the research physicist whose basic work had laid the theoretical foundation for the project. 'If a closed loop did unfortunately lock into being.'

'The general,' Addison Doug said, 'is using words he doesn't understand.'

'I researched the one I was unfamiliar with,' General Toad said. 'The technical psychiatric terms . . . know what they mean.'

To Addison Doug, Benz said, 'Where'd you get all those VW parts, Addi?'

'I don't have them yet,' Addison Doug said.

'Probably picked up the first junk he could lay his hands on,' Crayne said. 'Whatever was available, just before we started back.'

'Will start back,' Addison Doug corrected.

'Here are my instructions to the three of you,' General Toad said. 'You are not in any way to attempt to cause damage or implosion or malfunction during reentry, either by lugging back extra mass or by any other method that enters your mind. You are to return as scheduled and in replica of the prior simulations. This especially applies to you, Mr Doug.' The phone by his right arm buzzed. He frowned, picked up the receiver. An interval passed, and then he scowled deeply and set the receiver back down, loudly.

'You've been overruled,' Dr Fein said.

'Yes, I have,' General Toad said. 'And I must say at this time that I am personally glad because my decision was an unpleasant one.'

'Then we can arrange for implosion at reentry,' Benz said after a pause.

'The three of you are to make the decision,' General Toad said. 'Since it involves your lives. It's been entirely left up to you. Whichever way you want it. If you're convinced you're in a closed time loop, and you believe a massive implosion at reentry will abolish it—' He ceased talking, as tempunaut Doug rose to his feet. 'Are you going to make another speech, Doug?' he said.

'I just want to thank everyone involved,' Addison Doug said. 'For letting us decide.' He gazed haggard-faced and wearily around at all the individuals seated at the table. 'I really appreciate it.'

'You know,' Benz said slowly, 'blowing us up at reentry could add nothing to the chances of abolishing a closed loop. In fact that could do it, Doug.'

'Not if it kills us all,' Crayne said.

'You agree with Addi?' Benz said.

'Dead is dead,' Crayne said. 'I've been pondering it.

What other way is more likely to get us out of this? Than if we're dead? What possible other way?'

'You may be in no loop,' Dr Fein pointed out.

'But we may be,' Crayne said.

Doug, still on his feet, said to Crayne and Benz, 'Could we include Merry Lou in our decision-making?'

'Why?' Benz said.

'I can't think too clearly any more,' Doug said. 'Merry Lou can help me; I depend on her.'

'Sure,' Crayne said. Benz, too, nodded.

General Toad examined his wristwatch stoically and said, 'Gentlemen, this concludes our discussion.'

Soviet chrononaut Gauki removed his headphones and neck mike and hurried toward the three US tempunauts, his hand extended; he was apparently saying something in Russian, but none of them could understand it. They moved away somberly, clustering close.

'In my opinion you're nuts, Addi,' Benz said. 'But it would appear that I'm the minority now.'

'If he *is* right,' Crayne said, 'if – one chance in a billion – if we are going back again and again forever, that would justify it.'

'Could we go see Merry Lou?' Addison Doug said. 'Drive over to her place now?'

'She's waiting outside,' Crayne said.

Striding up to stand beside the three tempunauts, General Toad said, 'You know, what made the determination go the way it did was the public reaction to how you, Doug, looked and behaved during the funeral procession. The NSC advisors came to the conclusion that the public would, like you, rather be certain it's over for all of you. That it's more of a relief to them to know you're free of your mission than to save the project and obtain a perfect reentry. I guess you really made a lasting impression on them, Doug. That whining you did.' He walked away, then, leaving the three of them standing there alone.

'Forget him,' Crayne said to Addison Doug. 'Forget everyone like him. We've got to do what we have to.'

'Merry Lou will explain it to me,' Doug said. She would know what to do, what would be right.

'I'll go get her,' Crayne said, 'and after that the four of us can drive somewhere, maybe to her place, and decide what to do. Okay?'

'Thank you,' Addison Doug said, nodding; he glanced around for her hopefully, wondering where she was. In the next room, perhaps, somewhere close. 'I appreciate that,' he said.

Benz and Crayne eyed each other. He saw that, but did not know what it meant. He knew only that he needed someone, Merry Lou most of all, to help him understand what the situation was. And what to finalize on to get them out of it.

Merry Lou drove them north from Los Angeles in the superfast lane of the freeway toward Ventura, and after that inland to Ojai. The four of them said very little. Merry Lou drove well, as always; leaning against her, Addison Doug felt himself relax into a temporary sort of peace.

'There's nothing like having a chick drive you,' Crayne said, after many miles had passed in silence.

'It's an aristocratic sensation,' Benz murmured. 'To have a woman do the driving. Like you're nobility being chauffeured.'

Merry Lou said, 'Until she runs into something. Some big slow object.'

Addison Doug said, 'When you saw me trudging up to your place . . . up the redwood round path the other day. What did you think? Tell me honestly.'

'You looked,' the girl said, 'as if you'd done it many times. You looked worn and tired and – ready to die. At the end.' She hesitated. 'I'm sorry, but that's how you looked, Addi. I thought to myself, he knows the way too well.'

'Like I'd done it too many times.'

'Yes,' she said.

'Then you vote for implosion,' Addison Doug said.

'Well—'

'Be honest with me,' he said.

Merry Lou said, 'Look in the back seat. The box on the floor.'

With a flashlight from the glove compartment the three men examined the box. Addison Doug, with fear, saw its contents. VW motor parts, rusty and worn. Still oily.

'I got them from behind a foreign-car garage near my place,' Merry Lou said. 'On the way to Pasadena. The first junk I saw that seemed as if it'd be heavy enough. I had heard them say on TV at launch time that anything over fifty pounds up to—'

'It'll do it,' Addison Doug said. 'It did do it.'

'So there's no point in going to your place,' Crayne said. 'It's decided. We might as well head south toward the module. And initiate the procedure for getting out of ETA. And back to reentry.' His voice was heavy but evenly pitched. 'Thanks for your vote, Miss Hawkins.'

She said, 'You are all so tired.'

'I'm not,' Benz said. 'I'm mad. Mad as hell.'

'At me?' Addison Doug said.

'I don't know,' Benz said. 'It's just – Hell.' He lapsed into brooding silence then. Hunched over, baffled and inert. Withdrawn as far as possible from the others in the car.

At the next freeway junction she turned the car south. A sense of freedom seemed now to fill her, and Addison Doug felt some of the weight, the fatigue, ebbing already.

On the wrist of each of the three men the emergency alert receiver buzzed its warning tone; they all started.

'What's that mean?' Merry Lou said, slowing the car.

'We're to contact General Toad by phone as soon as possible,' Crayne said. He pointed. 'There's a Standard Station over there; take the next exit, Miss Hawkins. We can phone in from there.'

A few minutes later Merry Lou brought her car to a halt beside the outdoor phone booth. 'I hope it's not bad news,' she said.

'I'll talk first,' Doug said, getting out. Bad news, he thought with labored amusement. Like what? He crunched stiffly across to the phone booth, entered, shut the door behind him, dropped in a dime and dialed the toll-free number.

'Well, do I have news!' General Toad said when the operator had put him on the line. 'It's a good thing we got hold of you. Just a minute – I'm going to let Dr Fein tell you this himself. You're more apt to believe him than me.' Several clicks, and then Dr Fein's reedy, precise, scholarly voice, but intensified by urgency.

'What's the bad news?' Addison Doug said.

'Not bad, necessarily,' Dr Fein said. 'I've had computations run since our discussion, and it would appear – by that I mean it is statistically probable but still unverified for a certainty – that you are right, Addison. You are in a closed time loop.'

Addison Doug exhaled raggedly. You nowhere autocratic mother, he thought. You probably knew all along.

'However,' Dr Fein said excitedly, stammering a little, 'I also calculate – we jointly do, largely through Cal Tech – that the greatest likelihood of maintaining the loop is to implode on reentry. Do you understand, Addison? If you lug all those rusty VW parts back and implode, then your statistical chances of closing the loop forever is greater than if you simply reenter and all goes well.'

Addison Doug said nothing.

'In fact, Addi – and this is the severe part that I have to stress – implosion at reentry, especially a massive, calculated one of the sort we seem to see shaping up – do you grasp all this, Addi? Am I getting through to you? For Chrissake, Addi? Virtually *guarantees* the locking in of an absolutely unyielding loop such as you've got in mind. Such as we've all been worried about from the start.' A pause. 'Addi? Are you there?'

Addison Doug said, 'I want to die.'

'That's your exhaustion from the loop. God knows how many repetitions there've been already of the three of you—'

'No,' he said and started to hang up.

'Let me speak with Benz and Crayne,' Dr Fein said rapidly. 'Please, before you go ahead with reentry. Especially Benz; I'd like to speak with him in particular. Please, Addison. For their sake; your almost total exhaustion has—'

He hung up. Left the phone booth, step by step.

As he climbed back into the car, he heard their two alert receivers still buzzing. 'General Toad said the automatic call for us would keep your two receivers doing that for a while,' he said. And shut the car door after him. 'Let's take off.'

'Doesn't he want to talk to us?' Benz said.

Addison Doug said, 'General Toad wanted to inform us that they have a little something for us. We've been voted a special Congressional Citation for valor or some damn thing like that. A special medal they never voted anyone before. To be awarded posthumously.'

'Well, hell – that's about the only way it can be awarded,' Crayne said.

Merry Lou, as she started up the engine, began to cry.

'It'll be a relief,' Crayne said presently, as they returned bumpily to the freeway, 'when it's over.'

It won't be long now, Addison Doug's mind declared.

On their wrists the emergency alert receivers continued to put out their combined buzzing.

'They will nibble you to death,' Addison Doug said. 'The endless wearing down by various bureaucratic voices.'

The others in the car turned to gaze at him inquiringly, with uneasiness mixed with perplexity.

'Yeah,' Crayne said. 'These automatic alerts are really a nuisance.' He sounded tired. As tired as I am, Addison Doug thought. And, realizing this, he felt better. It showed how right he was.

Great drops of water struck the windshield; it had now begun to rain. That pleased him too. It reminded him of that most exalted of all experiences within the shortness of his life: the funeral procession moving slowly down Pennsylvania Avenue, the flag-draped caskets. Closing his eyes he leaned back and felt good at last. And heard, all around him once again, the sorrow-bent people. And, in his head, dreamed of the special Congressional Medal. For weariness, he thought. A medal for being tired.

He saw, in his head, himself in other parades too, and in the deaths of many. But really it was one death and one parade. Slow cars moving along the street in Dallas and with Dr King as well . . . He saw himself return again and again, in his closed cycle of life, to the national mourning that he could not and they could not forget. He would be there; they would always be there; it would always be, and every one of them would return together again and again forever. To the place, the moment, they wanted to be. The event which meant the most to all of them.

This was his gift to them, the people, his country. He had bestowed upon the world a wonderful burden. The dreadful and weary miracle of eternal life.

The Pre-Persons

Past the grove of cypress trees Walter – he had been playing king of the mountain – saw the white truck, and he knew it for what it was. He thought, That's the abortion truck. Come to take some kid in for a postpartum down at the abortion place.

And he thought, Maybe my folks called it. For me.

He ran and hid among the blackberries, feeling the scratching of the thorns but thinking, It's better than having the air sucked out of your lungs. That's how they do it; they perform all the PPs on all the kids there at the same time. They have a big room for it. For the kids nobody wants.

Burrowing deeper into the blackberries, he listened to hear if the truck stopped; he heard its motor.

'I am invisible,' he said to himself, a line he had learned at the fifth-grade play of *Midsummer Night's Dream*, a line Oberon, whom he had played, had said. And after that no one could see him. Maybe that was true now. Maybe the magic saying worked in real life; so he said it again to himself, 'I am invisible.' But he knew he was not. He could still see his arms and legs and shoes, and he knew they – everyone, the abortion truck man especially, and his mom and dad – they could see him too. If they looked.

If it was him they were after this time.

He wished he was a king; he wished he had magic dust all over him and a shining crown that glistened, and ruled fairyland and had Puck to confide to. To ask for advice from, even. Advice even if he himself was a king and bickered with Titania, his wife.

I guess, he thought, saying something doesn't make it
true.

Sun burned down on him and he squinted, but mostly he
listened to the abortion truck motor; it kept making its
sound, and his heart gathered hope as the sound went on
and on. Some other kid, turned over to the abortion clinic,
not him; someone up the road.

He made his difficult exit from the berry brambles shaking and in many places scratched and moved step by step in
the direction of his house. And as he trudged he began to
cry, mostly from the pain of the scratches but also from fear
and relief.

'Oh, good Lord,' his mother exclaimed, on seeing him.
'What in the name of God have you been doing?'

He said stammeringly, 'I – saw – the abortion – truck.'

'And you thought it was for you?'

Mutely, he nodded.

'Listen, Walter,' Cynthia Best said, kneeling down and
taking hold of his trembling hands, 'I promise, your dad and
I both promise, you'll never be sent to the County Facility.
Anyhow you're too old. They only take children up to
twelve.'

'But Jeff Vogel—'

'His parents got him in just before the new law went into
effect. They couldn't take him now, legally. They couldn't
take you now. Look – you have a soul; the law says a twelve-
year-old boy has a soul. So he can't go to the County
Facility. See? You're safe. Whenever you see the abortion
truck, it's for someone else, not you. Never for you. Is that
clear? It's come for another younger child who doesn't have
a soul yet, a pre-person.'

Staring down, not meeting his mother's gaze, he said, 'I
don't feel like I got a soul; I feel like I always did.'

'It's a legal matter,' his mother said briskly. 'Strictly
according to age. And you're past the age. The Church of
Watchers got Congress to pass the law – actually they,
those church people, wanted a lower age; they claimed the

soul entered the body at three years old, but a compromise
bill was put through. The important thing for you is that
you are legally safe, however you feel inside; do you see?'
'Okay,' he said, nodding.
'You knew that.'
He burst out with anger and grief, 'What do you think
it's like, maybe waiting every day for someone to come and
put you in a wire cage in a truck and—'
'Your fear is irrational,' his mother said.
'I saw them take Jeff Vogel that day. He was crying, and
the man just opened the back of the truck and put him in
and shut the back of the truck.'
'That was two years ago. You're weak.' His mother
glared at him. 'Your grandfather would whip you if he saw
you now and heard you talk this way. Not your father. He'd
just grin and say something stupid. Two years later, and
intellectually you know you're past the legal maximum age!
How—' She struggled for the word. 'You are being
depraved.'
'And he never came back.'
'Perhaps someone who wanted a child went inside the
County Facility and found him and adopted him. Maybe
he's got a better set of parents who really care for him.
They keep them thirty days before they destroy them.' She
corrected herself. 'Put them to sleep, I mean.'
He was not reassured. Because he knew 'put him to sleep'
or 'put them to sleep' was a Mafia term. He drew away from
his mother, no longer wanting her comfort. She had blown
it, as far as he was concerned; she had shown something
about herself or, anyhow, the source of what she believed
and thought and perhaps did. What all of them did. I know
I'm no different, he thought, than two years ago when I was
just a little kid; if I have a soul now like the law says, then I
had a soul then, or else we have no souls – the only real thing
is just a horrible metallic-painted truck with wire over its
windows carrying off kids their parents no longer want,
parents using an extension of the old abortion law that let

them kill an unwanted child before it came out: because it had no 'soul' or 'identity', it could be sucked out by a vacuum system in less than two minutes. A doctor could do a hundred a day, and it was legal because the unborn child wasn't 'human'. He was a pre-person. Just like this truck now; they merely set the date forward as to when the soul entered.

Congress had inaugurated a simple test to determine the approximate age at which the soul entered the body: the ability to formulate higher math like algebra. Up to then, it was only body, animal instincts and body, animal reflexes and responses to stimuli. Like Pavlov's dogs when they saw a little water seep in under the door of the Leningrad laboratory; they 'knew' but were not human.

I guess I'm human, Walter thought, and looked up into the gray, severe face of his mother, with her hard eyes and rational grimness. I guess I'm like you, he thought. Hey, it's neat to be a human, he thought; then you don't have to be afraid of the truck coming.

'You feel better,' his mother observed. 'I've lowered your threshold of anxiety.'

'I'm not so freaked,' Walter said. It was over; the truck had gone and not taken him.

But it would be back in a few days. It cruised perpetually.

Anyhow he had a few days. And then the sight of it – if only I didn't know they suck the air out of the lungs of the kids they have there, he thought. Destroy them that way. Why? Cheaper, his dad had said. Saves the taxpayers money.

He thought then about taxpayers and what they would look like. Something that scowled at all children, he thought. That did not answer if the child asked them a question. A thin face, lined with watch-worry grooves, eyes always moving. Or maybe fat; one or the other. It was the thin one that scared him; it didn't enjoy life nor want life to be. It flashed the message, 'Die, go away, sicken, don't exist.' And the abortion truck was proof – or the instrument – of it.

'Mom,' he said, 'how do you shut a County Facility? You know, the abortion clinic where they take the babies and little kids.'

'You go and petition the county legislature,' his mother said.

'You know what I'd do?' he said. 'I'd wait until there were no kids in there, only county employees, and I'd firebomb it.'

'Don't talk like that!' his mother said severely, and he saw on her face the stiff lines of the thin taxpayer. And it frightened him; his own mother frightened him. The cold and opaque eyes mirrored nothing, no soul inside, and he thought, *It's you who don't have a soul*, you and your skinny messages not-to-be. Not us.

And then he ran outside to play again.

A bunch more kids had seen the truck; he and they stood around together, talking now and then, but mostly kicking at rocks and dirt, and occasionally stepping on a bad bug.

'Who'd the truck come for?' Walter said.

'Fleischhacker. Earl Fleischhacker.'

'Did they get him?'

'Sure, didn't you hear the yelling?'

'Was his folks home at the time?'

'Naw, they split earlier on some shuck about "taking the car in to be greased".'

'*They* called the truck?' Walter said.

'Sure, it's the law; it's gotta be the parents. But they were too chickenshit to be there when the truck drove up. Shit, he really yelled; I guess you're too far away to hear, but he really yelled.'

Walter said, 'You know what we ought to do? Firebomb the truck and snuff the driver.'

All the other kids looked at him contemptuously. 'They put you in the mental hospital for life if you act out like that.'

'Sometimes for life,' Pete Bride corrected. 'Other times they "build up a new personality that is socially viable".'

'Then what should we do?' Walter said.

'You're twelve; you're safe.'

'But suppose they change the law.' Anyhow it did not assuage his anxiety to know that he was technically safe; the truck still came for others and still frightened him. He thought of the younger kids down at the Facility now, looking through the Cyclone fence hour by hour, day after day, waiting and marking the passage of time and hoping someone would come in and adopt them.

'You ever been down there?' he said to Pete Bride. 'At the County Facility? All those really little kids, like babies some of them, just maybe a year old. And they don't even know what's in store.'

'The babies get adopted,' Zack Yablonski said. 'It's the old ones that don't stand a chance. They're the ones that get you; like, they talk to people who come in and put on a good show, like they're desirable. But people know they wouldn't be there if they weren't – you know, undesirable.'

'Let the air out of the tires,' Walter said, his mind working.

'Of the truck? Hey, and you know if you drop a mothball in the gas tank, about a week later the motor wears out. We could do that.'

Ben Blaire said, 'But then they'd be after us.'

'They're after us now,' Walter said.

'I think we ought to firebomb the truck,' Harry Gottlieb said, 'but suppose there're kids in it. It'll burn them up. The truck picks up maybe— shit, I don't know. Five kids a day from different parts of the county.'

'You know they even take dogs too?' Walter said. 'And cats; you see the truck for that only about once a month. The pound truck it's called. Otherwise it's the same; they put them in a big chamber and suck the air out of their lungs and they die. They'd do that even to animals! Little animals!'

'I'll believe that when I see it,' Harry Gottlieb said, derision on his face, and disbelief. 'A truck that carries off dogs.'

He knew it was true, though. Walter had seen the pound truck two different times. Cats, dogs, and mainly us, he thought glumly. I mean, if they'd start with us, it's natural they'd wind up taking people's pets, too; we're not that different. But what kind of a person would do that, even if it is the law? 'Some laws are made to be kept, and some to be broken,' he remembered from a book he had read. We ought to firebomb the pound truck first, he thought; that's the worst, that truck.

Why is it, he wondered, that the more helpless a creature, the easier it was for some people to snuff it? Like a baby in the womb; the original abortions, 'pre-partums', or 'pre-persons' they were called now. How could they defend themselves? Who would speak for them? All those lives, a hundred by each doctor a day . . . and all helpless and silent and then just dead. The fuckers, he thought. That's why they do it; they know they can do it; they get off on their macho power. And so a little thing that wanted to see the light of day is vacuumed out in less than two minutes. And the doctor goes on to the next chick.

There ought to be an organization, he thought, similar to the Mafia. Snuff the snuffers, or something. A contract man walks up to one of those doctors, pulls out a tube, and sucks the doctor into it, where he shrinks down like an unborn baby. An unborn baby doctor, with a stethoscope the size of a pinhead . . . He laughed, thinking of that.

Children don't know. But children know everything, knew too much. The abortion truck, as it drove along, played a Good Humor Man's jingle:

> *Jack and Jill*
> *Went up the hill*
> *To fetch a pail of water*

A tape loop in the sound system of the truck, built especially by Ampex for GM, blared that out when it wasn't actively nearing a seize. Then the driver shut off the sound system and glided along until he found the proper house. However, once he had the unwanted child in the back of the truck, and was either starting back to the County Facility or beginning another pre-person pick-up, he turned back on

Jack and Jill
Went up the hill
To fetch a pail of water

Thinking of himself, Oscar Ferris, the driver of truck three, finished, 'Jack fell down and broke his crown and Jill came tumbling after.' What the hell's a crown? Ferris wondered. Probably a private part. He grinned. Probably Jack had been playing with it, or Jill, both of them together. Water, my ass, he thought. I know what they went off into the bushes for. Only, Jack fell down, and his thing broke right off. 'Tough luck, Jill,' he said aloud as he expertly drove the four-year-old truck along the winding curves of California Highway One.

Kids are like that, Ferris thought. Dirty and playing with dirty things, like themselves.

This was still wild and open country, and many stray children scratched about in the canyons and fields; he kept his eye open, and sure enough – off to his right scampered a small one, about six, trying to get out of sight. Ferris at once pressed the button that activated the siren of the truck. The boy froze, stood in fright, waited as the truck, still playing 'Jack and Jill', coasted up beside him and came to a halt.

'Show me your D papers,' Ferris said, without getting out of the truck; he leaned one arm out the window, showing his brown uniform and patch; his symbols of authority.

The boy had a scrawny look, like many strays, but, on the other hand, he wore glasses. Tow-headed, in jeans and

T-shirt, he stared up in fright at Ferris, making no move to get out his identification.

'You got a D card or not?' Ferris said.

'W-w-w-what's a "D card"?'

In his official voice, Ferris explained to the boy his rights under the law.

'Your parent, either one, or legal guardian, fills out form 36-W, which is a formal statement of desirability. That they or him or her regard you as desirable. You don't have one? Legally, that makes you a stray, even if you have parents who want to keep you; they are subject to a fine of $500.'

'Oh,' the boy said. 'Well, I lost it.'

'Then a copy would be on file. They microdot all those documents and records. I'll take you in—'

'To the County Facility?' Pipe-cleaner legs wobbled in fear.

'They have thirty days to claim you by filling out the 36-W form. If they haven't done it by then—'

'My mom and dad never agree. Right now I'm staying with my dad.'

'He didn't give you a D card to identify yourself with.' Mounted transversely across the cab of the truck was a shotgun. There was always the possibility that trouble might break out when he picked up a stray. Reflexively, Ferris glanced up at it. It was there, all right, a pump shotgun. He had used it only five times in his law-enforcement career. It could blow a man into molecules. 'I have to take you in,' he said, opening the truck door and bringing out his keys. 'There's another kid back there; you can keep each other company.'

'No,' the boy said. 'I won't go.' Blinking, he confronted Ferris, stubborn and rigid as stone.

'Oh, you probably heard a lot of stories about the County Facility. It's only the warpies, the creepies, that get put to sleep; any nice normal-looking kid'll be adopted – we'll cut your hair and fix you up so you look professionally groomed. We want to find you a home. That's the whole idea. It's just a few, those who are – you know – ailing mentally or physically that no one wants. Some well-to-do individual will snap you up in a minute; you'll see. Then you won't be running around out here alone with no parents to guide you. You'll have new parents, and listen – they'll be paying heavy bread for you; hell, they'll *register* you. Do you see? It's more a temporary lodging place where we're taking you right now, to make you available to prospective new parents.'

'But if nobody adopts me in a month—'

'Hell, you could fall off a cliff here at Big Sur and kill yourself. Don't worry. The desk at the Facility will contact your blood parents, and most likely they'll come forth with the Desirability Form (15A) sometime today even. And meanwhile you'll get a nice ride and meet a lot of new kids. And how often—'

'No,' the boy said.

'This is to inform you,' Ferris said, in a different tone, 'that I am a County Official.' He opened his truck door, jumped down, showed his gleaming metal badge to the boy. 'I am Peace Officer Ferris and I now order you to enter by the rear of the truck.'

A tall man approached them, walking with wariness; he, like the boy, wore jeans and a T-shirt, but no glasses.

'You the boy's father?' Ferris said.

The man, hoarsely, said, 'Are you taking him to the pound?'

'We consider it a child protection shelter,' Ferris said. 'The use of the term "pound" is a radical hippie slur, and distorts – deliberately – the overall picture of what we do.'

Gesturing toward the truck, the man said, 'You've got kids locked in there in those cages, have you?'

'I'd like to see your ID,' Ferris said. 'And I'd like to know if you've ever been arrested before.'

'Arrested and found innocent? Or arrested and found guilty?'

'Answer my question, sir,' Ferris said, showing his black

flatpack that he used with adults to identify him as a County Peace Officer. 'Who are you? Come on, let's see your ID.'

The man said, 'Ed Gantro is my name and I have a record. When I was eighteen, I stole four crates of Coca-Cola from a parked truck.'

'You were apprehended at the scene?'

'No,' the man said. 'When I took the empties back to cash in on the refunds. That's when they seized me. I served six months.'

'Have you a Desirability Card for your boy here?' Ferris asked.

'We couldn't afford the $90 it cost.'

'Well, now it'll cost you five hundred. You should have gotten it in the first place. My suggestion is that you consult an attorney.' Ferris moved toward the boy, declaring officially, 'I'd like you to join the other juveniles in the rear section of the vehicle.' To the man he said, 'Tell him to do as instructed.'

The man hesitated and then said, 'Tim, get in the goddamn truck. And we'll get a lawyer; we'll get the D card for you. It's futile to make trouble – technically you're a stray.'

' "A stray".' the boy said, regarding his father.

Ferris said, 'Exactly right. You have thirty days, you know, to raise the—'

'Do you also take cats?' the boy said. 'Are there any cats in there? I really like cats; they're all right.'

'I handle only PP cases,' Ferris said. 'Such as yourself.' With a key he unlocked the back of the truck. 'Try not to relieve yourself while you're in the truck; it's hard as hell to get the odor and stains out.'

The boy did not seem to understand the word; he gazed from Ferris to his father in perplexity.

'Just don't go to the bathroom while you're in the truck,' his father explained. 'They want to keep it sanitary, because that cuts down their maintenance costs.' His voice was savage and grim.

'With stray dogs or cats,' Ferris said, 'they just shoot them on sight, or put out poison bait.'

'Oh, yeah, I know that Warfarin,' the boy's father said. 'The animal eats it over a period of a week, and then he bleeds to death internally.'

'With no pain,' Ferris pointed out.

'Isn't that better than sucking the air from their lungs?' Ed Gantro said. 'Suffocating them on a mass basis?'

'Well, with animals the county authorities—'

'I mean the children. Like Tim.' His father stood beside him, and they both looked into the rear of the truck. Two dark shapes could be dimly discerned, crouching as far back as possible, in the starkest form of despair.

'Fleischhacker!' the boy Tim said. 'Didn't you have a D card?'

'Because of energy and fuel shortages,' Ferris was saying, 'population must be radically cut. Or in ten years there'll be no food for anyone. This is one phase of—'

'I had a D card,' Earl Fleischhacker said, 'but my folks took it away from me. They didn't want me any more; so they took it back, and then they called for the abortion truck.' His voice croaked; obviously he had been secretly crying.

'And what's the difference between a five-month-old fetus and what we have here?' Ferris was saying. 'In both cases what you have is an unwanted child. They simply liberalized the laws.'

Tim's father, staring at him, said, 'Do you agree with these laws?'

'Well, it's really all up to Washington and what they decide will solve our needs in these days of crises,' Ferris said. 'I only enforce their edicts. If this law changed – hell. I'd be trucking empty milk cartons for recycling or something and be just as happy.'

'*Just* as happy? You enjoy your work?'

Ferris said, mechanically, 'It gives me the opportunity to move around a lot and to meet people.'

Tim's father Ed Gantro said, 'You are insane. This

postpartum abortion scheme and the abortion laws before it where the unborn child had no legal rights – it was removed like a tumor. Look what it's come to. If an unborn child can be killed without due process, why not a born one? What I see in common in both cases is their helplessness; the organism that is killed has no chance, no ability, to protect itself. You know what? I want you to take me in, too. In back of the truck with the three children.'

'But the President and Congress have declared that when you're past twelve you have a soul,' Ferris said. 'I can't take you. It wouldn't be right.'

'I have no soul,' Tim's father said. 'I got to be twelve and nothing happened. Take me along, too. Unless you can find my soul.'

'Jeez,' Ferris said.

'Unless you can show me my soul,' Tim's father said, 'unless you can specifically locate it, then I insist you take me in as no different from these kids.'

Ferris said, 'I'll have to use the radio to get in touch with the County Facility, see what they say.'

'You do that,' Tim's father said, and laboriously clambered up into the rear of the truck, helping Tim along with him. With the other two boys they waited while Peace Officer Ferris, with all his official identification as to who he was, talked on his radio.

'I have here a Caucasian male, approximately thirty, who insists that he be transported to the County Facility with his infant son,' Ferris was saying into his mike. 'He claims to have no soul, which he maintains puts him in the class of subtwelve-year-olds. I don't have with me or know any test to detect the presence of a soul, at least any I can give out here in the boondocks that'll later on satisfy a court. I mean, he probably can do algebra and higher math; he seems to possess an intelligent mind. But—'

'Affirmative as to bringing him in,' his superior's voice on the two-way radio came back to him. 'We'll deal with him here.'

'We're going to deal with you downtown,' Ferris said to Tim's father, who, with the three smaller figures, was crouched down in the dark recesses of the rear of the truck. Ferris slammed the door, locked it – an extra precaution, since the boys were already netted by electronic bands – and then started up the truck.

> *Jack and Jill went up the hill*
> *To fetch a pail of water*
> *Jack fell down*
> *And broke his crown*

Somebody's sure going to get their crown broke, Ferris thought as he drove along the winding road, and it isn't going to be me.

'I can't do algebra,' he heard Tim's father saying to the three boys. 'So I can't have a soul.'

The Fleischhacker boy said, snidely, 'I can, but I'm only nine. So what good does it do me?'

'That's what I'm going to use as my plea at the Facility,' Tim's father continued. 'Even long division was hard for me. I don't have a soul. I belong with you three little guys.'

Ferris, in a loud voice, called back, 'I don't want you soiling the truck, you understand? It costs us—'

'Don't tell me,' Tim's father said, 'because I wouldn't understand. It would be too complex, the proration and accrual and fiscal terms like that.'

I've got a weirdo back there, Ferris thought, and was glad he had the pump shotgun mounted within easy reach. 'You know the world is running out of everything,' Ferris called back to them, 'energy and apple juice and fuel and bread; we've got to keep the population down, and the embolisms from the Pill make it impossible—'

'None of us knows those big words,' Tim's father broke in.

Angrily, and feeling baffled, Ferris said, 'Zero population growth; that's the answer to the energy and food crisis. It's like – shit, it's like when they introduced the rabbit in Australia, and it had no natural enemies, and so it multiplied until, like people—'

'I do understand multiplication,' Tim's father said. 'And adding and subtraction. But that's all.'

Four crazy rabbits flopping across the road, Ferris thought. People pollute the natural environment, he thought. What must this part of the country have been like before man? Well, he thought, with the postpartum abortions taking place in every county in the US of A we may see that day; we may stand and look once again upon a virgin land.

We, he thought. I guess there won't be any we. I mean, he thought, giant sentient computers will sweep out the landscape with their slotted video receptors and find it pleasing.

The thought cheered him up.

'Let's have an abortion!' Cynthia declared excitedly as she entered the house with an armload of synthogroceries. 'Wouldn't that be neat? Doesn't that turn you on?'

Her husband Ian Best said dryly, 'But first you have to get pregnant. So make an appointment with Dr Guido – that should cost me only fifty or sixty dollars – and have your IUD removed.'

'I think it's slipping down anyhow. Maybe, if—' Her pert dark shag-haired head tossed in glee. 'It probably hasn't worked properly since last year. So I could be pregnant now.'

Ian said caustically, 'You could put an ad in the *Free Press*; "Man wanted to fish out IUD with coathanger".'

'But you see,' Cynthia said, following him as he made his way to the master closet to hang up his status-tie and classcoat, 'it's the in thing now, to have an abortion. Look, what do we have? A kid. We have Walter. Every time someone comes over to visit and sees him, I know they're wondering, "Where did you screw up?" It's embarrassing.' She added, 'And the kind of abortions they give now, for women in early stages – it only costs one hundred dollars . . . the price of ten gallons of gas! And you can talk about it with practically everybody who drops by for hours.'

Ian turned to face her and said in a level voice, 'Do you get to keep the embryo? Bring it home in a bottle or sprayed with special luminous paint so it glows in the dark like a night light?'

'In any color you want!'

'The *embryo*?'

'No, the bottle. And the color of the fluid. It's in a preservative solution, so really it's a lifetime acquisition. It even has a written guarantee, I think.'

Ian folded his arms to keep himself calm: alpha state condition. 'Do you know that there are people who would want to have a child? Even an ordinary dumb one? That go to the County Facility week after week looking for a little newborn baby? These ideas – there's been this world panic about overpopulation. Nine trillion humans stacked like kindling in every block of every city. Okay, if that were going on—' He gestured. 'But what we have now is not *enough* children. Or don't you watch TV or read the *Times*?'

'It's a drag,' Cynthia said. 'For instance, today Walter came into the house freaked out because the abortion truck cruised by. It's a drag taking care of him. *You* have it easy; you're at work. But *me*—'

'You know what I'd like to do to the Gestapo abortion wagon? Have two ex-drinking buddies of mine armed with BARs, one on each side of the road. And when the wagon passes by—'

'It's a ventilated air-conditioned truck, not a wagon.'

He glared at her and then went to the bar in the kitchen to fix himself a drink. Scotch will do, he decided. Scotch and milk, a good before-'dinner' drink.

As he mixed his drink, his son Walter came in. He had, on his face, an unnatural pallor.

'The 'bort truck went by today, didn't it?' Ian said.

'I thought maybe—'

'No way. Even if your mother and I saw a lawyer and had a legal document drawn up, an un-D Form, you're too old. So relax.'

'I know intellectually,' Walter said, 'but—'

' "Do not seek to know for whom the bell tolls; it tolls for thee," ' Ian quoted (inaccurately). 'Listen, Walt, let me lay something on you.' He took a big, long drink of Scotch and milk. 'The name of all this is, *kill me*. Kill them when they're the size of a fingernail, or a baseball, or later on, if you haven't done it already, suck the air out of the lungs of a ten-year-old boy and let him die. It's a certain kind of woman advocating this all. They used to call them "castrating females". Maybe that was once the right term, except that these women, these hard cold women, didn't just want to – well, they want to do in the *whole* boy or man, make all of them dead, not just the part that makes him a man. Do you see?'

'No,' Walter said, but in a dim sense, very frightening, he did.

After another hit of his drink, Ian said, 'And we've got one living right here, Walter. Here in our very house.'

'What do we have living here?'

'What the Swiss psychiatrists call a *kindermorder*,' Ian said, deliberately choosing a term he knew his boy wouldn't understand. 'You know what,' he said, 'you and I could get onto an Amtrak coach and head north and just keep on going until we reached Vancouver, British Columbia, and we could take a ferry to Vancouver Island and never be seen by anybody down here again.'

'But what about Mom?'

'I would send her a cashier's check,' Ian said. 'Each month. And she would be quite happy with that.'

'It's cold up there, isn't it?' Walter said. 'I mean, they have hardly any fuel and they wear—'

'About like San Francisco. Why? Are you afraid of wearing a lot of sweaters and sitting close to the fireplace? What did you see today that frightened you a hell of a lot more?'

'Oh, yeah.' He nodded somberly.

'We could live on a little island off Vancouver Island and raise our own food. You can plant stuff up there and it grows. And the truck won't come there; you'll never see it again. They have different laws. The women up there are different. There was this one girl I knew when I was up there for a while, a long time ago; she had long black hair and smoked Players cigarettes all the time and never ate anything or ever stopped talking. Down here we're seeing a civilization in which the desire by women to destroy their own—' Ian broke off; his wife had walked into the kitchen.

'If you drink any more of that stuff,' she said to him, 'you'll barf it up.'

'Okay,' Ian said irritably. 'Okay!'

'And don't yell,' Cynthia said. 'I thought for dinner tonight it'd be nice if you took us out. Dal Rey's said on TV they have steak for early comers.'

Wrinkling his nose, Walter said, 'They have raw oysters.'

'Blue points,' Cynthia said. 'In the half shell, on ice. I love them. All right, Ian? Is it decided?'

To his son Walter, Ian said, 'A raw blue point oyster looks like nothing more on earth than what the surgeon—' He became silent, then. Cynthia glared at him, and his son was puzzled. 'Okay,' he said, 'but I get to order steak.'

'Me too,' Walter said.

Finishing his drink, Ian said more quietly, 'When was the last time you fixed dinner here in the house? For the three of us?'

'I fixed you that pigs' ears and rice dish on Friday,' Cynthia said. 'Most of which went to waste because it was something new and on the nonmandatory list. Remember, *dear*?'

Ignoring her, Ian said to his son, 'Of course, that type of woman will sometimes, even often be found up there, too. She has existed throughout time and all cultures. But since Canada has no law permitting postpartum—' He broke off. 'It's the carton of milk talking,' he explained to Cynthia.

'They adulterate it these days with sulfur. Pay no attention or sue somebody; the choice is yours.'

Cynthia, eyeing him, said, 'Are you running a fantasy number in your head again about splitting?'

'Both of us,' Walter broke in. 'Dad's taking me with him.'

'Where?' Cynthia said, casually.

Ian said. 'Wherever the Amtrak track leads us.'

'We're going to Vancouver Island in Canada,' Walter said.

'Oh, really?' Cynthia said.

After a pause Ian said, 'Really.'

'And what the shit am I supposed to do when you're gone? Peddle my ass down at the local bar? How'll I meet the payments on the various—'

'I will continually mail you checks,' Ian said. 'Bonded by giant banks.'

'Sure. You bet. Yep. Right.'

'You could come along,' Ian said, 'and catch fish by leaping into English Bay and grinding them to death with your sharp teeth. You could rid British Columbia of its fish population overnight. All those ground-up fish, wondering vaguely what happened . . . swimming along one minute and then this – ogre, this fish-destroying monster with a single luminous eye in the center of its forehead, falls on them and grinds them into grit. There would soon be a legend. News like that spreads. At least among the last surviving fish.'

'Yeah, but Dad,' Walter said, 'suppose there are no surviving fish.'

'Then it will have been all in vain,' Ian said, 'except for your mother's own personal pleasure at having bitten to death an entire species in British Columbia, where fishing is the largest industry anyhow, and so many other species depend on it for survival.'

'But then everyone in British Columbia will be out of work,' Walter said.

'No,' Ian said, 'they will be cramming the dead fish into

cans to sell to Americans. You see, Walter, in the olden
days, before your mother multi-toothedly bit to death all
the fish in British Columbia, the simple rustics stood with
stick in hand, and when a fish swam past, they whacked the
fish over the head. This will *create* jobs, not eliminate them.
Millions of cans of suitably marked —'

'You know,' Cynthia said quickly, 'he believes what you
tell him.'

Ian said, 'What I tell him is true.' Although not, he
realized, in a literal sense. To his wife he said, 'I'll take you
out to dinner. Get our ration stamps, put on that blue knit
blouse that shows off your boobs; that way you'll get a lot of
attention and maybe they won't remember to collect the
stamps.'

'What's a "boob"?' Walter asked.

'Something fast becoming obsolete,' Ian said, 'like the
Pontiac GTO. Except as an ornament to be admired and
squeezed. Its function is dying away.' As is our race, he
thought, once we gave full rein to those who would destroy
the unborn – in other words, the most helpless creatures alive.

'A boob,' Cynthia said severely to her son, 'is a mammary
gland that ladies possess which provides milk to their young.'

'Generally there are two of them,' Ian said. 'Your
operational boob and then your backup boob, in case
there is power failure in the operational one. I suggest the
elimination of a step in all this pre-person abortion mania,'
he said. 'We will send all the boobs in the world to the
County Facilities. The milk, if any, will be sucked out of
them, by mechanical means of course; they will become
useless and empty and then the young will die naturally,
deprived of many and all sources of nourishment.'

'There's formula,' Cynthia said, witheringly. 'Similac and
those. I'm going to change so we can go out.' She turned
and strode toward their bedroom.

'You know,' Ian said after her, 'if there was any way you
could get me classified as a pre-person, you'd send me
there. To the Facility with the greatest facility.' And, he

thought, I'll bet I wouldn't be the only husband in California who went. There'd be plenty others. In the same bag as me, then as now.

'Sounds like a plan,' Cynthia's voice came to him dimly; she had heard.

'It's not just a hatred for the helpless,' Ian Best said. 'More is involved. Hatred of what? Of everything that grows?' You blight them, he thought, before they grow big enough to have muscle and the tactics and skill for fight – big like I am in relation to you, with my fully developed musculature and weight. So much easier when the other person – I should say pre-person – is floating and dreaming in the amniotic fluid and knows nothing about how to nor the need to hit back.

Where did the motherly virtues go to? he asked himself. When mothers *especially* protected what was small and weak and defenseless?

Our competitive society, he decided. The survival of the strong. Not the fit, he thought; just those who hold the *power*. And are not going to surrender it to the next generation: it is the powerful and evil old against the helpless and gentle new.

'Dad,' Walter said, 'are we really going to Vancouver Island in Canada and raise real food and not have anything to be afraid of any more?'

Half to himself, Ian said, 'Soon as I have the money.'

'I know what that means. It's a "we'll see" number you say. We aren't going, are we?' He watched his father's face intently. 'She won't let us, like taking me out of school and like that; she always brings up that . . . right?'

'It lies ahead for us someday,' Ian said doggedlly. 'Maybe not this month but someday, sometime. I promise.'

'And there's no abortion trucks there.'

'No. None. Canadian law is different.'

'Make it soon, Dad. Please.'

His father fixed himself a second Scotch and milk and did not answer; his face was somber and unhappy, almost as if he was about to cry.

*

In the rear of the abortion truck three children and one adult huddled, jostled by the turning of the truck. They fell against the restraining wire that separated them, and Tim Gantro's father felt keen despair at being cut off mechanically from his own boy. A nightmare during day, he thought. Caged like animals; his noble gesture had brought only more suffering to him.

'Why'd you say you don't know algebra?' Tim asked, once. 'I know you know even calculus and trig-something; you went to Stanford University.'

'I want to show,' he said, 'that either they ought to kill all of us or none of us. But not divide along these bureaucratic arbitrary lines. "When does the soul enter the body?" What kind of rational question is that in this day and age? It's Medieval.' In fact, he thought, it's a pretext – a pretext to prey on the helpless. And he was not helpless. The abortion truck had picked up a fully grown man, with all his knowledge, all his cunning. How are they going to handle me? he asked himself. Obviously I have what all men have; if they have souls, then so do I. If not, then I don't, but on what real basis can they "put me to sleep"? I am not weak and small, not an ignorant child cowering defenselessly. I can argue the sophistries with the best of the county layers; with the DA himself, if necessary.

If they snuff me, he thought, they will have to snuff everyone, including themselves. And that is not what this is all about. This is a con game by which the established, those who already hold all the key economic and political posts, keep the youngsters out of it – murder them if necessary. There is, he thought, in the land, a hatred by the old of the young, a hatred and a fear. So what will they do with me? I am in their age group, and I am caged up in the back of this abortion truck. I pose, he thought, a different kind of threat; I am one of them but on the other side, with stray dogs and cats and babies and infants. Let them figure it out; let a new St Thomas Aquinas arise who can unravel this.

'All I know,' he said aloud, 'is dividing and multiplying and subtracting. I'm even hazy on my fractions.'

'But you used to know that!' Tim said.

'Funny how you forget it after you leave school,' Ed Gantro said. 'You kids are probably better at it than I am.'

'Dad, they're going to *snuff* you,' his son Tim said, wildly. 'Nobody'll adopt you. Not at your age. You're too *old*.'

'Let's see,' Ed Gantro said. 'The binomial theorem. How does that go? I can't get it all together: something about A and B.' And as it leaked out of his head, as had his immortal soul . . . he chuckled to himself. I cannot pass the soul test, he thought. At least not talking like that. I am a dog in the gutter, an animal in a ditch.

The whole mistake of the pro-abortion people from the start, he said to himself, was the *arbitrary* line they drew. An embryo is not entitled to American Constitutional rights and can be killed, legally, by a doctor. But a fetus was a 'person', with rights, at least for a while; and then the pro-abortion crowd decided that even a seven-month fetus was not 'human' and could be killed, legally, by a licensed doctor. And, one day, a newborn baby – it is a vegetable; it can't focus its eyes, it understands nothing, nor talks . . . The pro-abortion lobby argued in court, and won, with their contention that a newborn baby was only a fetus expelled by accident or organic processes from the womb. But, even then, where was the line to be drawn finally? When the baby smiled its first smile? When it spoke its first word or reached for its initial time for a toy it enjoyed? The legal line was relentlessly pushed back and back. And now the most savage and arbitrary definition of all: when it could perform 'higher math'.

That made the ancient Greeks, of Plato's time, nonhumans, since arithmetic was unknown to them, only geometry; and algebra was an Arab invention, much later in history. *Arbitrary*. It was not a theological arbitrariness either; it was a mere legal one. The Church had long since

– from the start, in fact – maintained that even the zygote, and the embryo that followed, was as sacred a life form as any that walked the earth. They had seen what would come of arbitrary definitions of 'Now the soul enters the body,' or in modern terms, 'Now it is a person entitled to the full protection of the law like everyone else.' What was so sad was the sight now of the small child playing bravely in his yard day by day, trying to hope, trying to pretend a security he did not have.

Well, he thought, we'll see what they do with me; I am thirty-five years old, with a Master's Degree from Stanford. Will they put me in a cage for thirty days, with a plastic food dish and a water source and a place – in plain sight – to relieve myself, and if no one adopts me will they consign me to automatic death along with the others?

I am risking a lot, he thought. But they picked up my son today, and the risk began then, when they had him, not when I stepped forward and became a victim myself.

He looked about at the three frightened boys and tried to think of something to tell them – not just his own son but all three.

' "Look," ' he said, quoting. ' "I tell you a sacred secret. We shall not all sleep in death. We shall—" ' But then he could not remember the rest. Bummer, he thought dismally. ' "We shall wake up," ' he said, doing the best he could. ' "In the twinkling of an eye." '

'Cut the noise,' the driver of the truck, from beyond his wire mesh, growled. 'I can't concentrate on this fucking road.' He added, 'You know, I can squirt gas back there where you are, and you'll pass out; it's for obstreperous pre-persons we pick up. So you want to knock it off, or have me punch the gas button?'

'We won't say anything,' Tim said quickly, with a look of mute terrified appeal at his father. Urging him silently to conform.

His father said nothing. The glance of urgent pleading was too much for him, and he capitulated. Anyhow, he reasoned, what happened in the truck was not crucial. It was when they reached the County Facility – where there would be, at the first sign of trouble, newspaper and TV reporters. So they rode in silence, each with his own fears, his own schemes. Ed Gantro brooded to himself, perfecting in his head what he would do – what he *had* to do. And not just for Tim but all the PP abortion candidates; he thought through the ramifications as the truck lurched and rattled on.

As soon as the truck parked in the restricted lot of the County Facility and its rear doors had been swung open, Sam B. Carpenter, who ran the whole goddamn operation, walked over, stared, said, 'You've got a grown man in there, Ferris. In fact, you comprehend what you've got? A protest-er, that's what you've latched onto.'

'But he insisted he doesn't know any math higher than adding,' Ferris said.

To Ed Gantro, Carpenter said, 'Hand me your wallet. I want your actual name. Social Security number, police region stability ident – come on, I want to know who you really are.'

'He's just a rural type,' Ferris said, as he watched Gantro pass over his lumpy wallet.

'And I want confirm prints offa his feet,' Carpenter said. 'The full set. Right away – priority A.' He liked to talk that way.

An hour later he had the reports back from the jungle of interlocking security-data computers from the fake-pastoral restricted area in Virginia. 'This individual graduated from Stanford College with a degree in math. And then got a master's in psychology, which he has, no doubt about it, been subjecting us to. We've got to get him out of here.'

'I did have a soul,' Gantro said, 'but I lost it.'

'How?' Carpenter demanded, seeing nothing about that on Gantro's official records.

'An embolism. The portion of my cerebral cortex, where

my soul was, got destroyed when I accidentally inhaled the vapors of insect spray. That's why I've been living out in the country eating roots and grubs, with my boy here, Tim.'

'We'll run an EEG on you,' Carpenter said.

'What's that?' Gantro said. 'One of those brain tests?'

To Ferris, Capenter said. 'The law says the soul enters at twelve years. And you bring this individual male adult well over thirty. We could be charged with murder. We've got to get rid of him. You drive him back to exactly where you found him and dump him off. If he won't voluntarily exit from the truck, gas the shit out of him and then throw him out. That's a national security order. Your job depends on it, also your status with the penal code of this state.'

'I belong here,' Ed Gantro said. 'I'm a dummy.'

'And his kid,' Carpenter said. 'He's probably a mathematical mental mutant like you see on TV. They set you up; they've probably already alerted the media. Take them all back and gas them and dump them wherever you found them or, barring that, anyhow out of sight.'

'You're getting hysterical,' Ferris said, with anger. 'Run the EEG and the brain scan on Gantro, and probably we'll have to release him, but these three juveniles—'

'All genuises,' Carpenter said. 'All part of the setup, only you're too stupid to know. Kick them out of the truck and off our premises, and deny – you get this? – deny you ever picked any of the four of them up. Stick to that story.'

'Out of the vehicle,' Ferris ordered, pressing the button that lifted the wire mesh gates.

The three boys scrambled out. But Ed Gantro remained.

'He's not going to exit voluntarily,' Carpenter said. 'Okay, Gantro, we'll physically expel you.' He nodded to Ferris, and the two of them entered the back of the truck. A moment later they had deposited Ed Gantro on the pavement of the parking lot.

'Now you're just a plain citizen,' Carpenter said, with relief. 'You can claim all you want, but you have no proof.'

'Dad,' Tim said, 'how are we going to get home?' All three boys clustered around Ed Gantro.

'You could call somebody from up thcrc,' the Fleischhacker boy said. 'I bet if Walter Best's dad has enough gas he'd come and get us. He takes a lot of long drives; he has a special coupon.'

'Him and his wife, Mrs Best, quarrel a lot,' Tim said. 'So he likes to go driving at night alone; I mean, without her.'

Ed Gantro said, 'I'm staying here. I want to be locked up in a cage.'

'But we can *go*,' Tim protested. Urgently, he plucked at his dad's sleeve. 'That's the whole point, isn't it? They let us go when they saw you. We did it!'

Ed Gantro said to Carpenter, 'I insist on being locked up with the other pre-persons you have in there.' He pointed at the gaily imposing, esthetic solid-green-painted Facility building.

To Mr Sam B. Carpenter, Tim said, 'Call Mr Best, out where we were, on the peninsula. It's a 669 prefix number. Tell him to come and get us, and he will. I promise. Please.'

The Fleischhacker boy added, 'There's only one Mr Best listed in the phone book with a 669 number. Please, mister.'

Carpenter went indoors, to one of the Facility's many official phones, looked up the number. Ian Best. He punched the number.

'You have reached a semiworking, semiloafing number,' a man's voice, obviously that of someone half-drunk, responded. In the background Carpenter could hear the cutting tones of a furious woman, excoriating Ian Best.

'Mr Best,' Carpenter said, 'several persons whom you know are stranded down at Fourth and A Streets in Verde Gabriel, an Ed Gantro and his son, Tim, a boy identified as Ronald or Donald Fleischhacker, and another unidentified minor boy. The Gantro boy suggested you would not object to driving down here to pick them up and take them home.'

'Fourth and A Streets,' Ian Best said. A pause. 'Is that the pound?'

'The County Facility,' Carpenter said.

'You son of a bitch,' Best said. 'Sure I'll come get them; expect me in twenty minutes. You have *Ed* Gantro there as a pre-person? Do you know he graduated from Stanford University?'

'We are aware of this,' Carpenter said stonily. 'But they are not being detained; they are merely – here. Not – I repeat not – in custody.'

Ian Best, the drunken slur gone from his voice, said, 'There'll be reporters from all the media there before I get there.' Click. He had hung up.

Walking back outside, Carpenter said to the boy Tim, 'Well, it seems you mickey-moused me into notifying a rabid anti-abortionist activist of your presence here. How neat, how really neat.'

A few moments passed, and then a bright-red Mazda sped up to the entrance of the Facility. A tall man with a light beard got out, unwound camera and audio gear, walked leisurely over to Carpenter. 'I understand you may have a Stanford MA in math here at the Facility,' he said in a neutral, casual voice. 'Could I interview him for a possible story?'

Carpenter said, 'We have booked no such person. You can inspect our records.' But the reporter was already gazing at the three boys clustered around Ed Gantro.

In a loud voice the reporter called, 'Mr Gantro?'

'Yes, sir,' Ed Gantro replied.

Christ, Carpenter thought. We did lock him in one of our official vehicles and transport him here; it'll hit all the papers. Already a blue van with the markings of a TV station had rolled onto the lot. And, behind it, two more cars.

ABORTION FACILITY
SNUFFS STANFORD GRAD

That was how it read in Carpenter's mind. Or

And so forth. A spot on the 6:00 evening TV news. Gantro, and when he showed up, Ian Best who was probably an attorney, surrounded by tape recorders and mikes and video cameras.

We have mortally fucked up, he thought. Mortally fucked up. They at Sacramento will cut our appropriation; we'll be reduced to hunting down stray dogs and cats again, like before. Bummer.

When Ian Best arrived in his coal-burning Mercedes-Benz, he was still a little stoned. To Ed Gantro he said, 'You mind if we take a scenic roundabout route back?'

'By way of what?' Ed Gantro said. He wearily wanted to leave now. The little flow of media people had interviewed him and gone. He had made his point, and now he felt drained, and he wanted to go home.

Ian Best said, 'By way of Vancouver Island, British Columbia.'

With a smile, Ed Gantro said, 'These kids should go right to bed. My kid and the other two. Hell, they haven't even had any dinner.'

'We'll stop at a McDonald's stand,' Ian Best said. 'And then we can take off for Canada, where the fish are, and lots of mountains that still have snow on them, even this time of year.'

'Sure,' Gantro said, grinning. 'We can go there.'

'You want to?' Ian Best scrutinized him. 'You really want to?'

'I'll settle a few things, and then, sure, you and I can take off together.'

'Son of a bitch,' Best breathed. 'You mean it.'

'Yes,' he said. 'I do. Of course, I have to get my wife's agreement. You can't go to Canada unless your wife signs a document in writing where she won't follow you. You become what's called a "landed Immigrant".'

'Then I've got to get Cynthia's written permission.'

'She'll give it to you. Just agree to send support money.'

'You think she will? She'll let me go?'

'Of course,' Gantro said.

'You actually think our wives will let us go,' Ian Best said as he and Gantro herded the children into the Mercedes-Benz. 'I'll bet you're right; Cynthia'd love to get rid of me. You know what she calls me, right in front of Walter? "An aggressive coward", and stuff like that. She has no respect for me.'

'Our wives,' Gantro said, 'will let us go.' But he knew better.

He looked back at the Facility manager, Mr Sam B. Carpenter, and at the truck driver, Ferris, who, Carpenter had told the press and TV, was as of this date fired and was a new and inexperienced employee anyhow.

'No,' he said. 'They won't let us go. None of them will.'

Clumsily, Ian Best fiddled with the complex mechanism that controlled the funky coal-burning engine. 'Sure they'll let us go; look, they're just standing there. What can they do, after what you said on TV and what that one reporter wrote up for a feature story?'

'I don't mean them,' Gantro said tonelessly.

'We could just run.'

'We are caught,' Gantro said. 'Caught and can't get out. You ask Cynthia, though. It's worth a try.'

'We'll never see Vancouver Island and the great ocean-going ferries steaming in and out of the fog, will we?' Ian Best said.

'Sure we will, eventually.' But he knew it was a lie, an absolute lie, just like you know sometimes when you say something that for no rational reason you know is absolutely true.

They drove from the lot, out onto the public street.

'It feels good,' Ian Best said, 'to be free . . . right?' The three boys nodded, but Ed Gantro said nothing. Free, he thought. Free to go home. To be caught in a larger net, shoved into a greater truck than the metal mechanical one the County Facility uses.

'This is a great day,' Ian Best said.

'Yes,' Ed Gantro agreed. 'A great day in which a noble and effective blow has been struck for all helpless things, anything of which you could say, "It is alive."'

Regarding him intently in the narrow trickly light, Ian Best said, 'I don't want to go home; I want to take off for Canada now.'

'We *have* to go home,' Ed Gantro reminded him. 'Temporarily, I mean. To wind things up. Legal matters, pick up what we need.'

Ian Best, as he drove, said, 'We'll never get there, to British Columbia and Vancouver Island and Stanley Park and English Bay and where they grow food and keep horses and where they have the ocean-going ferries.'

'No, we won't,' Ed Gantro said.

'Not now, not even later?'

'Not ever,' Ed Gantro said.

'That's what I was afraid of,' Best said and his voice broke and his driving got funny. 'That's what I thought from the beginning.'

They drove in silence, then, with nothing to say to each other. There was nothing left to say.